STUART CONDIE

THE
UGANDA
SAILS
WEDNESDAY

Red Door

Published by RedDoor
www.reddoorpress.co.uk

© 2020 Stuart Condie

The right of Stuart Condie to be identified as author of this Work has
been asserted by him in accordance with sections 77 and 78 of the
Copyright, Designs and Patents Act 1988

ISBN 978-1-913062-28-6

A CIP catalogue record for this book is available from the British Library

Cover design: Clare Connie Shepherd

Typesetting: Fuzzy Flamingo

Printed and bound in Denmark by Nørhaven

THE UGANDA SAILS WEDNESDAY

To all those who sailed on the SS Uganda (1952-1986)

SS *Uganda* Selected Crew and Passenger Lists

Crew – Officers
Captain
First Officer
Second Officer
Third Engineer James Scott
Chief Medical Officer Dr
  Sullivan
Purser
Assistant Purser Hancock
Chaplain Rev. Ian Tremwell
Cadet Mark Edwards
Chief Children's Hostess
Children's Hostess, Margot
Sister
Nurse Marion

Stewards
De Souza
Parminder
Diaz

First Class Passengers
Reg Worthington
Honour Worthington, his
  wife
Philip Doyle
Monica Doyle, his wife

Tourist Class Passengers
Heather Fontwell
Johnny Fontwell, her son
George Carmichael
Daphne Carmichael, his wife
Sophie Carmichael, their
  daughter
Norman Brown
Bob Saunders
Betty Saunders, his wife
Donald Kirby
Cynthia Kirby, his wife
Michael Kirby, their son
Mr Carruthers, Mombasa
  Harbour Master
Mrs Carruthers, his wife
Simon Carruthers, their son

Prologue

The seven of them were crammed into the Captain's cabin, all in tropical uniform except for the chaplain and harbourmaster who wore ill-fitting cream linen suits, with a dog collar in the chaplain's case. The Captain sat at the head of the table with a file in front of him, which he flicked through whilst the last of them were sitting down. No refreshments were offered despite the heat.

'Well now,' growled the Captain, 'this is a bloody mess, which we've had to investigate fully.' The officer handed him another file and the Captain looked around the table at all of them. 'I'll go through the findings and you can save any questions till the end.'

'To begin with, the treatment of the ill passenger was a shambles. The doctor had to be summoned and took his time getting to the hospital, whereupon he refused to treat the passenger and left. He was obviously drunk and required the sister to accompany him at all times to ensure a modicum of order. Or maybe the two of them were doing a spot of therapy of their own, eh?'

'Now look here, Captain...' said the doctor.

'Shut the hell up!' shouted the Captain. 'This is your last voyage with BI, you'll return to London straight away as a passenger. If you don't like it, remember that I don't have to give you an honourable discharge and I might choose instead to write to the General Medical Council asking for you to be struck off.'

There was a pause during which the doctor made a wheezing noise before the Captain continued. 'So, you left the treatment entirely to a nurse who was completely unsupervised. She did her best, but things went wrong, which I don't blame her for personally.' The nurse shifted in her seat, staring blankly at the table as the Captain turned to face her.

'There is also the question of the Distaval pills, which were found in large quantities in the passenger's cabin. However, since Sister should have been supervising this, and you have a good record with us, no action will be taken against you.

Then we come to the state of mind of the passenger, whom many of you said seemed quite febrile. The recent letter to the passenger that we found also seemed to be quite challenging. What did you make of this, Chaplain?'

The chaplain coughed and clasped his hands together. 'Well from what I could see, the passenger's private life was complicated, leading to a lot of stress, but then the cabin fire didn't help matters either.'

'Quite so. And lastly, Engineer, you were not implicated in the passenger's death but were witness to the cabin fire, their collapse and subsequent medical treatment. What are your thoughts?'

The engineer mumbled, 'Yessir. The passenger was certainly under a lot of strain.'

'As a result, I've concluded that nobody can be certain why the passenger died, but the circumstances do not reflect well on the company or many of its employees. For this reason, I've decided that, for the official paperwork, I will choose a version of the truth which does the least harm, namely that the passenger took their own life by a cocktail of pills whilst their mind was unbalanced by the fire and the letter recently received. The doctor will sign the paperwork to this effect.'

There was a long silence whilst the Captain stared at his audience, at the end of which the doctor nodded his assent.

'Lastly, there is the question of the passenger's remains. I've decided to follow the long tradition of burial at sea with a service tonight presided over by myself and the chaplain.'

'But given that we don't know the exact cause of death, the

normal procedure would be for an autopsy,' said the chaplain. 'The family is bound to ask for this.'

The Captain sighed. 'Have you not been paying attention, Padre? An autopsy would mean a coroner's enquiry, with many of you called as witnesses and a lot of uncomfortable questions, especially for the medical staff. Besides, we cannot keep a body on board till Mombasa in this heat.'

'There's space in the refrigerated cargo hold,' said the engineer.

'I think you'll find that's required for perishables,' replied the Captain quickly.

'Burial at sea is quite normal, we have a lot of cases in Mombasa,' said the harbourmaster. 'There won't be any problem with the paperwork.'

'But think of the impact on the family when they're told that their loved one has committed suicide and we've chucked her body overboard,' whispered the chaplain.

'Well maybe it was suicide, who knows, and there's a proper Anglican service for burial at sea, the same as on land, is there not? So that's what we're going to do. I must emphasise that we all stick together with this line, especially you, Chaplain. Anyone disobeying or tempted to speculate publicly on events will face disciplinary procedures. This would be especially unfortunate for those at the start of their careers with unblemished records.'

'Yessir,' the engineer replied. The nurse looked up briefly but remained silent.

The Captain stood up and handed the files to the officer. 'You have your orders and I'd like you all to come to the service late tonight as well.'

They all filed out, the last being the chaplain, who was beckoned over by the Captain.

'I know about your dirty little secret, Chaplain,' the Captain murmured. 'So make sure you give a good performance tonight, and sound convincing to the family.'

The chaplain gave a wan smile and followed the others down the narrow gangway. On the bridge, a new course for Kilindini Harbour was being plotted as they awaited the return of the Captain.

Chapter 1

March 1960 – Kiambethu, Kenya

Like a lot of things from Heather, there's no news for ages, then a bolt out of the blue.

> MY DEAREST WILLIAM. SURPRISE! CRISIS AT JOHNNY'S NURSERY SCHOOL. COMING TO KENYA SOONEST. WILL TELEX PASSAGE DETAILS. HOPE ALL OK. LOVE. HEATHER.

I re-read the telex from our London office and finger the torn bottom left-hand corner where I've ripped the paper from the cogs in my haste to hide it from prying eyes; telexes are charged by the character, and I can feel the sentences trying to burst out of their corset of parsimony. What kind of nursery school crisis would necessitate such a drastic step? Now Heather can drive, surely she can find another nursery school? When is 'soonest' exactly? Is Johnny coming too?

Her letters are quite different – very long and all-embracing as though the effort involved had exhausted the writer's energy and some time would have to elapse before another letter was possible. The drawings enclosed from Johnny are usually worth the wait, though – the stick people now have faces, clothes and names, though the last one only included Johnny, his mum and one of his friends from down the street, his father absent.

I'm standing on the veranda overlooking the grass and bushy borders leading towards the distant hills. This morning there's

1

a nagging breeze across my cheek and the green baize of the tea terraces ripples up and down over the rising ground with a faint sighing sound. On the horizon, the hills are misty and dark; above them, bulbous clouds are gathering their rain-filled skirts for a likely downpour. The sun is a pale yellow veiled by the clouds, but strong enough to begin burning the moisture off the ground. I glance at my watch, showing half past eight, then wipe the sheen of moisture from my forehead with a fresh handkerchief, though I know the sweat will only reappear later.

My wife is right about one thing, though, the telex certainly has come as a surprise. This is the first time that Heather has expressed the remotest desire to come to Africa, and she's usually dead against boarding school for Johnny.

'Really, why have a child and then abandon him?' I remember her saying, flicking the ash from her cigarette, staring at her mother. They were all in the garden allowing Heather to smoke as her mother didn't like the stale tobacco smell inside the house; it must have been last summer after her dad died and the arguments between Heather and her mother became more prolonged and heated.

'Good morning, William,' comes a voice from behind, making me start. I turn around and there is Dorothea, one arm up high hanging on the painted white doorframe to the veranda. She grins then drops her arm as she walks slowly over to me in that flowing movement she has, her legs striding purposefully. Dorothea has the shiny coffee-colour skin of a mixed-race woman, her hair tumbling down straight to her shoulders. She said her grandfather had worked on the Kenyan railway.

'You're jumpy today,' she says, tipping her head to one side and looking at me as though inspecting an interesting painting. I feel self-conscious that whilst I'm wearing an old grey checked shirt and a pair of long canvas shorts, Dorothea is dressed for a normal day at the office in a red blouse and black skirt. I'm not even sure she's seen my legs naked before, and sure enough her eyes flick down at them and she smiles a little smile.

'Well, it's Saturday and you don't normally come in at weekends,' I say, then feel foolish for stating the obvious.

'True,' she replies, running her finger along the wooden railing then shaking off last night's rain. 'I got behind yesterday, and it bothered me. Do you want some coffee?'

This is our little joke; we both secretly prefer coffee in the morning, not the otherwise ubiquitous tea. Taylor has banned everyone from drinking coffee up at Mabroukie and makes a public ceremony around drinking our estate tea, but then he drinks whisky most of the day and seems to think that this is perfectly acceptable, though the natives are not allowed it.

'Yes please,' I reply. 'Kenyan.'

'The best,' she says, shivering as she puts her arms through a loose white cardigan. I watch her as she opens the interior screen door, her narrow hips swinging in a fluid languid motion that none of the other African women seem to have. I've seen them on the estate looking at her through slit eyes.

The air around the plantation house seems crackly, despite the early hour and the dampness. There's no Jonas today, nor the two boys who look after the garden, nor Phyllis the housekeeper cum cook, as they don't work at weekends. It's Dorothea walking silently like a ghost around the house that seems to be creating the crackling – or maybe just me being unused to any change in my routine of solitude on a Saturday morning. Normally I cook an English breakfast and pore over the newspapers from home then write a letter to Heather and Johnny and deal with any issues arising from the factory or the workers that cannot wait till Monday.

Dorothea works in the office that extends over most of the ground floor of the plantation house. One room has all the files in boxes racked up on shelves on the walls; another is for storage of vehicle and machinery spare parts, packaged tea samples and anything else

3

that I don't like to leave unguarded. There is also a kitchen and pantry and another room used as a surgery for the workers when the doctor comes, as well as the office itself and a lounge area for visitors or the plantation manager at the weekends. The rooms are all whitewashed, with dark wooden exposed ceilings with ceiling fans hanging down and tiled floors. They are always cool, even in the height of summer, mostly due to the altitude and rains.

I leave the veranda in search of the promised coffee and find Dorothea at her usual desk in the office. There is a steaming mug in front of her as she pores over a book of accounts in neatly drawn columns, then looks up as she hears me approach.

'I put yours on your desk,' she says, pointing behind her, 'with the newspapers.'

I grunt and walk behind her to my separate office, though the door has been wedged open for as long as I've worked here. I like to hear everyone else move around and talk, though I usually don't listen.

'Has there been a telex today?' Dorothea raises her voice, still squinting at the accounts book, turning over a page. 'The paper feed was torn.'

'Yes, from Heather,' I reply. 'They're coming over.'

Dorothea turns quickly and waits for me to carry on, her eyebrows lifted expectantly, but when I don't say anything she gets up and moves to my office, her arm hanging from the doorframe again.

'Well,' she says smiling, 'this is news. Johnny as well?'

I nod and try to explain as best I can and she makes the strange tutting and tusking noise that she does when something unexpected happens. To try to avoid being asked difficult personal questions, I pick up the sheaf of papers from my in tray and start sorting through them, while Dorothea returns to sit at her desk. There's nothing much outstanding from yesterday and I feel bad about my curtness, so after about twenty minutes I emerge from my office.

'Coffee's good,' I say, coming over to her desk. 'Why exactly did you come in today?'

Dorothea leans back in her chair and stretches her arms. 'I wanted to check the books for Mabroukie to investigate that business with the workers not being paid last month, so I borrowed their books from the lady who replaced me.'

'Gabriella?'

'Uh huh,' she replies. 'Nice and quietly, without anyone noticing.'

I'm surprised at Dorothea's initiative, but then she had been furious when Taylor said she was to just do the Kiambethu plantation accounts and help out in the Mabroukie stores when Johnson was sick. She was used to doing both plantation accounts, not just ours. Maybe she's looking to be able to say, 'I told you so', but Dorothea doesn't strike me as that petty.

'Have you found out anything?' I ask.

She looks up from her desk. 'The cash from Kiambethu and Mabroukie can pay for all their suppliers and workers and leave enough over for head office…' Dorothea turns over the accounts pages inserting strips of torn paper and making faint pencil marks on the margins. 'Until recently, when the extra payments started at Mabroukie.'

I ask for more details, but Dorothea shakes her head and pleads for more time. I decide to leave her to it and propose a cooked breakfast, which Dorothea declines. In the pantry I find a joint of ham from yesterday under a muslin cloth and carve some slices to eat cold with fried eggs. This is comfort food to remind me of home and allows me the time to contemplate today's events as the eggs sizzle in the skillet. Perhaps Dad was right after all – maybe joining the family firm would have been easier than this; Africa feels like a continual struggle against Taylor, against the company, against the problems of getting anything done, and the threat of disease around the corner. And yet it's like a drug: when I do go

5

home I miss the sunsets, the heat, the earthliness of it all, the huge landscapes and the generosity of the people. By comparison, London is a blackened damp city where the people scurry around with their heads down.

I carry the newspaper and my large plate of ham, eggs and toast into the lounge, but Dorothea's clothes – a white cardigan, an umbrella and a purple headscarf – are strewn over various chairs and I decide to eat outside at the wicker table on the veranda, taking out the now crumpled telex from my shorts pocket to see if there is any meaning I've overlooked.

As I cut a slice of ham and dip it into the runny egg yolk, I ponder what we'd do with Johnny if he came over. There isn't much to occupy white children – the nearest family with kids is half an hour away and there's no suitable school. Heather hasn't said how long she wants to stay for, but I can imagine her being bored stupid after a matter of weeks. We could do trips to Nairobi and maybe the coast for a long weekend, but Taylor will probably be on my back if I take too much time off. Very few other ex-pats have brought their wives out, let alone young children. I know that the older ones go to an international school in Nairobi, but Johnny would be too young and the school is some way from the plantation.

What would Heather do? I just cannot see her fitting in with the few other ex-pat wives, most of whom have roles at the nearest Anglican Church or help with the running of the plantation house, but Kiambethu runs itself pretty well already. She would get bored with the women's conversations, the lack of anything to do and the stultifying social codes. It would be like the wretched tennis club all over again. Maybe she hasn't bought the tickets yet, as she would otherwise have mentioned this, and I could ask her to think again? If I send a telex to London today, Heather should get this via Dot sometime on Monday.

The cawing of the pied crows that roost in a tree on one side of the plantation house disturbs my thoughts and I watch a group of red parrots fly across the garden. I lay aside my knife and fork and look out beyond the garden to the flecks of orange and red on the foothills opposite, like tiny ladybirds, picking the best of the tea leaves, even at the weekend. The mists have retreated up the hills, just skirting the peaks now, and as the wind picks up a little I can scent the orange blossom from the garden and that pungent earthy smell you get after the rains.

I finish my ham and eggs, push my plate aside and pick up the *Times* that I'd dumped on the hanging chair; it's a few days old, having been brought by air to Nairobi airport then up in the post van to Mabroukie where Taylor has read it and drawn black biro lines around articles of interest, before handing the newspaper to Jonas to take with the other papers in the Land Rover to Kiambethu.

The ringed articles, usually on African colonial matters, are barely worth a glance and I turn to the front page where the second header is about Eisenhower setting up an anti-Castro army of exiles within the CIA. I muse over whether I could ever be recruited as a fifth columnist in England, before turning to domestic news – a paraffin heater fire in Kidderminster, a coalface collapse in Lanarkshire, and trade union discussions on bargaining rights – before sighing in frustration and returning the folded paper to the hanging chair.

Back in the office, I ask Dorothea to show me again how to set up the telex for transmission. She hovers at my shoulder and repeats the code for our London office, then puts her hands on her hips, expecting to be told something more.

'I'll do the rest, thanks,' I say and draft out a short telex using my best fountain pen with its blue paisley design on the top. After crossing out a few superfluous words, I slowly tap the message on the heavy metal keyboard, trying not to make any mistakes, then press the send key. There is a chattering as the cursor moves down a line and I return to my office with the draft and sift through my papers to see if there is anything urgent.

Dorothea walks over to my door with the accounts book in one hand, holding it up in the air to show what she wants to discuss. I beckon her to sit in the chair opposite me, and she pulls out a pencil, which has clipped her long hair behind one ear.

'Every month, starting last November, usually on the last Friday, five thousand pounds is taken from our bank account in Nairobi against an invoice from a transport company, but I don't know what it's for, and I've never heard of Redcar Logistics,' she says, slapping shut the accounts and putting them under her arm. 'I've noted all the details here.' She hands me an A4 sheet with jottings in her small neat handwriting. 'The invoices are all signed off by Taylor, so you could ask him about the payments.'

'Thanks, leave it with me, but don't tell anyone what you've been doing.' It will require careful thought as to how to proceed.

Dorothea turns around as she's leaving with the ledger. 'Why did you say "reconsider"?'

I've forgotten that Dorothea keeps all the telex copies; there is a pause while I tap my fountain pen on the blotter.

'I don't know what we'll do with Johnny.'

'Yes, I see,' she says, nodding to an inaudible tune. 'I can help if you want,' she continues with her clucking noise. 'But now I have to get to the market before it closes.'

'Enjoy your weekend,' I call to her as she moves around the office like a sound wave. I hear her picking up her belongings from the lounge, then clacking the veranda door behind her.

The telex draft stares up at me from the desk.

MY DEAR HEATHER. PLEASE RECONSIDER KENYA JOURNEY IF NOT YET BOOKED. LOVE. WILLIAM

I screw it into a ball and throw it into the bin; in the silence that follows I wonder if Heather ever feels as lonely as I do. Of course

I love her dearly, but sometimes I feel I don't know her any better than when we were first married; our enforced separation hasn't helped either. But then there are days here when my unhappiness is swallowed up by the vastness of Africa.

Chapter 2

24th March 1960 – SS *Uganda*, English Channel

There hadn't been a peep out of Johnny all night, just the creaking of the bunk bed as he'd shifted in his sleep; he'd wanted the upper bunk just because it was different, but Heather had worried that he'd fall out, and to keep him happy De Souza had found some bed railings.

'They're for babies,' Johnny had grumbled.

'All the sailors ask for them,' De Souza had replied, 'especially after a tot of rum!'

There was a knock at the cabin door and De Souza came in with some tea. Funny how the steward just wanted to be called by his surname, she wondered, watching him as he took the cup off the silver tray and left it on her wooden bedside table, frowning in concentration, then smiling, showing his single gold tooth. De Souza was younger than the other Asians, his moustache closely trimmed.

Aside from the double bunks, there was a low-level sink, two cane chairs and a wooden chest of drawers next to the bunks. In the corner next to the porthole was a matching tall cupboard together with a narrow writing table set against the wall opposite the bunks.

De Souza drew the curtain across the porthole and turned off the cabin lights. 'Did you get the welcome pack last night, madam?'

The A4 folder *Children on the Uganda* had explained about the children's playrooms, nursery and dining room, as well as the 'very popular' paddling pool. Other than the drawing room, children were not allowed in any public rooms and had to be quiet during the afternoon.

'I hope there are other children on board?'

'Oh yes, madam, about sixty or seventy this trip, I think. Lots of boys and girls for Johnny to play with. How old is he?'

'Coming up to five.' Heather remembered the letter which she'd had to put to one side. 'He should be in school this spring.'

Johnny ran his soldier along the edge of the writing table. 'Boys,' he said softly to himself.

There was a clunking noise and low voices outside the cabin. De Souza excused himself after reminding them that breakfast finished at 0900 and to attend the lifeboat drill afterwards. After quickly getting dressed, Heather and Johnny left their cabin and walked along a carpeted corridor, which she now knew were called alleyways, with steel walls whitewash bright. Heather realised she'd forgotten the map of the ship and tried to remember her route from dinner the night before but had to ask for directions from another white-jacketed steward. They went down a couple of decks via a metal staircase, Heather holding Johnny's hand, which he periodically shook off with vigour. The dining room had no windows but was brightly lit and with wood panelling along one side and linoleum flooring. Heather looked out for the Carmichaels whom she was grateful to have encountered the night before after the unpleasant conversation with the chief children's hostess who'd been officious and tried to convince her to go to the early dinner with Johnny.

Fortunately, Daphne had overheard the conversation and rescued them. 'Don't worry about her,' she'd said. 'She's just a stickler for rules.' Daphne, her husband George, and their thirteen-year-old daughter Sophie had sat at their table. Daphne had short wavy black hair in a bob, and after introductions, had enthused about the *Uganda* and the other passengers she knew on board.

'You and Johnny can eat with us in the normal dining room,' Daphne had said. 'No one minds as long as the children don't run amok, and I'm sure Johnny won't do that.' She'd squinted a little behind her round glasses before jumping up from her seat, waving furiously at another couple with a small boy, then sitting down again. 'The children's hostesses are normally very good, and Sophie can babysit – she often does that for pocket money.'

Now the stewards helped the two families reunite for breakfast. Heather ate with a reasonable appetite, but the *Uganda* was gently rolling, a languid motion that seemed harmless but gave Heather an increasing queasiness. 'I don't feel that great,' she said. 'I think I'll return to the cabin.'

'Go to the nurses,' replied Daphne. 'They'll give you something.'

'Nonsense,' said George. 'Best thing is to go on deck, sit down and watch the horizon.' He had a nice voice, thought Heather – quite deep but soft too. It seemed to go with his job at the agents in Mombasa – reassuring and measured. He was clean-shaven and dark-haired, just greying around the edges, with slightly bulbous eyes. Daphne was chatty but no-nonsense, which also went with her job, as a nurse.

'Don't forget the lifeboat drill at 10.30,' added George. 'A waste of time but still has to be done.'

Their daughter Sophie chose this moment to get up from the table and leave without speaking a word.

'She's annoyed that she's on the list as a child and has to mix with the younger ones,' said Daphne.

'I've had a similar problem – the crew had Johnny down as my husband for some reason,' said Heather. 'We'll see you at the lifeboats,' she added quickly, replacing her chair and beckoning Johnny to come with her.

Heather had to stop to lean against the alleyway walls several times on the way back to the cabin whilst Johnny was running along with his toy aeroplane, seemingly not caring at all. When she finally reached the cabin, it was just in time for her to throw up into the basin, which looked like it had been fixed at a low level for just that purpose.

'Yuk, Mummy,' said Johnny. 'What's the matter?'

Well, Heather thought, what indeed? If she said she was seasick, then it might make him feel the same way.

'Maybe the kippers,' she said, trying to think of something he hadn't eaten.

'Told you they were stinky,' he replied.

After a lie down, Heather felt recovered enough to read the on-board briefing for the *Uganda* – a dossier of procedures, facilities available and, roughly, what happened at each stage of the journey: it was a mixture of strict safety instructions in the event of dire emergency and the theatre of the absurd, such as the daily noon calculation of the ship's mileage and various deck games. According to Daphne that morning at breakfast, lots of passengers placed money on such things to alleviate the boredom.

'Where are my toy boats?' asked Johnny.

'I left them in the trunk, darling.'

'I want them.'

Heather referred again to the briefing pack on the writing table, to see how she could access the trunks that had been stored away. 'We can't get your boats till after lunch, but how about we go and look at some real boats now?'

While Johnny grizzled, Heather checked her appearance in the mirror. Her face was still pretty good, all things considered, she thought. She was tall and upright with what her mother had always called a distinguished look, though her nose was a bit too hooked for her liking.

De Souza didn't seem to be around, and Heather tried to follow the ship's map to get to their muster station. Eventually, after several flights of stairs, she found a door exiting to the boat deck, where the weather was gloomy with light rain and a wind that seemed stronger than last night. A youngish officer, with a closely cropped black beard and decked out in a bright yellow all-weather jacket, was sheltering with a group of passengers out of the wind behind a lifeboat. He introduced himself as the second officer.

'When the emergency siren is given, you come here, Muster station 3, port side of the sports deck.' He walked out onto the open deck and pointed at the sign on the bulwark, then consulted his watch; after a short pause, the ship's horn began blowing on and off and there was a whooping noise from the tannoy.

'The adults' and childrens' life jackets are located here,' he continued, after the testing of the emergency alarm had finished, pointing at a series of white boxes along the deck against the railings. Then, with the aid of a deckhand (who were also all Asian) in wellington boots and dark-blue boiler suit, he showed them how the lifeboats were lowered off their davits into the sea.

'Hello again,' said a man next to Heather. 'Don't you recognise me with my trousers on?' He had the air of an older, more upmarket version of Johnny's tutor Gerald about him, with a crumpled white linen jacket and mustard yellow neckerchief, and she had to laugh. Last night she'd seen him as she'd left her cabin, just his upper half visible as he'd leaned round the door of the adjacent cabin, and she'd had a feeling he had no trousers on. He'd then disappeared with a wave and a 'Catch up later', before closing his cabin door.

'Of course, next door, B17. Don't ask me for a bag of sugar, though,' she replied, introducing herself.

'Call me Norman,' he said, tipping his head sideways then noticing Johnny with his aeroplane. 'Is he yours?'

Did he always speak in these clipped sentences, she thought, or was it the usual class nonsense, a way of showing off to someone you're interested in? It was nice to feel noticed, but Heather didn't want any trouble on this ship, where everyone was watching everyone else and the tittle-tattle would follow her to Kenya and William. She did, however, like talking to men; they were less complicated, less judgemental, easier to manipulate as well when the occasion demanded, and had had more interesting experiences compared to housewives and nursemaids.

Johnny said hello to Norman.

'Well, who would have thought it?' said Norman, bending down to talk to Johnny. 'You shouldn't have a toy plane, young man, when we're on board such a fine ship.'

'My boats are in the trunk,' said Johnny, a bit too loudly over the continuing explanation of the lifeboat davits. A thin cloud of spray came over them as the ship rolled slowly to port and they could see the troubled grey-green water and the line of foam from the bow wake.

'Shhh,' said Heather. 'The officer's talking.'

'Fancy a coffee afterwards?' asked Norman.

The boat rolled sideways, and Heather felt her queasiness returning. 'OK, but where to go with Johnny?'

They agreed on the drawing room at 11.30 and Heather tried to quieten Johnny from making his louder plane noises. She wasn't entirely sure she wanted coffee in her condition, but she couldn't become a cabin recluse either. As the passengers drifted away from the lifeboat drill, Daphne waited behind for Heather and Johnny.

'Where are we now?' Heather asked, squinting through the murk at the smudge of a coastline as well as a few smaller ships pitching rather alarmingly in the Channel.

'Just off Dorset, apparently. I tried to wheedle some more information from an officer for George's estimate of the mileage run, but he looked a bit preoccupied. What he did say, though, was there'd be a storm crossing the Bay of Biscay tonight and to look out for the weather report.'

'God, that's all I need, with my dodgy tummy.'

They headed for the promenade deck where there was shelter from the rain with the deck partially enclosed or behind a steel screen with windows. George was waiting there for them, sitting amongst a cluster of deckchairs, and waved to them.

'Better off here, if you've got seasickness,' he said, signalling to a steward. 'Do you want to have a blanket and sit with us?'

Heather agreed and sat down with them. It transpired that George knew William through their work, having recognised the Fontwell surname.

'He's in tea plantations, isn't he? I've dealt with him on cargo exports.'

Heather started to feel worried at this development, though it wasn't a great surprise as William had always said that the Kenyan ex-pat community was quite small. She would have to be careful not to say or do anything that might embarrass William if he heard about it from a work colleague. On the other hand, she couldn't be offhand, and the Carmichaels could make looking after Johnny much easier for her. 'I can't stay long – I said I'd have coffee with Norman from my next-door cabin,' Heather said, to try to change the subject.

There was a short pause. 'Well,' said Daphne, leaning forward in a conspiratorial fashion, 'he's got a bit of a reputation, you know, but he normally doesn't go for mums.'

Heather didn't know what to make of this, but it didn't seem to be meant in a nasty way. 'Thanks, I'll report back all the gory details at lunch.' They both laughed then George started talking about the ship's mileage, which gave Heather and Johnny the chance to slip away.

'Nursery now, Johnny, just like at home.'

'On my own?'

'Only for a short while, darling.'

They went down inside the ship and found the tourist-class nursery on A deck where one of the children's hostesses, Margot from her name badge, welcomed them. She had a small round face and auburn hair, the strands of which were tucked under her hat, and was much younger than both the chief children's hostess and the dreadful Mrs Davenport from the nursery at home. Margot had the knack of diverting children's attention whilst their mums slipped away, and although Johnny had his 'much maligned' look, with lips pursed and eyes squinting, he didn't cry, and turned his back to concentrate on a rocking horse that Margot was showing him.

After leaving Johnny, Heather proceeded to the tourist-class drawing room, which she eventually found towards the stern of the ship on the same deck as the nursery. It had a low ceiling but was brightly lit, with windows along one side looking over the *Uganda*'s decking and the sea. Norman was waiting for her on a sofa underneath one of the windows and levered himself up to standing when he saw Heather.

'You made it then – I was about to give up,' he said, grinning.

'I had to leave Johnny at the nursery.' They both sat down on the sofa and, while Norman looked for a steward, Heather cast her eye around the room. There were very few other passengers.

The steward took their order then bowed and went away.

'Do you have children, Norman?' asked Heather, just to put him on the spot.

'No, confirmed bachelor. Never really considered family life whilst I was in the colonial offices in Nairobi.'

'What do you do there?'

'Security, that sort of thing.'

'Are you working on Kenya's independence?'

'Good God, no,' Norman harrumphed. Their coffee arrived in a large silver pot with china cups, saucers and sugar bowl; he signed for it with a quick flourish. 'In truth, I've been using my time in London to look for another posting from the Foreign Office, Far East maybe this time.' Norman drank some coffee, and Heather did likewise, but just then the ship pitched and they both had to dip their cups.

'I'm not enjoying this much,' she said, mopping up the spilt coffee with her paper napkin.

'Not me, I hope,' Norman murmured as he poured back the coffee from his saucer into the cup.

17

'No, it's the ship's movement.'

'Just teasing.' Norman uncrossed his legs and leaned forward. 'Now tell me why you're on the *Uganda*.'

'I'm going to see my husband at his tea plantation in Kenya. Our son misses him,' Heather replied, pushing her fingers through the hair on her temple.

'That's unusual, husbands normally accompany their families.' The ship lurched to one side and spray hit the windows behind their sofa.

'Going to have to go, Norman, I'm not feeling that well.' They stood and shook hands briefly. 'Another time, I hope.' Heather zig-zagged her way back to the nursery, waved at Margot and stood in the entrance door looking for Johnny.

'There he is, good as gold,' said Margot, as Johnny appeared from around the corner.

'How was the nursery, darling?' Heather asked as they made their way gingerly along the alleyway.

'I've been playing with Simon,' said Johnny.

On returning to the cabin, Heather rinsed out her mouth and laid on her back in her bunk, wiping the sweat from her brow with her hanky. Johnny was turning the pages of one of his Ladybird books.

'Johnny, get De Souza to bring us packed lunch. Not much for me, though.'

'Are you seasick, Mummy?'

'I'm afraid so.'

Johnny opened the cabin door, looked left and right then padded out. He returned a few minutes later with De Souza.

'You have the seasickness, madam? Take lots of fluids and, if it doesn't get better, see the nurse. I can get lunch from the galley if you want.'

'Sausages and beans,' said Johnny.

Heather rested and the steward came back ten minutes later with two paper bags and some napkins.

'Sorry, too rough to bring crockery, so here are some packed lunches instead.'

'Thanks, De Souza,' said Heather, who wasn't feeling at all hungry. She thought she ought to make an effort to engage the steward. 'I understand all the stewards are from Goa?'

'Yes, Goa, part of India.' De Souza proceeded to tell Heather how his family, like many others, had left their country after the partition of India to seek work in East Africa, and had found it with the BI line in Mombasa.

'Do you have children?'

'A boy and girl. Not much older than Johnny.'

Heather's eyelids started drooping and the steward quietly left; while his mother snoozed, Johnny ate his lunch, picking at the sandwiches, leaving the cheese but eating most of his apple.

'Mummy, can we get my toy boats now?' he said. Heather grunted and he touched her hair while she lay on the bunk. 'Please?'

Heather sat up gingerly; she felt slightly better but the ship was still moving about, disturbing her innards.

'OK, Johnny, but I'll have to go to the baggage area.' She swung her legs round and pushed herself up from the bunk to look in the mirror. 'What a fright!' she said on seeing her pale colour and the shadows beneath her eyes. Her forehead was clammy and loose hairs were sticking to it; she started by brushing her hair then washing her face in the sink and towelling her cheeks with a bit of vigour to get back some colour. Finally she reapplied her make-up.

'That's better,' she said to the mirror.

'Remember, Mummy, there are four boats.'

Heather kissed the top of his head and took the ship's map with her again. Eventually she found the 'Wanted on Voyage' baggage room down on B deck towards the bow. The door was open, and she put her head round.

'Can I help you?' It was the cadet they'd met on the first night, in his dark blue officer's uniform.

Heather explained that she wanted some toys from one of their trunks, and the cadet went in and out of the racking looking at the occasional trunk and suitcase label.

'B19 did you say?' He dragged the trunk into the clear area where she was standing. There was a booming sound and the ship shuddered. Heather fell into a chair next to her.

'You hear the noise more down here. Best stay seated, if I were you.'

Heather opened the giant lock on the trunk. The toys were easy enough to find as in this trunk there was only Johnny's stuff and what they were bringing to William. She felt awkward being alone with this young man in such a confined space, so she thought she'd better say something. 'Have you always worked for BI line?'

'Yes, I trained first on the *Chantala,* a much older more basic ship – the *Uganda* is newer and more comfortable. Have you finished with the trunk now?'

'Thanks. Let me buy you a drink when I'm feeling better,' said Heather and they introduced themselves. 'I'd better go, a touch of seasickness I think.'

'I'll take you to the nurse,' replied Cadet Mark Edwards. 'There's no point suffering if you don't have to and the coming storm will keep you in your cabin all night.'

They went up one deck and past the purser's office, which had a metal grill in front of it with a man seated behind a desk whom Heather recognised as the assistant purser, his face permanently set in a bemused smirk. They carried on towards the stern of the ship with Heather moving from one side of the alleyway to the other, her hands pushed out in front of her, whereas the cadet, carrying the toy boats, advanced in an ice-skating type of movement, before arriving at the hospital. The cadet opened the door and held it for Heather to go through. She noticed that he looked a little flushed.

'Marion, here's Mrs Fontwell with the old seasickness,' he said. The nurse was sitting at a desk with a pen in her hand when they came in. She wore a white uniform but no hat and was in her early thirties with sandy brown hair tied back in a bun.

'I'll be off now,' said the cadet, handing Heather the toy boats then making his mock salute again before closing the door behind him. Heather slumped into the chair offered.

'Just a few formalities first,' said Marion, pulling a printed form from her desk. She smiled and filled out the form, repeating everything she wrote down for Heather to agree to, then went over to a large glass cabinet, which she unlocked with the key already in the lock, then took the top two packets off a stack on one of the shelves.

'These pills, Distaval, are commonly prescribed for morning sickness but seem equally effective for seasickness. They might make you a bit giddy though.'

'Can I take a quantity of them and return what I don't use?' asked Heather.

The nurse hesitated and went back to refer to the stack in the cabinet. 'All right, but promise me you'll be careful how many you take. Just a half pill to start with, and then see how sleepy it makes you – no more than two a day, though, and just when you have to. There's easily enough here to last you the whole trip. Best thing is also to keep drinking fluids, no alcohol, and eat just bread or toast and soup. Try to stay out on deck when the weather allows.'

This sounded like a well-worn routine, as she spoke without pausing and with little eye contact. Marion then put her pen down, pushed the form into a wire tray and handed Heather a paper bag with the pills inside. Heather took this as a sign that the consultation was at an end, thanked the nurse, picked up the toy boats and left. She had to breathe in deeply and close her eyes momentarily to combat the nausea, then moved along the alleyway with one hand on the cold metal wall for balance.

'You were ages,' said Johnny on her return. 'Can I play with my boats now?'

'Sure,' replied Heather, taking one of the pills with a glass of water, just as the ship juddered from a big wave and she had to cling onto the doorframe. She watched Johnny playing on the floor with his toys, impervious to the ship's motion, then climbed into her bunk bed.

'Just going to have a little nap, darling.'

Her mind quickly slid into a shallow sleep with the tumbling narrative of a dream: she was back as a child going to her first day at school, but she had the wrong clothes on and was wearing slippers, standing alone as a group of children went round and round her in a circle.

Chapter 3

24th March 1960 – SS *Uganda*, Celtic Sea

Heather surveyed the nursery carefully with it's handful of children, mini cane sofas and chairs, together with small tables with decorated animal motifs in their plastic tops. The walls were plain but with painted roundels on them.

'They're pretty, aren't they?' said Margot. 'They're meant to depict nursery rhymes but in a nineteenth-century style.'

'Humpty Dumpty,' said Heather her face close to one of the roundels. She turned around to show Johnny, but he'd already run across to his new friend, a short boy with a pointed nose and pink cheeks. They circled each other, each talking then checking to see the other's reactions.

'Don't you get seasick?' Heather asked Margot.

'Sometimes,' she replied, 'but you get used to it when you're working. Don't worry, the storm will be finished by tomorrow morning.' Margot rubbed Heather's forearm.

'Thanks. I'd better go whilst he's distracted.'

Heather made her way slowly up to the promenade deck. The light was beginning to fade as the sky was completely covered in low dark grey cloud moving quickly over the ship. Heather found a deckchair and sat behind a glass screen, sheltered from the wind, trying to focus on the horizon, but it was difficult to see due to the size of the waves and the movement of the ship. The waves came in relentless peaks and troughs, their crests plumed with white foam and the ship now seemed to be pitching up and down more than rolling, which Heather found less disagreeable.

'White horses everywhere,' said a man leaning against the railing over the side of the ship. There was nobody else about and Heather assumed he was talking to her, but she didn't know what to say. The man turned and walked over and she saw that he was wearing a dog collar.

'I haven't seen you on BI before,' he said, introducing himself as Ian, the ship's chaplain. 'May I?' he said, pointing at a chair next to her. He had an open face with brown hair dragged across from a side parting and crooked teeth with signs of tobacco staining.

'First-timer. By the time I've worked out everything we'll be in Mombasa.'

The chaplain laughed. 'Why are you up here in the wind and rain?'

'Trying to hold seasickness at bay.'

'Come along to the film tonight, nine o'clock, in the first-class ballroom, that'll take your mind off things.'

'But I'm tourist class.'

'Don't worry, tell them you're my guest.'

Heather thanked him and explained she had to pick up Johnny. As they walked together, Heather talked about her son and William's tea plantation, though she thought it surreal to be chatting to a vicar while they both clung to the railings on the alleyways.

'See you tonight!' the chaplain said as he veered off.

Heather took Johnny from the nursery to the tourist-class dining room on C deck, which she'd had to look up on her ship's map. Entering the dining room, easily the biggest room she'd been in on the ship, felt like she was set for Sunday Night at the Palladium. A few heads turned as she descended and a steward escorted them to a vacant table; the open space and bright overhead lights were much more pleasing than the cramped children's dining room she'd been shown on the first day, though tonight most of the tables weren't occupied. When the waves buffeted the ship, the walls vibrated and there were noises from behind the swing doors of the galley area of plates and cutlery being dropped, accompanied by the galley staff shouting in their language.

'Sorry madam, no drinks or soup tonight, too difficult,' said one of the stewards.

Johnny pointed out his new friend with his fork and Heather waved in their direction, but his parents looked distracted. While she was wondering if she'd caused offence, George, Daphne and Sophie came and sat at an adjacent table and said cheerful hellos. Despite the daughter looking like she'd rather be elsewhere, Heather thought she had a pretty face, with thick dark-blonde hair cut short. Heather ordered Welsh rarebit and melon for afters for herself and Johnny.

'Would Sophie mind checking on Johnny tonight?' asked Heather.

'Are you going someplace?' said Daphne, leaning her head against one hand.

'The film show.'

'I thought that was just for the first-class passengers,' said George, perusing the menu.

'I bumped into the chaplain and he said it would be all right. I'm sure you could come too.'

'I'll look after Johnny,' said Sophie in a querulous tone.

'Or, Sophie,' said Daphne, 'why don't you accompany Heather, and we'll look in on Johnny?'

'Yes please,' she replied. 'What's on?'

'Sorry, no idea,' said Heather, 'and now I feel I've messed up your evening, Daphne.'

'I think its *North by Northwest,* rather appropriately,' said George. 'We've seen it before.' While he was talking, Daphne was mouthing something and surreptitiously pointing at her daughter. Heather got the gist that this would make Sophie happy and therefore be a good thing.

'That's that then,' said Daphne, rubbing her hands together and smiling. Heather arranged to pick up Sophie at 8.45 pm from their cabin, which wasn't far from her own. They carried on chatting while everyone finished eating and Johnny brought one of his boats onto the table.

'Funny thing happened today,' said Heather. 'De Souza said that someone had made comments about me having a young cabin steward when I'm on my own.'

George and Daphne glanced at each other. 'Yes,' said Daphne, 'we overheard Carruthers talking about this in the drawing room. That's them over there.' Daphne slightly inclined her head over her shoulder.

Heather glanced at Johnny's friend's family. That might explain their behaviour, she thought. 'De Souza explained that normally I'd have someone older but they'd assumed Johnny was my husband when they saw his name on the list,' she said to the Carmichaels.

There was an awkward silence whilst Daphne pinched her lips together and looked away. 'Some of the passengers are a bit finicky,' she said finally.

The steward came to clear the plates away on a trolley as Heather and Johnny got up and made their farewells. Back at the cabin, Heather made sure Johnny had a good wash with his flannel and brushed his teeth, then tucked him into his bunk, just leaving a side light on, and took out his nursery rhymes book.

'*Doctor Foster went to Gloucester in a shower of rain*,' she read. Johnny laughed as this was one of his favourites. '*He stepped in a puddle right up to his middle and never went there again.*'

This was followed by 'Jack Sprat' and 'Baa Baa Black Sheep', by which time Johnny's eyelids were wavering. His head slumped on the pillow, which allowed Heather to get dressed quickly and apply her make-up, having to put her face close to the mirror in the dim light. In the meantime, she could feel her sickness starting again and reflected on taking more medication; too much might mean falling asleep but she wanted enough to combat the nausea and so opted for a half pill. By now, Johnny was fast asleep and Heather wondered what to do for half an hour, before remembering the pile of magazines and books she'd brought with her. She reached for a magazine but the small poetry book that her sister had given her fell out. Heather picked up the blue hardback cover with the silhouette of a ship under full sail and flicked through the contents; at least the poems weren't too long and appeared easy enough to follow, but she tired of the effort involved and read the latest *Tatler* instead. At the appointed time, she checked on Johnny and kissed his forehead before leaving the cabin and walking sideways along the wall to her friends' cabin. She knocked gently, and the door immediately swung open to reveal Sophie in a long red floral dress, her hair clipped back behind her ears.

'Hi Heather, I'm so excited!' Sophie said, closing the door behind her without further ado. 'You look great!' she added.

Heather was surprised as she was only wearing a close-fitting white skirt and a belt with a large buckle, a violet open-necked shirt and a loose cardigan – not formally dressed as Sophie was. 'Hang on, honey,' she said, offering her arm to Sophie, in her best Cary Grant accent, which wasn't good at all, but recognisable enough to make her ward giggle.

They found the veranda ballroom eventually, after asking a steward, in the first-class area on the promenade deck. A projector was being set up in a side room, which looked as though it normally served as a bar. Assistant Purser Hancock was waiting at the entrance to the ballroom, with his twisted smile and sardonic air.

'The chaplain said you might come.' He nodded at Sophie. 'And who is this, if I may ask?'

'I brought Sophie Carmichael along,' said Heather, touching Hancock's hand. 'I hope that's in order.'

'All right,' Hancock smiled, 'just don't tell anyone.'

They found two seats together and sat down. 'This is nice,' said

Sophie, looking around her. The ballroom had a double aspect view through large windows to port and starboard, though the windows were now adorned in floor-length velvet curtains and the wooden dancing floor was covered by a thin rug allowing chairs to be set out without scratching it. The screen for the film show had been placed between the twin chandeliers over the dance floor, which meant that only the middle of the ballroom had an uninterrupted view.

'Is your mum all right looking after Johnny?' asked Heather. She thought she'd better get any conversation done now in case she fell asleep later.

'Oh yes, she loves small children. The problem is that I've grown up and she hasn't noticed. You're much more with it than my parents are.'

'All children think that other parents are more interesting than their own. I could have all sorts of faults you don't know about yet.'

'Ooh, do tell,' giggled Sophie. Heather smiled and shook her head and just at that moment Hancock came forward and briefly introduced the film before it started.

Heather had already seen *North by Northwest* but hadn't admitted it, as for her it was just a means of occupying her thoughts on something other than seasickness. As the film progressed in its dreamy fashion, she began to think of the oddity of her situation, on board a ship in the middle of the Bay of Biscay on her way to East Africa, waited upon hand and foot by a small army of Goanese and now watching a film involving an extended chase across America. The waves were crashing against the *Uganda* even harder and one of the stewards was now holding the screen from behind to stop it toppling over. The more Heather watched the film, the more it looked like a parody of her own situation; maybe she could escape her own destiny, or rather the one that others seemed keen to hoist upon her, and run away. But then, she didn't fancy being chased by knife-wielding baddies, which ended the parallel. Even so, she did empathise with Cary Grant's character, on his own against powers that were beyond his understanding. All that closed-in feeling, not trusting anyone, against the odds – she could relate to all that.

Heather's thoughts were interrupted by the lights coming on to permit the reel to be changed. A melee of people started to congregate around the stewards to get drinks, and Norman, in a red and cream stripy blazer, was talking with one of the junior officers. He turned around and beckoned Heather to come over.

'Excuse me a minute,' said Heather to Sophie, bashing her thigh on a displaced chair.

'That looked painful,' said Norman, 'you can show me the bruise afterwards.'

Heather laughed, which made her feel a little better.

'Drink?' Norman continued. 'Only plastic glasses, though.'

She ordered a Campari soda, since Norman was paying.

'Is that another child of yours?'

'No, I've just borrowed Sophie for the evening.'

'What did you think of Cary Grant?' He leaned over Heather and spoke out of the corner of his mouth. 'Did you fancy him even a little?'

'No, but I sympathise with him,' replied Heather twirling an end of her hair.

'I wish I were him,' said the junior officer. 'The adulation and money he earns.' They shook hands and he introduced himself as James Scott, the third engineer.

'Shouldn't you be bailing water and battening down the hatches?' asked Heather.

He laughed. 'Normally yes, but it's not my shift. And the hatches are well and truly battened down already, but thanks for asking.' He swirled his whisky and ice around in the glass and glanced at Heather.

Heather excused herself and rejoined Sophie.

'He's nice looking,' said Sophie, 'the younger one.'

Heather laughed. 'Ah, the Celtic look, you mean.' As the film was about to restart they both sat down and Sophie asked if she could try her drink. Heather hesitated before handing Sophie the glass.

Sophie carefully sipped the drink then crinkled up her face. 'That's rather sour, what on earth is it?'

The second part of the film saw an increasing amount of pitching from the ship, which led to the film coming in and out of focus as the screen moved and a crashing sound of bottles being knocked to the ground from inside the temporary projection room. The film wobbled a bit but then carried on, slightly askew to the screen, and there was a shot of Cary Grant in profile, the way he turned towards the camera, that reminded her of Mother's photos of her dad when they were engaged. He hadn't changed that much as he got older but then had gone overnight from being an active outgoing man with a lot of time for his children into a vegetative state lying in bed with half of his body shut down. Marjorie, her sister, had dealt with it, staying over with their mother and helping with the feeding and bed changing and trying to get him mobile to some degree. Heather had just pretended that it wasn't happening; she hadn't wanted to see her dad like that, it was just too upsetting, so she'd blanked most of it out, and hadn't helped much with the domestic arrangements. Heather decided she would write to Marjorie from the next port of call – Malta on 29th March – but any further thoughts were interrupted by a change in the timbre of the film music and the rolling of the credits.

'That was great,' said Sophie. 'Can you take me to the next one?'

Heather was starting to feel queasy again and stood up to go. 'Let's see what your mum says first, she'll be wondering if I've kidnapped you.'

They made their way back to B deck where Daphne briefly reported that Johnny had been sleeping when she'd looked in and

Heather returned alone to cabin B19. Her stomach was churning again, and her breath felt acrid as she knelt on the cabin floor next to the sink, took another pill and waited for the sickness. After a while it passed and she gargled some water and cleaned her teeth as quietly as possible. Johnny was murmuring in his sleep and Heather stood on the lower bunk, reaching up to stroke his hair.

'Mummy's here, darling. Sleep well.'

Johnny turned over and sighed, and Heather got down to her bunk and clambered in, exhausted. As she lay on her back looking at the imprint of her son on the bunk above, she reflected on how much she loved him, even though his birth hadn't been planned, and the glow from this thought comforted her as she succumbed to sleep.

Chapter 4

25th March 1960 – SS *Uganda*, North Atlantic Ocean

Heather woke up and was startled to find Johnny standing by the side of her bunk in his pyjamas, his hair askance but a grin on his face.

'You've been snoring!' Johnny said, poking his mother's cheek with the tip of a toy soldier's gun. 'Can we have breakfast now? I'm starving!'

Heather squinted at her watch; there was just about enough time to get to the dining room before it closed. She sat on the edge of the bunk drinking the tea that De Souza must have left earlier, sensing that something was different that morning, and wondering what it was.

'Are we at Africa yet?' asked Johnny.

'No, darling, ten more sleeps yet. Brush your teeth now and wash your face and hands.' Heather stood up and stretched then realised what it was: the crashing of the waves and the pitching of the ship had been replaced by a more moderate swelling and rolling. She felt much better, although the movement was still not that agreeable, so she took another half pill.

Heather brushed her hair in the mirror and thought that the shadows under her eyes had receded and her skin had a pinker and less clammy look to it. Just a bit of eye liner would have to do this morning and she forced a smile to see if there was any sign of crow's feet yet. She laid out some clothes for Johnny from the chest of drawers, then attended to her own wardrobe before hurriedly taking Johnny by the hand and making their way towards the main dining room on C deck – Heather taking care descending the steps with the heels she had on. They eventually arrived to find George, Daphne and Sophie just finishing off their fried breakfast.

'We'd almost given up on you,' said George.

Sophie smiled and said good morning to Heather, but Daphne frowned, said not a word and left with her daughter shortly after; this seemed like role reversal from the day before. Heather ordered an omelette for herself and runny fried eggs and sausage for Johnny.

'Stroll on deck?' said George after they'd finished eating and set aside their starched linen napkins. 'Should help with your sea legs.'

They walked up to the boat deck and stood on an area of bare wooden decking with white lines taped on it – George told her it was the sports deck, but the weather discouraged anyone from playing. The wind was less brutal than the day before but still gusty, and the sea heavy with only the occasional white horse, whilst the rain had been replaced by light cloud with sunlight reflecting from behind it. The air seemed warmer to Heather, promising spring.

The three of them stood at a railing and looked over the rear of the ship. George pointed out two yellow upright cranes on each side of the ship and two sets of booms folded up to go with them, together with electrical winches for the rigging. Between the cranes were a cargo hatch and the first-class swimming pool, which was covered over with a tarpaulin sheet, as well as a large mast with the BI black and white house flag fluttering in the breeze. Then there was another level change to A deck and the tourist-class swimming pool, also covered, and another cargo hatch. They were watching the Asian crew in blue overalls scrubbing the decks now the weather was better, when Mark the cadet came to join them at the railing.

'Where are we now, Mark?' Heather asked.

'Over there's Portugal,' he replied, pointing to a headland off the port side, behind their direction of travel, with a faint intermittent flashing just visible. 'The Fisterra lighthouse,' the cadet added.

George grunted and got out a mini notebook. Heather watched one of the Asians who seemed to be directing the others, an older man with brown spectacles and a grey moustache.

'He's the serang,' said Mark. 'See the red ring on his white cap?'

The deck crew were all wearing giant rubber boots and armed with stiff haired brushes which they washed out in buckets to get rid of the froth from the powder they were using.

'It's a bicarbonate to get the wood really clean,' added the cadet.

The crew seemed oblivious to the wallowing motion of the *Uganda* and chatted to each other in their language, with the occasional guffaw and wave of the arm.

'They're mostly from Bombay or Chittagong,' said Mark when George asked.

Heather looked back towards the stern of the ship past the cargo hatches and swimming pools where another superstructure rose up at the stern with a small pencil-shaped chimney and faint black plume. The cadet explained about the crew accommodation and mess area with the galley above. 'Smell the curry?' he added.

'Yuck,' said Johnny, 'it's stinky like the kippers.'

Heather laughed; she could indeed smell an unusual aroma, but as she'd never eaten curry she didn't know what it was. She ruffled her son's hair and put her arm around his shoulders. '*And what did we see?*' she sung to him. '*We saw the sea.*'

They looked at the wash from the bow spreading across the sea on both sides of the ship in a giant V shape, then at the white cauldron of foam churned up by the propellers at the stern. Behind them was the massive black funnel with two white hoops; when the wind gusted, some of the smoke from it would pass over them, a warm but oily sensation, smelling of the ship's fuel, bitter and dusty. Then the wind would change again, and it would be back to the wet saltiness of the sea.

'Why is the funnel so large?' she asked the cadet. 'It looks out of proportion.'

He shrugged his shoulders. 'Some say it looks ugly, and others regard it as a distinguishing feature.'

'Never heard it put that way before,' said George, smiling. He then turned to Heather. 'Let's go and find Daphne, she's got some people for you to meet.'

The cadet waved his hand and went off down the short staircase to the Promenade deck to speak to the deck crew. George led Heather and Johnny along the boat deck forward towards the bow.

'What was Daphne upset about at breakfast?' asked Heather, holding Johnny by his hand as they strolled side by side.

'Sophie said you'd given her a glass of Campari last night, which her mum would never have allowed. You can imagine how that went down.'

'Well I only allowed her a sip, actually.'

'Daphne's a bit cross about it,' said George, looking out over the horizon. 'Don't mention this to her, but she doesn't like you seeing Norman unaccompanied either.'

A short snorty laugh escaped Heather's lips before she could put a hand over her mouth. 'Sorry, it just seems a bit Victorian.'

George shrugged his shoulders in amusement. 'Don't worry, it'll all blow over.'

They made their way to the tourist-class smoking room, on the port side of A deck.

'Daphne likes a little puff with the chaplain. The men don't much like having women in there, but that's part of the fun,' said George. 'However, definitely not for Johnny.'

Heather pondered why Daphne could see the chaplain but she not talk to Norman; it felt like Daphne was being possessive. 'Don't worry – I'll take Johnny to the nursery,' said Heather and set off.

She saw Margot at a distance and left Johnny quickly.

When she returned to the smoking room, she had to look through the fug of tobacco to make out the Carmichaels, who had a sofa and chairs underneath the windows and near a bar in the corner of the room. As well as the smoke, there was an aroma of leather and tobacco with a trace of salt in the air. Heather went over to sit with them and was introduced to an older couple, Betty and Bob Saunders.

'We've heard a lot about you,' said Bob in a slow Scottish voice. It sounded to Heather that he might have had elocution lessons. His wife giggled nervously.

'I thought we could go and have an extended lunch in the dining room today, to cheer ourselves up after the storm,' said Daphne. 'What's more, Sophie has agreed to take Johnny to the children's dining room for lunch, as a thank you for the film.'

'Did you enjoy the film?' the chaplain asked Heather.

'It took my mind off the sickness, though it was a bit hard to follow at times with all the ship's movement.'

'Well, when I was on the *Kenya*, the projectionist passed out, it was so hot,' said Bob. He then proceeded to give a minute by minute account of this incident in his halting voice, inflating himself up and pausing at moments which he thought were of particular import.

'I'm going to powder my nose,' Heather whispered to Daphne.

'I'll come with you,' she whispered back and made a little hand signal to George.

Inside the ladies' toilet – which was off another alleyway – they both stared at the mirror set in wood panelling, touching up their hair. 'Sorry about Sophie's Campari – it was only a sip,' said Heather.

'Yes, but it undermines the way we're trying to bring her up.'

Heather protested her innocence, thinking that there must be an ongoing problem between mother and daughter, which she had unwittingly inflamed.

'How come George knows so much about the *Uganda*?' she asked after a long pause as they both adjusted their lipstick, pursing their lips and glancing at each other via the mirror.

'He's in charge of Smith Mackenzie, BI's agents in Mombasa. Don't show too much interest in him, though, people might take it the wrong way.' When Heather glanced again in the mirror, Daphne's usual studious smile had gone, replaced by a flinty glaze, face lined in a warning, whilst Heather had two patches of red on her cheeks, her usual sign of anger.

Daphne's air of nonchalance had returned by the time they went outside on deck. 'Your punishment is to talk to Bob and Betty. We've known them from a couple of journeys and can't seem to get rid of them.'

Charming, thought Heather, who felt like she'd been told off and punished like a naughty schoolgirl. She was on the point of replying when the door to the smoking room opened. 'News-sheets just in, ladies,' called out the chaplain, holding the door open for them, then handing them both a sheet of typing, which looked as though it had been copied off the radio verbatim. The three of them remained standing while Heather and Daphne read the headlines, which were extensions of topics already in the news when they left home – further unrest in South Africa following the Sharpeville shootings, unrest in Alabama over whether blacks should be allowed to ride on buses, and unrest at home with more demonstrations against the H-bomb. The world of the *Uganda* seemed far removed from all this death and destruction.

Heather put down the sheet on one of the wooden tables and the three of them went to rejoin the others at their table, pulling up heavy leather chairs to sit on.

'Just to change the subject,' said Daphne in a bright trill voice. 'Who wants to get *Lady Chatterley's Lover* then?'

Betty Saunders made a small 'eek' noise and looked at her shoes, whilst her husband Bob cleared his throat as though he were trying to spit something out, then added, 'Isn't it banned?'

'Cynthia says it's already been published in Europe, so I think we should search for it on our shore visit in Valletta.' Daphne smiled and peered at each of the others in turn. 'Just think, we'll be able to read it before anyone else in Britain, if we get in quick before the trial ends.' She clasped her handbag shut.

The chaplain had a wry smile on his face. 'I feel I should read it too just to see what all the fuss is about.'

George came back with a tray of drinks. 'I'm starving after that enforced fasting yesterday. Who's for early lunch?'

'I need to check on Johnny first,' said Heather. 'Where's Sophie, by the way?'

'Sulking in our cabin, probably,' said Daphne, lighting up a cigarette offered to her by the chaplain.

★★★

At the nursery, Heather was met on arrival by Margot, who looked a bit flustered. 'Sorry, Mrs Fontwell, Johnny's got upset over something – I've calmed him down but he's still a bit grumpy.'

Heather went over to Johnny who was sitting on his own in a toy car facing the wall and refusing to turn around even though he'd seen her. She carefully picked him out of the car and wiped his runny nose and blotchy eyes with her hankie.

'Come on, brave sailor, time for lunch.'

'Not a sailor.'

Heather put Johnny down as he was getting too heavy to carry and led him by the hand to Margot who was standing at the entry door.

'It just suddenly flared up with a lot of pushing and shoving with his friend Simon and I had to separate them.' Margot's face was puckered as though she was about to burst into tears as well.

'Don't worry – I'll try to get to the bottom of it.' Heather and Johnny left and went back to their cabin so Heather could tidy up her son a bit. She had a sense of déjà vu about the nursery – it was almost the same as the incidents back home, with Susan Briggs pushing Johnny all the time, then him retaliating. So much for Heather telling everyone that the nursery problem had led to her deciding to take them both to Kenya – the same pattern had now resurfaced on the ship before they'd even got to Africa. Was this down to Johnny or something else?

'Was Simon nasty to you, darling?' asked Heather, as casually as she could manage.

'Yes,' Johnny replied, not looking at her. 'He said he didn't want to play with me any more.'

Heather then remembered that Simon's parents were the Carruthers, who'd already made comments about her steward.

'Never mind, Johnny, maybe you can find another friend tomorrow,' she said, just to try and cheer him up. 'Let's go and see Sophie. You can bring a couple of your boats, and a book as well, if you want.'

They left their cabin and walked round to the Carmichaels'; Heather knocked, and Sophie opened the door just a crack, smiling when she saw them. Heather leaned forward to try to talk to Sophie without Johnny hearing.

'He's a bit out of sorts – I don't know if I should leave him with you.'

'Don't worry, I can always come and find you,' she replied. 'Come in and tell me what I should wear.'

Heather looked around their cabin; the layout was the mirror opposite to her own but much tidier with clothes packed away and no toys strewn around. She helped Sophie pick a dress but wasn't entirely sure the one she chose wasn't her mother's, which led to Heather offering to lend Sophie her wardrobe.

'Rather!' Sophie replied wide-eyed.

On reflection, Heather realised that many of her clothes wouldn't fit Sophie due to their difference in height, but it was nice to see Sophie smiling and enthusiastic.

They headed off for the children's dining room but when on arrival Heather told Johnny she'd see him after lunch, he scrunched up his face in disappointment. Heather squatted on her haunches to get down to Johnny's level. 'Sophie will look after you and maybe even help you read a story.' She rubbed his right arm to try to reassure him, before Sophie led Johnny away by the hand, bending over and whispering to him.

Heather scampered off on her way to the tourist dining room again, feeling guilty. She thought about the incident in the nursery but couldn't decide if it was something to do with her or something to do with Johnny, which might in turn have something to do with her. Had she brought him up well, or was she too laissez-faire? Was it a problem that William was abroad, and Johnny didn't have a father figure to look up to? Maybe a brother or sister would make him more balanced?

Alternatively, maybe Johnny was just the way he was and there was nothing that could be done about it. After all, she hadn't much liked Mrs Davenport and the same might apply to the Carruthers were she ever to talk to them, so these episodes were probably all about Johnny growing up, getting used to people he didn't like and finding ways of dealing with them.

As Heather was walking quickly along the alleyway, she noticed that she seemed to have got used to the *Uganda*'s gentle rolling and was now subconsciously leaning and tacking to compensate for it. Less welcome was the heartburn and tightness she felt in her stomach; she belched since no one was looking and decided to walk more slowly.

The steward took her to the Carmichaels' table, which was a foursome in one corner of the room. The chaplain was also with them.

'Is it our turn to be saved today, Reverend Ian?' said Heather once she'd sat down.

'Especially from the Saunders,' said Daphne who was scrutinising the wine menu. 'We don't normally have wine at home but it's much cheaper on board. Who'd share a Chablis with me?' Everyone agreed it was a fine choice.

Heather skipped the starter to catch up with the others, and chose the fricassee of veal with mushrooms as a main.

'There's always the cold buffet if you want something quick as a starter,' said George, pointing over to a side table and chill cabinet on the other side of the room.

'No thanks, I've got to leave room for dessert,' she said.

When the main courses arrived, Heather was about to tuck into her veal when the smell of the chaplain's fillet of whiting Chantilly wafted over to her, almost making her throw up. Normally she loved fish, so she supposed this was related to her sickness and tried to breathe through her mouth to repulse the nausea.

'Didn't you like the veal?' asked the chaplain as the plates were collected by the steward.

'Still a bit, you know…' said Heather, patting her stomach. 'But tell me, Ian, about your duties on board.'

'Well, there are the Sunday services and the daily rounds of anyone in the hospitals, but then I have individual sessions with anyone that needs them and generally wander round and people watch. Actually, I spend as much time with the crew as they are away from home for long periods of time and can get homesick, or worried by bad news they get in the post. The Goanese are all Catholic, so I can tend to them from a religious as well as pastoral perspective, but the rest of the crew aren't Christian or English speaking, so it's difficult to help them.'

Desserts were served and Heather managed to eat her macaroon trifle and tried not to look at George's tapioca, which resembled glutinous vomit but at least had no discernible odour. Heather told the chaplain about Johnny's falling out with Simon and her suspicions that the boy's parents were behind this. 'What do you know about them?' she asked.

'They're Plymouth Brethren members,' replied the chaplain,

41

'which means socially very conservative, so for instance they believe pre-marital sex is a punishable sin.'

George looked up midway through a spoonful of tapioca and Daphne's mouth dropped open.

'I hope Johnny hasn't played up with Sophie,' said Heather, to try to diffuse the awkwardness.

'Despite being a little madam with me, she's quite good with young kids,' replied Daphne. 'Shall we leave the men to their smoking, and go and find our children?'

After a long search, they found them on the sports deck; Sophie was showing Johnny the rudiments of deck quoits, mostly trying to stop him letting go too early and accidentally throwing the quoit over the side of the ship. There was another boy on the deck with his mother and Johnny was now kneeling down and rolling the quoit to him.

Daphne introduced Cynthia and her son Michael, and the three mothers sat in deckchairs against the bulwark, watching their children and enjoying the occasional rays of sunshine between the clouds which raced across the horizon. The sea was also calmer, so the *Uganda* had more of a gentle roll than the previous wallowing motion.

As Daphne wrapped a silk scarf around her head, Heather wished she'd thought of that, too. She listened to Cynthia and Daphne talking about mutual friends and events in Mombasa and noticed how Cynthia's severe expression, not helped by the horn-rimmed glasses, vanished with her radiant smile, and decided that, although she seemed quite serious, at least Cynthia was independently-minded and somebody who could probably be relied upon.

With the woom woom of the turbines vibrating through the deck below her, Heather began to daydream of the pulse of the ship's heart, a reassuring regularity day and night whilst the crew and passengers carried on regardless, each wrapped up in their own duties or thoughts.

'Sophie and I have to go now,' said Daphne, getting up from her chair and straightening her skirt at the back. Sophie remained seated, looking steadfastly out to sea as though she hadn't heard. Her mother held out her hand, but the girl remained seated.

'I want to stay.'

Daphne dropped her hand and looked her daughter up and down. 'If you must, though it's not really convenient,' she replied and left abruptly without saying goodbye to anyone.

'Thanks for looking after Johnny,' said Heather.

'S'nothing,' Sophie replied, shrugging her shoulders, 'believe me.'

Heather asked Cynthia about the practicalities of living in Kenya with a young child, and she realised that it would be much easier living in either Mombasa or Nairobi rather than a tea plantation up in the hills. The conversation became rather fragmented in the increasing warmth of the sun, not helped by Sophie's continuing silence.

'Time for Johnny's nap,' said Heather. 'He never thinks he needs one, but he always does.'

As they all walked down together to B deck and their cabins, Heather reflected on how helpful Daphne had been on the first night of their journey after she'd argued with the children's chief hostess over dining with Johnny, and how willing she'd been to accept her into her circle of friends. Since then, for reasons Heather didn't fully understand, she'd managed to upset Daphne by talking to Norman, and giving Sophie a sip of alcohol, and now Heather worried about how Daphne would react to this recent scene with Sophie and potentially take it out on her. Cynthia was quieter but by comparison much easier to get on with and Heather decided she quite liked her.

They took the stairs from the sports deck down to A deck, but as they passed the smoking room one of the stewards came out and held the door, offering a momentary view inside the fug. Heather saw Daphne standing, her back to them, talking to a couple who were sitting smoking at a table. The door then closed, and they carried on down the stairs, with Heather wondering if, in that one second's image, she'd imagined Daphne talking with Mr and Mrs Carruthers, but then the man's bloated face and red skin rash were hard to confuse with anyone else.

They went their separate ways to their cabins on B deck and whilst Heather lay back on her bunk with her hands behind her head, Johnny fell asleep on his bunk above almost immediately. She thought that maybe she was worrying too much about people she hardly knew, and whether she should consider matters much closer to home.

Chapter 5

March 1960 – Kiambethu, Kenya

The plantation house was built after the war and looks both architecturally pleasing, with its double frontage of two-storey whitewashed brick buildings, but also functional with the discoloured sloping tin roof linking the two wings. There is an expansive and lush lawn around the house, encompassing the steps, and bush laden borders on both sides. I can hear the whoosh of water hoses spraying rhythmically over the long borders.

Dorothea calls out to me from the house, one hand pulling up her black skirt and the other held out for balance whilst she descends the short flight of steps between the two short columns that form the low entrance. 'Ahh,' she shouts, running from the bottom of the steps towards me to avoid being sprayed by the hoses. 'Wait!'

I cannot help laughing. 'Whatever is it, Dorothea?' I ask as she reaches me then bends forward to regain her breath. I look at her black hair, finer and straighter than the other estate workers, and she catches my eye as she stretches upright.

'The workers' – she puffs a little – 'they've not been paid again. Ben called me from the factory.'

'I see,' I reply, remembering Dorothea's recent scrutiny of the accounts.

'Since you are seeing Taylor, maybe you could ask him,' she continues, wrinkling her nose. Her face is a compromise between her absent black father and her Indian mother.

'Of course, don't worry.' I lightly clasp her shoulders, touching

45

her bright yellow oversized blouse. 'What's the situation with those payments you were looking at?'

'I spoke to Gabriella and she confirmed they were paid every month. Taylor just showed her the invoices and said they were for logistical support. She didn't like to ask anything more.'

I turn away and admire the view over to the hills, a clear blue sky today. 'I'll be back for lunch then off to both the factories.'

She puts her hands on her hips. 'We should find out more, though, William, about that company.'

'Yes,' I reply. 'I've got it in hand but I don't want to implicate you any more. Give me a few days and I'll tell you what I've found out.'

'Be careful with Taylor, don't confront him, just say the workers need to be paid,' she almost whispers, holding onto my shirt sleeve.

'I know.'

Dorothea lets go of my arm and smiles her distinctive smile; she's the only Kenyan I know with straight white teeth. 'Good luck,' she says, then turns back to the house, this time walking slowly but in long measured steps, looking up at the trees as they hiss in the breeze, her body flowing like water.

I walk down to the dirt track where Jonas is waiting for me in the Land Rover: a battered dark green short-wheelbase version, no synchromesh, a leftover from the war. The engine is already running, a choking rattle, when I reach him.

'Mabroukie factory, boss?' he says, slowly purring each syllable.

'Yes,' I reply. 'I hear the workers haven't been paid again?'

'Uh huh,' says Jonas, bending down to depress the four-wheel-drive yellow lever as we have to go down the slope from our plantation, then up another hill, and much of the track is rutted.

The workers in the fields, mostly women but some men too, wave as we pass. Only their heads and shoulders can be seen as they bob up and down picking the top leaves off the tea bushes and tossing them into the wicker baskets strapped to their backs.

The women have colourful headscarves and are still wearing cotton jerkins to combat the early-morning chill. Our plantation is fringed by native forest, a jungle of trees at different heights, some with wisps of residual mist, and on a clear day you can occasionally see the snow and ice of Mount Kenya.

'How's your sister doing, Jonas?'

'Not her chatty self.' He starts humming in a low flat bluesy kind of tone.

'Does she want to talk about it?'

'To you'n me maybe, but nothing official.'

'So he'll get away with it?' I lean forward to look at Jonas.

'Uh huh,' he replies as he makes a sharp left downhill turn, the gear grinding despite Jonas double declutching. 'With this man, you pay or else.' He makes a quick slicing action with one hand before reinstating it on the steering wheel.

I shunt the sliding window forward to get some air in the cab, even though it means inhaling the dust from the red-brown soil churned up by the thick ragged tyres of the Land Rover.

'Can she get another job?'

'Not on Mabroukie. Maybe somewhere else in Limuru.' He spits out of his window then hangs his arm out as the road is now flatter.

'I'll see what I can do. Is she…' I pause as I don't want to say it.

'With child? She says no.'

I sigh in relief, and Jonas starts humming again.

The Land Rover is now on a paved road much further down the valley, where there are small fields of maize and vegetable plots. A telegraph line follows the border of the road and Jonas meanders around the larger pot holes. We pass a whitewashed brick building with windows but no glass where school children are walking into the yard, dressed in navy blue uniform but no shoes.

About ten minutes later there is a white wooden signpost with black lettering marked 'Mabroukie', and Jonas crunches down a gear to make the turn. This estate is lower than ours and the trees are commercially planted softwoods in dark green swathes across the lighter green tea bushes; the tea rolls over the hills as at Kiambethu, but the estates are much larger and organised into square blocks with mud tracks in between. Here there is one owner, Brooke Bond, whereas we have in addition a variety of local farmers.

Again the workers are out everywhere, like coloured flies crawling over the leaves, but the sun is gaining in strength as the morning progresses with just a few cotton wool clouds advancing across the wide open sky.

'How were our yields yesterday?' I ask.

'Good, like last week,' Jonas purrs slowly, 'ten per cent up.'

The Land Rover is straining against the slope and the ruts in the mud road, the engine racing every time a wheel spins. Jonas double declutches down again and we are jolted back in our seats.

There is a small factory down on the left-hand side. It's a large rectangular tin shack with one third open but covered and the rest on two storeys. There is a queue of tea pickers outside the open area with their wicker baskets on the floor in front of them.

We carry on up the hill and I look behind at the dirt cloud following us; tea bushes fill the horizon with only the occasional windbreak of dark green forest. There are wooden signs by the roadside announcing the name of each plantation, which is then given to the tea produced: they are all British names like Coronation, Ludlow and Edinburgh. After a further ten minutes we pass through a set of high cast-ironwork gates and on to a gravel drive that forks in two with signs pointing to the factory and plantation house; the Land Rover takes the former and the road becomes rough again as we descend behind a strip of thick pine forest and into the compound of the factory, which looks like the one we passed earlier, only on a much bigger scale.

I jump out of the Land Rover and slam the door. 'Let's have a look round first,' I say to Jonas, and he slowly gets out and carefully closes his door. We have a look at the fermentation area first, several long wide trays half the length of the open part of the building. Tea is being offloaded onto the nearest empty trays, whilst the other trays are graded by the length of time the tea has been fermenting.

Jonas picks up a handful of the more fermented leaves and absentmindedly sniffs them, shaking his head and flaring his nostrils; he discards the leaves then walks over to one of the ovens, which has been fired up. I can smell the charcoal from the furnace, which a workman checks by opening a door underneath the oven, then bending down to peer in. The heat radiates out until he closes the door and ambles away, wiping the sweat from his face with a blackened rag.

The oven is solid cast iron, blackened and greased, with a metal plaque marked 'Wishaw Machinery' and a couple of switches and some dials.

'It's too hot,' says Jonas, feeling the front of the oven, disregarding the thermometer dial.

A man in a foreman's jacket ambles up to the oven and checks the dial. 'One ninety degrees, perfect,' he says. 'Oh, it's you,' he adds, staring at Jonas then walking off again.

'Have you calibrated the thermometer?' Jonas shouts at the retreating foreman who just waves a hand without turning.

'Come on,' I say, 'it's time to see Taylor.'

'I'm staying in the compound,' Jonas replies and walks back alongside the fermenting trays. I have little option but to leave him and make for the open metal staircase behind the ovens. The Blakeys on my heels ring out on the stairs as I climb up to Taylor's office, which is on the first floor with a view onto the open area below. Taylor has a dour Scotsman who runs the factory and acts as his bagman as well, and I pass through his office first. He's sitting at his desk scrutinising a ledger and calling out numbers to a black foreman standing next to his desk.

'Doug,' I greet him.

He looks up and stops speaking, but then just carries on reciting the numbers; the foreman glances up and nods almost imperceptibly to me as I pass through into Taylor's office, which is bigger and with leather chairs around a teak desk. Taylor is stroking his chin looking out through a wide glass window over the factory. He has a dumpy physique with balding wiry ginger hair and rather peculiar sideburns linked to a moustache.

'Ah Fontwell, our weekly meeting already?'

'Indeed.'

'Let's try some of our black tea, just settled.' Taylor steps outside his office, claps his hands and shouts, 'Service.' He returns to his chair, larger than the others, and asks me about last week's yields. I tell him the good news but instead of offering a compliment he just stares at me with a blank expression, only looking away as a young Kenyan woman brings in a wicker tray with a white china teapot and two cups and saucers. She is wearing a long orange dress and puts the tray down on a low side table with two chairs; her hand trembles slightly when she pours the tea, a dribble going in Taylor's saucer.

'Sloppy,' says Taylor just as she is leaving.

'Sorry Baas,' she mumbles and closes the door.

I sit in one of the chairs and try the tea, first without, then with a little milk. After a few gulps I take the lid off the pot and sniff the mash of unbroken leaves. 'It doesn't taste quite right for the top quality.'

Taylor puts his cup and saucer down too hard on the teak desk and jolts the cup from the saucer. 'Since when were you a tasting expert, Fontwell?'

I stand up and look out over the factory floor; he's trying to unsettle me, as usual, with his unpredictable behaviour and nasty little barbs, but I've learned that the best thing is to slow things down.

'Have you checked the thermometers on the ovens? They're ancient. We've replaced ours at Kiambethu.' I look at his reflection in the glass window.

'Fontwell, we've been over this before. I'm not investing in new equipment, the company hasn't got the money for it.' He swivels sideways in his chair.

'It's just a new thermometer. Surely with the better yields we can afford that.'

He swivels round again, this time to face me, his finger pointing. 'And another thing, your wage bill is too high, your black foremen in particular.'

I turn round and speak before I have a chance to think properly. 'Well at least they don't assault the women workers.'

There is a silence whilst Taylor twists his mouth from side to side and preens his ginger moustache.

'Has someone complained?'

'No, but…'

'I thought not. So, how do you know what's happened? These are just whispers, family feuds, with you dancing to the niggers' music.'

I'm furious but don't want to show it, so I turn around again and look out at some freshly picked leaves being unloaded onto a sorting tray where a gang of women are grading the leaves, their fingers moving across the tray like beetles. I listen for their songs but can only hear the electric fans on each side of the office whirring around, and smell the leather chairs and Taylor's sour sweat.

'How's Gabriella settling into her new job?' I ask.

'Who?'

'The accounts clerk who used to be at Kiambethu.'

'Oh, her.' Taylor takes a slurp of tea and puts his cup down with a clatter. 'At least she's not mouthy like the half-caste I sent you.'

I try the tea again; it definitely has a bitter aftertaste that you wouldn't expect with orange pekoe.

'Well, I'm pleased with Dorothea, she's very forensic with the accounts.' I pause, watching Taylor as he takes another mouthful of tea. 'Nothing would get past her.'

'I'm sure you're right,' Taylor says more softly.

Yes I am, I think. There was something about the way Taylor's small eyes darted around in that last exchange that makes me sure he's up to something, but I don't want him to know I know, so I decide to talk about the tea price and the various grades we can offer this year. Taylor is quite knowledgeable in this area and he relaxes and smiles and talks more expansively.

'You should think about your future, Fontwell,' he says, steepling his fingers together.

'Well that depends on the future for Kenyan tea, with independence around the corner,' I reply, trying to summon some enthusiasm.

'Ah,' he chuckles and then looks out over the factory again. 'I can't imagine that going well, can you? But in the meantime, we can make a decent amount of money while the sun shines, then piss off home, what?' He holds out his hands like it's a huge joke.

I shrug my shoulders and force a laugh; it's really too depressing a picture to contemplate.

'But I meant your *immediate* future,' Taylor says as he gets up, flinging open the door and clapping outside again. He then returns to the office, leaving the door open. 'Think about it and discuss it with Mrs Fontwell when she gets here. I'm happy to be flexible.'

As he slumps back in his chair, I take this as my cue to leave, but then hover at the door, with my hand on the frame. 'The Kiambethu workers haven't been paid again.'

'No, I think the foreman forgot. Get the money from Doug, it's all been prepared.' He smiles, a strange twist to the corner of his mouth, glad no doubt our meeting's over.

I pass the girl in the orange dress walking slowly up the metal staircase, her eyes downcast, then find Jonas in the compound outside and ask him to go and get the pay packets as I can't face the dour Scotsman again.

Jonas doesn't smile on the journey back to Kiambethu, just hums a lot, the sack of money between us. I start to think about the time Heather and I had agreed to meet in the restaurant at lunchtime in Exeter at the end of the summer following our graduation; she'd been at St. Lukes teacher training college so was a year ahead of me. I'd been expecting us to decide what we'd do next, perhaps go on an extended trip around Europe as neither of us had planned very much. I'd been disappointed not to have met her parents at her graduation, but she said the PGCE wasn't like a normal batchelor degree and they hadn't come. I was also ready with some other ideas of my own, maybe about going to London, where she could teach and I'd find something else. I was so in love with her but anxious also about what she saw in me, so anxious that I wondered about the unusual location (we usually met in pubs or the students' union, never a restaurant, as we couldn't afford it) and whether she might be about to call it off so we could go and pursue our own dreams.

Instead she'd announced she was pregnant, that there was no doubt. It took me completely by surprise.

'Don't worry, we don't have to get married if you don't want to. I don't want to entrap you,' she'd said in all seriousness.

But the more I thought about it the happier I became. 'No, I want us to get married. I love you so much,' I'd said and got down on one knee and proposed to her. I'd been wondering about doing this but assumed we'd graduate and meet each other's parents before getting engaged.

'Sorry there's no ring. We can go and get one right away.'

She held my hand but her face had that frozen look that meant she was thinking still. 'You can get up now, William.' As I returned to my seat, she cut some of her lamb chop and took a mouthful, slowly chewing.

'What do you want to do then?' I asked, unable to even look at my quiche.

'Well bang goes my first teaching placement as I'll be obviously up the duff when I go for interview.' She paused and then spoke more slowly. 'But I *am* looking forward to being a mum, so we should see my parents and announce our engagement before my bump shows.'

I took that as a yes and wanted to shout from the rooftops about it, but we never did get the engagement ring.

The Land Rover jolts me back to the present as it stops at the junction with the village road, the tyres scraping the yellow gravel.

'At least we got the money,' Jonas says, tapping the sack then engaging first gear.

Chapter 6

26th March 1960 – SS *Uganda*, Gulf of Cadiz

Heather gradually came to her senses as the light crept in between the edges of the blind and reinforced steel plate of the porthole; it was brighter than before and earlier. She got out of her bunk, trying not to shake Johnny above, put on her slippers and a dressing gown and went for a pee in the toilet down the alleyway. She had flushed the toilet and turned to stretch when the nausea rushed over her as if it had been waiting and gathering in strength all night. The suddenness took Heather by surprise even though all she had to do was turn round and lift the lavatory's wooden seat; the spasm racked her stomach, then her tightened muscles relaxed as the moment passed, and she could breathe again. Perhaps it was the smell of sea water and urine from the bowl that had set it off, or the strange gurgling and slopping noises of a ship's toilet.

Heather stood up straight and washed her face, then swilled some water around her mouth and spat it out. She leaned on the basin with both hands and breathed slowly and deeply to relax, something she'd learned from her antenatal classes when she was pregnant with Johnny. As she left the toilet, she met De Souza reversing out of her cabin with a tray and a cup of tea, in the process of carefully closing the door.

'Good morning De Souza, can I take that?'

He smiled and handed her the cup and saucer. 'I wondered where you were.'

'I'm feeling better now the sea is calmer.' Heather held the cabin door open and was about to enter.

'Tomorrow you'll have a new steward, madam, someone older.'

Heather frowned and spilled some of the tea in the saucer. 'Why? I'm very happy with you.'

De Souza shrugged his shoulders almost imperceptibly, his silver tray under his arm. 'Thank you but the assistant purser has already made arrangements.'

'I'll speak to him then,' said Heather.

De Souza bowed and walked off down the alleyway to the stewards' area, a little cubby hole she'd noticed yesterday when the door was open.

★★★

Up on boat deck there was an easterly wind blowing warm air across from the Iberian Peninsula. Instead of the sound of the occasional passenger, there was now constant chatter as chairs were brought out and drinks requested. The Indian deck crew had just finished applying a brown stain to the teak railings, leaving warning signs not to touch, and were now polishing brass fittings around the deck doors and stowing away the tarpaulin covers from the tourist and first-class swimming pools. There were hose pipes filling the two pools and a couple of deckhands were splashing around inside, cleaning the blue sides of residue from the previous voyage and removing any debris in a net. Johnny made a fuss about wanting to go in, even though he couldn't swim, so Heather promised to look for a buoyancy aid of some sort. They both went to look for the shop near the hospital on B deck.

When they returned, the pools had both been filled and the surface of the water was dancing in the sunlight. However, as the shop had no buoyancy aids, Johnny either had to swim with Heather holding him, or hang onto the side of the pool, neither of which kept him happy for long.

Heather was lying in a deckchair wondering what to do next

when she spotted De Souza and another steward coming out of a doorway marked 'Crew only', which led to their quarters at the stern of the ship. She waved at them as they passed, and De Souza came over.

'I spoke to Hancock just after breakfast and he said that it was all a misunderstanding and you could stay as my steward after all,' she said, touching the sleeve of his white jacket.

'Very good, madam,' replied De Souza, beaming. 'And how is Master Johnny today?' he added, turning to her son.

'He's cross as he hasn't got a bathing ring,' replied Heather without waiting for Johnny to reply.

The two Goanese spoke to each other in their language, then De Souza said to Heather, 'There's a bathing ring and some water wings in storage. I'll look for them.' He walked back to the crew area, skirting the cargo hatches and derricks, whilst the other steward waited.

'Here we are,' said De Souza on his return moments later. He presented Johnny with two bright blue water wings and a ring with one half white and the other red.

Johnny smiled his grin that showed the gaps in his teeth. He turned the ring over and over again, examining it. 'Girl colours,' he said, but looking as though he'd live with it.

'Thanks very much,' said Heather, waving to them as the two stewards both made their way back to their crew area at the stern.

Now Johnny was happy with his wings and ring, Heather could watch him and read her magazines at the same time, but instead she found herself thinking about the day when she and Johnny had made an impromptu visit to her sister in Beckenham. Although Heather was in the middle of travel preparations for Kenya, it felt like several months ago; she'd gone ostensibly to ask for Marjorie's approval or at least for her understanding for the trip. Instead, she'd found her sister in tears about her newly diagnosed inability to have children, and Marjorie was so upset that she was quite naturally unable to think of or talk about anything else. Now Heather had to reflect on how she could assist Marjorie and hopefully her sister would reciprocate so they could help each other, as they'd always done before.

But first she would have to talk to her sister about when her father was ill; then she'd have to confess about Gerald. But how could she help Marjorie now that she was far away on a ship bound for Kenya? Heather felt like she'd abandoned Marjorie again in her hour of need, just as when their father was ill – so how could she make up for this?

Heather laid aside her magazines and practised her breathing exercises again to try to quell her inner anxiety then sat up and waved at Johnny. Her son was grasping the edge of the pool with his water wings on his upper arms and his ring presumably around his waist. 'Watch me!' he said.

Heather smiled but her mind was elsewhere. On balance, Heather thought she would write to Marjorie, but it would need careful wording.

'Drink, madam?' asked one of the stewards, a younger man with smooth dark skin and black sleeked-back hair. Heather asked Johnny what he wanted, then ordered a lemonade and a gin and tonic.

'Thanks, Parminder,' she said, making a show of reading the badge on his lapel. He smiled shyly, showing a crooked set of teeth.

She decided to write the letter the next day, and whilst thinking about Marjorie, thought she'd give the sea-poetry book another chance.

'Shall I read you a story?' Heather asked Johnny. He nodded, and she crouched down under her chair to retrieve the book from her beach bag, then skimmed down the contents list till she found something suitable for a five-year-old.

'The owl and the pussycat,' she said, moving to sit beside him on the edge of the pool.

The Owl and the Pussycat went to sea
In a beautiful pea-green boat,
They took some honey, and plenty of money,
Wrapped up in a five-pound note.

It was a pleasure to read and the cadence was obvious for Johnny – more like a nursery rhyme than a poem. At the end, Johnny clapped his hands and went off for another paddle. Their drinks arrived, and Heather leaned back and wrote 'Johnny likes' against the poem.

She sensed someone looking at her and glanced up: it was Mr and Mrs Carruthers who'd arrived unnoticed by Heather and were now sitting in chairs against the wall of the first-class pool. He's an ugly man, she thought, with thinning hair and pock-marked skin – heavily built, unlike his gaunt wife with her too prominent cheekbones. They both quickly looked away, the wife returning to her book whilst he gazed out to sea, frowning.

'Again,' said Johnny, who'd got out of the pool via the steps and was dripping beside her. She sat him next to her then repeated Edward Lear's nonsense poem.

'That's us, Johnny, we've gone to sea,' she said, opening her arms out wide and flat. 'And this is our beautiful green boat.'

'Naaaaa,' said Johnny.

Heather wrote, 'Us en route to Kenya' next to the first verse.

★★★

The sports deck area, where they'd been the day before, was another favourite place for Heather. She could sit in one corner next to Johnny's nursery just in case of problems, and look down on the two swimming pools. However, that afternoon, whilst Johnny was having his nap after lunch, Heather had moved a little way along the boat deck towards the funnel, under the lifeboats, where very few passengers came – probably put off by the doors off the deck all being marked 'Crew only'. She was glancing through her poetry book again when one of the doors opened and a crew member almost fell over her chair.

'Hello, Heather isn't it?' It was James Scott, the engineer that she'd met at the film.

'That's right. Am I allowed here?'

'Of course, but the deck's a bit narrow. There's more room up top – let me show you.'

He led her up a staircase to a flat area with a green metallic deck next to the funnel. They walked around the funnel to get a panoramic view of the sea and the smudge of coastline on the port side. Heather felt the beat of the ship through the exhaust fumes being pumped out through the funnel and high above them.

'There's Spain and Gib around the corner,' James pointed out. 'You get the best views from up here – apart from the bridge, of course – but you don't want to be downwind of the funnel or you'll get the smuts.'

Heather laughed. 'That sounds nasty.'

The officer smiled. 'I'm collecting names for the two ship tours tomorrow – the engine room in the morning and the bridge in the afternoon. Since you showed such great interest in the cargo hatches, would you like to come along?'

'Why not – so long as Johnny can come too.'

The engineer twitched slightly.

'My son.'

'Of course, that's great.' He then shimmied down the staircase, which Heather thought might have been him showing off for her, then turned, smiled and waved goodbye.

She gazed out to sea for a few moments – it really was a three-sixty-degree view, with a couple of fishing vessels between them and the coast, a tanker further out on the starboard side, and their wake disappearing in a straight line behind the ship. If you looked straight down at the water next to the ship, it seemed to be moving quickly, but if you looked at the horizon, the *Uganda* appeared static. Heather felt goosebumps on her arms as the breeze got up; she pulled the sleeves down on her cardigan and reflected that Johnny was probably awake by now.

***

That evening in the dining room, Heather and Johnny were on the Carmichaels' table as usual, though there was no sign of the chaplain.

'They made a fuss about me and Johnny last night,' said Sophie in her querulous told-you-so voice. 'Said we were too young to be dining without our parents.'

'We've been over this once already,' said her father. 'Let's just enjoy our meal. In any case, we've something to celebrate – I managed to win the ship's mileage competition today.' George grinned at everyone around the table, clearly expecting plaudits, but instead everyone groaned. 'Yes, I got it to within two miles, so I've won a pound to spend on drinks at the dancing tonight.' George pulled out an envelope with a short letter from the first officer and a green one-pound note for everyone to see and admire. Daphne ignored him and rummaged in her handbag for a cigarette.

Heather had forgotten about the band playing for the first time that evening. 'What should I wear?' she asked Daphne.

'It's quite informal and George doesn't dance, so we usually end up just listening to the music.'

'I've seen Dad dancing,' said Sophie. 'Just listening is much better for everyone.'

Daphne stared at her husband then lit up, blowing a puff of smoke away from the table. 'We'll pick you up at nine, if you like.'

Heather agreed and then told the Carmichaels about the fuss with her steward. 'God knows what I've done to so offend them – and what right have they got to try to change my steward?'

'Carruthers is the harbourmaster in Mombasa – ex-RN – so he can make life quite difficult for BI if he puts his mind to it,' said George, pushing away his main course and leaning back in his chair. 'I'd keep away from him if I were you.'

Heather had left half of her chicken curry as the taste was too alien to her, and took another one of her seasickness pills with a glass of water. 'I spoke to Hancock about De Souza and told him I wanted to keep him, and not have someone else "more suitable for a lady travelling on her own".' Heather spoke the last phrase in a mock upper-class accent, a bit like Mrs Davenport's.

'What did Hancock say?' asked Daphne after she'd taken a sip of her Chablis.

'He assured me De Souza would stay and that would be the end of it.'

'Let's hope so,' said George. 'Just going to see what desserts they have in the cabinet.'

'De Souza is so happy he agreed to look in on Johnny tonight,' continued Heather.

Johnny smiled at the mention of his name and held up one of his toy boats.

★★★

'Here tonight, playing for the first time on the outward-bound journey, is the Sonny Souto band!' The purser turned, and with a flourish of his arm introduced the band's first number, 'Come Fly with Me'.

The stewards wove in and out of the tables, brandishing their white gloves and silver trays as though it was they who were dancing, not the passengers. They seemed to shine under the chandeliers in the smoke-filled room. Heather looked around at the lounge, which had had the tables and chairs moved over to one side to create a small dance floor, with the band squashed in the corner next to the bar. Curtains had been drawn across the windows, which Heather thought was a shame as you now couldn't see the sea.

The dancing and the music with the hubbub of the lounge reminded Heather of when she and William were engaged and used to go dancing up in the hotels of the West End – the Dorchester, the Waldorf and the Savoy. She'd loved that time, which she'd almost forgotten about till tonight.

'Ho ho,' said the purser at the end of the song, 'we know you don't mean it, Sonny. Only the Americans want to fly, us British still prefer the sedate luxury of the *Uganda*.'

The passengers all laughed and held up their glasses for more drinks. What a fool, thought Heather. I would have taken the plane if I could – it would have saved me an awful lot of trouble. She turned to speak to George.

'What do you think will happen with the East African colonies, George?'

'Oh no, must we start on this topic, it could last hours,' said Daphne, rolling her eyes.

George looked pained. 'In brief, they'll get their independence pretty soon. A lot of the French African colonies already have, and Ghana too in 1957, so it's inevitable, really.'

'What will happen to the East African ex-pats?'

'The civil servants will be sent home but those in commerce will probably stay on – at least that's what I'm hoping. What does your husband think?'

'To be honest I'd rather he was back home with Johnny and I.'

The volume from the music increased and Heather gave up on the conversation for the moment. She spotted Norman coming over to their table.

'Mind if I join you?' he asked, though he had pulled up a chair before anyone had replied. 'Well this is better, now we've passed Gib, what? The aroma of the Mediterranean, longer days, warmer weather, quieter seas and the sensual Frank Sinatra! Feels more like an adventure now, what do you say, ladies?'

Daphne laughed. 'What have you been drinking, Norman?'

'A cup of bonhomie,' he replied, smiling. Heather thought he was quite nice looking with blue eyes, swept-back hair and a deep bass voice, but the way he surveyed women up and down was a bit off-putting. Daphne liked Norman; Heather could tell by the way she looked at him when she thought no one else was paying attention.

'Nobody dancing, how come? What about you, Heather?' asked Norman, standing up and offering her his hand. Daphne's face sagged as she looked down at her drink and swilled around the lemon slice in the remaining dregs.

'Ask Daphne,' said Heather. 'I need to pop to the ladies first.'

A shadow momentarily came over Norman's face, but he of course offered his arm to Daphne who smiled and took it. Heather left the lounge, but just to walk slowly around the deck; she spotted the constellation of the plough where there was a gap in the clouds, but it was too cool outside to linger, so she returned to the lounge.

'It's a shame you don't like dancing,' said Daphne to her husband. Norman was now nowhere to be seen so presumably hadn't danced long with Daphne.

'Yes dear,' said George and signalled to a passing steward for more drinks.

★★★

Heather lay on her bunk listening to Johnny snuffling above her and reflecting on the evening. After Norman had returned, she had danced a little with him, which had been great fun. Norman was a very good dancer – he'd confessed that he'd entered a few competitions when he could find the right partner, 'Like you,' he'd added. His dancing was tactile, hand very firmly in Heather's lower back, but not too showy and he was very attentive to Heather's movements, seeking to match his own to them if required. Daphne had looked on with a sour look on her face, though eventually managed to bully George into dancing as well, but then still flicked glances across the floor at Norman.

'Fancy a gander on deck?' Norman had asked Heather, as she'd known he would.

'I don't think that's a very good idea, Norman,' she'd replied in a firm voice.

Norman held up his hands in professed innocence and they'd both laughed and walked over to the bar.

'You only live once, eh?' he'd said, putting on his linen jacket.

'What are you doing in Malta, Norman?'

He'd hesitated and wiped the palm of his hand with his thumb. 'Visiting the NATO bureau, otherwise I'd have offered to show you round. I know Malta from the war.'

'What was that like?'

'Grim; you wouldn't believe how awful it was, continual bombing for two years. I was lucky, I was in the subs, but when we were in harbour it was nerve-wracking. That's why I live for the day.'

'Will you return home and settle down eventually, Norman?'

'Only with the right person, Heather.' He'd laughed but she could tell he was proposing something.

'Maybe in another world, Norman. I know someone who might take you up, though.'

'Daphne, you mean,' Norman had nodded. 'But she's not my type.'

After that they'd returned to their table, though Norman then moved away to talk to some friends, his hand brushing against hers.

'Why are you talking so much with Norman?' Daphne had accused, frowning, her face in a pink blush. 'You shouldn't do that, you're married, what will people think?'

Luckily, the conversation had finished when George returned to their table, dabbing his face with a napkin.

At least De Souza seemed happy when she'd returned to B19 – Johnny had been as good as gold, he'd said.

Chapter 7

18th March 1960 – Orpington, Kent

'Johnny,' Heather shouted up the stairs, one hand on the solid oak bannister. 'Time for nursery, darling.'

Down he came; he could manage one step at a time now, but had to hold onto the railing, though this was a bit high for him. She smiled and opened her arms for him at the bottom of the stairs. Heather always thought he was a bit short for a four- to five-year-old, but the doctor had said not, and his pale skin and thin limbs were just like all the other boys she saw. She loved him for his thick black hair left a little long, and the ginger freckles below his pale blue eyes.

Johnny grinned back as his mum enveloped him in a big hug. She could feel the buckles of the leather satchel on his back, so she knew he was ready to go.

'We're going in the car again.'

'No bunny jumps,' said Johnny, pushing her shoulders away but still smiling.

'No, that's right, I can drive much better now.' Heather remembered how long this process had taken, from convincing William, who'd been doubtful to start with, then deciding what to do about a car; William's Rover was too big and difficult for her to manoeuvre and now spent its life in the garage. She'd eventually found a second-hand Mini that William said was affordable in the *Advertiser* and started lessons with Percy. They hadn't gone well to start with, but then she'd got the knack of the clutch and had passed her test three weeks ago.

'Mummy?' said Johnny, looking at her.

Heather shook off her thoughts, smiled at her son, then picked up her car and house keys, took Johnny's raincoat off its peg in the hall and opened the front door. Johnny ran out and stood next to the red Mini, waiting for her to unlock the driver's door and tip the seat forward so he could clamber in the back.

The nursery was at a local Presbyterian church, which had been built after the war in a nasty red brick; it was angular and square-looking with a squat tower and posters outside conveying Jesus' saying of the week. Heather managed to drop Johnny off at the bunker-like hall to one side of the church without having to go in.

After a three-point turn, which was easy enough in a wide road with a Mini, she returned home. Heather liked her large detached house with its spacious garden and was glad that she lived in a new house, built in 1956, paid for by William's parents, of course. His father had had what everyone called, but not to his face, a 'good war' working in his own shipping firm with its links to the colonies to provide food back home; it was deemed to be essential for the war effort, so he'd never had to enlist.

As a result, Heather had never wanted for anything, was simply not required to work, and her parents had loved William from the outset. When his father had retired, William had decided that he didn't want to stay in the firm and changed job to work for Brooke Bond.

'There's no future in shipping any more,' he'd said, though Heather didn't really know why and his father had certainly been very disappointed.

Heather walked up the driveway to her house with its mock Tudor inlaid wooden beams and tile frontage and looked up at the thickening sky and felt the air colder now; the weather was about to turn. She sighed and opened the front door. What was she going to do? William wasn't due to come home till August and his company wouldn't want him to return earlier. She could tell him that Johnny was upset about going to school, but that didn't reflect well on her, and in any case didn't sound a very convincing reason for him to come home early.

As she tugged the front door key out of the lock and turned to close the door, she looked at the single parade of shops opposite her and the green, around which all the houses had been built. Half of the newly planted trees looked like they were dead, though there were now daffodils poking through the grass in clumps. A woman in a grey coat was sitting on a bench with a perambulator, rocking it gently as another child kicked a ball around in a rather aimless fashion.

No, she'd have to go out there; but then that would take several weeks and the company would be unlikely to pay for a flight. Maybe he could meet her somewhere on the way for some sightseeing? Egypt perhaps? But then Heather remembered the Suez crisis and that horrid Nasser man, and she'd have to bring Johnny who might get ill if they left the ship.

Heather forced a smile and looked at herself in the hall mirror; she was still good looking, she thought, just like the photos of her mother when she was younger, her dark brown hair pushed out and her skin unblemished and with an olive tone to go with her hazelnut eyes. Of course, her nose was a bit aquiline, but she was tall and carried herself well, she thought, as she stared at herself. Heather then adjusted her hair, pursed her lips to get the lipstick evenly applied, and pushed her chest out to show her breasts to best effect, her new brassiere a pleasing pointed shape.

She passed through the lounge and into the dining room; this was her favourite room in the house, smaller than the lounge but snugger and more informal, with Johnny's toys and his books in one corner. A couple of streaks of sunlight came through the French windows and fell diagonally across the dark-stained dining room table, burning first brightly then fading away with the clouds' advance. This was where Johnny had had the fishbone stuck in his throat and made those ghastly rasping noises before Gerald had hung him upside down and bashed it out. Dear Gerald.

She'd have to see the doctor next just to make sure it was all right for her and Johnny to travel to Kenya; she thought about driving but it was less than half a mile away on the other side of the green, and the rain was holding off for the moment. As Heather walked along the pavement of her street up towards the main road, a small green bus's engine was idling opposite the parade of shops and she was glad she no longer had to worry about its unpredictable arrival and departure to get into Orpington. It hadn't been easy to learn to drive – not just the mastering of the clutch but the frowning of the other mothers in the nursery. 'My husband looks after that' or 'We haven't got a car', or 'What's wrong with the bus and train?' they'd said, though Heather thought they might secretly be envious. Then there'd been the time she'd taken Johnny to nursery as part of her driving lesson and they'd made remarks about her instructor – God knows why, as his home-knitted jumpers and tubbiness didn't make him attractive at all.

At the far end of the oval-shaped green, there was another street linking to the main road, which was bordered by semi-detached houses; the doctor's surgery was one such, its walls pebbledashed with a cream paint overlaid, and the ground floor given over to one waiting and two consulting rooms. One of the three doctors, the junior and unmarried one, lived above.

The waiting room was draughty and had drab linoleum on the floor; the patients were lined up in two rows opposite each other, with the secretary behind a desk and filing cabinets at one end. The row opposite was almost entirely taken up by mothers with their babies or toddlers, apart from an elderly couple who must have lived on the main road. There was a lot of crying and coughing, which Heather tried to ignore as she settled down for a long wait.

After half an hour, Heather thought it might be her turn next and the door to her doctor opened and the woman in the grey coat she'd seen earlier emerged with her perambulator and young boy. Heather saw that the woman was much younger than she'd first thought, without make-up and her hair sticking up on one side. The boy asked for his ball as they tramped out of the surgery and Heather was called in.

After taking her pulse and blood pressure, plus tapping her chest and listening with his stethoscope, the doctor said she was well enough to travel and told her what vaccinations were required. He then gestured towards the door and shook his rather cold hand with Heather's. Outside, the boy was kicking his ball in front of him as his mother and her baby crossed the green diagonally.

'Mind the dog's mess, Thomas,' she shouted to him.

Back home it was time to phone Dot, William's assistant in their London office. Heather didn't like doing this but sometimes it was the best way of contacting him, so she lit up a Craven A and smoothed out her pink dress to calm herself. She knitted her brow thinking through what she wanted to say, and then dialled the number. Dot answered and they exchanged the usual preliminaries.

'Can you telex William a message? I'd like to come out soon. Johnny's been suffering a bit at nursery and I think we both need a break. We could all return home with William in August as he intended.'

'Well, I know he's difficult to track down, but I'll send him a message if you like. Just spell it out again for me, exactly what you want to say, but keep it brief.'

Heather spelt out her message to Dot and then asked, 'Would it be possible for us to make the journey by plane, rather than by sea?'

'Sorry, Mrs Fontwell, but we only use air travel for urgent business or if the extra expense warrants it. I don't think even William could get it at his grade.'

Heather was on the point of saying that it *was* urgent but managed to restrain herself.

'And, to be frank Mrs Fontwell, the sea passage is quite pleasant, by all accounts; most of the ex-pats really look forward to it. I wouldn't trust those Comet aircraft either – have you seen the latest film *Cone of Silence* – it tells you all about those terrible crashes.'

'Well, I guess I'll have to take the ship then,' said Heather, exhaling a big puff of cigarette smoke.

'Just get Thomas Cook to book the passage and quote our business account in Leadenhall Street,' replied the secretary in an enthusiastic voice. 'There's the usual financial limit, though.'

'Thanks Dot, you're a star,' Heather said, and rung off, grinding down the cigarette into a china ashtray then retrieving her diary again.

Well, the only thing would be to see what ships were going when, and whether they'd even have a berth for her and Johnny. When William had left before Christmas and they'd been to the party in London, his colleagues had said how busy the ships were at the time. Heather twirled her pen around, tapped her cheekbone, and let out a long sigh.

There was now only just enough time left to call the travel agent in Bromley and at least see what her options were.

'Can you tell me the next sailing to Mombasa?' she asked, all in a rush.

Heather could hear the girl slowly turning over the brochure pages. 'Union Castle line goes there in three weeks' time, the um…' there were more page flicking noises… '*Edinburgh Castle*, a nice ship.'

'Listen, I need a ticket as soon as possible.'

'I'll have to phone our shipping office then, Mrs Fontwell. Can I call you back?'

Heather slowly replaced the receiver and prayed that there would be something available. She then picked up the copy of the *Times* delivered that morning and looked up the liner movements; there was a Union Castle ship leaving tonight but that didn't help her planning for something in the next week. She lit up another cigarette, taking a long drag on it, and whilst contemplating her options the phone rang – it was Thomas Cook.

'Last-minute cancellation for two next week on BI line, tourist class. Any use?'

This is my way out, Heather thought. 'Yes, for myself and my almost five-year-old son.'

'OK – I'll get Sidney to put a hold on that then. Can you come in tomorrow before we close at midday to sort out the paperwork? Your husband's firm is paying, I assume?'

'That's right,' said Heather. 'When does the ship arrive in Mombasa?'

There was a clunk as the phone was put down followed by a thud and the flicking of pages. 'April the tenth. I've got the brochure on the BI line and another one about the ship, which you can look at tomorrow.'

'What facilities are there for children aged five?'

Heather could hear the girl flicking through the brochure.

'Well there are normally quite a few children on these ships. They have their own dining rooms and nurseries on board, but it's probably best if you look tomorrow at the brochure. By the way,' the girl added, 'BI have two ships going to East Africa. Yours is the SS *Uganda*, a very friendly ship, apparently. I'm sure you'll both love it.'

Chapter 8

27th March 1960 – SS *Uganda*, Western Mediterranean

'I don't know, I'm not really a churchgoer,' said Heather, sitting drinking coffee in the tourist-class lounge. It was a relief to walk around open space, feel the sea breeze and relax in relative tranquillity after the heat, noise and confinement of the engine-room tour. She'd left Johnny at the nursery.

'Well,' said Daphne, 'I'm sure Reverend Ian would appreciate our support.'

Heather blew air over her too-hot coffee and lifted an eyebrow towards Daphne.

'In any case,' continued Daphne, 'it's quite uplifting, even if you're not religious, isn't that so, dear?' She turned to look at George who was reading the ship's order of the day, with his glasses balanced on his forehead.

'What Daphne means is that it's a good chance to nose around the first-class drawing room,' replied George, still reading the sheet of paper.

'Really, George, whatever will you say next,' replied Daphne, flicking some imaginary crumbs off her skirt.

'I *am* religious, it's just that I don't like church,' said Heather. 'But I'll come along to support Ian – Johnny can stay a bit longer in the nursery.'

'How was the engine-room tour?' asked George, putting down the sheet. 'The last one made me quite claustrophobic.'

'True, but at least real work is being done there, the officers and

74

the crew working together, all with their job to do, men harnessing a machine, the employment of science, that sort of thing.'

They finished their coffees and walked up two staircases to the promenade deck then along the enclosed walkway to the entrance to the first-class area. There was the same oil tanker running parallel to the *Uganda* but otherwise no coastline or other shipping to see. There were dark and light patches on the sea as the sun moved in and out of cloud, a light salty breeze rippling the sea's surface, gently pitching the ship and causing the occasional burst of spray.

One of the stewards opened the door for them and George explained they had come for the Sunday Service. They carried on walking forward on plush blue carpet, past the wood-panelled first-class writing room, where a lone gentleman in a green tweed suit sat at a desk with a fountain pen in one hand and a blotter in the other, admiring the spidery writing he'd so far completed. Heather reminded herself to write to Marjorie that afternoon or Monday, to catch the post in Malta.

In a small vestibule, the chaplain was handing out service sheets and greeting the passengers with a handshake. In front of them were the Carruthers, awaiting their turn to talk to the chaplain, the husband wearing a grey morning suit and his wife a long blue dress; they whispered something between themselves then turned around when they heard Daphne talking.

'Sorry about the business with your steward,' he said, but the corner of his lip curled up.

'Yes, I sorted it out, thanks,' Heather replied, hands on hips, aware that she was looking down on the man.

His wife dragged him forward to be greeted by the chaplain. 'Don't make a scene,' she whispered.

The Carmichaels and Heather stayed well back, but the Carruthers' greeting from the chaplain was quickly concluded.

'Reverend Ian, where have you been hiding?' said Daphne, smiling.

'Sorry, had a lot to do with the crew,' he replied. 'Everything all right here, with…' He tipped his head back towards the retreating Carruthers.

George shrugged his shoulders and motioned Heather to come forward and shake the chaplain's hand.

'You're looking much better, Heather,' said the chaplain. 'Pop by and see me when you get a moment.'

They moved into the drawing room, which was a large circular shape surrounded on three sides by the promenade deck with a wide view over the sea and the cargo area in front of the fo'c'sle, with the occasional cloud of spray coming over the bow. The deep sofas and chairs, all in a oatmeal linen with floral sprays of blue and gold, had been pushed back under the windows with their full-length curtains of silk brocade, again in oatmeal with blue and gold. In the centre of the room there was a magnificent Wilton carpet with floral design, sitting under a backlit circular recess in the ceiling.

Some ordinary wooden chairs had been put in lines for the congregation, with a gangway up the middle facing a wooden lectern and a piano, where a Goanese was seated in his white band suit flicking through the sheet music in front of him.

'There's the Captain,' said Daphne, pointing out to Heather the officer in uniform seated behind the lectern as George sought somewhere for them to sit together. The Captain was probably in his late fifties, short and squat with thick grey hair, and looking down at his notes. George beckoned them over and they sat down next to Bob and Betty Saunders, who smiled effusively and chatted, thankfully to George.

Heather looked up at the pale peach ceiling and noticed the little punkah louvres dotted about; of course, this was the air-conditioning referred to on the morning tour, no wonder the temperature was so cool in this room. As she waited for the service to begin, Heather reflected that Daphne had seemed quite smug about the conversation with Carruthers and that it was her, after all, that had persuaded Heather to come along. She was feeling rather disgusted by this un-Christian thought when the Captain and Reverend Ian stood up, the latter announcing the first hymn. There was a rustling as the passengers also stood and referred to their service sheets, then the piano played the introduction to 'Eternal Father, Strong to Save'.

Heather looked in her handbag for the poetry book; yes, there it was. She sang along but thought the third verse the best:

Most Holy Spirit! Who didst brood
Upon the chaos dark and rude,
And bid its angry tumult cease,
And give, for wild confusion, peace;
Oh, hear us when we cry to Thee,
For those in peril on the sea!

She wrote the date and *'somewhere in the Med'* underneath this verse. There was then a Bible reading from the Captain, who knew his lines almost by heart and was able to cast his eye over the congregation as he read, followed by some prayers and another hymn. Ian then delivered a sermon about the need for each individual to recognise their failings and confront them by talking to friends and loved ones. He told the parable about the two debtors and how the woman 'with many faults' could be forgiven because she kissed Jesus' feet with tears and then anointed them – so love could always lead to forgiveness, whatever the tariff. Heather admired the way he spoke without notes, moving around in front of the congregation from one side of the room to the other, using his arms to make points, his voice rising and falling like an actor's.

This was not a parable that Heather was familiar with, but she felt the murmuring in the congregation. Maybe the faulty woman was a lady of the night or loose, which might have offended some of the passengers, but whatever the details, Heather felt there were parallels with her own circumstances.

At the end of the service, the Captain stood at the lectern and talked about the programme for the next few days and that the collection would be going, as usual, to the Mission to Seafarers. He spoke quietly but clearly expected to be listened to, then clicked his fingers whilst pointing towards the back of the room. Heather turned round and noticed that cadet Mark was holding out a collection pouch with a wooden handle.

Reverend Ian walked slowly down the gangway, nodding to a few people, and into the vestibule. Heather noticed the ease with which he moved amongst the passengers; he'd greet them with a smile, touch their sleeve or shoulder, lean in to them to talk on a personal level, then retreat slightly to laugh at whatever they had to say. The chaplain reminded Heather of a younger version of a friend of Daddy's that she'd long lost contact with; what did it mean, she wondered, this desire for solitude but also his easy gregariousness?

The Captain followed the chaplain and made a show of dropping a ten-bob note into the pouch proffered by the cadet. Heather waited whilst the queue moved away, and admired the astonishing variety of wood panelling around the walls of the lounge, of which she recognised birch, ash and elm. Over the mantelpiece was an oil painting of a French chateau with tree-lined avenue and a group of huntsmen conversing with some pedlars in the foreground.

They were amongst the last to leave as the Saunders had been chatting; Heather made a few polite remarks but was overawed by the luxury of the room that the others had obviously seen before.

'I enjoyed your sermon,' said Heather to the chaplain, and looking down at his hands noticed the lack of a wedding ring, not even the ghostly marking of an absent one.

★★★

'Come on, Johnny, we're going to see the Captain on the bridge,' said Heather as her son dallied over the end of lunch. There were few other passengers left by now, and the stewards were standing around the walls of the dining room waiting to clear the tables.

'Can I come with you?' asked Sophie.

'Yippee!' said Johnny. 'Mummy, is it a bridge over the sea to Africa?'

They all laughed. 'No, Johnny, it's where the Captain looks out over everyone and tells them what to do,' said George.

Johnny frowned. He didn't like people laughing at him, but he still wanted to see what the Captain looked like.

'You can bring your toy ships along,' said Heather, standing up to go. Daphne announced she wanted to lay in the sun up on deck. so the rest of them, including Sophie, set off up to the sports deck then forward along the boat deck between the lifeboats and the officers' cabins and mess rooms. Eventually, they found the outside stairs up to the bridge and Heather went to hold Johnny's hand as the stairs were narrow and steep and the sea appeared alarmingly to be moving beneath them if you looked down.

'No, Sophie's hand!'

Sophie giggled and took Johnny's hand as he slowly took each step at a time.

As they opened the teak door to the bridge, they were met by the Captain himself who invited them to admire the view. They looked out of the bridge in the direction the ship was heading, seeing the bow wash spread out on either side of the ship and the fo'c'sle rise and fall. There were fishing vessels either side of the *Uganda,* as well as another cargo ship heading away from them in the distance on the port side and a small oil tanker ahead of them to starboard.

'Is that the same ship we saw earlier today?' asked Heather, pointing at the tanker.

'Yes, I saw it, too,' said Sophie, looking excited.

'Well, Number Two?' said the Captain, turning to another officer on watch, who was staring out to sea with a pair of binoculars. He let his binoculars down and turned towards them – it was the same officer they'd met at the muster station exercise.

'That's right, the *Lampusa*. We're following her into Valletta,' he said with his robotic voice.

'I knew that really,' the Captain said, talking softly behind his hand as they walked into the chart room. 'Just checking he was alert, eh!' He showed the group of about ten passengers the charts for the day ahead, how the voyage was plotted towards Malta, and the radio navigational beacons and lighthouses they were expecting en route.

'Don't you just navigate by radar?' an elderly gentleman asked.

'No, radar's for surveillance of other ships and the shoreline.'

'Can we see the radar?' George asked.

'We don't usually bother with it in good visibility in the Med. Let me show you the wheelhouse and communications instead.'

They moved out of the chart room and returned to the main part of the bridge where another officer was holding the wheel. Behind him, mounted onto a backing panel, was an array of dials and instruments where James Scott, the third engineer, was noting the readings on a clipboard.

Scott explained the functions of each of the instruments and the Captain then allowed each passenger to take the wheel and see how hard it was to move the rudder. Johnny went first and had a box to stand on and the first mate's hands to help him.

'Hi Heather,' whispered Scott as she was waiting her turn. 'Sorry to miss you this morning, been doing instrument checks all day.' He looked at her out of the corner of his eye, surprised by her attractiveness, though she had little natural beauty, more a poise and athletic physique.

After everyone had had their turn on the wheel, the Captain took them all into his day room for a glass of champagne or orange juice. The room had light-wood panelling and display cabinets with dark-wood chairs and desk-height cupboards that extended around two sides; there were also half a dozen deep armchairs with blue floral patterns that some of the older passengers were collapsing into, having stood for so long. Heather ran her hand along the chair backs and wondered if anything ever got lost behind the deep cushions, then noticed Cadet Mark tapping gently at the door with an envelope in his hand. The Captain moved over to the door and turned his back to the passengers to block their view, but Heather was nearest and could see him take the envelope and open it to reveal a ten-bob note inside, before folding the envelope and putting it inside his jacket.

'Remember, next time,' he said to the cadet and turned back to the tour party, catching Heather's gaze as he did so. 'Clever of you to notice the tanker,' he said, but without a smile. Then he noticed Johnny sitting on the carpeted floor, pushing his toy boat. 'Hasn't your mum got a watchful eye?' he said to Johnny, bending down to him, then raising himself up again. The Captain gave a big smile when he realised that everyone was looking at the two of them. 'Now, ladies and gentlemen, the cadet will accompany you to the radio room on the deck below to conclude this afternoon's tour.'

The group slowly filed out down a staircase, but just as they were leaving, Heather noticed that the officers on the bridge were now all surveying the horizon with their binoculars.

'Come on, Sophie,' she said, 'let's get some tea.

Chapter 9

March 1960 – Kiambethu, Kenya

Yesterday I asked Jonas if his sister was settling in at Kiambethu after I'd had her moved from Mabroukie. Needless to say, Taylor had made a fuss, said I was too soft with the niggers, as he liked to call them. I'd told him it was because Jonas wanted to be with his sister, which was partially true. But then Taylor had demanded that someone else be sent from Kiambethu to replace Jonas's sister. After talking with Jonas, we'd decided on a worker who already had family on the mother plantation, and who would be better protected from Taylor's schemes.

So the swap had happened a few days ago, and Jonas said things were going fine until this afternoon when he came to see me in the office.

'Sir, can you come this evening to the workers' cottages, far side? Something is going on.'

So here Jonas is again in the office, at the time agreed. Dorothea looks up from her ledger and shakes her hair back; she doesn't like to get involved in issues with the estate workers as she thinks they distrust her and clam up in her presence.

'Good luck,' she says drily with a half smile as we leave.

Outside, I ask Jonas what he thinks of Dorothea, but he just laughs and his teeth gleam in the remaining light. We get in the estate Land Rover and set off across the dirt roads linking the tea plantation, houses and drainage ditches, the engine wheezing with the corroded exhaust pipe. It's dark by the time we arrive and Jonas takes me into a single-storey white building; there's a hurricane lamp outside, which he shakes to check for paraffin and lights with a Swan Vesta. Inside it smells of urine and rotting vegetables.

'Follow me, please.'

We reach an oblong room with no windows, the only light coming from the doorway; cream-coloured paint is flaking off the walls to reveal a previous rendition in ochre and bare plaster. A bare light fitting hangs from the ceiling, but there's no bulb.

Around the walls of the room are a dozen cots on castors where children of all ages up to about ten are sleeping. Some are babies face down, snuffling and lightly snoring, others are infants sucking their thumbs, all with skins of various shades of brown, as well as older children, about Johnny's age, who are sharing cots with the sides removed. The floor is beaten earth covered with dust underneath the cots and there are dark splash stains on the walls with rubbish pushed against them. The room smells of sweet sweat; it's stuffy and airless.

I look at one of the older boys, lying on his back with his arms flung out sideways, one across the shoulders of the boy next to him sleeping on his side. His chest expands and contracts in his grubby off-white vest, and the two of them look peaceful enough as they shift in the cots then resume their heavy breathing. There are no cot mattresses, just layers of rough towels and tunics of varying colours, probably harbouring fleas or bed bugs. I leave the room in a quandary to look for Jonas, but instead find myself facing a Kenyan woman who is leaning languidly against a filthy wall.

The woman pushes off from the wall and walks slowly up to me, her face suddenly breaking out into a smile. Her right-hand fingers travel down the yellow strap of her singlet and her thumb massages the side of her breast, drawing my attention to the nipples poking through the material of her singlet.

'Jumbo bwana,' she whispers, looking around behind me, and I can only grunt in reply. The woman's skin is a glistening dark black, the occasional light reflecting off her arms, chest and throat. Her broken teeth shine. 'I keep you company, free your spirits of the darkness,' she adds, shuffling up close to me, patting the lapels of my shirt and grazing her fingers on my neck. With her proximity, I notice her left eye is slightly swollen and bloodshot.

I know I'm being propositioned, that this is not something I can do if I'm trying to stop prostitution amongst the tea planters, that it doesn't seem right to be here amongst the squalor of their sleeping quarters, but then it's been a long time with this aching and my loneliness, and I linger over the moment before stepping back and replying, 'No, no thank you.' I feel very stiff and British, rubbing the back of my neck, but try not to show my awkwardness.

'Very clean,' the woman adds, in a rising tone of desperation. I gather she must be talking about herself rather than the oblong room or the corridor, which are anything but clean.

'I've come to have a look round here.' I point towards the room, 'Check the facilities and make sure all the women are happy.'

The woman nods and now rubs her hips with her hands, still staring at me. I don't think she's understood me well, so I wait for Jonas, who I can see is now walking down the corridor between the pools of light from the hurricane lamps. He strides across to meet us, carefully avoiding a box of old clothes and a heap of dust and rotten jack fruit that someone has swept up, leaving tracks across the corridor. The woman and Jonas exchange a few words of Swahili before hugging each other briefly.

'Who's looking after the children?' I ask.

Jonas peers into the oblong room and shrugs his shoulders. 'All the mothers, they take it in turns, whoever is awake. Rehema too,' he adds nodding towards the woman.

I feel in my pocket and hand Rehema a couple of East African shilling coins. She frowns at me, still holding the coins, jinking them together in her upturned hand. Was this not enough or have I insulted her with the money?

'Yes, this is my sister,' Jonas pauses and picks up one of the hurricane lamps 'I told you her story.' He wipes the back of his hand across his face.

The shadows flicker around the walls as Jonas swings the lamp around, the flame rising and falling. Now I understand and reach out to shake Rehema's hand; the muscles on her bare arm are tense and lined in the half light. She smiles at me, nods, then looks away.

'Nice to meet you,' I say, feeling very ill at ease, before I step backwards next to Jonas who is shuffling with impatience.

'Well, what has happened?' I ask him. He speaks in Swahili again to Rehema and she replies, her eyes darting all around the room.

'They came this afternoon, the foreman and the money man from Kiambethu,' says Jonas, 'with another white man, a visitor. Now they doing with our women workers what they did up there, starting with Rehema, because they know she is weak.'

'You mean Doug, the money man?'

'Uh ha.'

'Does he lie with the women as well?'

Jonas shrugs. 'Sometimes. The foreman threatens them with a machete if they make trouble, then pays the woman. They are frightened so they hiding now.'

We walk down the corridor and I notice another room that I missed before, stacks of wood along one end under two unglazed windows, the night air rippling through, prickling my skin. The far wall and ceiling are blackened by wood smoke.

'Kitchen,' says Jonas, 'and washing too.' There are two giant tubs, one wooden, the other galvanised, set against an adjacent wall.

We march further down the corridor and out through a low wooden door into the night. I stop to shut the door then squeeze my eyes closed, trying to breathe normally, and concentrate on listening; the tea plants hiss in the breeze and an owl hoots from the trees at the bottom of the field. My mind is awash with so many thoughts squirming and rushing backwards and forwards that I can't think what to do next, other than go back to the plantation house and Dorothea, then try to sleep away a few months forward to better times; but I know I will never be free again, of these tumbling thoughts, the memories or my responsibilities skulking behind everything. I open my eyes and the tea plants are shimmering in the lunar light. Jonas looks away, leans down and blows out the hurricane lamp, then stands it next to the door, his face black against the whitewashed wall.

'What kind of estate worker house is that?' I ask, to return to more prosaic matters, my voice rasping in the half light. 'It's nothing like those next to the plantation house.'

Jonas laughs, but not from joy or surprise, more a harsher cynical tone. 'Those are what you English call show homes, I think, for when the inspectors or the Brooke Bond visitors come. The houses further away have no plumbing or electricity, only open wood fires and no proper windows. There are usually three big families in two rooms so the children get put in one and the adults in another. Then the women selling themselves have to hide amongst the children or go outside under the trees.'

Now I realise the prostitution is more endemic than I thought, pimped by Taylor, though indirectly through his henchmen, the same kind of structure as the invoicing fraud – and the scene with the blind man in the New Testament, cured by Jesus, comes to mind. I mention this to Jonas.

'St John, chapter nine, first I was blind then I could see,' he replies.

I realise how little I know about Jonas's life outside the plantation, that he must be an avid churchgoer. 'So Taylor is behind all this. In the morning...' A wave of fatigue rises up and prevents me saying more.

Jonas laughs, this time a slower, softer kind of chuckle. 'Don't worry, plenty time tomorrow. Let's go back and get some sleep.'

We head off to the Land Rover parked on a bank next to the dirt track. As I open the door, I realise how casual this all is and ask Jonas, 'Johnny will be safe here on the estate, won't he?'

Jonas looks at me across the roof of the Land Rover, squinting in the silvery light. 'Don't worry, he'll be a lot safer here with the village people than with Taylor, who'd sell anyone he could.'

'Have we still got those shotguns, Jonas?'

He looks alarmed. 'Yes, for shooting rats. Two guns, locked in the plantation house.'

'I'll speak to Doug, tomorrow. Let's go.'

We both close the grey metal doors and the Land Rover sets off along the track, rear wheels spinning out mud before regaining traction. When we get back to the plantation house, Dorothea is closing the office by pulling across the roller doors on the filing cabinets. She comes and stands close to me, shoulder to shoulder.

'Well, what happened?' she murmurs in a low voice.

I give her an account of events and she clicks her tongue. I can smell the coconut oil on her hair, and something else, a spice of some sort.

'She's trouble that Rehema. You should have left her at Mabroukie.'

'Rehema's not the problem, it's the white men up the hill.' Whatever I do seems to backfire on me.

'Yes them too.' Dorothea holds up her hands and jangles the office keys.

***

As the engine noise tails off, the silence of the tea estate retakes the night. Inside the sleeping area, Rehema is lying on her mattress on the floor; she thinks about the boss's face, the shadow lines and the darkness of his eyes, and feels his sadness. Of course her brother told her about him and the half-caste Indian woman who has slithered her way into his spirit like a serpent, but she never met the boss before, so misplaced him for another Taylor white worker sent for sex before returning to them plantation house the other side of the mountains. Rehema wonders if Mister boss found her attractive, her breasts still upright despite her children, if he wanted her like the other coming bwana, whether she could free his spirits and hers too so they fly free and high like the storks.

Jonas told her before to stop laying with these bloated white men, weighed down by their guilt and unhappiness, but then she's cranky too sometimes, so maybe she could make happy the boss and Jonas too. Then there are all the men on Taylor's pay; despite Fontwell boss, Jonas has no idea. How does he think she gets food and clothing for her little ones? She listens out for any children crying but there's just snuffling, the creaking of the cots and the occasional sleep talk, so she lifts the glass of the hurricane lamp, blows out the orange flame and smells the soot of the wick. Hakuna matata.

***

The next day, I call Doug and ask him to come over to the plantation house at Kiambethu to talk over the accounts. He's not keen to do this.

'I think I found a way to improve things but wanted to talk the details over with you first,' I add in as cheerful a voice as I can muster. This sounds like I might be agreeing to join Taylor's scheme, and sure enough Doug agrees a time.

I ask Jonas to get me one of the shotguns before he heads off to pick up Doug in the ancient Land Rover, then station myself next to the borders where the trees are, shotgun on my shoulder. It's hot today, even in the shade, and sweat stains appear on the underarms of my thick cotton shirt as I listen to the calls of the birds and hope the breeze will pick up soon. I'm poking around in the undergrowth to see if there really are any rats to shoot at when I'm disturbed by Doug, standing on the edge of the lawns.

'Doesn't your boy do that?'

'I like to keep in practice with the guns,' I reply, stepping back onto the lawns to face him. 'You see down there in the hollow' – I point with the shotgun – 'That's the dirt track to the other side of the estate, so it's quite easy to see, from the dust or headlights, if there are any cars going that way, which there rarely are. Apart from yesterday afternoon that is.'

I pause and I can see Doug shift his shoulders and look back at me.

'Don't follow you. What's this got to do with the accounts?'

'Oh nothing at all,' I reply. 'Just saying I don't like clandestine visitors, that's all, it might lead to extra security measures and that risks a misunderstanding.' I swing the shotgun and fire into the undergrowth.

Doug ducks and puts his hands over his ears. I swing the gun around again and point it at him. 'You can do what you like on your plantation, but no more unofficial visits here, Doug, otherwise...' I pull the trigger again but there is only a click.

A groaning noise comes from Doug and he jumps up, throwing his arms about, realising there was only one cartridge. 'There's something wrong with you, William,' he shouts as he runs back to the Land Rover where Jonas is waiting.

Chapter 10

28th March 1960 – SS *Uganda*, Western Mediterranean

'Is honesty always the best policy?' Heather asked Reverend Ian as they sat in the tourist-class smoking room. There was something about the male atmosphere – the deep leather chairs, dark wood panelling, the mixture of cigar and cigarette smells and the murmured conversation – that was comforting to her. She was wearing her best nautical outfit that morning, the first time it had felt sufficiently warm to do so, a navy blue top embossed with a white ship's wheel and a cream-coloured skirt – but no tights, oh joy, so she'd had to shave her legs in the bathroom after breakfast. William had always complimented her on her pegs, as he called them, shapely without being muscly he'd said last summer, which now seemed like a century ago.

The chaplain put down his coffee cup, took out a pipe from a side pocket of his grey herringbone jacket and started filling the pipe from a tin of tobacco. 'Usually,' he replied, squashing down the tobacco into the pipe bowl with a small metal device, 'but the occasional white lie might be justified.'

Heather nodded and shifted in her seat.

'Why do you ask?' the chaplain continued, then sucked on the pipe to exhale large clouds of blue smoke.

Heather wondered where on earth to begin; she really didn't do white lies – just great whoppers, but thankfully very rarely.

'Well, did you know,' Heather replied, 'that after the Captain puts his ten bob in the collection for the Sunday service, with such aplomb, he then removes it afterwards?'

'Mmm, I didn't know that,' said the chaplain, puffing and staring out at the reflection of the sun dancing on an azure sea as the ship gently rolled.

Heather thought about how Mark the cadet had squirmed on his bar stool when she'd confronted him last night. He said he'd forgotten to return the money earlier, which was why the Captain had been short with him, but Heather had reassured him that no one else could have noticed the money being handed back and she wouldn't mention it to a soul (the chaplain didn't count as he was bound to secrecy).

'Well, it would get expensive after a while,' said Ian, engulfing himself in more blue smoke, 'and the aim of encouraging charity is a noble one.' They both finished their coffees and Reverend Ian insisted on paying. 'Not that I get this paid back,' he added, waving the chit, as they both got up to leave. They walked slowly along the promenade deck towards the stern, enjoying the warmth of the Mediterranean sun tempered by the slight breeze.

'About Carruthers,' said Ian. 'I couldn't explain this properly in front of the Carmichaels, but he thinks that a woman's place is in the home and doesn't like you travelling on your own.'

'Why not? It wasn't my idea for William to be in Kenya.'

'He's got it into his head that you're unsettling the men on the ship, like Norman or George, for instance.'

'Well really,' said Heather rather crossly, 'who the hell is he to judge me?'

'I did speak to him but his faith is strong.'

Heather was furious – she hated this kind of judgemental intolerance, especially when it threatened her or her family. But nothing much would be gained by public displays of anger, so she decided to keep quiet and away from Carruthers.

'Is anything else troubling you?' Ian stopped walking and turned to look at her.

She stared at the hazy sun then returned his gaze. 'Not exactly, but I need to write to my sister from Malta and try to straighten out a few things.'

The chaplain knocked his pipe on the teak railing to get rid of the tobacco remnants then turned to lean his back against the railing, away from the sun that was blinding him. 'Are you going ashore in Malta?'

'Daphne has this madcap idea about finding a copy of *Lady Chatterley's Lover.*' They both chuckled.

'I'm sure it'll be published soon in England, so I won't join in your search, but I always go to the Catholic and Anglican cathedrals in Valletta; they're both magnificent. If you wanted to accompany me we could find the Carmichaels afterwards for lunch.'

'I'd like that,' said Heather and made her excuses to leave. It was too bright to write outside and she didn't want to be interrupted, so she returned to their cabin, sat down at the writing table, and pulled out some of the ship's writing paper and a ballpoint pen. The reflections of the sun on the water danced around the walls and ceiling of the cabin, wavy lines always in motion.

The beginning of the letter was easy enough – just where they were, what they'd been doing, what it was like on the *Uganda*, the weather, the other passengers and crew and so forth. Then it got more difficult to write, more personal, and Heather concluded that maybe, after all, honesty would be the best policy for this letter.

We've never really talked about when Daddy was ill. I know you faced most of the burden of looking after him and for this I will always be grateful. It cannot have been easy when his death was so drawn out and painful for him despite the drugs. I'm afraid I was not much use at the time; yes, I was on my own as William was in Kenya, and yes Johnny was only a toddler at the time and needed a lot of my attention, but I still feel that I could have done more, especially when Daddy was at home with you.

To be frank, that Daddy's illness was terminal was just too

difficult for me to face; he'd meant everything to me when I was
younger. I know you and Mother felt that I was his favourite, but it
wasn't deliberate or sought after, just that we seemed to have a lot of
things in common. If it hadn't have been for Daddy, I don't think
I would ever have gone to Exeter; Mother was quite against it and
often said she thought I was wasting my time away. So I think I
blanked out most of the time he was ill – I should have been more
engaged emotionally but somehow I had to survive.

Anyhow, to come to the present day and my predicament,
which I wanted talk to you about when we were last in Beckenham
but Johnny was present so I couldn't say much. Needless to say, it
is also the real reason why I've had to board the Uganda at short
notice.

Heather tapped her teeth with the end of the pen, then folded the
unfinished letter and put it into the slim drawer underneath the
writing table. The rest will have to be done this afternoon, she
thought, as Johnny needed to be picked up.

At the nursery, Margot was wiping down one of the low giant
petal tables with a wet cloth and looked up at Heather's arrival.
'Johnny plays a lot now with Michael and is well behaved.'

Heather looked around the nursery – there were few children,
probably as most of them were outside on deck.

'Is everything all right – you look a bit worried about something?'

Heather knew what it was, she'd felt it creeping up on her,
her childhood phobia, but she wasn't ready to confront it again. It
related to a childhood incident when Daddy had read to her about
the trolls, creatures from Nordic mythology, and the picture in
her book, with its long hooked nose, elephantine wrinkled skin
and missing fingers, had terrified her. Daddy had just laughed and
got another book instead, but her mother had insisted that she
confront this fear, and reread the book, and had then started using
the picture as a punishment if she'd done something wrong. The

confrontation approach did not work and she'd started wetting the bed and having nightmares about the trolls and their crooked fingers and spider's web hair. One day the book just disappeared and wasn't referred to again, but the trolls seemed to have made a permanent mark on her dreams, re-emerging at times of anxiety and during her teenage years, then re-appearing last when her father had been ill.

The seasickness pills seemed to help for some odd reason, but she'd forgotten to take one this morning. 'I'm fine, thanks,' she replied, 'just a bit preoccupied.' Heather was asking Margot how long she'd worked on the ship and how she'd got the job, when Johnny came careering into her legs, almost knocking her over.

'Easy tiger,' said Margot, 'don't go bashing into your mum.'

A tall man came in and rather abruptly grabbed Johnny's friend Michael and propelled him up into the air.

'Daddeeee!' screamed the child in delight whilst Johnny looked on wistfully. Heather introduced herself and Donald Kirby let his son slither to the ground through his arms.

'Cynthia told me about you,' he said so softly that Heather had trouble hearing him. 'And of course I know your husband up at Mabroukie.' He scratched his wrists and Heather noticed the red sores of eczema just visible underneath his long shirt sleeves.

'The boys seem to get on well together,' said Heather.

'Yes, always a worry on board,' Donald replied. 'Must go now, sorry.' And he marched quickly out of the nursery, his son running after him.

Heather frowned and wondered if she'd said something wrong.

'Don't worry, he's always like that,' said Margot giggling. 'Very shy.'

'Oh well, time for lunch!' said Heather, swinging Johnny once round by his arms then neatly landing him near the door.

In the dining room, Daphne was very excited about the shore visit to Malta. 'George spoke to one of the officers, didn't you, dear, so we know how to find the shopping area, and he gave us a couple of restaurants to look out for.' George smiled and nodded. 'But before then we need to search for the book.'

'What book?' asked Sophie, putting down her knife and fork, chewing the last of her lamb chops.

'Just a work thing your father is researching,' replied Daphne trying to sound casual but failing.

'Why are you talking about it so much then?' said Sophie, her eyebrows furrowed. 'You're never normally so interested in Dad's work.'

'While you're shopping, Reverend Ian has invited me to explore the two cathedrals,' said Heather, to try to divert the flow of Sophie's annoyance.

'I've done that,' said George, 'it's really worthwhile.'

'What about Johnny?' asked Daphne, wiping her spectacles.

'You'll come with me, won't you, darling?' said Heather, flicking her head round towards her son.

Johnny looked up from his fish fingers and stared at his mum. 'Is this Africa yet?'

'No, but at least you'll be able to run around a bit,' said Heather, nodding at him.

Johnny gave a toothy smile and picked up his toy boat.

'Can I come with you, Heather?' asked Sophie in a pleading voice.

'Of course,' Heather replied. 'We can all meet up for lunch after your parents have finished shopping.'

'I don't think that's a good idea,' said Daphne, rubbing the corner of her mouth with her napkin. 'Heather will be busy and I'd like you to come with us.' While George was asking the steward to keep their wine bottle for dinner, she threw down the napkin on the table and shot Heather a defiant look.

★★★

A white awning had been pulled across an area to one side of the swimming pool to keep the deckchairs in the shade. Johnny wore a blue pair of swimming trunks and a white T-shirt as Heather was worried about his pale skin and the Mediterranean sun; even at the end of March it felt as hot as an English summer. He'd made a fuss about his bright red hat, so Heather had been to buy another one in the shop.

Johnny was now proudly wearing his recently purchased *Uganda* hat, and playing with his boats under the awning. There was a pleasant breeze, which ruffled the canvas material and took the burning edge off the sun. Heather took out her sea-poetry book in search of inspiration to finish her letter; from the index she saw that there was a poem 'The Sea' by D H Lawrence, which was appropriate given all the fuss about his blasted book. Why couldn't it be published? Heather couldn't imagine that it would describe anything more than an affair with a gardener – what was so bad about that? Doubtless these things happened, so why try to pretend otherwise?

She read the poem and enjoyed it, but it seemed relentlessly bleak; there was nothing that resonated with her, so she turned the page and looked up to see Johnny putting on his armbands and ring; she put down her book and blew up the armbands for him as they looked a bit deflated.

Heather sat down again and turned over the pages of the poetry book but many described stormy weather and sailors dying at sea; she considered this and decided that as most of the poems were from the nineteenth or early twentieth century, it was a reflection of the perils of sea faring at that time – in open wooden sailing ships at the mercy of the wind and tide. The *Uganda* felt more like a floating hotel or ex-pats club, which would plough through anything the weather churned up.

The poems by Carl Sandburg and Edna St Vincent Millay were more accessible but then they'd been written more recently;

finally Heather read a poem by Longfellow that seemed to fit her circumstances better.

> So comes to us at times, from the unknown
> And inaccessible solitudes of being,
> The rushing of the sea-tides of the soul;
> And inspirations, that we deem our own,
> Are some divine foreshadowing and forecasting
> Of things beyond our reason or control.

'*This could be me,*' she wrote in the margins, but then laid down the book and thought she really ought to finish the letter to Marjorie, so carried on with a new page, her eyes flicking up and down to check on Johnny as she wrote.

After twenty minutes had elapsed, Sophie came down the stairs towards the swimming pool; she carefully turned around to come down backwards, holding onto both railings, and then jumped the last two steps. She was wearing a one-piece swimming costume, yellow flowers on red, with a white towelled dressing gown on top – the standard *Uganda* cabin issue – but hanging loosely. Sophie held up her hand against the sun and peered around the swimming pool then noticed Johnny in the pool. I wonder if she needs glasses, thought Heather, but hasn't yet admitted it for fear of them making her look like a geek, the last thing a teenage girl would want.

Sophie splashed Johnny from the side of the pool, the boy squealing in delight, trying to manoeuvre himself to splash back, but Sophie had already darted off and slumped down in a chair next to Heather.

'Nice costume,' said Heather.

'What about yours, though, no one else has got a two-piece,' replied Sophie, blushing and pulling back a strand of her fair hair. She will look stunning in a few years, thought Heather, when she's got rid of her scowl and filled out a bit.

'I'm going to wear my bikini when it's back from the laundry.'

'Really?' Sophie replied, her voice raised, sitting upright in the chair.

'Just joking, my figure's not good enough for that.' They both laughed. If only she knew, thought Heather.

'I'm excited about Malta tomorrow,' said Sophie, turning over to look for her sun cream. 'Mum said shopping was cheap.'

'Have I upset your mum?'

Sophie twisted her mouth as she struggled to find the right words. 'She doesn't like me being with you too much.'

Further conversation was interrupted by Johnny who had managed to get out of the pool, scoop up some water in his hands and throw it over Sophie's lap, who screamed then knocked his hat off. Everyone around them smiled.

***

At dinner, they were obliged to share with Bob and Betty Saunders. Heather tried to focus on the menu; she couldn't contemplate anything seafood as the salty sliminess of it now disgusted her, so it would have to be guinea fowl forestiere followed by poire belle Hélène. Heather slapped the menu shut.

'Ah, Heather,' said Bob in his slow wheezy voice. 'Do you play golf?' The way he pronounced the last word sounded like 'goff'. Before Heather had a chance to reply, he'd carried on. 'Our club has just started a ladies section, off the winter tees. It's been a great success but' – Bob shrugged his shoulders and grinned – 'they can't go in the bar.'

'Well, I'm more of a tennis player myself.' Heather leaned forward and whispered, 'And we go to the same bar as the men.'

Betty giggled insanely in a little girl's voice, whilst George managed to turn his snigger into a coughing fit. Daphne stared at Heather with her mouth open and a quizzical look on her face.

'Indeed,' said Bob, who was laughing in the nervous and pensive way that people do when hearing a joke they don't understand. He picked up the wine menu, squinted at it close to his face then spoke to George. 'I thought the Graves 56 tonight?' The women were not consulted on such matters, even though Daphne was having fish.

'What about some Riesling for Daphne?' asked Heather.

'Oh, that German stuff is far too sweet for fish,' said Bob, chuckling at an unknown private joke of his.

'The Alsatian Riesling is dry and good with fish,' said Heather. 'Do you know which one to choose?'

'Yes, of course,' said Bob, waving his hand at the steward who was waiting against the wall. And so the meal started; the service was excellent, as usual, the stewards padding silently between the diners, serving from the left with white gloves on their hands. After the mains had been cleared, the desserts were served, and everyone compared notes.

'I always wondered,' said Betty in a rare interlude, 'what it would be like eating poire belle Hélène, if… your name was Helen! It would be like… you were eating yourself!' She tee-heed in her girl's voice whilst George laughed so energetically that his glasses fell into his ice cream.

No wonder Bob spends all his time at the golf club getting cut, thought Heather who was trying her best to laugh politely, but her tone was too strident and high pitched. She regretted not ordering cheese and biscuits.

'Who's for coffee in the lounge after?' said Daphne, smiling in her blustery, lets-change-the-subject way.

'No thanks – I'm going on deck to listen to some records,' said Sophie.

'But it's classical music tonight,' said Bob, with his classical sounding like 'clarsical'.

'Mark's organised it for us young people,' replied Sophie, putting her hand over her chest.

'Well, in that case I'll take Johnny too,' said Heather, putting her napkin on the table. 'Even though it's past his bedtime.'

'Yippee!' said Johnny.

Daphne frowned but said nothing.

★★★

The night was soft and clear with no moon and a full viewing of the stars. Heather lay in a deckchair and stared up in wonder at the brilliance of the display, especially the silvery nebula of the Milky Way, something she'd never seen in London under smog-edged cloud and street lighting. She wanted to reach out across the light centuries and touch the gaseous swirls, but the noise from the passengers brought her back to Earth.

They were on the sports deck, Sophie and Johnny and her, with about fifteen others, mostly older children and teenagers plus a few parents lurking in the background. A couple of stewards, their white uniforms glowing, hovered next to the railings in case drinks were required. Sophie was wearing a dark peacock-feather cocktail dress, which Heather thought was far too old for her and would have looked better on Daphne, but her eyes were glistening in the half light of the boat deck as she flicked her head around, surveying but never settling. Heather tried to work out who Sophie was attempting to look at without being seen.

On the starboard horizon, the dark outline of a coast was just visible, with daisy chains of lights encircling the low hills.

'That's Cape Serrat,' said cadet Mark after Sophie had asked. 'We're ten miles off the Tunisian coast, you don't always see it.' He was busying himself getting some extra deck lighting organised, an array of light bulbs off a rubber lead. There was an RCA record player on a table at the back of the deck nearest the lights, facing the stern of the ship and plugged into the same rubber lead. James Scott was sorting through some singles and squinting at the record player. He plugged in a microphone to the record player and handed the device to Mark. There was a crackling sound as Mark extended the cable and brought the microphone up to his mouth.

'Ladies and gentlemen, girls and boys, whilst the rest of the ship reclines to classical, up on the boat deck we're gonna be movin' and groovin' to rock and roll!' There was gentle laughter and applause in response and Mark passed the mike to James who introduced 'Rock around the Clock'. A few younger children ran around the deck randomly and some tried to dance with their parents holding both hands.

A Little Richard record went on next, but it was still the same group dancing; the older children and parents just shuffled around the perimeter, unsure of what to do next. Heather spotted nurse Marion and walked over to her with Johnny, who'd so far resisted all efforts to dance.

'Not dancing, little man?' said Marion. Johnny shook his head, frowning with his arms crossed. Marion ruffled his hair and turned to Heather. 'Well, you look much better than the last time I saw you.' Heather smiled and they chatted easily about the ship. For the first time, Heather felt relaxed; there even seemed to be a scent of pine and herbs, maybe thyme, in the air, instead of the usual brine. Could the smell of land reach that far? It had been months since the warmth of last summer and she felt her skin respond, easing and stretching.

'Are you trying for another?' Marion suddenly asked. Heather tensed as she thought of a suitable reply. 'Sorry, that was a bit tactless,' said Marion, touching Heather's arm.

Heather smiled. 'Well, it depends when William comes home.'

'I understand,' said Marion, slanting her head sideways and winking.

'Shall we dance?' said Heather. 'Since the two young officers have gone to so much trouble. Shall I be the man?'

'Why not,' said Marion, smiling.

They danced rock and roll style to 'Hound Dog', both hands together, turning sideways and twirling. Heather noticed that Marion was a good dancer, understated, not flashy but fast and always in the right place. Mark announced Chuck Berry's 'Roll Over Beethoven' and Sophie ran over to Heather and grabbed her arm. 'Can you teach me?' she asked, breathless.

'No, but Marion will, she's a better dancer,' said Heather.

Marion stepped forward and led them off slowly, talking her partner through where to put her feet, slowly increasing the speed. Sophie wore an expression that was both a broad smile and a grimace of concentration as she squashed her lips over one corner of her mouth.

Mark asked Heather to dance and, as they joined in, others started as well, some rather tentatively. Heather laughed as Mark stumbled when the ship rolled unexpectedly; he blushed then dashed off to grab the microphone as the turntable arm lifted at the end of the record.

'Here's another Chuck Berry number just for Master Fontwell. It's called "Johnny B Goode"!' Mark pointed at Johnny but was looking at Sophie, who squealed in laughter and clapped her hands.

Johnny squirmed in his seat but acquiesced when Heather came over and whispered in his ear. As they were slowly dancing, Heather telling Johnny where to go, Johnny bumped into his former friend Simon who was dancing with his mother, Mrs Carruthers. They both stopped and stared at each other before their mums pulled them away to carry on dancing. Not a word was exchanged, but Mrs Carruthers' face was lined and tight and she didn't look at Heather, instead moving away as though frightened she might catch something.

At the end of the record, they all swapped partners: James Scott took hold of Sophie, and Marion went with Johnny. James bent down to Johnny and said, 'Well, will you?'

'What will I?' replied Johnny, confused.

'Be good!'

They all laughed and in the briefest pause before 'C'mon Everybody' started, Heather thought she heard someone mutter, 'Like his mother', but then Mark marched over and started to dance with her and she wondered if she'd misheard it.

After a few more records, James Scott called for an interval so everyone could have a breather and the stewards could bring some drinks. The lights of Tunisia were now much further away, barely visible. Another ship, dark and low with only navigation lights on, passed in the opposite direction on the starboard side, silhouetted against the distant shoreline. The *Uganda* rolled a little as she went through the wash a minute later and a gentle breeze picked up, enough for Heather to reach for her cardigan. She looked again for the Milky Way but it was no longer visible. A few more passengers came onto the sports deck through the doors leading forward or up the stairs from the swimming pools below, amongst them the chaplain and Johnny's friend Michael, accompanied by Cynthia; Johnny jumped up and ran over to meet them. Cynthia left the two boys who went over next to the record player, whispering in each other's ears, and came and said hello to Heather and Marion.

'Donald not here?' asked Heather. 'I met him earlier today.'

'Yes, he said. Neither of us dances much, but I like listening to the music and Michael was very insistent.' Cynthia was wearing a short dress, which showed off her well-toned legs, and she seemed a bit more relaxed than the last time they had met.

More records were played that were less rock and roll – 'There Goes My Baby' followed by 'Living Doll' – but somehow the mood had changed. There were fewer people dancing, and more standing and talking. Heather and Cynthia met the Reverend Ian and they leaned over the railings and talked about the arrangements for the following day.

'Are they playing this one for you?' a sneering voice interrupted them. It was Mr Carruthers; his face was flushed and his skin seemed even more pock-marked up close. Over his shoulder Heather could see his wife and son dancing slowly.

'What?' said Heather, who hadn't been listening to the current record.

Carruthers took a long drag on his cigarette then threw it overboard between the chaplain and Heather, staggering in the process. 'That's why the lady is a tramp.'

'What the hell do you mean by that?' said Heather, standing upright and staring him full in the face.

Carruthers waggled his finger, a bubble of spittle in the corner of his mouth. 'Shouldn't swear in front of the vicar.'

Reverend Ian just looked at Carruthers, mouth open, like he wanted to say something but had forgotten what it was.

'Stop that,' said another voice. It was James Scott, standing right behind Carruthers, his face hidden in shadow.

'What's that?' replied Carruthers, turning around with difficulty, his voice raised.

'Don't throw your lit cigarette overboard – they get blown back in and cause fires.'

Carruthers wavered, shook his head then slowly walked towards his wife and son, who'd now stopped dancing but were still holding hands.

'Well done, James,' said the reverend, softly.

'I'm always telling passengers this,' James replied, glancing in turn at the three others.

'Forget about the cigarette, why was he so rude?' asked Cynthia, putting her arm around Heather's shoulders, despite their difference in height.

'I wish I knew,' replied Heather, biting her lip. 'He just has it in for me.' She was determined not to cry for such a horrid man.

'It started as soon as he arrived,' said James, corralling them all against the railing so no one could overhear. 'He wanted a first-class cabin, but there weren't any left, so then he wanted some of the BI staff returning home to be downgraded. When this wasn't possible, he started complaining about Heather travelling alone and the business with the steward. Frankly, he's just bitter and twisted, as well as drunk a lot of the time, and is taking it out on you.'

'Because she's a woman on her own,' said Cynthia. 'I know the type.'

Johnny appeared at Heather's side. 'Mummy, I'm tired now, can we go back?'

'Yes, I think that's enough for tonight,' she replied, taking him by the hand and looking round to find Sophie, who was talking to Mark.

Chapter 11

29th March 1960 – Malta

Heather was being shaken from side to side as the men carrying her along the dusty track tried to avoid the potholes and rocks in their path. There was little shade on the track and Heather felt the sweat on the back of her neck and the dirt in her mouth. The shaking was getting worse now as they descended the hill, and her head was being rolled from side to side.

'Mummy, mummy,' a thin reedy voice rose from above the men's murmuring, and Heather took a deep breath in and surfaced in a splutter from her dream. 'The ship's bumped! Are we crashed?'

'What ship?' thought Heather until she remembered the *Uganda*, her disappointment filling in the void left by the departing male litter carriers. She opened her eyes and saw Johnny's face right in front of hers, his small hands on her shoulders, his hair tousled up at the back. He needs a haircut, when was his last one, she wondered. 'It's dark. What time is it darling?'

'I thought you were dead!' he shouted, but laughing as well. 'You sleep good.'

Heather realised that the ship was *not* moving, not even the slight roll of the last few days, none of the awful pitching in the storm, and there was none of the *woom woom* of the turbines. It was funny how something *not* happening could be so noticeable, she thought.

Malta, that was it, they'd arrived, of course. Now she heard the distant whir of electrical machinery, the occasional shout, and a scraping noise quite near their cabin. They'd definitely docked, though the light had an artificial grey and silver tone to it, without the usual reflection of the sun on the waves dancing across the cabin ceiling.

Heather sat up sideways across her bunk; she'd got used to being hunched over to avoid banging her head on Johnny's bunk above, and now pulled back the single sheet that covered her and swivelled her legs round to touch the floor.

'Don't worry, darling, we're safe in port, we haven't crashed.' Heather rubbed her eyes then looked at her son standing in front of her. 'But how did you get down from your bunk?'

'Used ladder, careful like you said,' he replied, looking unsure if this was the right answer, then carefully put on his slippers. 'Wee wee,' he added before reaching up to open the cabin door and heading down the alleyway to the toilet.

Heather shifted off the bunk bed and stood up, but the nausea started welling up again almost immediately. She looked in detail at the green loamy soap, the yellow flannel hanging from the metal railing on the side of the sink, the stainless steel taps and noticed how the chrome was starting to wear on the spout, the cream rubber bung hanging by its chain until the bile had subsided. She stood up and slowly stretched her arms and shoulders outwards and upwards and looked between the porthole and the blind at the tendrils of sunlight appearing over an adjacent warehouse.

'Madam?' came De Souza's voice. Heather turned round and saw him framed in the cabin doorway, which Johnny must have left open, a towel draped around his forearm, head on one side and a frown on his dark face. 'Can I help at all?'

'No thanks,' mumbled Heather, her mouth full of toothpaste.

De Souza nodded slowly then turned and left, silently padding down the alleyway. Heather took another sickness pill and wondered about calling off the shore excursion but decided she felt better, and the pills hadn't let her down yet. She closed the cabin door quietly and lay back down on her bunk.

'I need to sleep a bit more, darling,' she said to Johnny when he'd returned. 'Why don't you lie with me and read your nursery rhyme book?'

Johnny took off his slippers, found his book on the table then jumped in. Heather put her arm around him, opened up the book and re-read 'Doctor Foster' with Johnny joining in with her; on the opposite page was 'When The Boat Comes In', which she'd never read before but recognised as a folk song, so tried to sing it with a Geordie accent.

'No Mummy, read,' said Johnny.

'All right, darling,' Heather replied and read him the next verse in her normal voice. By the end, Johnny's head had fallen forward and she thought she'd close her eyes for a moment.

★★★

There was a frenetic knocking at the cabin door and Heather woke up and looked at her watch; it was already nine o'clock. She got up and put a dressing gown on. Johnny had also woken and was rubbing his eyes.

'Madam, the chaplain was worried when you missed breakfast,' said De Souza after Heather had answered the door.

'Excursion leaves in twenty minutes,' Reverend Ian shouted down the alleyway. He was wearing a white linen suit with a blue shirt and his usual dog collar.

Heather leaned out and waved to him. 'Sorry, slept in. Where shall I meet you?'

Ian lifted his panama hat in greeting. 'Gangway on port side of A deck.'

'What about Sophie? I promised to take her.' This had been only after Daphne had relented, probably under pressure from her daughter.

'We haven't got time now.'

Heather groaned, but was secretly relieved to be without the complication of Sophie and their relationship with her mother. She waved goodbye to Ian and stepped back into the cabin. 'Can you help Johnny a bit please, De Souza?' She grabbed some underwear from one of the cabinet drawers, took her wash bag and left to get dressed in the toilet.

De Souza hesitated then slowly walked into the cabin and closed the door behind him; he picked up Johnny's clothes from the back of the chair that Heather had already laid out for him the night before, and handed them to the boy as he stripped off his pyjamas.

'I can do it,' said Johnny.

In the toilet, Heather attached her new pointed bra behind her back then stepped quickly into her knickers and pulled them up. She tousled her hair with one hand, gave it a few strokes with her brush then put on the dressing gown and belted it up.

As Heather returned to the cabin, De Souza was patting Johnny on the back.

'Your sleeves are on backwards,' he whispered then backed out of the cabin, closing the door softly as he went.

The boy laughed. 'Mummy, the man said…'

'Yes, darling, now put your shorts on properly, and brush your teeth, quick as a flash.'

***

They were sitting on red metal chairs in a pavement café, half in shadow, half in full sun. Johnny was eating a cornet with chocolate and vanilla ice cream, studiously wrapping his tongue around the cone to catch the ice cream before it melted. Heather reflected on the morning so far: the three of them had rushed off the ship and down the gangway, with the Carmichaels having already caught the tour bus. Ian had said they could walk but hadn't got very far before passing a kiosk on the quayside where Johnny complained about being hungry and missing breakfast. He still had his grumpy look from being told that Sophie wasn't coming with them.

'Who's the funny man?' he'd said, looking at Reverend Ian. Heather had started to explain when Johnny had said, 'I want a sausage roll,' and pointed at the glass display cabinet on the kiosk. Heather had bent down and peered at the oddity of seeing sausage rolls so far from home, but in the end they'd all eaten one, the pastry crumbling over their lips as they'd walked slowly past another cargo ship then on through the exit gates of the port.

'It's still a British colony,' Ian had said. 'Just.'

After this impromptu breakfast on the move, Ian had found a taxi and taken them to St John's Co-Cathedral. Heather had been worried about subjecting Johnny to two cathedrals in one morning, but in the event the chaplain had been really good with him. Ian had explained about the knights of St John and showed Johnny their white marble tombs; they'd then looked at the Caravaggio painting of the beheading of John the Baptist, less gruesome than Heather thought it might have been. Ian had pointed out details in the paintings on the ceiling, the Maltese crosses, a sculpture of an angel blowing a trumpet; the smell of incense was everywhere, wafting out in grey clouds from huge hanging silver burners.

They'd flopped down in the café afterwards. 'I need a rest before the Anglican cathedral,' said Heather, ordering Johnny an ice cream from the waitress, a young girl with dark hair and skin, wearing a white blouse and maroon skirt. Heather watched her son with his ice cream; his freckles seemed to have come out more in the sun and she admired the single mindedness with which he tackled the slowly dripping cornet. 'I'm worried another cathedral might be too much for him. Won't you want to go to a service there?'

'I'd like to take communion, but don't worry,' Ian said. 'You can leave after a few hymns – they'll understand.'

Their coffees arrived, strong and very bitter, and Heather had to ask for milk and add sugar, which she didn't normally do.

'Do you go to church at home?' asked Ian.

Heather shook her head and thought how to reply without upsetting the chaplain. 'I quite like the service, but many of the parishioners are much older. For the women, it's all about flower arranging, cleaning rotas and coffee mornings and I'm not really interested in those kinds of things. Sorry.'

Ian smiled. 'Don't be.'

'Finished!' said Johnny with a big toothy grin. Heather smiled and ruffled his hair then took one of the paper napkins to wipe off the creamy circle of chocolate from around his mouth.

The waitress walked over to their table and placed the ashtray with the bill clipped on in front of Ian, then stood back and turned to Johnny.

'You liked ice cream?' she asked. Johnny nodded vigorously.

'He's lovely, you must be happy parents,' the waitress continued, lisping slightly, with her hands on her hips, looking around the table. A lock of her hair moved in the slight breeze and she pushed it back with her hand.

Ian laughed and Johnny jumped in his chair.

'Ah, you not the daddy,' the waitress said, pointing at Ian's dog collar. 'You a priest!'

Well, of course the waitress was right, she thought, her son was lovely and Reverend Ian didn't seem to mind being considered his father.

'Time we went,' said Ian shortly afterwards. They walked slowly along a street overlooking the Grand Harbour on top of fortifications, which ended abruptly at the water's edge. The sun was dazzling and the surface of the harbour a deep, untroubled blue. Heather stopped to put on her sunglasses and Johnny's sailor's hat. They reached the cathedral, which had neo classical columns on one side and a tower with a steeple on the other. Ian led the way past some palm trees outside then up the steps passing between the columns and into the entrance. Inside was completely unlike the Catholic cathedral: there were no paintings anywhere and it had a plain white ceiling and a chequerboard stone floor with dark wooden pews.

'It reminds me of churches in the City of London,' Heather whispered, but Ian wasn't listening, instead looking directly ahead of him with a puzzled expression on his face. He strode forward ten yards and embraced a fellow clergyman in his early forties, clean shaven with black glasses, hair thinning on top. They clung to each other's arms and were close enough together to be able to talk quietly without being overheard. Ian pointed towards Heather and Johnny, and they both came over and introductions were made.

'Mrs Fontwell is from the ship,' said Ian, blushing. He then turned around and said to Heather, 'Reverend Mandusa is an old friend with whom I need to catch up on some ecclesiastical matters. Why don't you and Johnny have a look round and stay for some of the service at least?'

In the background, the organ music started and a vicar slowly mounted some circular steps around a gothic pillar to the wooden lectern.

Heather had the feeling she was in the way, so she smiled and took Johnny's hand to find a seat at the back of the cathedral. The service was in English, but the congregation was sparse with many of the pews empty, and the priest's voice echoed across the expanse of the chancel, the gaps being filled with shuffling and coughing noises. A ray of sunshine came through one of the clear side windows showing up swirls of dust as the first hymn started. Heather and Johnny sung along with the hymns and listened to the readings made from a brass stand with an eagle atop holding a large bible. The faithful, mostly elderly people, then queued to receive bread and wine, their shoes scraping against the stone floor, like the noise of sandpaper on wood. The organ was playing gentle background music, almost as though the organist was humming songs randomly then transposing them to the keyboard, and the servers could just be heard uttering, 'The blood of Christ' and 'The body of Christ' as the elderly faithful genuflected in front of them, then struggled to their feet.

Johnny was fidgeting in his trouser pocket, then brought out a toy soldier and put it onto the stained wooden shelf of the pew in front of him. He turned to look at his mother; Heather shook her head. 'But Mummy, I'm bored,' he whispered.

Whilst the last few communards were still queuing in front of the altar, Heather and Johnny left their pew, with Heather making the sign of the cross towards the altar before leaving. She found a bench under the colonnade, which looked out towards the harbour, and sat down, whilst Johnny ran up and down the colonnade holding up his soldier before eventually rejoining his mother on the bench, panting. She read to him from a *Famous Five* book, whilst he took out his handkerchief and mopped his face and around the back of his neck.

'I'm hot,' he said, and indeed Heather could see the heat shimmering off the white stone forecourt in front of the cathedral. Luckily, Ian had given her some cartons of orange drink from the Carmichaels' packed lunch and Johnny slurped his down while they were waiting.

How my life could have changed, thought Heather. I could have taken up with Gerald and become his lover, a couple living in sin. But where would they have lived? Not with his parents, not in their married home in Orpington; Gerald had wanted to rent somewhere in Dulwich, a nice town house, he'd really pleaded with her. But what, she'd thought, was right for Johnny?

She loved Gerald, his quirkiness and his learned ways, his books and theatre and his yearning for travel, and in that moment of weakness she'd gone to bed with him, willingly, even energetically. Of course, he had saved Johnny's life, probably; Heather wasn't sure that on her own she'd have had the presence of mind to dislodge the wretched fish bone. Normally she was quite practical, but when it was anything to do with Johnny she just froze in fear, a fear of losing him and her own life with it, she couldn't help it.

Did she no longer love William? He seemed like a stranger to her because most of the time he was in Kenya and, when he was home, he always seemed distracted about Africa but unable to talk about it. She didn't dislike William, she just felt disconnected from him – and she thought this feeling was probably mutual. Maybe he had a mistress in Africa, someone who could devote herself to him more than she could. Maybe if she hadn't got pregnant with Johnny, and felt obliged to accept his proposal, a truer love might have emerged. Or not.

She'd almost said yes when Gerald had begged her, but she hadn't liked to see him demeaned like that; it didn't seem fair on him, so she'd taken a week to decide. Then it became clear that it wasn't all about her, it was all about Johnny. He wouldn't have liked a new dad or a new house, though a new school would have been a bonus. Separation from William would also have been very messy – he might have insisted on naming Gerald and all the courtroom drama that would have entailed, or even had a go at getting custody. She'd asked and realised the odds were not with her, that she would have had to move to another area, find new friends and tell a few more lies.

But now she was beginning to feel that she regretted this decision. Gerald would have been a good husband and treated Johnny well, and yet she thanked him by dumping him as forcefully as she could and sneaking away without any explanation. Well, tried to. Now she thought about him in moments of weakness, despite promising herself that she'd not do this, that a clean break would be best, that the trip to Kenya would take her mind off Gerald and she could rekindle her affections for William.

Heather glanced up as Ian emerged from the doorway of the cathedral, combing his hair; his cheeks were flushed and his forehead a sheen of sweat. 'Sorry, Heather, I have to stay a little

114

longer, so can I get you a taxi?' Ian shepherded them together and motioned towards the small square at the front of the cathedral. 'Apparently they congregate here.'

The one taxi waiting was an elderly cream-coloured Ford Prefect, with the bonnet up, presumably to cool the engine, and an overweight and unshaven driver leaning on a side panel reading his newspaper.

'Civil Service Club please,' Ian said to him as they arrived.

The driver slowly stood up and folded his paper. 'Very good,' he said in a gruff voice.

Ian turned to Heather, patting her arm. 'I arranged it with George and it's got the best roast beef in Malta,' he said. 'By the way, did you manage to post your letter?'

'God, with all the rush this morning I forgot, but hopefully I still have it.' Heather opened the canvas bag she used for the pool and began to delve amongst all her and Johnny's things. She could feel her heart pounding; how could she be so stupid as to forget something this important? At last she found the ship's envelope, already addressed, though she knew the letter inside was still incomplete, having only added a few paragraphs last night in bed.

'It's not quite finished and I've no stamps,' Heather sighed in frustration and pulled the sheets of paper out. 'Sorry about the swearing, Ian, it's just that it has to go today.'

'Finish it now,' said Ian, 'and I'll post it before I return to the ship.'

The taxi driver muttered something, unfolded his paper again and pointed at the meter. Heather grimaced then took the last page of the letter and leaned on the roof of the taxi to start writing.

Dirt and dust of Malta enclosed as I have to finish this epistle in a hurry before we go. Please think carefully about what I've said, it's taken a lot out of me just writing it. Always remember that I love you, little sister, and always will, whatever rocks life throws at us.

'There,' she said, folding the pages, putting them inside the envelope and tucking the flap in. 'Sorry to bother you with this,' she added, handing him the unsealed letter.

'No problem – I'll see you later,' said Ian, putting the letter in his jacket pocket as Heather and Johnny got inside the taxi. It smelled of strong tobacco smoke and body odour with an overlay of sweet cologne water that the driver must have recently sprayed. The seats were PVC and there was little room in the back, quite unlike the leather and walnut of William's luxurious Rover that spent most of the time in their garage at home. The driver closed her door, which gave a loud complaining squawk, then jumped in the front and started the engine; the taxi pulled away, juddering, leaving behind a drifting plume of blue smoke.

Heather smiled at Johnny, held his hand and considered her thoughts. Ian had clearly been unsettled by Reverend Mandusa and it was unlike him to brush them off like that, normally being very attentive. Yet Ian could also be a little distant and formal, but Heather supposed this was down to his ministry. She wondered what his domestic situation was, given the lack of any wedding ring.

The taxi came to an abrupt halt, jolting Heather out of her thoughts. The taxi driver turned round to face her, his tobacco smell wafting across.

'This club,' he announced in the rasping voice of a heavy smoker. Heather realised she didn't have any Maltese money on her and began rummaging in her purse in the hope that he would take pounds.

'Man paid,' the driver said, raising his eyebrows and grinning, then getting out to yank open the groaning door for Heather and Johnny.

'Do you know any English bookshops?' Heather asked after managing to get out of the car without her skirt riding up too much.

'Many.'

Heather hesitated. 'I'm looking for *Lady Chatterley's Lover*, do you know it?'

The taxi driver laughed loudly and wiped his hand across his mouth. 'Of course. Big seller for English. I know where get it. When you finish lunch?'

'Three o'clock,' she replied, pulling down her skirt.

'Good. I come then – bye bye sailor,' he said to Johnny with a mock salute, then drove away leaving a cloud of blue smoke mixed in with the dust and smell of cabbages cooking.

Heather saw the sign for the Civil Service Club in the shadows of a side street and was glad to get out of the harsh sunlight. She pushed opened the wooden door with frosted glass panels and entered. Directly in front of them there was a giant photographic portrait of the young smiling Queen Elizabeth in her robes, and lined up exactly underneath was a heavy mahogany desk with a woman seated behind it. She wore a grey cardigan and had steel-rimmed glasses with her hair pulled back in a tight bun.

'Are you a member?' she said in stockbroker English.

'I've come for lunch, booked by the Reverend Tremwell.'

She looked Heather up and down as though deciding whether she passed muster or not. 'Some of your party are already in the restaurant.' She squinted in a leather-bound reservation book in front of her, running her finger along a line of names. 'Is Reverend Tremwell not with you?'

'No, he can't make it.'

'Oh, this is rather irregular,' said the woman, sighing.

'If you say so,' said Heather, fidgeting with her handbag then taking Johnny's hand.

'Is he well behaved?' said the woman looking at Heather again with her poker face.

'Who? Reverend Ian?' Heather stooped over the desk.

The woman tutted and shook her head, pointing at Johnny.

'No children in the bar area, and those in the restaurant should be well behaved at all times.' She spoke like she was quoting a rule book.

Heather stared at the woman and thought about slapping her but managed to control herself. 'Quite,' was all she could trust herself to say then turned and walked through another glass door marked 'Restaurant', dragging Johnny behind her.

'Heather!' said George, standing up when he saw them enter. 'We've ordered roast beef for everyone, hope that's OK. Where's Ian?'

'He met another vicar at the Anglican cathedral,' said Heather. 'Bit of a mystery really.'

'Well, Sophie's had a miserable morning,' said Daphne, 'putting up with her awful parents.'

'Yes, it was terrible,' said Sophie, her arms folded and forehead creased in annoyance.

Heather sat down and looked round the restaurant; it was like a staff canteen with a hatch and swing door along one wall where all the food emerged from. The walls were whitewashed but had grey smudges, and the floor had a green carpet with occasional cigarette burns and discolouring where presumably food had been spilled then a patch of the carpet cleaned. Around the walls were black and white photos of London, some of which still had bomb damage visible.

Most of the tables were occupied by men and women in office wear, some pale and indifferently dressed in jackets and ties, obviously British, others more Mediterranean looking with casual but stylish clothing. There was the usual hubbub of restaurant conversation but punctuated by the noise of the waiters. The service was not what you'd call discreet; there was shouting in Maltese through the kitchen hatch, and when the swing door opened it was always presaged by a warning cry from the waiter, usually with a retort from whoever was on the other side of the swinging door.

The trolleys were pushed at an alarming speed, with the stacks of plates and racks of cutlery rattling as the trolley wheels spun round crazily.

'Fiv-A roast-A beef-A,' shouted the waiter when their trolley arrived. Five servings on the plates were handed out together with one tureen of steaming green vegetables and another with roast potatoes, onions and parsnips. 'Plates very hottA!'

Johnny was grinning at this loud display and sat back in his chair to avoid touching the plate.

'I've arranged for a taxi to take you at 3pm to a bookshop where there are supposedly copies of *Lady Chatterley*,' said Heather to Daphne.

'That's marvellous!' said Daphne, grinning widely. 'Maybe you can take Sophie and we'll look after Johnny?'

After eating the roast beef, the Carmichaels decided to have a go at the jam roly-poly. Heather decided against it, whilst Johnny got down from the table to look for his toys, and there was just enough time for George to pay. As they left, the grey-cardigan woman frowned at them and pointed at Heather's taxi driver.

'Is he yours?' she said, as though the driver were a missing sock.

'Ah, Lady Chatterley?' the driver said in his raucous smoker's voice, ignoring the receptionist and bowing to Heather, his newspaper tucked under his arm.

Heather shook his hand briefly as the driver seemed to be expecting this and explained that he would be taking Daphne and George to the bookshop.

'After all that food, we're walking back to the port,' said Heather. The taxi driver gave her some rough directions before leaving with a grate of his gears and she and Sophie set off in the warm afternoon sun.

The *Uganda* was due to leave at six that evening, giving them enough time for a gentle walk back; they found a pavement café near the port and took half an hour to try on some swimsuits.

Heather turned her back in the changing room as Sophie wriggled into something too small for her but which showed up the buds of her young breasts.

'Maybe not,' she said. Sophie looked disappointed but Heather then helped her find a T-shirt and they bought a ball for Johnny to use in the pool.

★★★

Having missed leaving London in the rain, Heather was keen to witness the *Uganda*'s departure from the Grand Harbour of Valletta. She and Johnny peered over the railings on the sports deck and watched as the last of the provisions rolled up one of the gangplanks and in through the shell door. Mark the cadet was on deck with his radio and explained how the larger cargo, on palettes with netting around, had been loaded earlier that afternoon and the ship had already taken up fuel from a lighter – 'a sort of grubby oil barge' – which had moored alongside. Diesel for the generators had been supplied by hoses from a road tanker.

The cadet disappeared as the tugs arrived and it was time to cast off. She could hear the deckhands shouting at the rear of the ship and then the winding noise of the capstan starting as the Maltese crew on the wharf edge let go the bow ropes, which dropped in the water with a splash; by now the ship was slowly swinging around, the stern, still tied to the shore and the tug nudging the bow out, pointing towards the harbour entrance. There was an officer below them, next to the rear cargo hatch, speaking into a radio set; the deckhands let go the rear lines and the ship gradually eased away from the quayside. Now the ship's engines started up, with a wash appearing alongside the wharf propelling the *Uganda* sideways; the noise died down as the ship was now fifty yards from the quayside, skewed sideways with the tugs pushing against her to straighten her up.

There was a loud blast from the horn, which made Heather and Johnny jump, then the familiar feel of the turbine as the ship moved forward, gathering momentum. The whining of the capstans had finished and the crew were standing waiting for any further orders. A few locals on the quayside waved and some of the passengers waved back.

Heather and Johnny looked forward alongside the shoreline in the soft fading light. On the port side was the centre of Valletta with yellow sandstone buildings packed tightly together and the twin towers and dome of St John's that they'd visited that morning poking through. The setting sun was hidden behind the city but the sky above was a pink and grey herringbone pattern. On the starboard side were two inlets where cargo ships were tied up and a fort guarded the shoreline.

As the *Uganda* gathered pace, the tugs dropped back, their job done, but the pilot boat, a tiny orange blob, still followed at a distance as they approached the twin breakwaters. The horn went off again to warn away the colourful fishing boats. Further along the deck, Bob and Betty Saunders, together with nurse Marion, were waving frantically to some small figures on the shoreline and Heather thought of the Stevie Smith poem 'Not Waving but Drowning' that she'd read, and decided she should jot this memory in the margins of her anthology.

'Always emotional, uplifting somehow.' It was the chaplain who'd appeared unexpectedly, still in his linen suit. He took a pipe out of his pocket and tapped it on the railing.

'What's more important, the journey or the destination?' replied Heather.

Ian smiled. 'Indeed,' he said, checking his trouser pockets for tobacco.

The ship was now passing between the breakwaters; Heather could see local men fishing on the port side, their backs to the ship and lines cast out into the open sea. Some of them turned and waved as the *Uganda* slid by at reduced speed, her bow wash a gentle ripple on the water. The three of them stared at the setting sun, now visible without Valletta to hide it, as the bottom of the orb touched the sea and the reflection glittered on the surface. The vibrancy of the pink colour of the clouds had now diminished but had been replaced by the dazzling reflection. Already a third of the sun had gone and Heather couldn't bear to see it all disappear, so she took Johnny over to the starboard side to show him the pilot going down a rope ladder dangling from the shell opening to meet the pilot boat which was now hugging the ship in the shadows.

'Will he fall in?' asked Johnny, jumping from side to side.

'Certainly not!' Heather replied, giving him a stern look.

There was another blast of the horn and Heather could feel the *whoom whoom* increasing and the ship turning east towards the night. The rope ladder was hauled back into the shell door, which then closed with a grating noise.

Heather walked back over to Ian, who'd now lit his pipe and was puffing contentedly. 'So what happened at the Anglican Cathedral?' she asked.

'It's a long story.'

'I'll tell you mine if you tell me yours,' said Heather with a wry smile.

Reverend Ian glanced at Johnny. 'Later, maybe.'

★★★

Dinner was a quiet affair with most of the passengers tired from their day excursions; Daphne was, however, the exception. She was glowing from her adventure of finding a US copy of *Lady Chatterley*. All conversations about the book had to be conducted by leaning low over the table, glancing around to make sure there were no eavesdroppers, then calling the book *LC* in whispered tones.

'Honestly, Mum,' said Sophie, 'it's not a state secret.'

'I'm thinking of Johnny,' snapped Daphne.

The gloss was rather taken off this when Heather pointed out that by the time they got back home the book might have been on sale in the UK for some time, assuming the court case went the publisher's way. Johnny, meanwhile, was playing with a plastic figure of a Maltese knight that George had bought him and not listening to the conversation at all.

'Well, I'm going to enjoy reading it,' said Daphne in her matter-of-fact voice.

'We're all having cold meats and salads tonight, thanks Parminder,' said George to the young steward that now seemed to attend to them regularly. He smiled, showing his crooked teeth.

'I think it's important to be broad-minded about these things,' continued Daphne, as though George hadn't spoken, balancing her spoon in her hand before tackling the scooped melon in a glass.

'But what's in it that's so shocking?' said Heather. 'The lady and the gardener is a pure fairy story, like the beauty and the beast.'

Daphne frowned and put down her spoon. 'The point is that it's talking about things that are never normally talked about. I would have thought you'd have got that.'

Heather didn't want to argue with Daphne, so she asked for more details about the bookshop and the conversation passed into less troubled waters. At the end of the meal, Heather tucked Johnny into his sheets and climbed up the ladder to read him a story from his nursery rhyme book, but his eyelids were already drooping and she felt thwarted at being unable to read to her son. He was soon fast asleep and she could see his eyes flickering behind their lids. It had been a long day for him with no afternoon nap and lots of walking.

She'd agreed to meet the others in the lounge but she first had to tidy up all the clothes, towels and toys strewn around the cabin from the rush that morning; Heather didn't want De Souza to think she was slovenly. Then she freshened her make-up, sprayed some more perfume and closed the cabin door behind her. With a stab of worry, she opened it again to make sure Johnny hadn't awoken, then reclosed it and made her way up to A deck.

Heather entered from the main staircase and spotted the chaplain standing at a table where George and Daphne were seated having coffee.

'I'm glad I found you,' Heather said to Ian.

The chaplain smiled and touched her arm. 'It's been a tiring day, so let's catch up tomorrow.'

Heather agreed and they both carried on chatting with the Carmichaels.

Later, in her bunk bed, she felt herself swaying with the *Uganda* as it rolled; it was strange how her body seemed to seek the movement and settle back into a familiar groove after a day spent on solid rock. Heather thought she'd better take another sickness pill just in case and while standing at the sink swallowing a glass of water she stood on tiptoes to admire her son sleeping, facing the wall away from her. She returned to her bunk, taking care not to make too much noise, and pondered how Ian had initially been keen to hear her story, but now she wanted to hear his account he seemed more evasive. Maybe his story was just as difficult to confess as hers.

Chapter 12

20th March 1960 – Orpington, Kent

Johnny and Heather were having breakfast at the small table in the kitchen; Heather had finished her bowl of cornflakes and was staring out into the dripping garden. She watched a blackbird on the lawn pick up a twig in its yellow beak and fly off low to the copper beech in the angle of the boundary fence; this reminded her that she'd have to find someone to look after the garden while they were away.

As Heather drank from the cup of tea in her hand, she turned and leaned against the draining board and indulged in her favourite occupation – watching her son when he was unaware of her attention. But Johnny always seemed to sense this and today was no exception as he looked up from dipping his soldier into a soft-boiled egg, his freckled face in a grin. Just at that moment, the sun came out and a watery beam lit up the kitchen's buttercup walls and cream gas cooker: it was a perfect picture. Heather bent across the table and wiped a trail of egg yolk from the corner of her son's mouth with her serviette. His face scrunched up and he pushed her arm away.

'Shall we read Daddy's letter now?' asked Heather.

Johnny nodded and started scooping out the egg white with his teaspoon.

'I'll go and get it,' Heather said. She walked down the corridor to the hall, and sifted through the stack of letters from yesterday's post left on a narrow glass shelf. William tried to write every week, but the mail was slow, even when it came by plane, so his news was often several weeks out of date. It felt a bit like looking at the stars at night, in the knowledge that even though they shone brightly, they might by now no longer exist due to the time taken for the light to arrive on Earth.

Heather found the brown padded envelope and opened it with a wooden dagger from Kenya. As usual, it contained a variety of material, some for her and some for Johnny. She passed Johnny his letter, which he ripped open in some haste, knocking his teaspoon to the floor. He tipped the contents onto the breakfast table.

Heather's letter was written on official paper headed *The Mabroukie Tea Estate* and dated two weeks ago. It smelt musty. The handwriting was William's – careful and neat, with lots of short loops, no problem to read at all. Although it started *My Darling Heather* it read like a newsletter, with lots about the tea business, how the office workers were doing, what the locals were up to, the weather, the state of his plantation house and so on. Heather grew increasingly impatient reading it and found herself flying up and down the pages.

'Look what Daddy sent!'

On the table was a square piece of cloth about the size of a handkerchief; it was coloured orange and green with vertical line patterns.

'It's got a woolly feel – maybe for teapot warming,' said Johnny, now holding the cloth up in the air.

'Mmm,' said Heather. 'It could be from Dorothea, Daddy's housekeeper. We'll have to send her another photo of you, the last one must be a bit old now.'

'And a flag,' said Johnny, the cloth now back on the table. The flag was a yellow lion on a green background, with *Mabroukie* written underneath, and was pinned to a thin stick.

Enclosed with Heather's letter were some newspaper cuttings from the *East African Standard*. There was a photo of William outside the tea plantation, with black African workers surrounding him, all grinning and wearing a ragtag of clothing, some traditional, some Western. She squinted at the photo: there was Dorothea next to William, lighter-skinned and straighter-haired than the other Africans, quite a good-looking woman. Heather often wondered if William had ever been tempted to take a mistress, and whether there were any *droits de seigneur* for the white bosses, but then maybe it was best just not to know about such things, so long as your husband didn't come home with the pox.

Now the prospect of going to Kenya was closer, she looked at the clippings again, to try to divine what it might be like; the countryside looked quite lush, even European, not like pictures she'd seen of the savannah grasslands. There were some other articles, mostly about the rise of nationalism and a conference in London in the autumn on constitutional reform. Heather only skim read these – the political situation seemed a lot calmer than when the Mau Mau were killing the whites, though William had been posted to Kenya after that insurgency been put down.

'Look at this photo of Daddy,' said Heather, placing the article to the side of his boiled egg. Johnny looked at it, turning his head from side to side.

'Daddy with black people,' he said. 'When will he come home?'

'Would you like to see him soon?' asked Heather, looking up from re-reading her letter.

Johnny nodded in an exaggerated fashion.

'Well, let's hope we can go and visit him soon then. Would you like to go to Africa?' she asked. The nodding was even more vigorous. 'All right, well get ready for Sunday school now, wash your face and hands and clean your teeth like I showed you.' Johnny pushed back his chair, jumped off it onto the patterned lino floor and ran through the open door to the stairs in the hallway. She could hear him clumping up the stairs, banging his hands against the balustrade.

Heather tidied up in the kitchen, putting the perishables in her new fridge, then closed the door and walked into the hall. As she touched up her lipstick and patted her hair in the hall mirror, Heather thought of her sister, Marjorie. She didn't always see eye to eye with her, but she was at least discreet and somehow had a more practical grip on day-to-day matters than Heather. However, Marjorie could be overly critical from her vantage point of the elder (and therefore somehow wiser) sister, which Heather found difficult to digest. As her and Ralph didn't yet have a telephone, Heather would have to go and see her on spec and hope Marjorie was in.

'Are you ready yet, Johnny?' she called up the stairs. There was complete silence, which was not a good sign, but then he was not even five, after all, so she walked up the stairs to see what progress he'd made.

Johnny jumped up when she came into his bedroom. He had a toy soldier in one hand, and a sheepish grin on his face. He'd crumpled up the rug next to his bed to make a relief model for his soldiers, who were facing each other in two groups.

'It's the Red Indians against the British,' he said. His hair was sticking up at the back and there was a milk stain around his mouth. He had obviously not been to the bathroom. Heather sighed; she felt she was useless at the discipline stuff, and shouting at children seemed so, well, like bullying, though with some adults you just couldn't help yourself.

'Come on, Johnny, time for Sunday school.'

'I don't want to go, I've got a tummy ache.'

'You probably ate too much for breakfast, darling.' Heather wasn't a strict mum but knew this ruse quite well. 'Why don't you want to go?'

Johnny wrinkled up his nose and cheeks. 'Susan keeps pushing me,' he replied. 'I don't want to play with a girl. I just want to play with boys, like you said I could at my next school.' He looked closely at the green plastic soldier he was holding.

Heather smiled; it was almost like she was making this story come true by some weird process of osmosis. Maybe she could get things to work out after all. She took Johnny by the hand and walked with him into the bathroom, where everything was blue apart from the white tiles and ceiling; Johnny loved it – there were toy boats and fish hanging off round clear-plastic suckers on the sides of the bath. Heather had moved all of William's shaving kit and aftershaves to a small cupboard under the bath, so she had one long glass shelf under a mirror for her soaps and creams and another for her son, most of which she'd purloined.

She washed Johnny's face with a flannel, got him to dip the bristles of his blue brush into the tin of powdered toothpaste, then quickly flicked his hair with a black wetted brush before he could object. Once he'd finished his teeth, she accompanied him down the stairs.

'I can do it,' he said, with one hand on the railing.

What would it be like with a school uniform to contend with, she wondered, as he struggled with his brown lace-up shoes? Then it was on with his raincoat and out of the door, with Johnny insisting on opening the hip-height wrought-iron gates across their driveway. Heather had decided to take the car to church but, as she didn't know the way to Marjorie's house in Beckenham, they'd have to take the train after.

They slipped into the back row at the church amongst a group of other mums. It was the same church where Johnny came for nursery, and many of the mums had also been at Heather's antenatal classes.

'You've passed your driving test now?' the one next to her whispered, whilst the others turned and waved at her. She knew most of them reasonably well and they seemed friendly enough, but you could never tell with these suburban women. She'd even been to one or two coffee mornings, but the conversations had all been about their children, and, really, how could you spend hours doing that all the time?

Johnny shook his hand away from hers and joined the other children walking up the aisle and away to the side entrance to the hall and Sunday school. He passed in front of the reading lectern made of a giant brass eagle and underneath the wooden board with the paper gothic numbers slotted in denoting the hymns of the day.

As the service began, Heather thought what she'd achieved so far and what remained to be done before the passage. Yesterday she and Johnny had taken the train to Bromley South, walked up the High Street, past Importers, her favourite coffee shop, then past Medhurst the department store, before arriving at Thomas Cook in the Market Square.

'Oh, the *Uganda* sails Wednesday,' the girl had said, pushing her wire-rimmed glasses up her nose. 'Not much time left for packing.' This was a rather obvious understatement, Heather had mused, as she filled out all the forms, went through the payment from William's head office in Aldgate, and booked their luggage and the train tickets via Liverpool Street to London Docks. There'd been no time to order any foreign currency, so she'd just taken some Thomas Cook travellers cheques, then read the brochure again just to make sure there wasn't anything she might have forgotten. The brochure had a picture of the ship carving a path like an arrow across a flat expanse of deep blue sea, a colour never seen off Britain's shore where cool greens and muddy browns predominated.

The service was finished now, and Heather said goodbye to the other mums and hurried out from the back row, with a quick deposit into the offertory – a maroon pouch held by one of the elders– followed by a handshake with the vicar. The church hall doors were opening just as Heather walked quickly across the adjacent car park; she could hear some parents following her, talking in low voices. Heather pulled open the hall door with a vague smile on her face as she struggled to pick out Johnny from the children milling around inside. Heather eventually spotted him sitting on his own on one of the cane chairs in a row against the roughly whitewashed brick wall, his head bowed low and his eyebrows in a frown.

Heather went over to him. 'Whatever is the matter?' she asked, bending down to his level.

He shook his head and looked away.

'Mrs Fontwell,' a strident voice called.

Heather turned around towards the kitchen area, which had been sectioned off from the hall with rough wooden planking and had a serving hatch and single door, both outlined in yellow. The Sunday school leader, Mrs Davenport, was walking across from the kitchen dressed in her usual tweed jacket and knee-length skirt; Heather noticed she was wearing a new pair of horn-rimmed glasses that made her expression even crosser-looking than it normally was.

'Can I have a word please?' she said in her clipped accent, steering Heather into the kitchen through the door. An older lady in a green pinafore was drying up some plates in a languid fashion and looked startled when she saw Mrs Davenport enter; she slowly put down the enamel plate she was drying on the steel draining board and left, closing the door behind her and leaving Johnny outside. It smelt of steam from the giant tea urn and washing-up suds.

'Johnny has been very naughty today,' said Mrs Davenport, hands on hips. 'He pushed poor little Susan Briggs over and made her spill her squash. And…' Mrs Davenport drew in a long breath, 'hasn't said sorry to her or me.'

'Well, I know…'

'The thing is, Mrs Fontwell, we don't like this kind of behaviour in our church, and have to crack down on it straight away.'

'Have you asked Johnny why he did it?' said Heather, as the leader paused for breath.

'He won't speak to me.' Mrs Davenport looked straight at Heather. 'Now, unless things improve…'

'Mrs Davenport, I've been unhappy for some time with your standards here and Johnny won't be coming any more.' Heather

131

pushed past Mrs Davenport, left the kitchen and found Johnny outside, staring at the floor. 'Come on, darling, let's go home now,' she said, taking his hand to leave.

'What do you mean? Our standards here are excellent.' Mrs Davenport had followed Heather out into the main hall, a small bubble of spittle and a trace of pink lipstick stuck to her front teeth.

'And by the way,' replied Heather, 'Susan Briggs is neither poor nor little.'

The older lady with the green pinafore was staring at Heather as she strode away and banged the entrance door open. There was silence as the door clacked shut afterwards.

Outside, Heather walked along the pavement and took a side road to locate the Mini.

'You're pulling me,' said Johnny.

'Sorry, darling,' Heather said, dropping his hand and leaning against their car. She opened her bag, pulled out a packet of Craven A, the last that Gerald had given her, and lit up with her small square silver lighter. 'Shall we go to the sweet shop?' Heather asked, holding out the cigarette with one hand to keep the smoke away from her son.

'Cor, yeah.'

They parked at home and Heather gave Johnny sixpence to go to the newsagent and tobacconist on the parade of shops opposite their house, which Heather knew had the bubblegum that Johnny liked for the aircraft cards that came with them. She waited for him on the pavement outside their house, stubbing out her cigarette on the pavement and kicking the fag end into the gutter, then watched him as he left the shop, examined his card then slowly crossed the road.

'What happened with Susan?' Heather asked. 'You can tell me, I won't be cross.'

'Gloucester Meteor, got this already.' Johnny held up the card for Heather to inspect.

'Oh yes, so you have.'

There was a short pause as Johnny chewed his gum. 'She was pushing me again. Then she said, "Your mummy's loose."'

'What?' Heather's voice was a tone higher. The anger she'd felt on Friday was burning again as she thought of Mrs Briggs, a shrivelled woman with greying hair who normally said very little. Perhaps the child had heard it from one of her mother's friends. But who were they thinking of? The only men she'd ever met were her doctor, her driving instructor, who'd never come in the house, and Gerald, Johnny's tutor. How dare they speak about her in front of their children like that? Heather breathed in deep breaths, almost as though in labour, and reflected that she'd done the right thing by leaving.

'You said you wouldn't be cross,' a little voice said.

'I'm not, Johnny,' she said, putting on a smile, 'at least not with you.'

'What's it mean, loose?' he asked in his about-to-cry wavering voice.

'It just means different, but don't repeat it. Anyhow, we're going on a ship to Africa to see Daddy in a few days.'

Johnny smiled. 'No more nursery?'

'That's right, no nasty Mrs Davenport.'

'No pushy Susan either.'

Heather chuckled. 'But first we have to go and see Aunty Marjorie.'

'What, now?'

Heather nodded then took out her compact mirror and patted her hair. 'She's expecting us for Sunday lunch,' she told him, which was completely untrue, but she thought it made her sound better organised and a better mother.

Johnny looked up at his mum, then down at his aircraft card and pondered.

'Righty-o,' he eventually said in a moment that was so William that Heather wanted to cry.

Chapter 13

30th March 1960 – SS *Uganda*, Eastern Mediterranean

Today was hot, the sky a deep blue and visibility the best they'd had yet. It was perfect for the swimming pool in the morning before the sun got too raw and Heather had to worry about Johnny burning.

The Carmichaels had agreed at breakfast to accompany Heather and Johnny and they'd also met Cynthia and her son Michael. Daphne was reading *LC*, as she still insisted on calling it, and had even put brown paper around the outside cover so nobody could see the book's title. She was wearing a navy blue one-piece that went halfway down to her knees and had extra flaps around the waist to make sure nothing too revealing would be on show. Just in case of prying eyes, Daphne was also wearing the white *Uganda* dressing gown and she'd instructed Sophie to do the same. This plus her Paisley headscarf and sunglasses meant there was very little naked skin to see apart from her ankles and meant she looked like a cross between a cleaning lady and a hair salon assistant.

'This is quite racy,' said Daphne in a whisper to Cynthia, motioning towards the book. 'Do you want to read it after me?'

'I'm not sure. What's it like otherwise?' Cynthia didn't look or sound like a woman who sought approval with her wide forehead and dark eyebrows as well as a steely look behind her wire-rimmed glasses. She wasn't wearing a swimming costume but a plain yellow summer dress.

'Would Donald read it?' asked Daphne.

'I doubt it – he's more interested in newspapers and journals.'

Daphne glanced at her husband who was reading the daily news-sheet. He smiled benevolently and handed the sheet to Heather.

'Where is Donald today?' asked George, adjusting himself in his white plastic chair.

'He doesn't like the sun much.'

Heather read the sheet and wished she hadn't. A fire in Glasgow killed nineteen firemen; the last steam train ran in America but England still had lots of them; troubles in South Africa and America with gruesome reports of the Ku Klux Klan and demonstrations in Alabama.

'All very depressing,' she said, handing the sheet to Cynthia. 'I think I prefer my poetry book.'

'Read one out, Heather,' said George. Daphne looked askance at him.

Heather agreed but wanted to check on Johnny first; he was playing with Michael – they both had toy boats and had abandoned the pool and removed their sun hats. She told Johnny he had a choice: either to play in the shade or put his hat on. To get rid of her, he scowled then shuffled sideways into the shade at the back of the pool.

Heather sat down again and flicked through the poems. Many were too long or too Victorian but eventually she found John Masefield's 'Sea Fever' where the language was straightforward and she was confident about reciting, so she started the first verse; George had his eyes closed and was nodding his head whilst Cynthia was staring wistfully at the bleached wooden decking; even Daphne had put the brown-paper-wrapped *LC* on her lap and her head was tilted to one side. Sophie unwrapped herself from her dressing gown and was looking towards the two boys, whilst Heather finished the poem.

'Bravo, Heather,' said George, opening his eyes.

'Do any of my fellow rovers have a merry yarn to tell?' asked Heather, referring to the penultimate line. 'Cynthia?'

'Good lord no!' she laughed. 'You read very well, Heather, quite a natural, better than most teachers can.' Heather denied it but was secretly pleased by this remark, and wrote 'read this aloud after Malta' against the page of the poem.

'Well, I know a story from Dartmoor from my youth,' said George, 'though I won't be able to tell it as well as Heather.'

'Not that one, Dad, it's a bit ghoulish,' said Sophie, but Cynthia and Heather encouraged him enough for him to start.

Late one night, a young couple were driving home in the pouring rain from a party. They decided to take a country road with a view to spending some time together. [George winked at this point.]

Suddenly the car hit a tree fallen across the middle of the road. The boyfriend got out to see what had happened and reported back that the front wheel was badly damaged and the car couldn't be driven. He said he'd seen a light a mile or so back and would go to fetch help; his girlfriend wanted to come with him, but he insisted she stay and keep warm and dry in the car. He made her promise to lock the doors and not get out until he returned.

More than an hour passed and the boyfriend had not returned. The girl began to worry and thought about going to look for him, but remembered her promise and decided to wait a bit longer. She put on the radio to try to take her mind off things and then the local news came on.

There was a story about a breakout from the nearby prison. People were warned to lock all their doors as the escapee was considered extremely dangerous. The girl became even more fearful but decided to stay put and wait for her boyfriend.

She then fell asleep but was awoken by an insistent tapping on the roof of the car. She looked out of the windows to see if her boyfriend had returned, but could see only swaying trees, the moorland beyond, and the wet night. Fearful from the news story, and mindful of her promise, she stayed in the car, deciding the tapping must be from an overhanging bough and so managing to doze off again.

She awoke as dawn was breaking and noticed a police car coming over the crest of the road. She got out, flagged it down and a policeman opened the passenger door.

'Stay right there and don't turn round,' he commanded, but the girl couldn't help herself.

Over her car was an upside down figure, his feet tied to an overhanging tree, arms dangling down, his fingers just touching the roof of her car when the wind blew in the branches. She recognised the blood-stained clothes of her boyfriend.

George finished slowly and with an obvious relish.

The women groaned with delight at the finale.

'Well that yarn wasn't very merry,' said Heather to George.

Sophie rolled her eyes and got up to go to the pool, but Johnny interrupted the conversation. 'Is it true?' he asked in a trembling voice, pulling on Sophie's arm. Michael was standing next to him with his hand in his mouth.

'No, darling,' said Heather, jumping up to take Johnny's hand and rub his back. 'It's just a silly story.'

'Told you,' said Sophie to her dad, hands on hips.

'Sorry, ladies, I didn't realise the kids were in earshot,' replied George, the smile disappearing from his face. Daphne shook her head and carried on reading *LC*.

The sun had encroached on where they were sitting and a couple of stewards, one of them De Souza, were now putting a white canvas awning across one side of the deck. Heather hugged Johnny then asked Cynthia about her work.

'I'm a secondary-school teacher near where we live,' Cynthia said, adding that she'd been lucky, that her father had sent her to teacher-training college where she'd been one of the very few girls specialising in maths. 'Not that I use high-level maths much anymore,' she continued, smiling. 'I seem to specialise in the dullards, those whom no one else wants to teach.'

'Isn't that frustrating?'

'No, quite the opposite, it's very rewarding.' Cynthia swirled the ice around in the bottom of her glass. 'Many of them thank me after they've left school.'

Heather related how her father had also suggested her going to university, and that she completed her PGCE, but had never starting teaching after falling pregnant with Johnny.

'I would have found *that* very frustrating,' said Cynthia.

Heather told Cynthia that her life had simply become absorbed by her son, although now she did mind that she'd never started her teaching career.

Finally it was time for lunch; the dining room felt much warmer, though there were now some electric fans whirring in each corner of the room. After salads and a variety of desserts, they agreed to meet later in the lounge for coffee, giving Heather the chance to take Johnny for the nap he increasingly needed as the temperature rose and he was doing more physical activities.

'I didn't like Uncle George's story,' he said as Heather tucked him under a single sheet. She stroked his hair, reassured him, and when she promised she'd play deck games with him that afternoon he seemed to calm down.

The tourist-class lounge also seemed stuffy with the sun right overhead and Heather decided with Daphne and Sophie to go up to the boat deck, look for some shade and hopefully whatever breeze there was off the sea. After finding some deckchairs in the shade of the funnel and lifeboats, they settled down to read; they'd all changed into summer dresses, but Daphne still wore her odd headgear and had her copy of *LC*.

The twangs of shuttlecock on racquet followed by clapping at the end of each point drifted up from the sports deck below. Cynthia was playing with George against a couple in their forties that Heather didn't know. The ship barely moved, just a slight and occasional roll, which added to the excitement for the badminton players. Heather got up to watch, but the players now decided they were too hot and congregated under a canvas awning against the railings.

George waved to Heather with his racquet. 'We're winning,' he said, raising his voice. Heather waved back but felt self-conscious, so remained on the upper deck.

'Good afternoon everyone, warm enough?' came a familiar voice. It was Norman, dressed in a very crisp white set of tennis shorts and shirt, and holding a gin and tonic in a tall glass, which had just been brought over on a tray for all the players by one of the stewards.

'Cheers, Norman,' said George cheerfully, taking a slurp from his glass.

'Cigarettes?' said Norman. He broke open a fresh packet of Craven A and offered them round; most of the players lit up. They wiped themselves with their beach towels to get rid of the sweat, then consumed their drinks and stretched their legs.

Daphne and Sophie got up from their chairs and came over to see what was happening. 'Hello, Norman,' Daphne shouted, waving her arm frantically. Norman looked up, tapping the side of his head with his racquet to each of the three women. A door slammed shut behind them and out came James Scott from the engineers' mess area. The crew had now swapped to tropical white uniform, which Heather thought rather accentuated the third engineer's sandy colouring.

'Just starting my shift,' he said.

'Everything tickety-boo?' said Heather, when a thought occurred to her. 'Fixed the radar yet?'

There was a short pause and James grimaced a little. 'How did you know about that?'

'Woman's intuition,' Heather replied.

James chuckled. 'Well you'll be pleased to know that it's fixed now, as the spare parts were waiting for us in Valletta. Don't go telling anyone about it being broken, though. What are you reading, Mrs Carmichael?'

'Oh nothing,' replied Daphne, putting her book behind her back. 'Silly women's novel.'

'Not *Lady Chatterley* then?'

Now it was Daphne's turn to look embarrassed. 'How did you know?'

James Scott laughed and tapped the side of his nose. They chatted a little before he looked at his watch. 'Better start my rounds now. I could begin here with the lifeboats.'

He checked the davits and the winding gear, then peered under the plastic covering of each of the lifeboats, and the three women went and sat down again. After a while, the engineer started sniffing the air and walking between the lifeboats to look over the railing down the side of the ship. 'Can you smell something burning?' he called over to them.

Heather could only distinguish the oily smell of the funnel and the brine. 'Maybe the people smoking on the sports deck?' she suggested.

'Yes!' said James then swung his legs down the staircase without touching the steps and barged past where the badminton team were drinking and smoking.

'I say…' said Norman as his drink got spilled onto his wrist.

James pirouetted over the side of the ship next to the players. 'There's a fire in one of the cabins, B deck,' he cried, then headed for the staircase next to the tourist lounge. Heather felt a twinge of anticipation and ran after him.

'Wait for me,' shouted Cynthia, while the other badminton players stood watching, drinks in their hands.

They ran down three sets of stairs to get to B deck, by which time James Scott was way ahead of them. He turned to the starboard side where he'd seen the smoke and rushed down a passage leading to four cabins and started knocking on doors, but then dashed back without waiting for a reply and headed into the next passage where he bumped into Heather.

'That's our cabin!' she shouted, 'Nineteen!' There was a tiny wisp of grey smoke coming out from under the door. She opened the door with her key and James barged in first; inside, flames jumped up as the air brought a current of oxygen into the room. It was dark except for the flames and the light filtering in through a haze of smoke from the porthole.

'Johnny!' shouted Heather, but she couldn't get by James who was blocking the doorway as he adjusted his eyes to the darkness and smoke. He crouched along the ground and felt the bunk beds to see if there was anyone in them, then went down low to look under the beds.

'There's no one here!' he shouted.

Heather turned on the light switch, but the light just reflected off the smoke casting a feeble pall over the room. In desperation, she flung open the clothes cupboard but that too had no one inside, and she started coughing.

'Out of the cabin, Heather,' shouted James who now had a fire extinguisher handed to him by De Souza. He bashed the knob on top and sprayed a stream of white foam around the flames consuming the porthole curtains, the carpet beneath, and the bedding at the bottom edge of the bunks. The steward went to the sink, turned the cold tap on full and sprayed water around by putting his finger under the nozzle. The flames had now gone but the ceiling of the room was filled with billows of black smoke which moved around in currents of air. There was a small group of passengers outside who'd heard the noise and knocking on doors.

Heather left the cabin and knelt down in the alleyway, still coughing, and Cynthia put her arm around her.

'Where's Johnny?' asked Cynthia.

'Don't worry, he's safe,' said De Souza, his voice muffled by the towel he'd now put over his face.

James came out of the cabin, his white uniform now smeared all over with black streaks and burn marks, and sprayed some foam on the steward's back.

'Aaii!' said De Souza, turning round sharply.

'You were smoking a bit there,' said James. He then turned to the passengers and put down the extinguisher on the floor. 'All over, nothing to worry about.'

De Souza now had his towel draped around his shoulders and Heather asked him where her son was.

'I saw Johnny come running out of your cabin. He said there was fire, so I put him in the store cupboard then found the fire extinguisher.'

De Souza led Heather and Cynthia along the alleyway and found Johnny sitting in a storeroom on a shelf amongst piles of white towels. His face was blotchy and his hair standing on end, but his pyjamas looked scruffy rather than dirty; he was, however, barefoot and the soles of his feet blackened.

'Darling, are you all right?' asked Heather, sitting next to Johnny and putting her arm around his shoulders.

'Mummy, I dreamed about the boy and girl in their car at night. I dreamed there was a monster dog that attacked the boy, knocked him down and ate his face. Then, then…' Johnny had been speaking quickly but now faltered. 'Then the girl left the car to escape the mad dog and ran through the woods but they started crackling and she couldn't breathe as she was running too quick and and…'

Heather stroked his brow. 'Yes darling?'

'Then I woke up and it was all smoky and I hadn't played with matches, but I got down careful like you showed me and went outside. The Indian man found me.'

'Well done, darling, you did really well.'

'It was Uncle George's story what gave me the dream, I didn't like it.'

'Never mind, Johnny, it's just a story. Maybe he'll tell you another one that's nicer.'

They returned to cabin B19 where James was talking to the bridge on his radio and the clean-up was already starting.

'Thank you, James. Just look how filthy your white uniform is,' said Heather. James smiled and thought better of telling Heather that her face had black smudges and her hair looked like a crow's nest. 'Now you two should see the nurse in case of smoke inhalation or burns.'

'What about all our possessions? We'll have to move, won't we?' said Heather.

'Don't worry about that, I'll talk to the staff while you go to the hospital; it's only just down the alleyway. Can you take them, De Souza?'

When they'd left, a couple of stewards started throwing the burnt curtains and bedding into a white canvas laundry bag. James Scott had been joined by the assistant purser, and the third engineer was demonstrating how the lighted cigarette must have been blown into the cabin porthole and then set fire to the curtains, which had then dropped to the floor and set the carpet alight. Now the black smoke had dispersed out of the porthole and cabin door, the state of the room was clearer; most of the mess was from the fire-extinguisher foam and water from the tap and concentrated around the sink, writing table and the ends of the bunk beds.

'Where will they go?' asked Cynthia who had been joined by Daphne. 'The carpet and curtains need changing and the writing table and chair are burnt.'

'There's one cabin free, a cancellation from Valletta,' said Hancock, lifting up a clipboard with a cabin plan and lists of names.

'Shall I move their clothes?' asked Daphne. 'Otherwise they'll get smoke damaged.'

'Don't worry, we'll see to that.' Hancock had a long aquiline nose but otherwise a pleasing face with a hint of humour always present. He laughed to himself as he again checked all the cabins listed with his pen. 'Every smoky cloud has a silver lining, though. From today the Fontwells will be in first class.'

Chapter 14

30th March 1960 – SS *Uganda*, Eastern Mediterranean

In the meantime, Heather and Johnny were being seen by Marion in the hospital. Doctor Sullivan had also been called in to try and reassure the passengers that there was nothing to worry about. He was a very tall man with thick brown glasses who at first appeared rather distant, but his Scottish accent had a mellow tone that his patients found reassuring if rather hypnotic, so he really was the right man for the occasion.

Dr Sullivan decided to examine Johnny on a couch behind a screen with Heather sitting beside him on a chair. He took the boy's blood pressure, listened to his heart and lungs by means of a stethoscope, looked in his ears with a torch on his head, flipped his eyelids up and down, and finally asked Johnny to spit in a bowl then cough whilst he listened to his chest area. The doctor then pronounced him perfectly fit and healthy and sent him to wait with the nurse.

Heather went through the same procedures with the doctor. She thought she noticed the sour smell of drink when the doctor bent his face close to hers.

'Eyes a bit red, BP a little high, but nothing much to worry about. It might be wise to get a chest X-ray in Mombasa just to be sure. The nurse will finish off and give you some cough linctus, otherwise you're free to enjoy the rest of the journey.'

The doctor came out from behind the screen and went over to the sink to wash his hands. 'I'll see the steward and the engineer at the end of their shifts,' he said to Marion. With that, the doctor dried his hands on some paper towels, chucked them in a metal bin then went into a side office to fill in the patient notes in the buff-coloured folders he was carrying.

'What a horrid thing to happen to you,' Marion said to Heather. 'Is there much damage to your possessions?'

'I don't care about any of that, I'm just so grateful that Johnny escaped when he did and is unharmed. When I think…' Heather covered her face with her hands and shook her head, sobbing quietly. She couldn't believe how quickly it had all happened, how disaster had been prevented only by some quirks of fate, Johnny hearing the story and being disturbed by it, then dreaming and waking up; James Scott being on deck smelling the burning, acting on it straight away and putting out the fire. She remembered being on deck at night dancing to records when there'd been the incident with Carruthers' cigarette; it now seemed portentous.

Truly the fates must be on our side today, she thought as she managed to bring her sobbing under control. I should be looking after Johnny better, give him more attention and try to be less, what Marjorie called, *self-absorbed*.

She slowly drew her hands away from her face, but the blinding white of the hospital ward was still there with the shiny cupboards and sparkling Formica surfaces, light bouncing off everywhere. Marion had her arm round her shoulders and brought herself around to speak to Heather. 'Do you want a sedative?' she asked, her eyes flicking from one side to the other as she checked Heather's pupils.

'No, *you* probably need one though, I must look a fright.' Heather picked a tissue from the blue box proffered by Marion and wiped underneath her eyes; it came away wet and black and Heather wasn't sure if it was from the smoke or her eye liner.

'Are you better now, Mummy?' asked Johnny.

'Much, thank you, Johnny. Just being silly.'

The door opened and the Reverend Ian stuck his head round, smiled, then slowly the rest of him entered the room. 'Hancock just told me what happened.'

Heather and Johnny were sitting hunched over their chairs with Heather blowing her nose.

'I'll just put some linctus on those burns,' said Marion, getting up and opening a cupboard door for a brown bottle and some cotton wool. She quickly shook the bottle and applied the yellow fluid to the red marks on Heather's hands.

'Sorry,' said Heather, 'I suddenly feel exhausted.'

'I'll catch you later,' said the chaplain, 'when you're feeling more up to it.'

The chaplain left and Marion put a blanket around Heather's shoulders. There was a knock at the door, which Marion answered. 'Wait there a moment.' She left the door half open and turned inwards. 'Come on then, Johnny, let's go and see your new cabin.' Marion held out her hand and Johnny slowly slid off his seat to take it. The nurse opened the door and took him to Sophie who was waiting outside whilst Cynthia ran in and interlinked arms with Heather, her pale face now streaked with black lines.

'I've got some good news for you!' said Cynthia, smiling.

The five of them, Marion holding Heather in case she fainted, Sophie holding Johnny's hand, and Cynthia bringing up the rear, walked tentatively along the alleyway. Outside the hospital, it felt stuffy and airless, the ship shifting languidly. They passed through a small door marking the entrance to first class then further along still on the starboard side of the ship and down a short passage on the left. Marion knocked on a cabin door and entered; a steward looked up from where he was bending over fixing sheets on a bed. The room wasn't much bigger than B19 but the shape was inverted and there were two single beds instead of bunks. The fittings were, however, of much higher quality: there was wood panelling on all the walls, the ceiling was backlit from an alcove, and the porthole was covered by a see-through plastic sliding window, which would have prevented the fire they had suffered in tourist class. In addition, the carpet was thicker and with a flecked pattern, the chairs were deeper and wooden built rather than wicker, and there were extra wall lights and an electric fan not in their previous cabin.

'So this is first class,' said Heather, sitting on one of the chairs.

'No other cabins left, apparently,' said Cynthia, rubbing Heather on the arm.

'I'm Diaz.' The new steward introduced himself in a hushed voice. He was short and stocky, probably in his early fifties, with thick grey hair and large brown, rheumy eyes. 'I sorted your things. Those from cupboard and chest of drawers I put back in cupboards and chest of drawers. The rest, I thought, smelled of smoke so they're in this box, waiting for laundry.' He motioned to a large cardboard box with red sticky tape around it that looked like it had once contained tins of mushrooms. There was another thick white plastic bag next to it that looked crumpled and lightly loaded.

Diaz followed Heather's gaze. 'Damaged things in the bag. Please check it all, we can always change them around.'

Heather felt the beginning of a headache coming on; she didn't feel like rummaging through her stuff in front of the others, and rubbed her brow.

'Why don't you get some rest now?' said Cynthia. 'I've got those sedatives from nurse Marion, she said you might need them. Johnny can always come and see Michael.'

Heather yawned, bent over to talk to Johnny, and asked him if he was feeling well and happy enough to spend a little time with Michael. He smiled and nodded with his eyes down as he sensed everyone was looking at him.

Just as Johnny was leaving with Cynthia, he asked for his boats. Heather was sitting on the bed feeling the newly starched and ironed sheets and couldn't think what to say.

'Here's your plane,' said Diaz, picking up the grey and white

Vickers Viscount from the top of the chest of drawers and handing it to Johnny. The boy took it reluctantly and turned over the fuselage in his hands, noticing the black fingerprints underneath; but when Cynthia offered him her hand, he walked out of the cabin with the others.

Heather stripped off down to her underwear then slid inside the bed. It felt strange to be without Johnny in the bunk above with the creaking and shuffling of the mattress. She thought again about Johnny in the cabin as the flames danced around the bottom of his bunk, smoke rising to the ceiling then creeping around the cabin and falling down in curling black wisps to meet his head lying against the pillow. She could see him coughing then turning over, his eyes flickering as he dreamed about George's story.

The sheets felt cold to touch and damp from being unoccupied for over a week, so Heather got up and closed the porthole and sliding window then returned to bed. She felt tired but at the same time tense, so she lay on her back and tried to calm herself. However, this didn't work, primarily as she couldn't think of something calming, so she found her beach bag that Cynthia or Daphne must have rescued from the boat deck and retrieved her poetry book. The poem to read was obvious this time, though it took her a while to find it as she knew neither the title nor the author, just the first line.

The boy stood on the burning deck
Whence all but he had fled;
The flame that lit the battle's wreck
Shone round him o'er the dead

She read Felicia Hemans' poem through to the climax of the boy's death, followed by the postscript, which explained how Casabianca, son of the Admiral, had remained at his post during the Battle of the Nile, then died in the explosion as the flames reached the gunpowder hold. She pondered how a child could have been involved in a naval battle and the senseless loss of his life for no purpose, now glorified in a poem. On rereading the second verse she thought it fitted Johnny's poise and character well, but shivered again when she imagined the smoke and flames.

'Just like Johnny in the cabin fire,' she wrote against the first verse, using the pen from her beach bag. *'Luckily not the same ending,'* she wrote at the end of the poem, then closed the book. Her headache was slowly getting worse so, without looking at the label, she shook out two of the pills from the small brown bottle that Cynthia had left on the bedside table, and tipping her head back swallowed them down in one with a glass of water from the sink.

She clambered back into the bed and thought again about Reverend Ian; she hadn't had a proper conversation with him since Malta and maybe now was the right time to confess to someone who would have to keep it confidential and might even be able to help her. She relaxed and murmured to herself.

★★★

There came the sound of voices: it was Cynthia and Donald Kirby, the first time she had seen them together, with Diaz hovering in the background.

'Thank God you're awake,' said Cynthia, sitting on the edge of the bed. 'How many pills did you take?'

'Two,' said Heather, yawning and stretching.

'It says only a half on the label,' said Donald, scrutinising the bottle. 'We were quite worried.'

Heather sat up with the sheet pulled around her, and rubbed her eyes.

Cynthia turned her head. 'Thanks, Diaz, everything's all right now,' she said, closing the door behind him and returning to the side of the bed next to Heather.

Heather wanted to sit up and pull her legs round but remembered she only had her underwear on. She looked at her watch: it was almost nine o'clock and she'd slept about three hours. Still, her headache had gone, though now she felt heavy-limbed and dull of mind. 'It's nearly Johnny's bedtime.'

'We'll go and get him now.'

'Glad you're better,' said Donald, rubbing his wrists as they both left, enabling Heather to get up and get dressed.

Heather considered what to wear and thought that a cocktail dress was what was required, something bold to banish the worries she had and show the other passengers that she was back to normal, whatever that meant. She chose one that had a dark green floral print because it reminded her of a Rousseau painting she had seen with a tiger hidden in the jungle and she imagined herself as the tiger. She was just applying make-up to her paler-than-usual face when Cynthia came back with Johnny.

'The Carmichaels are all dying to hear your story,' said Cynthia, smiling. 'Come and find us in the bar, assuming you don't mind mucking in with tourist class now.'

Heather got up from her chair and gave Cynthia a hug; she could smell her soap and lily of the valley eau de cologne and felt Cynthia's shoulders tense then relax as she brought her arms up to reciprocate. 'I can't stop thinking about how this day could have ended,' Heather murmured in her ear. They separated with Heather promising to see them later. After Cynthia had gone, Heather gave Johnny a big hug as well.

'Mummy, you're squeezing me,' said the boy, then he smiled at his mum. 'Are we staying here now?'

'Yes, darling, a much nicer cabin,' she said, throwing her arms out.

'I liked the double-deck bed,' Johnny replied, pouting a little.

'Yes, but it's all stinky and smoky from the fire now.'

Heather found Johnny his pyjamas and wash kit and watched

him in the mirror as he changed; she did find him beautiful and bright as in the poem, but then, she supposed, any mother would. Johnny brushed his teeth then started looking in the cardboard box and plastic bag as Heather finished applying a touch of blush to improve her colour.

'Mummy, where are my ships and books?'

Heather looked in the white plastic bag to see what had been damaged most. They were predominantly objects that had been lying around when the fire had occurred – some of Johnny's toys and books as well as his pants and socks and a collection of Heather's knickers and tights as well. The nursery rhyme book was wet and charred around the edges when Heather took it out of the bag, but Johnny made a fuss about keeping it, so she put in on the ledge between porthole and sliding plastic frame to try and dry it out. The toy boats had been partially melted in the heat and recast into strange elongated shapes, but there was a blue one that was still recognisable as a liner, so she took it out and gave it to Johnny.

'Not sure where the others are.'

Johnny got into bed with his blue liner and charred book and Heather reread him 'The Owl and the Pussycat', at the end of which his eyes were already drooping.

She waited a while until she was convinced he was fully asleep, then reduced the lighting to just one side light and contemplated what to do for babysitting. Sitting at her desk she realised there was a white call button marked 'Steward' in front of her on the wall next to the light switches; she pressed it, half expecting to hear the ringing of servants' bells somewhere in the distance, like in a manor house.

After a minute or so, there was a knock at the door and Diaz entered. Heather asked about babysitting Johnny.

'Of course, madam. I'll look in every thirty minutes or so and listen up for any crying.' He had a gentle but slightly sycophantic voice.

'Is De Souza well after the fire? I haven't thanked him properly.'

Diaz shrugged slightly and replied, 'Fine, no problem, madam.'

Heather went back along B deck towards tourist class, retracing her steps to her old cabin. There was little sign of anything untoward from the outside, other than the door feeling bevelled when she smoothed the palm of her hand over it.

She walked onto the tourist-class lounge via the familiar staircases, her body now subconsciously blending into the movement of the ship, leaning against any roll, knees slightly flexed and hands out ready to steady herself. Seeing the Carmichaels and the Kirbys together with Reverend Ian in the lounge, just as they had been the night before, gave Heather a sense of déjà vu. In some ways it felt exactly like twenty-four hours ago, the same group of people, the same sounds and smells, the same place. Yet in another sense the moment felt quite different as the events of the afternoon had almost led to her son's death, and anything involving fire and water felt as though there were primeval, even biblical, forces behind it.

'What do you want, Heather?' George shouted from the bar, waving at her.

'Campari soda please, George,' she replied, walking over to the bar to see if he needed any help.

'Can I try some of Heather's?' Sophie asked her mum. Daphne rolled her eyes and was about to say something, but thought better of it and gave her permission.

George passed over the pink fizzy drink to Heather, then took a tray for the rest. The conversation passed to recounting the details of the cabin fire and their treatment in the hospital. The chaplain asked what Dr Sullivan had said and Heather told him they'd all been checked out and passed clear.

'Sorry about frightening Johnny with my story earlier,' said George, putting his whisky down. Sophie and Daphne tutted.

'Don't be,' replied Heather, 'you saved his life.' She had to explain that the bad dream had caused Johnny to wake up and leave the cabin, and that otherwise he might have breathed in all the smoke.

'It reminds me of a Russian proverb I heard a long time ago, about the songbird and the cow,' said Donald in his quiet voice, his long legs extended out from his chair. There was a pause as he drank some of his beer.

'Go on, Donald,' said Cynthia, gently.

'It was a hard Russian winter and a songbird got really cold and flopped to the ground in exhaustion, ready to die. Along came a cow and dropped a load of dung right on the bird, which then warmed up and found a few tasty grubs to eat. The bird was so happy at this turn of events that it started singing, but a nearby hungry fox heard the songbird, jumped in and ate it.'

There was a collective gasp of breath followed by another pause.

'But what does the proverb mean?' asked Heather.

'Well, firstly, that being dumped on can have good results. Secondly, if you're in a mess, don't make a song and dance about it.'

George laughed very loudly, but Donald remained expressionless.

'That was almost as bad as one of George's ghastly stories,' said Daphne.

George shrugged and grinned and they all took another sip of their drinks.

'We should thank James Scott,' said Heather. 'He was really quick off the mark and would have saved Johnny if he'd still been in the cabin.' The others all murmured their agreement.

While Heather passed Sophie the remnants of her Campari soda to try, the chaplain spoke quietly to her. 'There's hardly anyone in the smoking room.' They both left with Daphne arching her eyebrows towards them.

The chaplain found a table with two leather armchairs in the corner; he was wearing a short-sleeved light-blue shirt and dog collar, with black cotton trousers. He draped his grey herringbone jacket around an adjacent chair before sitting and fumbling in his pockets for pipe and tobacco. 'Johnny had a lucky escape, but you must have found it very traumatic.'

'Enough about me. What happened in Malta?'

'Not much, really. I hadn't seen Mandusa for some time, so we had some catching up to do.' Ian leaned forward, his pipe in his hand, to continue. 'He was born in Malta but his father's British. I first met him when he was training in an adjoining parish to mine in Lincolnshire. We became good friends but then he had to go back to Malta, and I hadn't seen him since.'

'Why didn't you keep in contact if he was such a good friend?'

Ian shrugged his shoulders. 'I was never much of a letter writer.'

'You've never considered getting married?'

'I'm not really the marrying sort, Heather,' he replied, looking directly at her. 'If you see what I mean.'

There was a long pause and a steward came over, but the chaplain waved him away. Heather's mind was awash with thoughts; she actually didn't really see what he meant but didn't want to admit this, or press the chaplain on the matter. He could mean he was married to the Church, or simply that he preferred to be a batchelor, or both. Alternatively, he could mean he was homosexual, but then Heather barely knew what this meant. She understood that homosexual acts were illegal and remembered her father reading the newspaper one day, with an article about police round-ups in London. It had never been a suitable topic for conversation at home.

The reverend put his pipe in his top pocket and stood up to leave. 'Wait,' she carried on, 'you haven't asked about my confession yet.'

Ian shrugged his shoulders then sat down again and wrung his hands.

'You didn't read my letter, did you?' asked Heather, now recalling that she'd handed it to him unsealed.

'I don't make a habit of snooping, but I sensed something was troubling you and that you might have wanted me to read it.'

Heather looked askance, torn between anger that her private letter had been read by almost a complete stranger and her fear that Ian now had knowledge that she'd struggled so hard to keep secret.

'Don't worry, Heather, I'm compelled to keep everything confidential or I could get thrown out of the Church.'

'Well I hope you posted the bloody thing afterwards.' Heather struggled to suppress her anger and saw a tiny blob of her spit land on the lapel of his jacket.

'We can talk again when you're a bit calmer.' Ian touched her forearm then walked away through the seaward door and out into the night without looking back, his pipe still unlit. Heather clenched her fists and then let her fingers loose before leaving in the other direction.

Chapter 15

31st March 1960 – SS *Uganda*, Eastern Mediterranean

The dawn felt like it was heralding a new beginning for Heather: they had a new cabin and a new steward and somehow the fire had shifted the chemistry in her head, giving her a new filter, colouring her view differently. Even the light this morning was harsher, perhaps unsurprising given that they were due in Egypt the next day.

Heather rolled over and looked at Johnny's bed; compared to the bunk beds he seemed far away but, of course, at home he had his own room and was even further away. Johnny had his back to her, fast asleep, but she could still see his sticky-up hair and the navy blue pyjamas with mini teddy bears on that Marjorie had bought him at Christmas. Heather thought about the letter she'd written and where it was now, on another ship going back to England, maybe another BI liner or mail ship; she'd ask James Scott, or Mark the cadet, they'd know. She'd heard George tell Daphne that tomorrow was the halfway point, but that still left ten more days before they got to Mombasa.

Johnny started shuffling in his bed, mumbling some words and kicking out his legs. There was a knock at the door, which then opened a crack.

'Morning tea, madam?' came Diaz's soft voice as he opened the door further with a tray in his hand.

'Can you leave it on the writing table please?'

Diaz grunted and shuffled over to put the tea and sugar bowl down. 'What would you like, Johnny?'

'Squash please,' he replied in a muffled voice. Heather turned and looked: he was under the covers playing with a hidden toy. Diaz padded out of the cabin and Heather quickly got up, put her *Uganda* dressing gown on and took a sip of the tea. She could feel the tannin taste on her tongue and at the back of her throat.

'Smell this, Mummy,' said Johnny, holding out his blue plastic liner, the one saved from the cabin fire. She took it and sniffed a burnt chemical aroma; her stomach recoiled at the combination of this and the taste of the tea. She could hear Diaz speaking in his own language to another woman in the alleyway as she washed her face in the sink and gargled some water from the tap.

When Diaz re-entered the cabin to hand Johnny his squash, there was an Indian-looking young woman behind him, with black tousled hair and a wide nose. She was wearing a white military-style top stitched up to the neck with black wide trousers but had no shoes on; at first Heather thought it might be Diaz's wife, but she was too young for that and there were no female stewards on board.

'Hello, I'm Monica, from the cabin next to yours,' she said in a well-educated southern England accent, holding out her hand. 'Just thought I'd say hello, after all your heroics.'

When they shook hands, Heather noticed how thin and cold her fingers were.

'No after-effects from the fire?' Monica asked.

'No,' replied Heather, not liking to talk about herself. 'I like your top, very unusual.'

'Oh, my pyjamas you mean. Yes, they're from Goa,' Monica replied, pulling at her neck self-consciously.

Heather made her excuses in order to get Johnny ready, took another anti-sickness pill, and eventually they made it to breakfast in the first-class dining saloon. As in tourist class, the dining room was on C deck, but this time forward rather than aft, so they simply had to go down one deck from their cabin. As they opened the door from the staircase vestibule, Heather immediately noticed the chill of the air conditioning after the stuffy feel of the cabin with the sliding window closed; she thought she'd have to get over the fear of another cabin fire and open the window and porthole now that the air was warmer.

'Mrs Fontwell and Johnny.' It was the purser whom she'd seen previously at the Sunday service; he did a half bow but his grin made it feel slightly mocking. He was older than his assistant, salt and pepper hair going bald at the back. Probably a company man with that self-assurance, Heather thought.

'I trust you're well after your experience yesterday. British India have decided to upgrade you to compensate for any inconvenience, so welcome to first class and if ever I can be of any help…' He held out his hand motioning her to one of the Goanese stewards and gave another mock bow. Heather didn't know what to make of him.

The dining saloon was panelled in much the same way as the drawing room, from what she could remember of it from the Sunday Service: silver birch, cob casings and cherry wood against a pale peach background, with the roof raised up and panels painted all around it. The room was dominated by two paintings, one of which she assumed to be of an African harbour with a fort, and the other she recognised as the Thames between Blackfriars and Southwark bridges. Heather wondered why any passenger would want to look at the latter, which would probably be well known to them; then she realised they both represented an end point of a journey, and maybe a colonial who'd been in Africa a long time would quite like to be reminded of home before he arrived there.

The food was pretty much the same as in tourist class but the service was very attentive. There was a dining room for children in an alcove next to them, but the steward explained that it wasn't really used at breakfast. Johnny looked around him, frowning and keeping his face low against the table.

'They're looking at us,' he said, putting his semi-melted blue liner onto the white starched tablecloth.

'Nonsense, darling,' Heather replied. Although no one was overtly staring, which would have been very bad manners, she could nevertheless tell that he was right from the slight lapse in the murmuring of conversation when they'd arrived, and the way the other passengers averted their gaze when Heather looked up. The only exception was Monica, sitting opposite a young man hunched over some papers at a table on the other side of the room; the two women smiled at each other.

Heather tucked into her bacon and eggs and watched the staff working. The rigmarole of the morning welcome was normally the preserve of the head waiter, an upright, well-tanned man in a black suit. His gestures were even more extreme than the purser's; where possible, he accompanied every group to their table in a way that looked like he was doing ballroom dancing, one arm high up and twirling around to avoid the other tables. He seemed quite effeminate, which reminded Heather of the last conversation with the chaplain. Was he one of those as well?

Heather cringed at her reaction last night; she'd been rather tired and that usually led her to behave in *more impulsive ways than usual* she could hear her sister Marjorie saying in her dry tone. Yes, she had obviously upset the chaplain, especially after he had so kindly given her and Johnny his time in Malta. But reading her letter had also incensed Heather – it felt like a deeply personal invasion of her privacy, like being touched when you didn't want to be. Her mother had read her diary once when she was thirteen, *'Just to make sure you were all right'*, but it had infuriated Heather, led to a shouted argument and her running away to spend the night at a friend's house.

'Sorry to interrupt, Mrs Fontwell,' said the grinning purser. 'I took the liberty of moving your baggage to the first-class baggage room, just in case you need to retrieve anything. Also, this is Mrs

Worthington, who wanted me to introduce you.' He did another bow and stepped backwards to reveal a lady with white hair and steel-framed glasses.

'Just wanted to say hello and hope you're well after the fire. We don't have many children in first, so it's nice to see a little boy as well.' She spoke quietly with a Lancashire accent.

Heather reassured her that they had both recovered and with no serious injuries. Just to prolong the conversation, she asked Mrs Worthington about the African harbour painting.

'That's Fort Jesus in Mombasa, my dear. It's splendid, isn't it, over those three panels? You've not been out to Kenya before then?'

Heather explained about William's job and wanting to go to Kenya before he came home for good, whenever that would be. This, of course, was a charade, but it was a story she could easily tell, and it sounded plausible.

Mrs Worthington then quickly moved on to Johnny; she asked him his name, how old he was, where he went to school and who his favourite teacher was. Her manner was open and frank and she seemed interested in Johnny's answers, and used to talking with, rather than down to, children. Johnny spoke clearly but kept looking at his lap, though he seemed happy to answer the torrent of questions.

'We've got grandchildren, you see, and I spend quite a lot of time with them,' said Mrs Worthington. She then made her excuses and returned to her table where there was an older portly man seated, presumably her husband, who lifted his teacup as a greeting.

Heather and Johnny returned to their cabin and got changed for the morning activities which, according to the daily sheet handed to them by Diaz, included Sports Day; Race Night was also 'on the cards', which Heather thought must be a joke of some sort. She found her canvas bag and filled it with hats and sun tan lotion, plus swimwear for Johnny and a couple of books for herself.

Heather wanted to go to the morning activities with her friends and decided to head for the Carmichaels' cabin to see who she could find. She and Johnny walked along the alleyway from their cabin and opened the door to go back into tourist class. Heather waited for Johnny who was dawdling and running his hand along all the teak railings; while she was waiting, the door to the hospital opened and Mr Carruthers stepped out. He didn't see them at first, while taking the same direction, but Johnny shouted 'Mum' and he turned his head.

'Can I help you, you seem lost?' he asked in a sarcastic voice, his eyes flicking up to the first class sign hanging on the door. 'Sorry to hear about your... um, accident.' Carruthers didn't look in the least bit sorry with his nasty leering grin.

'No thanks, I'm not lost, I've got a cabin in first class now,' she replied, trying to be as cool as possible.

Carruthers stared at her, frowning, his grin now dissipated.

'After the fire,' she added, then took Johnny's hand and walked on down the alleyway past the hospital. She wondered what took him there – piles, constipation or even the trots, she mused as she turned into the passage for the Carmichaels' cabin and knocked on their door.

George answered in a tennis shirt and shorts. 'Morning, Heather,' he beamed. 'Tired of all that luxury already?'

Heather laughed and Daphne appeared at the door. 'I'm glad you've come, Heather, Sophie wants to rest in bed all day and says Sport's Day's not for grown-ups.'

'Come on, Sophie, you can be in my team,' she shouted in through the door.

'Shall we meet on the sports deck?' asked George. Heather agreed but said she might be at the swimming pool nearby and would look out for them.

Up on deck, the thermometer against an outside wall already read 82 degrees even though it was only ten o'clock and the canvas awnings were stretched wide over the whole decking area. Heather thought she'd take Johnny to the pool to occupy him in the meantime; they'd both put on their swimming costumes underneath their clothes, but then Heather thought she'd go in the first-class pool as it was slightly larger, had a better view over the sea and she could avoid seeing Carruthers again. Johnny didn't seem to notice the difference between the two pools and was impatient to get in the water. 'I can do it,' he said when Heather made to take his outer clothes off. Instead, she blew up his blue water wings; the red and white ring hadn't survived the fire.

They found a couple of chairs at the back of the pool area against a bulkhead where they left their bag and clothes. Johnny carefully went down the steps backwards as he'd seen the crew doing throughout the ship, but he wasn't as confident without the ring and clung onto the side of the pool. Heather followed him in and rested in one corner of the pool where she could spread out her arms along the side; the corner she'd chosen was in the sun and she lifted her head and angled it away from the sun but looking up at the sky. There were no clouds, just an aching deep blue, and she pulled the sunglasses down off her forehead to counter the glare.

It was a perfect moment; the ship rolled very slightly, tipping the water from up and down the sides of the pool, creating a buoyancy that was not unpleasant. Heather could feel the sun warming her arms and the water rising up and down her body with the ship's movement, but she still kept her eyes on Johnny as he inched his way round the pool to her. They threw the inflatable ball to each other, just short distances so as not to annoy the sole other user of the pool, an elderly man with a purple plastic cap slowly swimming from side to side in about three or four strokes.

'Ahoy there, Heather,' came Sophie's voice from behind her. Heather turned around and could just see her head sticking up above the edge of the pool, presumably by standing upright on the railings of the tourist-class pool below her. They both waved and

Heather flagged down a passing steward to ask if he'd let Sophie into the first class pool.

When she arrived, Sophie was wearing long khaki shorts with a blue polo shirt. She was frowning. 'Thought I'd never find you,' she muttered. 'I didn't realise you'd be up here. Dad is being really stupid about entering lots of races.'

'He's probably just pulling your leg.'

'Look at me!' said Johnny, doing a doggy paddle stroke. 'I can swim!'

Heather got out of the pool by levering herself up on the side and gave Johnny a hand to do the same.

'No two-piece today, Heather?' said Sophie, watching.

Heather quickly put on her white gown. 'Don't think they're ready for that here,' she said smiling and looking around at the much older clientele in the deckchairs who only dared show off their wrinkled arms and legs.

'Dad said to come over in half an hour, so can we have a drink here beforehand?'

They all ordered then sat back in the shade. Sophie wanted a Campari but Heather said it was too early, maybe later at the race night.

'I'm bored,' said Johnny, fiddling with the straw in his orange juice.

'In that case,' said Heather, 'Sophie will read you a story.' She rummaged in her bag and handed the poetry book to Sophie, with a page open. 'Here, this one, I saw it last night.'

Sophie looked at the book. 'The Walrus and the Carpenter?' she asked, turning the page in some doubt and clearing her throat a bit self-consciously.

Heather smiled and asked Johnny if he was ready.

The sun was shining on the sea
Shining with all his might

He did his very best to make
The billows smooth and bright-
And this was odd, because it was the middle of the night.

Johnny cackled and clapped his hands. Heather looked over the dark blue flatness of the sea merging into the endless horizon. Was this the same water that had tormented her throughout the Bay of Biscay, throwing the ship around and making her sick? She made a note to this effect as Sophie carried on reading, her face now free of its habitual frown, and the Walrus, the Carpenter and the Oysters were introduced. Johnny picked up his liner boat when it became apparent that the ending was nowhere in sight.

'Let's stop there, thank you,' said Heather, watching Sophie turning back the ends of her hair behind her ear, then closing the book and putting it on Heather's bag. 'We should go and see what's happening with sports day.'

There was a small crowd up on the sports deck, mainly parents of children onboard whom Heather recognised from tourist class. The tarpaulins had been pulled across the whole deck area and there was a table with a white cloth in the corner where a selection of drinks had been laid out, and three stewards, one of them Parminder, in attendance.

James Scott was unrolling some wires going to a speaker, which had been set up at the opposite end to the drinks table. He plugged in the amplifier and another cable to a power socket whilst cadet Mark Edwards was spooling out the lead to a microphone with a bulbous grey end. Assistant purser Hancock was talking to the waiting parents and children; he had a confident manner, a bit like the chaplain, but was eager to find humour in whatever situation he could. He squatted down on his haunches to speak to the more diffident children and motioned for more drinks where there were empty glasses.

A rhythmic tapping on the microphone by James Scott was the

sign for Hancock to step up and announce the beginning of the sports day. He grasped the microphone and hunched forward in a conspiratorial pose, scanning the groups of participants with his hand on his forehead to shield his eyes from the sun.

'What a motley crew you are,' he said in a piratical West Country voice. 'First off we have the dry games for children – the potato race, the sack race, the obstacle race then the run to Mummy race for the little 'uns. Then, Gawd help us all' – Hancock made the sign of the cross – 'the parents' races, back by popular demand. There will be Daddy's blindfolded potato race' – whereupon a few fathers cheered – 'and Mummy's sack race…' A few groans followed. 'Then to the pool where you'll all be keelhauled and survivors made to walk the plank!' There were cheers all round encouraged by the crew, officers and stewards alike.

***

Heather and Johnny had lunch with their friends in the tourist-class dining room; Daphne updated them on the latest plot twists in *Lady Chatterley*, and told them all what a splendid book it was, sensitive and written from a woman's viewpoint, even if by a man.

'Odd, though, considering he was probably homosexual,' said Cynthia.

'Oh, Cynthia, the children…' said Daphne, leaning over and trying to cover her daughter's ears.

'Get off, Mum!' said Sophie, who'd spent most of the meal so far in silence, cutting and repositioning the food in front of her.

'Don't mind Johnny, he's not even listening,' said Heather. Johnny looked up from where he'd been playing with a soldier in his lap, in expectation of something about to happen.

'Talk about *bête noire,* though,' continued Cynthia, quite unaware of the ripples of annoyance coming from Daphne. 'He was accused of everything under the sun the authorities could think of. First he was damned because he ran off with a married German woman, then he was accused of being a spy signalling to German submarines, then a homosexual and now a pornographer.'

'Have you studied Lawrence then?' George asked Cynthia; he was affecting great interest in the conversation but Heather suspected was trying to divert it towards less troubled waters.

'Well, a little,' replied Cynthia dabbing her cheeks with her napkin. 'Amateurish, though.'

'What should I read of his?' asked Heather, trying a sip of coffee.

'Most people like *Women in Love* but I would start with his short stories.'

'Shall we enter our two boys for the fancy dress competition?' Heather asked Cynthia, tapping her arm with the palm of her hand.

'No, Mummy,' said Johnny, 'that's for girls.' Michael next to him nodded in sympathy.

'Just watch then?' said Heather in a pleading voice.

The two boys both shook their heads violently. They all then agreed to meet again for dinner to be followed by race night.

The afternoon was much hotter than on previous days and there was little by way of a breeze as the sea was calm. Heather and Johnny retired to their new cabin and slept for an hour and a half.

Johnny was keen to see Michael again, so Heather went back to tourist class and took him to the nursery. The chief hostess, Whiffie Smithie as Daphne called her, was hovering at the nursery door. She greeted Heather in her curt manner and asked why she wasn't at the first class nursery.

'Well, he's made friends here,' replied Heather, looking around at the children inside, 'and he won't know anyone in the first class nursery.'

Smithie paused momentarily then smiled weakly and walked away. Johnny, meanwhile, had spotted Michael and was off, not noticing that his former friend Simon was watching him from astride the rocking horse.

Heather left the nursery and made her way outside to the aft cargo hatches and swimming pool. Really, she thought, I'm going to have to stop looking at all the children's dolls and I can't let the troll phobia stop me from taking Johnny to the first class nursery, the real reason why I haven't been there yet. The heat hit her as soon as she opened the door to the deck, so she walked around to the port side where the promenade was partly in shadow; someone called out her name.

'Hello!' said Sophie, breathless, having run from the swimming pool. 'I've been looking all over for you.'

'Fancy some tea? It's too hot out here in the afternoon. We could go to the first class lounge if you like?'

'Cor, yes please!'

'You'll have to be my guest and behave yourself, young lady. No Campari this time.' Sophie could tell that Heather was gently teasing her, so she laughed and they walked along the side of the ship on A deck, past all the better first-class cabins. A brown smudge on the horizon denoted the presence of another ship but otherwise the sea seemed empty and limitless. There was another deck door, which was stiff and heavy, but they managed to open it and plunge into first class; at the end of a short passage, they found the grand staircase going up to the public rooms, with their walnut wood panelling and marine oil paintings.

'Remember coming here before?' asked Heather.

'Yeah, the Sunday service,' replied Sophie as she signed a leather padded book to denote that she was Heather's guest. 'Seems like a century ago.'

In the lounge, the head waiter came across to them. 'Ladies,' he screeched, 'afternoon tea?' He led them forward to a vacant table, then withdrew with a mini-twirl as a steward came forward with two menus and drew back their chairs for them.

They ordered tea and cake and sat back and enjoyed the air conditioning and the view over the forward cargo hatches to the bow and destination Egypt beyond. Heather went over and chatted to Mrs Worthington then returned to Sophie and sat down just as the tea and Madeira cake was arriving. The steward poured the tea then left them.

'So, how was your day then?' Heather asked Sophie.

'I'm never going to children's activities again – it's too embarrassing with Dad.'

They both drank some tea in silence.

'Heather, can I ask you something?' Sophie pulled her hair back behind her ear.

Heather knew exactly what she was going to ask and that she'd been contemplating this all day.

'What's homosexual exactly?' asked Sophie, leaning forward so she could speak without being heard.

'They're men who prefer other men to women.' Heather held her cup of tea in front of her and blew across the surface.

Sophie looked worried. 'But there are lots of men like that, in pubs and at football matches.'

Heather laughed and wondered how far she should go; she wasn't, after all, responsible for Sophie's sex education. 'Sexually, I mean.'

'Oh.' Sophie thought for a while. 'How does that work?'

Yes, a good question, thought Heather. She smiled at Mr Worthington who seemed to be looking at her but in a curious rather than hostile manner. Heather felt suddenly tired, even though she'd had her nap. 'Shall we look at the rest of first class when we've finished?'

Chapter 16

1st April 1960 – SS *Uganda*, Port Said, Egypt

The harbour was teeming with small craft – mostly wooden clinker built open boats painted blue or red with lavish curls along the gunwales – that looked suitable only for fishing or transporting around Port Said. Heather and Johnny had agreed to go ashore with the Carmichaels, and Norman.

'You'll get pestered a lot, so form a large group with plenty of men,' Hancock had said, whilst supplying them with some Egyptian pounds from the purser's office. 'It's fixed to the British pound in theory but you'd be better off flashing around some roubles these days,' he'd added laconically with a twist to his mouth.

The purser had walked by. 'Anyone for the pyramids?' he'd asked, as though it were a game of tennis on a lawn in a country house instead of a hot and dusty overnight trip by bus. He then apprehended George who was telling some lady passengers that the trip had been cancelled after a sandstorm had covered the pyramids. 'No wonder the numbers are down,' the purser finished with a gloomy expression.

George smiled and puffed out his stripy shirt that looked like a deckchair cover. 'Well I didn't expect anyone to take that too seriously, given today's date.'

The purser glanced at the wall chart in the office opposite, then claimed that he'd known all along it was an April Fools' joke.

'The passengers don't want to be in hostile territory more like,' muttered Norman. 'Nasser has turned the country against us since the Suez crisis.' He was wearing a dusty grey jacket with beige linen trousers and carrying a straw trilby.

'Or maybe they didn't like their country being invaded,' Heather said, just to see his reaction. George coughed and Daphne looked at Heather in alarm. Norman wagged his finger and gave a long lecture on why it had all been the Americans' fault, how they'd let down Britain and France as usual. Heather suspected he was bluffing.

'Mummy, can I see the giant pyramids?' asked Johnny, tugging on Heather's arm.

'Not today, Johnny – we'll go another time, with Daddy.'

The promise managed to quieten Johnny who began to poke around inside Heather's beach bag trying to find the packed-lunch sandwiches wrapped in greaseproof paper.

'Don't eat anything ashore other than the packed lunch and only drink out of sealed bottles,' Hancock had said, 'unless you want to reacquaint yourselves with the hospital.' He'd winked at Heather.

Heather looked out from the newly opened service hatch and squinted into the morning sun reflecting off the water; she could hear the continual slopping noise against the *Uganda* and felt a light breeze, which took the edge off the heat. One of the ship's launches, with a white hull and orange plastic sides, drew alongside and they all walked down the gangplank that was pulled in diagonally against the hull. Heather walked on the outside with one hand on the railing, the other holding Johnny's hand as they descended. Johnny knocked on the white steel with his hand. 'Ow!' he said as he grazed a knuckle against a rivet.

From right up close, the ship's hull towered above them and Heather noticed the faint smudges of grey and green. All the passengers started to assemble in the launch and she spotted Monica and her husband next to the chaplain, all three clinging onto white plastic bags with their packed lunches. An officer came down the gangplank and took the helm from an Indian serang. Heather didn't recognise him – he was close-shaven bald, late forties, probably, but his skin was well creased, so possibly younger, with a close-cropped grey beard to match his head.

'I'm the first officer, for those who don't know me,' he said in a West Country accent. 'The bumboats are here in number, so keep your arms away from the side of the launch.'

A group of open boats began congregating around the *Uganda*. They had their decks panelled over, so the oarsman and vendor stood or sat in a little square of space surrounded by their goods, mostly stacks of leather cushions. The vendor would stand and shout up to the passengers and crew peering over the deck railings.

'Souvenirs of Egypt!' shouted one. 'Nice jellabiya, tarboosh hat, leather products!' He threw a rope up to the promenade deck where Heather was surprised to see Mrs Worthington catch it, a bemused deckhand next to her.

'Jellabiya please, for ladies!' she shouted.

A pannier was filled with clothes and the rope pulled up to the deck by the deckhand.

Meanwhile, another boat with food on board approached the launch. 'Drinks for hot sun, ladies!' a young man announced, standing in the boat as it rocked in the wash of the harbour, arm outstretched showing bottles and cans. A second Egyptian had his back to them, tending the oars, adjusting backwards and forwards as Daphne bartered, then eventually bought a can of coke.

'Time to go,' shouted the first officer, and the serang pushed the bow of the launch away with a boathook; the officer throttled up the engine and took them away from the side of the ship. After the *Uganda*, the launch felt very low in the water as the sea gurgled past the passengers just inches away; the boat pitched slightly, pushing a spray of water over the bow, causing some of the women passengers to scream.

'Oops,' said the first officer, 'that'll keep you cool!'

They made a long sweeping turn and pulled alongside a low-planked pontoon linked to a concrete jetty; the serang jumped ashore with the painter and pulled the launch in snug.

'Mind your step. Our agent is ready for your tour – please be back by three.'

They all stepped gingerly from the launch aided by arms from the first officer and the boatman. Heather felt strange being on solid land again – much as she had done in Malta – the ground appearing to tilt when it didn't really, and having to adjust her walking style.

There was a dark-blue coloured bus on the harbourside with two men standing next to it: one was bending down polishing the radiator grille and chrome bumpers, which were gleaming in the sun, whilst the other waved at them and slid open the side door of the bus.

'City tour, Uganda!' he announced. The other, younger Egyptian, with a surly expression on his face, stopped his polishing and walked round to the other side of the bus and got in the driver's cab. But before the group could board the bus, some other local men who'd been sitting on a bench in the shade of a palm tree, quickly walked over to them.

'Hello please British, we are the famous gully-gully men, yes,' said the leader, with a gold-tooth smile under a greying thin moustache. He ruffled Johnny's hair. 'Look out for us when you get back,' he said, 'on top deck.'

The tour guide beckoned them to join the bus, and showed them inside; it was hot, despite all the window blinds being pulled down, and not helped by the low ceiling. The bench seats were made of plain wood and the guide then handed out some cushions to sit on, but it was still nothing like the luxurious seating of the *Uganda*.

The guide then went outside and turned the engine over with a starting handle. It caught straight away, coughing as it turned, before roaring into life and vibrating the whole bus. With a grinding

173

noise as first gear was engaged, the bus then moved jerkily forwards and clouds of sooty smoke crept along the ground to where the gully-gully men had resumed their seats under the palm tree. The guide switched on two electric fans, which blew air down the bus, then stood up and shouted their itinerary over the engine and fan noise.

They were first shown the offices of the Suez Canal Company, a magnificent building in Arabic style, with whitewashed walls and three cupolas that looked like the domes of mosques. It was set right on the harbourside with rather ugly tall radio towers all around and the Egyptian flag flying from the central largest cupola. The bus paused briefly for photos then moved on.

'The De Lesseps monument,' announced the guide, pointing out a plinth at the end of a short jetty protruding into the harbour, with several ships at anchor in the background. A dhow with its diagonal mast was slowly making its way down to the sea.

'But the plinth is empty,' queried the chaplain, his brow furrowed.

'Removed for safe-keeping after return of canal to Egyptian people,' replied the guide, nodding as though this was quite normal. Nobody wanted to take photos, so the bus moved on again, stopping at the lighthouse, again overlooking the harbour.

'First concrete building in world,' said the guide as the driver spat out of his side window. The lighthouse was set back from the waterfront, a small copse of cypresses in front; it was very tall and thin, built in a hexagon shape with white segments painted onto the concrete and narrow slits for windows going up each side. Again there was only a short pause due to the heat and the clamour of street sellers around the doorway, calling in several languages and lifting up arms full of scarves and linen shirts.

The next stop was the Latin cathedral; with its high brick walls and square tower, Heather thought it looked like a waterworks in Bromley, though the style was art deco, with multicoloured bricks and it was set in a wide boulevard of palm trees. Inside it at least had the benefit of being cool and tranquil, the beggars only being allowed as far as the top of the steps outside. Back on the bus they toured around the busy streets.

'Can we have a drink soon?' asked Monica.

'Yes, very soon, lady!' said the guide, who turned and said something to the driver whereupon the bus picked up speed and left the centre for a residential area. They looked at apartments built after the 1956 bombing and a chemical plant financed by Russian money, the bus not stopping. Heather was beginning to feel sick, though she was unsure whether it was the heat, or the erratic jolting of the bus, or both. She was about to ask the guide to stop when the bus drew up outside what looked like an old colonial wooden house of two storeys.

'Tea house; old French trading post,' said the guide and led them up some stairs to a low table on a veranda facing a patch of scrubland and a long mound of earth, behind which Heather could see a funnel and mast and a bridge deck slowly moving left to right.

'Suez Canal!' said the guide, pointing at the strange tableau of the tops of moving ships in the background.

Mint tea was produced for everyone, poured from giant silver teapots into small glasses with Suez Canal written on the side, the server letting down a long stream of tea into each glass with minimal spillage. Some dates and baklava were also furnished on chipped brown floral plates. The passengers drank the tea whilst Johnny had squash from a small carton.

'Can we eat these?' Reverend Ian asked, showing his greaseproof-paper wrapped sandwiches.

'Yes, no problem,' said the guide, waving him away and then joining a group of Egyptian men on an adjacent table. A plate of flatbreads and cold roasted peppers, aubergines and courgettes was brought out for the locals. The passengers' sandwiches, apples and chocolate biscuits seemed rather dull by comparison. Heather thought she had to try the baklava, which she found rather syrupy but tasty; Daphne looked on, turning up her nose. Conversation was desultory as the overhead fans whirred noisily and a few flies buzzed around. The guide returned from his meal and started talking about the industrial progress of Egypt, but the midday heat made it difficult for the English group to concentrate. Eventually the guide brought a scruffy receipt with a number written on it and Norman paid the makeshift bill, putting his roll of Egyptian pounds back in his trouser pocket. Heather asked the guide for the toilet.

'Of course, madam, I show you,' he replied, beaming.

'I'll come with you,' said Norman, 'in case there's any funny business.'

They went out the back of the teahouse where the guide unlocked a door to a white-painted wooden shed; a swarm of flies was disturbed and the stench was choking.

Heather went into the cubicle, which had a Western-style toilet, filled to the brim with soiled paper and turds. The toilet was not, however, connected to any form of plumbing, so was purely ornamental; she held her breath and quickly peed into the toilet bowl, trying not to touch anything, and squatting above rather than sitting on the seat. She quickly pulled her pants up, adjusted her yellow skirt and walked out quickly, breathing again in long deep bursts to calm herself and avoid being sick.

Heather told the others about the toilet and they decided to wait till they got back to the ship. The bus seemed even hotter than before, though the electric fans afforded some relief as the engine started.

'Last stop, the new airport,' announced the guide. 'No photos please.'

After ten minutes, they passed a flat area with a high mesh and wire fence, behind which was a collection of silver military planes squatting in the heat, the sun intermittently reflecting off their fuselages. On the left there were three large hangars, and on the right a concrete terminal building.

Norman was in the seat in front of Johnny and Heather, staring at the military area, his hand shielding his eyes from the bright light. Heather was shocked to see that he was using a pair of miniature binoculars, crouched down behind the seat in front.

'Hmm MiG 17s and 19s, bloody death-traps,' he whispered. 'Plus a few Badgers and Ilyushin 28s. Usual Soviet junk.' He put down his binoculars then raised them rapidly. 'Wait a minute, though, what's this, a Bear? Surprised there's enough runway length for it.'

'A bear in Egypt?' asked Heather, though she realised it was a kind of aircraft.

'Just wait till they see this.' Norman had now swapped his binoculars for a small camera but was still crouched down in his seat. Heather could hear the shutter clicking.

As he was putting his camera away, Heather saw that the driver had spotted Norman in his rearview mirror and exchanged a few words in Arabic with the guide, who now came down the bus, his smile vanished.

'What you doing?' he asked. Norman showed him his binoculars.

'Just wanted to see better, eyesight no good these days,' he replied in a casual drawl.

The guide grunted and returned to the front; there was no further commentary as the bus returned them to the wharf opposite the *Uganda* at anchor. The heat was even more intense and Heather noticed the burnt oily smell that the ship had when in steam. There was a black film drifting behind the funnel and the ship had turned around on its anchor chain over the afternoon and was now showing port side to the dock.

'We're ready to go,' said the first officer as they boarded the launch. 'We're in convoy for the canal, with a tanker and mail ship in front of us, but if we're not formed up at the right time we'll lose our slot.'

There were some empty open boats tied to the bottom of the gangway. 'Gully-gully men on board, sir,' said the serang to George when he asked.

Sure enough, on the boat deck under the white tarpaulin covers, there was a group of passengers and the same Egyptian men they had met earlier on the shore. Heather spotted Mrs Worthington and went over to speak to her; she was wearing a cream-coloured jellabiya with dark green and blue embroidery around the edges.

'It's ideal for this heat, dear, and I got it for a very reasonable price. We can't be bothered with the shore excursions when it's hot like this; we've done them all before, but I've always wanted a jellabiya, and I got a few souvenirs for the grandchildren for when we eventually get home.' She introduced Reg, her husband, who was portly with little hair left and a pair of thick brown-framed glasses; he had a kind voice and announced they were on their last tour of duty. Heather was about to ask them more about Africa when the leader of the gully-gully men butted in.

'Please to borrow your watch, kind sir.' He spoke very loudly and bowed in a theatrical fashion. There was then a pause while the leader held up the watch then shook it. 'But this tells wrong time, sir,' he said to Reg, laying the watch on the palm of his hand. 'It needs to be fixed, yes?' He smiled and showed his gold tooth.

One of the other gully-gully men approached. 'I can fix, I good workman,' he said, nodding his head as he surveyed the audience. With a swirl of his cloak he laid the watch on the deck and produced a hammer.

'Little adjustment now,' said the leader to the audience while his accomplice swung the hammer down and smashed the watch face. There was a collective 'Ahhhh' of horror from the crowd, some of the children screaming and holding onto their mothers' skirts.

'Thank you, Tariq,' said the leader, bowing slightly and picking up the watch from the deck. He held it up to his ear and frowned, then tapped it with his index finger. 'Working perfectly now.'

In the meantime, Reg had been gazing on as though this was all nothing to do with him. Heather wondered if he had followed events or been dozing.

'You rascals!' Reg said suddenly, shaking his fist.

The leader walked back to Reg and handed him his watch. 'Please look carefully, is it working well now?'

Reg grunted and put the watch to his ear, then squinted at the watch face. 'Seems to be, you blackguard.'

The leader took a bow and the audience applauded. Reg put his watch back on and did up the leather strap, which judging by its bright ochre colour had been purchased recently.

Then chicks were produced from behind passengers' ears, out of their jacket pockets, and even out of Johnny's blue ship. The gully-gully men then did their final bows and circulated a sisal basket for change to be placed in, while one of them played his discordant trumpet. The leader made a big show of walking around the passengers urging them to be generous then examining the contents of the basket in disgust.

'Not enough money!' he shouted. 'But one man has given his wallet to make up the difference.' The leader then produced a wallet from within his cloak and began shaking it theatrically.

'Hoi!' said Bob Saunders, 'that's my wallet you got there!' He walked forward to claim his wallet but the leader was waiting for him and went over to the railing and chucked the wallet over the top and into the sea, where it landed with a small splash, followed by an even bigger 'oooooohh' from the crowd. Bob looked like he was about to cry, his jowls crumpled. 'My winnings!' he wailed, staring out into the harbour. The crowd fell silent, waiting to see what would happen next.

The gully-gully leader shrugged his shoulders, put his hands in prayer and looked up at the sky. There was then a loud blast from the ship's horn, which made the leader jump, and the other Egyptians sniggered before the trumpet man started again.

'Don't worry, sir, tall lady over there has your wallet.' The leader was pointing at Heather who was standing next to Daphne, George and Betty; the latter had her hand against her throat as though she were about to pass out. The women all held their palms up in ignorance of the missing wallet. Meanwhile, the gully-gully men collected up the bags of souvenirs they'd been selling, and made towards the stairs down to the shell door.

'But I haven't got it,' said Heather, checking all her pockets, her face aghast. 'Oh, wait a minute, here it is,' she exclaimed pulling the wallet out of the beach bag she had on her shoulder. Bob lunged towards her, grabbed the wallet and began to count all the notes. Betty let out a squeak of delight and looked over his shoulder.

Heather leaned down on her haunches and laughed at the absurdity of it all. Johnny was looking very puzzled, so she hugged him and whispered into his ear, 'It's magic, darling, nothing for you to worry about.'

Johnny frowned and began to complain about the heat and how thirsty he was; his face looked pale and blotchy and Heather recognised the signs of not having his nap, so took him back to the cabin where it was noticeably cooler as they were on the shady rather than sunny side of the ship and the curtains were drawn. He fell asleep almost immediately without having a story. Heather decided to rest on the other bed and she too dozed off.

Chapter 17

March 1960 – Nairobi

I have to find the right spot in a café opposite the side of the bank, shaded under the awning but with a clear view over the columned entrance. The bank stands commanding over a swarm of green- and cream-coloured buses parked in untidy rows in the Hardinge Street bus stance. Dust swirls around the pavements as the construction of the new Ambassadeur Hotel, a fifteen-storey skyscraper the other side of the bank, is just being completed and the buses kick up a lot of black fumes when their engines start. As a result, there is a constant background noise of traffic punctuated by the drivers shouting to each other and the clatter of construction.

Dorothea had told me the day the regular monthly payment was made to Redcar Logistics, which was yesterday, and I guessed Taylor might go to the bank the day after. In case anyone asked, I'd also arranged to see an ex-pat couple two days before in Nairobi, Allan and Patricia Welham, whom Taylor had introduced me to, calling them 'good sorts'. I wanted to ask them about possible arrangements for Johnny, how Heather might be occupied, and generally how the Welhams managed their family life in Kenya, though I knew it hadn't turned out quite as planned for them.

Their home, Jessop House on Lower Kabete Road, was very impressive. It looked like a cross between an English mock-Tudor manor and a Swiss Alpine lodge, with wooden beams and an oversized chimney built onto the front of the house.

'We're just lodging here until independence when it will become part of the embassy,' Allan said wistfully, staring at the parquet floor with a glass of whisky in his hand. They seemed a bit put out when they realised I wasn't going to change for dinner into formalwear, and seemed to have decided to downgrade the conversation to rather stilted and unflattering observations about Nairobi.

Welham was the Trade Commissioner, so I asked him what he'd do after independence. His mouth twisted as though he was drinking his whisky sour, though he'd really only topped it up with ice.

'Perhaps you'll move into the embassy, you might even be able to stay here,' I added, opening my arms to encompass the wood-panelled dining room and heavy wool curtains with heads of tigers and antelope, and washed-out watercolours of savannah hunting scenes on the walls.

'Good Lord, no,' Patricia spat out, having spoken previously in a mild but laboured voice. I felt awkward, as though I'd said something indiscreet or ill-conceived. 'Back to Blighty for us. The country will go to the dogs when the blacks take over and who would want to witness that after we've worked so hard to get things running properly?'

'Best thing for you, Fontwell,' said Allan, trying a more considered and confidential tone, 'is to advance yourself as much as you can in the meantime. Nothing will last more than a couple of years now. Hasn't Taylor spoken to you about his projects? Everyone is looking out for themselves these days.'

Patricia rang a silver bell next to her wrist and a Kenyan girl came in. She was wearing a crisp blue dress with her hair tied back in a white scarf, her legs thin and bony. There was silence while the girl stacked up our plates, her face downcast as she concentrated on not losing her balance.

'Thank you, Mathilda,' Patricia said. 'Mulatto,' she added after the girl had gone. 'Her mother got into trouble so we gave the eldest daughter a serving job, not that she's much good at it.'

'Who's her father then?' I asked. There was a pause as Mathilda returned with a dish with a lemon meringue and cake knife balanced on it in one hand and a jug of cream in the other. The tension whilst we watched the girl place these on the table was almost unbearable. The tart slid slightly off the plate and Mathilda quickly pushed it back on with her thumb. Patricia's intake of breath was virtually a snort as the girl scuttled back through the kitchen door.

'We don't know her father, some sordid affair in town apparently. Probably, you-know, for money.' Patricia stood up, cut the meringue into slices and served everyone.

'Where does your plantation deposit the takings?' asked Allan in a low voice.

'National and Grindlays,' I replied.

'Well, talk to the branch manager, he'll put you straight.'

'I had to make this myself,' Patricia said to nobody in particular and sat down. She wiped her forehead with her serviette and pushed the jug of cream towards me. The room seemed to have become hotter despite the ceiling fans. 'Take some before it curdles,' she added, at last looking me in the eye. Her face seemed blanched and devoid of emotion.

'Delicious,' I said – and it was.

Over coffee I decided to ask about more personal matters.

'What things do you do to keep Anthony occupied in Nairobi?'

'Well, you know our son doesn't live here any more,' said Patricia, a cigarette held askance. 'He was at the Duke of York school but there's no point now as we don't intend to stay for much longer – a year at most.'

'That's the school you can see from the railway line in the Ngong Hills? It looks pretty big.'

'Yes,' said Allan, 'it's a good school, but the numbers are falling. Such a shame after they built the new lecture theatres and tower building. God knows what will happen to it after independence.'

'But what could I do with Johnny when he comes over with Heather?'

'Oh don't worry about that,' said Patricia, touching the side of her hair. She must have been to the hairdresser for what Heather called a bouffant – all piled up at the back. 'There's lots of things. Anthony best liked going to the game park – we always went there at half-term and hired a guide for a few days. Otherwise he did enjoy the drive-in cinema, though there's a proper one being built now on Government Road.'

'I took him sailing once out at the dam,' said Allan. 'There were lots of other kids in small dinghies, going around the reservoir. Not much variety and the wind is unreliable, but it's a good way to keep cool and have a swim afterwards. But how long is he here for – he'll need to go to school, won't he?'

'Yes – in September, anyhow. Until then I thought he might have some private tuition or find a pre-school.'

'You should send him to the Duke of York by train,' said Patricia. 'He can fit in with all the European boys. You must have seen them in town with their maroon uniform and shorts from Ahmed's. The boys are allowed two hours' shopping every week in Nairobi.'

We retired to the drawing room thereafter, but with the gold braided curtains drawn the room was quite gloomy; the huge open fireplace with carved mahogany mantelpiece really served for the men to put their feet on the fender and lean against bookcases and architrave. I accepted a cigar whilst Patricia lit up another cigarette with a gold-plated flintlock lighter. The smoke swirled around the framed photos of various government officials, including Welham, hunting parties and East African railways and ports. I caught Allan checking his watch when he thought I was perusing a dusty copy of *Hard Times*, so when Jonas arrived I was relieved to see him; I could tell the Welhams had been expecting a chauffeured car with a driver or at least a taxi, rather than an African foreman in his boiler suit driving a mud-splattered Land Rover. I knew then more surely than ever before that I'd never fit in with these colonial people.

I don't have to wait long outside National and Grindlays before

I spot Taylor over the rim of an old copy of the *Times of London* I found lying on a table at the back of the café. He's wearing a duck-egg blue linen suit with a white fedora hat and sunglasses, arriving via a side street, looking all around him like an agent from *The Third Man* before stepping between the columns of the bank. I finish my African-style coffee with condensed milk and flick through the newspaper headlines. After only five minutes Taylor's out again, frowning at the mounting sun, patting his jacket pocket, then retracing his steps, head down, in a quick walk. I pay for my coffee and go through the columned portico and into the bank.

The air is cooled by the swinging fans high up on the ceiling and the marble flooring. One clerk is halfway through stamping a sheath of forms, so I choose the other who is closing the cash drawer.

'Did I just miss Mr Taylor? I thought I saw him leave.'

He stares at me through the metal grille, the light glancing off his glasses.

'Yes, he's just left, I'm afraid. It's Mr…'

'Fontwell, Kiambethu plantation. I'd arranged to meet him here about our payroll.'

'Ah, I thought I recognised you. Well he was here on another matter, actually.'

The clerk smiles and turns as two other figures emerge from an adjacent desk hidden to one side. One is presumably the manager, judging by his starched collar and silk waistcoat, and the other is Allan Welham. I wave in recognition and retreat hastily as he responds rather half-heartedly, peering over his half-moon reading glasses, a leather-bound ledger in one hand.

I relax outside and breathe deeply; there is the street smell of body odour mixed with overripe fruit and a hint of something new and fragrant, so I look around and spot a silk floss tree on the corner of Government Road, its pink orchid-like flowers just starting to blossom. I realise the lights have changed and cross quickly without any clear idea of where I'm going, a Ford Anglia tooting at my tardiness. Now there is a long line of palm trees and I find myself at the New Stanley Hotel and the Thorn Tree sidewalk café where I once saw Dorothea sitting with an African, presumably her husband. She had smiled briefly but seemed preoccupied enough to put me off going to talk to her. In my mind, it's still Dorothea's café.

I order a tea with strawberries and cream as many of the other white clientele have done, junior officials and mothers with grown-up children, some of whom are wearing the maroon jackets of the Duke of York school. Without thinking, I'm sitting at the same table Dorothea had, and I reflect on how she'd first uncovered the irregularities, though the scale seems now to extend way beyond the one scheme that Taylor was running with dummy invoices. Yet I need more concrete evidence otherwise it would be their word against mine; the last piece to investigate is the dummy company, which has to be real to some degree and therefore set up and managed by somebody. Dorothea had told me that the registered office was in the port area of Mombasa and the accounts filed were anodyne with the ultimate ownership opaque – another company in Kampala. I decide to take the next train to the coast and damn the expense and time wasted – at least whatever I find will finish the matter once and for all.

★★★

I'd made some phone calls and set up meetings with our agents in Mombasa, Smith Mackenzie. My friend Donald Kirby who helps the estate with packaging and finding new markets would normally have come with me but is away in the UK and may well be returning soon with BI, most probably on the *Uganda* with Heather at this very moment. First stop is the Smith-Max offices, as everyone calls them, a pleasant two-storeyed L-shaped building on the corner of a street behind the port area, painted in cream and maroon and with colonnades on the ground floor of both sides. A Union flag hangs from the apex of the building on the first floor. I'm shown to the offices of Mr Tomkinson; a tall man gets up from behind his walnut desk and shakes my hand. There is the obligatory photo of our young queen on the wall and a coat stand with a lone panama hat cocked to one side. Tomkinson is dressed in a cream suit and his skin is the colour of cane sugar, but wrinkled and loose around his hands and wrists, and his face like an old walnut.

I explain my plans for Kiambethu and ask for his advice; he is friendly and refers to 'these troubled times' with a smile on his face. Then he says he has noticed that Heather is on the manifest for the *Uganda* arriving the week after, and we indulge in small talk.

'Can you help me find the offices of Redcar Logistics?' I ask as I'm on the point of leaving. He turns and looks me in the eye.

'Why do you want to go there?'

I shrug my shoulders and talk about admin checks.

'Personally I wouldn't touch them at all,' he says in a quiet voice as we walk along the corridor, 'but I believe they're in the port authority building in Kilindini, Britannia House.'

As I descend the steps from Smith-Max I look back and notice that Tomkinson is jotting something down in what looks like a small diary.

I take a taxi, an old Austin A30, to the port authority building, an austere brick building painted over in white with rounded metal window frames, probably built in the 1920s. The air smells of drain water and rotting cabbages.

Reception cannot help me regarding Redcar Logistics and I get sent to the Harbourmaster's office on the third floor, where I find Carruthers' secretary. I've met the captain briefly before at an evening reception in Nairobi, but my only memories are of his skin rash and an alarming propensity to drink; judging from the photos on the wall, someone who thinks more of his RN wartime on destroyers than of his family.

His secretary is rather stout and greying with horn-rimmed spectacles. She doesn't smile and shakes her head when I mention Redcar.

'That's the Captain's domain, and he's away.'

I ask when he'll be back and who else can help me.

'Sorry, no one that I know of.'

When I ask to see the offices she sighs and picks up some papers on her desk.

'Down in the basement, but it's locked up.'

I finally find the office with a small nameplate at the very end of a basement wing where many other rooms are either empty or being used for storage of equipment; it's just a two-roomed module like all the others in the building but with wood instead of glass partitioning, so it's impossible to see inside and the single door is locked. There is a flap for letters, which I stoop down to look through, but without a box the correspondence just falls to the floor. I can see a small mound of letters on a dark-yellow linoleum with some plain tables and chairs.

There doesn't seem much point examining the basement office any more, so I return up the stairs to see if somebody else might help me with Redcar Logistics. I look again at the door to the Harbourmaster's office. The veneered wood and brass handle are not important – it's the sign that reminds me of something.

HARBOURMASTER CAPT A CARRUTHERS
SECRETARY MISS T MONKS

I open the door swiftly on an impulse, causing his secretary to look up in alarm, midway through typing something.

'Sorry, what did you say Captain Carruthers' first name was? A for...'

'Alfred, but he doesn't like to be addressed—'

'Thanks!' I cry out in joy. Alfred Carruthers. A classic crossword clue for Redcar, formed by joining the last and first three letters of the two names. Redcar Logistics, nothing to do with the town in Yorkshire after all, but all to do with Carruthers and created in all likelihood by Donald Kirby who would have had the brains for it and been bullied by Carruthers into doing so, probably against his will.

I spot the *Kenya* on dock number one about to leave and watch from the top floor of the port offices. Two gangways are pulled away from the ship's white hull by the stevedores, wearing baggy half-trousers, T-shirts and dirty black boots; they have red rubber gloves tucked into their belts and they move slowly in the full sunlight, mopping their glistening brows, the white of their handkerchiefs contrasting with their black skin. The transit sheds back right onto the wharves and comprise long low grey buildings with the railway line behind. I hear the steam engine for the passenger train to Nairobi shunting backwards and forwards as it picks up coal and water, coughing up puffs of white smoke and hissing. A lonely figure climbs down the access ladder on the crane nearest to me, its jib gently swinging still.

The *Kenya* sounds its siren and its engines vibrate into life with a churning of water at the stern, and the bow ropes are uncoupled by the linesmen; there's an electrical whir as the ship's capstans take up the slack and the lines get pulled into the harbour waters then onto the side of the ship. One tug pins the *Kenya*'s stern to the quayside against the old tyres used as fenders whilst the other has a hawser attached to the bow pulling the liner away from the quayside. They both have black oily smoke emanating from their pencil-shaped stacks, now facing the harbour entrance with Fort Jesus above it.

The liner drifts slowly into the shipping lane and I can now see the ship behind on the quayside, which I recognise as the *Rhodesia Castle* that I took to Mombasa on my last trip out. It was a friendly ship with just one class, a large red and black funnel, and grey- and-pink painted hull, sleeker somehow than the BI ships.

The forward tug on the *Kenya* has dropped its hawser and steamed to one side leaving its protégé to pick up speed slightly, a ripple for a bow wave, now passing a long line of all the other BI ships docked that day, mostly in the company colours of white with black trim. The liner passes behind a tangle of masts, rigging and overhanging cranes and is now more difficult to pick out from the debris of the port.

In the distance towards the harbour entrance is the headland of Shelly Beach and I can just spot the Likoni Ferry, little more than an open-decked barge plying cars and passengers across the narrows, scampering across before the *Kenya* arrives.

I wonder where Heather and Johnny are now, and what they'll make of the letter I've left for them on the *Kenya,* bound for Aden.

Chapter 18

1ˢᵗ April 1960 – SS *Uganda*, Suez Canal

'We've just entered the canal, madam,' said Diaz taking a cup of tea and a glass of juice from his silver tray and placing them onto the writing table. 'Hello, little man!' he added, waving to Johnny who'd just got up and was sitting on the corner of his bed, his hair dishevelled and his face looking red and sticky. Mother and son got ready quickly so they could go and watch the passage of the canal. Heather brushed both his and her hair, then got Johnny to wash his face whilst she applied a lick of toothpaste and touch of make-up. In the toilet, Heather noticed there were still flecks of blood in her urine, but she felt fine, so thought no more of it.

They both climbed up to the boat deck, Heather holding Johnny's hand when he allowed her to, and they found a space against the teak railing in the shade, though the sun was by now quite low on the horizon, a pale milky glow. On one side of the canal there were flat fields criss-crossed with channels of water and green crops standing tall, whereas the other Arabian side was barren with only yellow sand and rock.

The banks of the canal looked like the same continuous mound of rock and soil that they had seen from the teahouse, but nearest to them they had been cemented into a rough low wall. On each bank there were also orange marker buoys at regular intervals, presumably to mark where the deep water started. Every now and then they passed a group of men wearing filthy togas working on repointing the wall as well as a dredger with a line of buckets on a chain, which was pumping sandy water over the top of the wall into an adjacent field.

The passage was a lot narrower than Heather imagined for such an engineering marvel of the world used by most ships travelling east to avoid the long detour round the Cape of Good Hope. Ships could only pass in single file in one direction at a time and even then had to watch their distances to the marker buoys, so Heather now understood why they were grouped into convoys.

In front of the *Uganda* was a cargo ship with derricks at the rear and a Dutch flag flapping in the breeze at the stern, whilst behind was a small oil tanker – Heather thought it might be the one they'd seen off Malta. She then noticed Cadet Mark in his sunglasses, as he was leaning over the side, and asked him.

'Yes, it's the same Russian tanker that was shadowing us in the Med.' He kept looking away from her towards the canal bank.

'What are you doing?' she asked, her hand on her forehead shielding her eyes from the low sun. He went back and looked over the side again.

'The bridge has asked me to check the distances from the marker buoys. Then I've got to go to the fo'c'sle to prepare for nightfall.' He seemed distracted.

'What does that involve?'

Before he could answer there was a static noise and a bleeping from the radio set in his hand. 'Cadet Edwards,' he said, in a self-conscious whisper, his mouth right against the radio, then turned round and peered over the side again.

'Ten feet,' he shouted into the radio and Heather looked over the swell as an orange buoy bobbed by, close to the ship, and then swung around in the wake. The cadet ran over to the other side of the deck and shouted into the radio again, then ran back. Heather thought she felt the ship turn and noticed that the red ensign on the stern mast was no longer in the centre of the passage of the canal.

'Five feet!' Mark shouted this time as the next orange buoy bounced by very close to the stern, and the turn was abandoned.

'Ten feet!' shouted Mark, his voice a lot more subdued.

Surely they must have a pilot on board as they did in Malta, Heather mused.

'Ten feet!'

'I'm getting cold, Mummy,' said Johnny. She looked at him and realised he only had shorts and a T shirt on – which had been fine for the heat of midday and afternoon but now the wind was stronger, blowing across the ship, and the sun's heat had all but evaporated. A sudden squall blew across the *Uganda* again and Heather felt the ship shift in the shallow waters of the canal.

'Five feet!' This was followed by some indistinguishable voices and scraping sounds on the radio and the stern turned again, but only slightly.

'Contact!' shouted Mark who by now was leaning over and facing the stern. There was a long metallic scraping sound off the ship followed by a strange silence; Heather looked towards the following tanker and realised that the wash from the *Uganda*'s twin propellers was absent and the familiar whoosh of the turbine was muted. Looking down the straight line of the canal and the pairs of marker buoys going back on each side every hundred yards or so she realised that one was missing on their side of the ship.

'Two feet!' shouted Mark again and the wash started again as the ship nudged slowly towards the middle of the channel then turned again to go straight. They now seemed nearer to the other bank, from whence the wind was coming, and Mark moved over to that side. There was a spectacular sunset on the starboard side of the ship as the orange sun was segmented by pencil-thin cirrus clouds low on the horizon and the light seemed refracted everywhere, casting long shadows from the mounds on the side of the canal and the white tops of wooden buildings set back from the canal. They were passing a long line of palms, which had been planted just the other side of the African canal bank.

'Let's go back to the cabin and get ready for dinner, Johnny,' said Heather, bending down to rub the goose pimples on her son's arms.

'That tickles,' said Johnny and they both laughed. As they walked over to the doors leading to the stairwell, Heather noticed that the deck was now completely empty and the sun's glow just an afterthought below the horizon. Mark had also disappeared, presumably for the fo'c'sle, which she now knew was the part of the superstructure behind the bow.

★★★

The first-class dining room was more glamorous – gilding and chandeliers rather than the plain wooden panelling and inset lighting of tourist class – and there were senior officers at each table with the head waiter dancing in attendance. Nevertheless, Heather preferred tourist; the passengers were more interesting somehow, more extrovert, more varied in their situation and their demeanour. In first there was less conversation and more educated remarks about the journey or the landmarks; everyone seemed perfectly nice, just stiffer and more withdrawn. There was none of the coarseness of the Carruthers or idiocy of the Saunders, but Heather imagined the first-class passengers were better educated and might have interesting stories to tell; they just didn't want to tell them in front of their wives and children or maybe even the stewards and officers.

So Heather and Johnny again finished their meals as quickly as was decent and went off to find their friends in tourist class; they waited a while in the lounge before Cynthia and the Carmichaels turned up. Heather agreed to meet them again later after she had put Johnny to bed. 'I've so much to talk to you about,' she said to Cynthia, resting her hand on her arm.

Sophie beamed at Johnny and ruffled his hair and he and Heather left. Back in the cabin, Heather read 'The Owl and the

Pussycat' and a few opening verses from 'The Walrus and the Carpenter' before her son went to sleep. She flicked through the poetry book for something for her to read and came across a Walt Whitman poem 'Song for All Seas, All Ships'. She thought about the *Uganda* in amongst the row of ships in the night, travelling in the same direction at the same speed – a bit like the Atlantic convoys during the war – but of all different nationalities.

> *But do you reserve especially for yourself and for the soul of man,*
> *one flag above all the rest*
> *A pennant universal, subtly waving, all time, o'er all brave sailors*
> *All seas, all ships.*

Norman and George would probably say it was the red ensign, but on a ship crewed by Indians, Heather thought the pennant meant something more than that. She remembered the view from the teahouse over the canal, the ships seemingly moving over land not sea, and the fatigue swept over her again like an influx of warm suffocating air, and she fell asleep.

When she awoke, it was over an hour later, and she realised it was the noise of the anchor chain clunking and scraping somewhere up in the bow area, but resonating throughout the ship, that had nudged her out of sleep.

'Dreadfully sorry I took so long,' Heather said to the group of friends in the tourist lounge. There were the Carmichaels, the Kirbys, Engineer Scott and Norman. 'Why have we dropped anchor?' Heather asked the engineer. He suggested they all went up to the bar on the promenade deck to have a look.

Norman bought everyone a drink and they stepped outside into the night. The narrow passage and the mounds alongside had gone and they appeared to be floating on an inland lake. On the horizon on their side of the ship the stars were showing, but directly overhead it was cloudy, a crescent moon only occasionally peeping through. Heather thought it was a fairy tale view with the blackness of the desert and the deck lights of the other ships in the convoy shimmering on the water.

'Great Bitter Lake,' said James Scott. 'This is where the northbound and southbound convoys pass each other. We're anchored up now waiting for the northbound, which is a bit later than anticipated, so we may be here for a few hours.'

'Ships that pass in the night,' said Cynthia softly, looking down into the water.

'Like us,' Donald murmured. There was a pause while everyone contemplated the water hungrily slopping against the ship and the darkness as the moon faded behind a cloud.

'Longfellow,' Cynthia added, turning round to face them.

'I don't remember seeing it in my poetry of the sea book,' said Heather.

'No, it's from 'Tales of a Wayside Inn', a much bigger work.' Cynthia looked up over their heads before continuing, a frown of concentration on her face.

> Ships that pass in the night, and speak each other in passing,
> Only a signal shown and a distant voice in the darkness;
> So on the ocean of life we pass and speak one another,
> Only a look and a voice, then darkness again and a silence.

'That's marvellous, Cynthia, you've memorised it whilst I just narrate from a book,' said Heather. 'What does it mean?'

George coughed and shifted upright, raising an eyebrow. 'Well, aside from this highbrow literary stuff, estimating the ship's distance is getting more difficult with these delays.'

Daphne groaned. 'Really, George, you mustn't take it so seriously.'

George laughed. 'I don't, it just keeps me interested in what's going on.'

'What happened about the buoy we ran over earlier?' Heather asked James, thinking that maybe George was right to divert them from a philosophical discussion, though she did want to ask Cynthia about Longfellow when the two of them were alone together.

'What do you know about that?' he replied, stuttering a little.

'Well done, girl,' said Norman in a low murmur, 'keep the crew on their toes.'

'I saw it on deck. I hope Mark isn't in any trouble.'

'No, it's not that.' James looked down at his shoes then across the lake.

'So was the pilot at fault?' said George, taking a swig of his beer.

'Well, that's the thing. So, don't repeat this,' replied James.

'No trouble, old boy,' said Norman tapping his nose. 'Do go on.'

'The pilot came on board before we entered the canal and he asked for his usual cigarettes. But then he wanted vodka, being Russian you see. Captain refused at first but then the pilot threatened to drop us off the convoy so we had to give him a bottle, after which he went back to his cabin until we were ready to weigh anchor.' James finished his beer and tipped the foam over the side.

'Normally we get rid of the pilot quite quickly, once we're steaming down the main channel. There's not much navigation involved, really, though it can be tricky with cross winds. Anyhow, this time the Russian came up to the bridge as we were about to enter the canal, already quite drunk, and started throwing his weight around. The captain put up with it for a while, either ignoring him or pretending to be following his instructions, until the pilot starting drinking in front of us, out of his vodka bottle. Then he pushed the first officer off the wheel and tried to steer the ship himself, so there was a scuffle while we dragged him off and handcuffed him. In the meantime, we'd lost our course and were right over on port side, too close to the marker buoys.'

'Good God,' said Norman. 'Where's the Ruskie now?'

'Locked up. We radioed and said he was ill, but it sounded like they knew what that meant. We'll drop him off at Suez and if they mention the buoy we'll say he did it.' With that the engineer bade them goodnight.

A silence followed, punctuated by the occasional clanging of metal and voices carried over from the other convoy ships. They looked at the lights from the *Uganda*'s superstructure dancing on the water, until the Kirbys said they were ready for bed.

'Just before you do, Kirby,' said Norman, steering Donald to one side, 'can you help me understand this telegram? It's like a riddle.' Heather strained to listen to the conversation as Norman carefully unfolded a scrap of paper.

'Rem shake up typeface well,' Norman read out.

Donald looked at the ground, stroking his chin. 'Who's it to and from?'

'To Carruthers on board, from his office in Mombasa, dated a few days ago. He dropped it – naturally I returned it to him.'

'Let me reflect on it,' said Donald, and they rejoined the others and made their way to the bar to drop off their glasses. As they were leaving, Heather took George by the elbow.

'Do you work with Donald in some way?'

George turned around to check no one was in earshot. 'Yes, he fixes prices and contracts for tea and coffee exports from Kenya, and he's very good at it too, despite his shyness.'

'Oh, there you are,' came a voice from behind, making them jump. Daphne interlinked her arm with George's and pulled him away, arching her eyebrows at Heather.

Gosh, thought Heather, I've really annoyed her again.

Chapter 19

2nd April 1960 – SS *Uganda*, Port Suez

The light was shining brightly through their window blind and she could still hear the slapping and gurgling noises that the sea made when the *Uganda* was stationary. There was a soft knock on the door and Diaz padded into their cabin, setting down tea and lemon barley water on their bedside tables, and then hovered, his silver tray in hand. What did he want? thought Heather; she could see that his brown eyes were always moving around, searching and shifting for opportunities. Was it greed or nosiness?

'Diaz, do we tip every day or at the end of the voyage?' asked Heather, still lying in bed watching his reaction.

The steward licked his lips quickly. 'As you wish, madam,' he replied, backing out of the cabin like an unctuous servant.

So that was it, thought Heather, swinging her legs across and down onto the carpet to get up. Johnny was playing under his sheet, talking to himself.

'Johnny be good, Johnny be quick,' said Heather, managing to catch him by surprise. 'Race you to the toilet!'

'Nyyaaah!' said the boy, also jumping out of bed, running to the cabin door and flinging it open.

Heather stretched and put on her *Uganda* bathrobe – in first class it was silk rather than cotton. She felt a little out of sorts and her tummy was gurgling as she walked over to the toilet, which Johnny had just vacated; the bleeding still seemed to be there, though just a few streaks. On her return to their cabin she took another anti-sickness pill.

The printed weather forecast from yesterday had promised cold nights and hot days, so they decided to dress lightly, and Heather took her beach bag with sun cream and hats, books and a selection of Johnny's toys including the fire-damaged blue liner and a plastic Red Indian and cowboy.

They looked out from the promenade deck over the town of Suez where the *Uganda* had anchored early that morning. The wind from yesterday had died down and they could feel the warmth of the sun on the white metal of the deck railings; there were no gully-gully men but instead a small flotilla of feluccas filled with young boys in white robes were bobbing up and down around the shell door; all were wearing maroon red tarbooshes, which were being raised up and down to indicate their desirability.

'Missie, missie,' one shouted as soon as Heather peered over the railings.

'Here Johnny, looky see,' shouted another.

'How do they know my name?' asked Johnny.

Heather laughed. 'They're very good salesmen.'

They went in for breakfast and met Mrs Worthington dressed again in her jellabiya; she was sitting at the table wearing a scarab bracelet and a gold necklace adorned with red stones. Reg was sitting adjacent to her, reading the daily news-sheet.

'See what I bought!' said Mrs Worthington excitedly. 'I got up early to get the best bargains from the boatmen.'

Reg smiled and shrugged his shoulders. 'We have a trove of Egyptian trinkets at home – all "genuine Pharaohs' tombs", or "belonged to Cleopatra". Rogues, the lot of them.'

'I know they're not real, it's just a bit of fun,' Mrs Worthington replied, tutting a little.

Heather laughed and said the jewellery looked great on her – which actually was true. 'But Reg, were you in on the gully-gully act yesterday?'

Reg leaned back and made a gurgling noise in his throat. 'Was it that obvious? I'm going to have to improve my game.'

Heather's eyebrows rose and she patted her lips with her napkin.

'Don't worry, I'm not "in on it" directly,' said Reg, still holding his knife and fork and about to attack a sausage. 'We've done a number of these journeys, and a few years back they just asked me if I'd play along a bit, you know, ham it up. I haven't the faintest idea how they do their tricks, and don't want to know, it's all part of the theatre. In exchange they give us good prices on anything that Honour buys.'

Mrs Worthington looked a bit sheepish. 'Is it wrong, do you think?'

'Don't be silly, Honour,' replied Heather, grinning.

After breakfast, Heather and Johnny went back into tourist class and climbed up the stairs to the swimming pool. Cynthia was there with Michael, as well as the Saunders. Daphne and George were over at the railings looking at progress with departure and Heather and Johnny went to join them; there was a short blast on the ship's horn and a thin black haze emerged from the giant funnel with its BI colours of two white rings on a black background.

'We're just stopping to pick up the Cairo excursion passengers and the ship's mail,' said George.

'There's the launch now,' said Heather pointing. The small boat with the orange canopy swung around parallel to the *Uganda*, picking up a deckhand from a remote jetty where he'd untied the ship's mooring ropes, then continuing in a wide arc to the *Uganda*, avoiding the feluccas and coming alongside the gangplank that had been lowered down from the shell door below them. The second officer was at the helm this time, his eyes narrowed in the sunlight, with his hat on the seat beside him. There were only a handful of passengers who'd braved the excursion and the rest of the launch was taken up with several grey sacks, some large cardboard boxes and a black briefcase. The officer helped the passengers off the launch then handed the boxes and sacks to a pair of waiting deckhands who took them up the gangway, walking slowly behind the passengers.

At the rear of the ship, the Indian crew were working the electrical capstan to winch up the loose mooring ropes; no sooner had the launch begun its ascent up the side of the ship to its berth above the decks than the clanking of the anchor chain being pulled up started. The two deckhands then started folding up the gangplank, with the second officer running up behind them and into the shell door. They could just see him wiping his brow with a handkerchief then carefully putting his hat back on, checking that the motif was in the middle.

'He's in a hurry so we must be late,' said George. There was another longer blast on the ship's horn and the murmuring vibration from the turbines restarted. The felucca men waved frantically and started rowing back to the harbour to escape the stern wash from the ship's propellers.

The Carmichaels returned to the swimming pool area and Heather stood everyone a coffee, which Parminder went away to collect, bowing and making his broken-tooth smile.

'Got all your money back then, Bob?' Cynthia asked with a small smile.

Bob grimaced and sucked his teeth. 'That was awful – I was sure he'd thrown my wallet overboard.'

Betty trilled but otherwise remained silent. Coffee arrived when Heather noticed Cadet Mark standing on the boat deck above, looking out to sea. She climbed the stairs and went over to ask him what he was up to.

'Just trying to blow the cobwebs away.'

'James Scott mentioned the business about the pilot.'

Mark raised his eyebrows and put his hands in his pockets. 'Yes, he left at first light looking a bit grey. The Captain even confiscated his cigarettes.'

'Any repercussions about the buoy?'

'I don't know yet – the second officer has only just come back from the harbour office.' Mark yawned and put his hand across his mouth. 'Excuse me but I've been up most of the night.'

'Oh yes, you said you were going to the fo'c'sle.'

'We have a split searchlight for the night transit of the canal,' said Mark, more animated now, like he'd suddenly woken up. 'It's right up in the bows, behind the BI badge, which I have to crank open first then adjust the searchlight angle so that it shines on both banks. But it's bloody cold up there and last night there was a strong breeze blowing, so I had to wear a duffle coat and balaclava. I've got some free time now until evening watch.'

'Come and have coffee with us if you like.'

'Thanks,' the cadet replied, his eyes glittering.

They returned to the tourist-class swimming pool area where the coffees had just arrived, so Heather ordered an extra one. Johnny and Michael were in the pool together, though Heather noticed that Michael had no buoyancy aids so presumably could swim.

Daphne was lying on a lounger with her back to Heather and Mark. 'Finished!' she announced in a loud voice, clapping her brown paper-covered book closed then placing it with a flourish on a plastic table next to her. 'Who wants to read it next?'

'What is it?' asked Mark.

'Oh, sorry Mark, didn't see you there,' replied Daphne, adjusting her white gown. 'It's more of a woman's book really.' Daphne took her hat off and shook out her hair, moving the book under her chair in the process.

'Mummy calls it *LC*,' said Sophie, squinting into the sun, acting nonchalant.

'Actually Mark, I'm glad you've come,' said George, sitting up in his chair, 'as I need some advice on the ship's progress.'

Sophie muttered something under her breath.

'We're only about an hour or two behind schedule,' the cadet replied, sipping his coffee and glancing at Sophie who had her new swimming costume on again.

Heather had decided not to bring her two-piece costume this time; she was watching Johnny in the pool and was conscious that in her red summer dress she was not best equipped to jump in and save him if necessary. In the end, she decided that it might look peculiar if she didn't put her swimming costume on, so she excused herself to get changed and asked Sophie to keep an eye out for Johnny.

On her return, Heather noticed Cynthia leaning with her back against the angle of the teak railing and the corner of the bulkhead partially in the shade from the promenade deck above. She was wearing a floral swimming costume with a light cotton gown over it, staring at the cargo cranes above the pool, her hand against her forehead.

'What's the view like?' asked Heather.

'Nothing special,' Cynthia replied, turning her head to check. It was true, the view in the Gulf of Suez was not so different to that in the canal; on either side of the ship there were dark-brown cliffs with little sign of life and only glimpses of the rocky desert behind. The ship had picked up speed and seemed to be doing its normal (according to George) 17 knots on placid yellow brown waters streaked with meandering trails of foam.

'Penny for your thoughts?' asked Heather.

Cynthia sighed and examined her hand. 'Don't tell Daphne, but, it's Donald. This is his last tour of duty, but I'm worried about how he's going to cope.'

'Cope with what?' said Heather, placing a hand on Cynthia's sleeve.

'Donald's very shy, as well as being agoraphobic, so he tends to stay mostly in our cabin and has meals at odd times on his own. I was worried things were getting worse, so I handed in my notice as a teacher in order to accompany him.'

Heather leaned against her as they both stared out at the cliffs now receding into the distance as the Gulf opened out.

'He wasn't very happy about me coming out – thinks I'm spying on him – but what could I do?'

'I can see that.'

'It's very hard on Michael – he doesn't understand what's going on or why he's got to leave school in Guildford where he's very happy. I've always wanted a sibling for him, but that's…' she opened out the palms of her hands '…been very difficult. I'm so glad he's met Johnny.' Cynthia turned to Heather and smiled.

'Me too. It's difficult travelling as a single parent, nothing is geared up for it,' replied Heather. 'So meeting all of you has been great.'

'Do you want another child, too?'

'I'm a bit unsure.' Heather bit her lip and considered what she might say. 'I don't really know what William thinks about it, and another child might be difficult to manage.'

'But you don't work, do you?'

'No, but maybe it would be good for me if I did.'

Their conversation was interrupted by a blast of a ship's horn, from another liner, the *Asia*, which passed by, the *Uganda* rocking unpredictably in its wash. Norman appeared from one of the deck doors.

'Lunch anyone? I don't want to sit on my own.'

They all laughed at the implausibility of this and gathered their possessions to go.

'Oh, Heather, I almost forgot,' said Betty Saunders, 'I think there's a letter for you in the purser's office.'

Heather made her excuses to leave, with Norman looking like he wanted to ask her something but thought better of it. At the office, the purser himself produced Heather's letter with one of his trademark mock bows. 'Air mail,' he said, holding the letter by its corner as though it were diseased. 'You can always send it via our own ship's mail at a fraction of the cost, you know.'

'Yes,' said Heather smiling brightly, 'but then it would take forever.'

It was an aerogram on the thinnest possible blue paper and she recognised her sister's handwriting. Heather tried to imagine her folding the paper over, then licking the edges to seal it before taking it to the post office. The prepaid stamp of the young queen's head reminded Heather of home, not that she missed it very much.

She thanked the purser, stuffed the letter in her bag to read later and decided to take lunch in first class to take advantage of the air conditioning. It was much quieter than tourist class and Heather asked the waiter for her and Johnny to be taken to a spare table next to where Monica Doyle was sitting.

'This is my husband,' said Monica, smiling, and they all shook hands, even with Johnny, who turned to his mother in shyness. Monica explained they were going to Kenya for the first time and her husband had been sent out with a firm of accountants to audit the books of firms in Nairobi and Mombasa.

'I must apologise to you, Monica,' said Heather, sitting down at the adjacent table and having her napkin put on her lap. She hesitated, hoping that the discussion would not become too awkward. 'For the state I was in when we first met.'

'Are you better now?' asked Monica, cutting a portion of cheese and placing it carefully on a cracker biscuit.

'Yes, thanks,' replied Heather, waving a hand dismissively. 'So you're Goanese, like the stewards?'

'Well, I was brought up in Goa, then my parents moved to England,' said Monica. 'We're going to see my extended family in Kenya – some of them moved there after independence, with all the troubles.'

'It sounds complicated,' said Heather, but also watching Johnny to make sure he behaved. 'You don't have the red dot.' She touched her forehead in the middle.

'No, I'm Catholic, not Hindi.'

Heather placed their lunch orders, and they then talked about their children before the Doyles paid their respects and left.

Heather tried to eat as little as possible as she was convinced her waistline was starting to bulge a little, but then she felt hungry for certain dishes. The Brown Windsor soup went down well whilst the prawn cocktail almost made her retch when she saw it. The cheese soufflé omelette was perfect, but the pork chops looked a bit too slimy when they went to an adjacent table. She certainly couldn't face the *Uganda* coffee any more, but a glass of dessert wine really hit the spot.

After they were both back in their cabin and Johnny had gone to sleep, Heather took out the letter from her bag and lay down to read it. She carefully unstuck the edges to make sure she didn't tear across any of the writing, which was in blue fountain pen, then unfolded the whole letter and took in a deep sigh.

There was a lot of preamble about having to use airmail and how Marjorie had phoned BI to find out about mail via the ship's offices en route. Malta was too soon but Suez would work; this was typical of Marjorie – she was both quite determined and resourceful as well, leaving as little to chance as possible; this normally made Heather feel both admiring and inadequate in equal measures, but today it irritated her, though she knew this was unfair.

I thought a lot about our last meeting; I don't think either of us were on tip top form – I know I wasn't. I've seen the GP again and he's recommended someone for us to see at the hospital but it doesn't sound hopeful – surgery is not the norm and can lead to complications and infections, with uncertain success rates. This specialist is apparently an expert in manual physical therapy, which doesn't sound like a barrel of laughs but is better than being butchered, I suppose. Our doctor says the blockage probably came after the appendicitis I had two years ago.

Heather read on about the prospects of adoption…

It would be quite nice to adopt a baby, a new start, but the process can take some time and usually you get offered older children. I'm unsure I want this – trying to undo the damage others have done – or maybe we need more time to consider it properly as we'd set our hearts on having children of our own.

Enough of our problems; I've thought about your leaving for Kenya so suddenly and I can't help feeling that there is something more behind this than the nursery business you mentioned.

Do write and tell me how you're getting on and I'll of course try to help where I can.

Otherwise Mummy is entering some of her flowers into the local fete and is as busy as ever with the National Trust local area…

Heather felt suddenly fatigued and refolded the letter; there wasn't much more to finish anyway, so she turned on her side and dozed off.

Chapter 20

3rd April 1960 – SS *Uganda*, Red Sea

'Hot today, madam,' said Diaz to Heather, with his sad voice and drooping eyelids. He was probably disappointed over the lack of any tip following their last conversation and his hand was slightly trembling as he handed her a cup of tea followed by the daily activities sheet, which Heather quickly scanned. It had the typical Gestetner-produced grey smudges, black blobs and a typeface that varied from bold to faint within a couple of lines, but from the headline date Heather realised it was Sunday. This meant she'd been on the ship a week since the last Sunday service, which felt like a month ago – before she'd met Ian properly and had only just got to know the Carmichaels, before Malta, Suez and the cabin fire.

Heather felt that her life was on a slow burn, a glowing fuse that was slowly playing out, creating an aroma of cordite and white smoke, and all the time there was Johnny living his life by the minute, and William working away on the plantation.

Whilst her nausea had reduced she now had vaginal bleeding, which though not excessive was always there to greet her, a red calling card in her pants every time she went to the toilet. The situation made her apprehensive, and Heather was not someone given to worry; she thought about talking to Marion – the nurse had seemed nice enough once she'd got to know her better at the dancing evening and might be able to reassure her. Then it came in a flash to Heather as to how to approach the matter, and she smiled as Diaz took Johnny's empty glass away.

'Best to stay in air-conditioned rooms and have a long siesta this afternoon,' said Diaz.

'Sorry, I was miles away there,' said Heather trying her assertive voice. 'How is De Souza, by the way? I haven't seen him recently.'

'Me neither,' said Diaz, puffing out his chest. 'He's in tourist class.'

Heather smiled but thought this remark rather irksome and decided to talk about something else. 'How do the older passengers, like Mr and Mrs Worthington, deal with the heat?'

'Well, some of them have deluxe cabins with air cooling. Otherwise, they sleep a lot in the day, but many of them are used to this from living in Africa, I think.' Diaz nodded, as though agreeing with himself, then cleared away the tea things and left the cabin.

And then there was Marjorie's letter. Heather could see how her sister had meant well, and after all, she was right, it was a strange thing to do, to up sticks at short notice with a small boy and head to Africa. So Marjorie was observant, well meaning, and willing to help, none of which she should be criticised for, yet the net effect on Heather was to make her feel guilty about Marjorie's infertility. But if her sister was envious, what was Heather supposed to do about that? Feeling sorry for her wouldn't make Marj's misfortune any easier.

Heather simply didn't know what William thought about another child, though whenever she'd raised the issue of a sibling for Johnny before, William had never said no, but then he hadn't exactly enthused about the idea either. He seemed to regard it as purely for the mother to decide.

She looked at the reflections cast by the sun on the white blind covering the porthole, dancing rivulets of water swaying with the motion of the ship, though of course it was the Red Sea, a branch of the ocean between two expanses of sand and rock, the fault line between Jew and Saracen in the recent Egyptian crisis, not some gargling English brook.

Pull yourself together, Heather murmured to herself, it's just because you don't feel well physically on top of the stress of this journey, always being on show, being judged by others, stuck in the closed-in world of the ship and its occupants, some of whom didn't seem to like her much. To try to divert herself she thought about what family life in Kenya might be like for her and Johnny. The fire had reminded her how much she loved Johnny but still she had her doubts over how good a mother she was in reality.

'What's the matter Mummy?' asked Johnny, a small voice behind her. Heather was shocked to realise that there were two tear tracks down each side of her nose, a silent expression of her remorse. She quickly wiped them away with the cuff of her pyjama top and turned to face Johnny.

'I washed myself and brushed my toothipegs like you said,' he continued.

'Well done, darling. Auntie Marj has written with some sad news, but nothing to worry about really. You get dressed now, shorts and T shirt for another sunny day!'

'Can we go swimming again?'

'After breakfast, could you go to the other nursery, the one in first class, but not for long though? Then we can go swimming straight after.'

Johnny crinkled up his face, considering the deal, then assented and went to look for clothes to wear.

They had breakfast in first at a table next to the Worthingtons.

'I find this part of the voyage rather tiring,' said Mrs Worthington who was no longer wearing her jellabiya but an all-white skirt and blouse, which gave her a rather pale look. She looked older today, her face a little sunken and eyes withdrawn. 'We mostly just drink, sleep and lounge around during the day.'

'Well, nothing wrong with that,' said Heather, 'but I doubt if it would suit Johnny!'

The first-class nursery was about the same size as in tourist, but with far fewer children, so the noise level was lower and there was less chance of children colliding. It also meant that it was easier for Heather to examine the other children and their dolls, though she was now forced to admit to herself that her troll phobia was returning; the thought of this was too much, so she instead looked around at the nursery walls, which were decorated with painted roundels depicting five nursery rhymes. Johnny said these were too babyish for him, but Heather noticed him glancing at them nevertheless. The tables had animal motifs cast into the plastic tops and one of the hostesses took Johnny round to examine each of them and judge what his level of reading was like.

'Mummy, this is Chris,' said Johnny. He was sitting at a table next to Johnny, with his back to Heather, and she noticed his hair was long for a boy. Chris then turned round and revealed herself to be a girl holding a brown plastic doll with garish hair and a hooked nose, a troll, which she held up in the air to see.

Heather screamed and almost fainted but managed to stagger out of the nursery towards the nearest ladies toilet where she locked herself in a cubicle. She could hear her son calling her outside, sounding a bit panicky, whilst the hostess came in to find her.

'Mrs Fontwell, are you all right? What was it that frightened you?'

After doing some deep breathing, Heather explained through the cubicle door about her phobia, though she felt ridiculous in doing so, and eventually came out.

'Don't worry, we'll make sure it doesn't happen again, you should have said before, people have all sorts of fears these days,' said the young hostess. Heather thanked her for her concern and left the toilet to find Johnny and reassure him that everything was fine, though she herself still felt a bit wobbly.

Eventually she was able to leave her son at the nursery and decided to explore the first-class area a bit more thoroughly to try to take her mind off things. She started in the smoking room; like the other public rooms it spanned the width of the ship on promenade deck and was double the size of the tourist-class equivalent. It was generously panelled all round, including pillar casings, door surrounds and frieze in woods of different colours, some pale, probably ash, and others yellower and darker, possibly walnut. The central feature was the wide stone fireplace on the forward side of the room, with a carved relief cut into veneered panelling above it with a theme of the tobacco plant. On the bulkhead opposite the fireplace was a fine pair of elephant tusks, laid sideways against each other, inviting the spectator to imagine the elephant that used to proudly convey them.

Heather moved closer to the tusks to examine them.

'The ship's just been given those,' came a lazy voice. Heather turned to face a white-haired older man, probably in his sixties, with a rugged clean-shaven face and a dimple in his chin. He explained that they were a gift from the Kabaka of Buganda, of whom Heather had never heard.

'He's the king of a semi-autonomous part of Uganda but will probably get the chop with independence. Shame, I liked him.'

Heather rested her bottom against the back of a chair and asked him if he still lived in Uganda.

'Used to, but then I moved into sisal production in Tanzania.' He coughed slightly and made to leave. 'Mind the sandstorm this afternoon,' he added.

Heather picked up the weather forecast sheet from the shelf in the broadcasting room next door, which featured a radio, turned off for the moment, then decided to go to the morning service, to be held again in the splendour of the first-class lounge.

In the anteroom, as with the previous week, there was a long queue of passengers, many of whom were wearing their Sunday best – suits for men and long dresses for women. Heather suspected several were coming simply to experience the air conditioning and luxurious fittings rather than for any spiritual uplift. When her turn came she shook hands with the reverend Ian.

'I hope you're not still cross with me.'

'No, of course not,' Ian replied, his eyes flicking back to scan the passengers behind her. He was wearing a grey herringbone jacket with his regulation black shirt and dog collar underneath.

Heather nodded and moved into the drawing room, marvelling again at the silk curtains and Wilton carpet, though feeling less overawed than at the last service. She noticed the Captain was sitting on a chair in front of the dais, fiddling with some notes; this time Cadet Mark was absent and the second engineer, the Scottish one from the engine room tour, was standing at the entrance to the drawing room with the collection pouch clasped behind his back, looking around him.

The Carmichaels and Kirbys were sitting together and Heather managed to find a seat next to them.

'Sandstorm this afternoon, so stay inside,' said George. 'They might lock the boat deck doors.'

'Is that safe, locking us all in?' muttered Cynthia.

The service followed the same format as the previous Sunday. The first hymn was again 'Eternal Father, Strong to Save' accompanied on the piano by one of the Goanese members of the band. This was followed by some prayers led by the chaplain who perched on the edge of his seat, clasped his hands together and closed his eyes. The Captain, on the seat next to him, squinted at the chaplain with one eye barely open, copying all his actions, as though he was unsure what was coming next.

At the conclusion of prayers, the chaplain stood up from his perched position and announced, 'Our next hymn will be "Will Your Anchor Hold".' There was a round of shuffling and rustling as the congregation arose from a variety of prone positions and picked up the service sheet, followed by murmuring at it being something new. The Captain looked askance at Reverend Ian as though this was an outrageous departure from the Sunday norm, and the pianist brought out some sheet music and placed it on the stand in front of him, before striking up the introductory stanza.

> *Will your anchor hold in the storms of life?*
> *When the clouds unfold their wings of strife?*
> *When the strong tides lift and the cables strain,*
> *Will your anchor drift, or firm remain?*

The congregation sang hesitantly, occasionally warbling off time or note but then gradually got the hang of the chorus line, which the pianist was confident enough to play with more gusto.

'Well that was a new hymn for us, written by Priscilla Owens in 1882, taking inspiration from St Paul's "Epistle to the Hebrews", which the Captain will read to us a little later. But it sets the theme for the day – will your anchor hold in your life? In other words, are we more defined by how we react to the difficulties that life throws at us, rather than how we live from day to day? Will you stay true to yourself when tide and wind push you askance or will you just go with the flow?'

Heather listened very carefully to Ian's address; she was troubled by it on two counts. First, had its provenance got anything to do with her, even in some small measure? She felt ill at ease with being spoken about in this way, even anonymously, as she didn't want to be set up as an example to others even if she did meet whatever standards were being referred to. In short, she didn't want to judge or be judged and her situation was her business and hers alone.

The other thing that bothered her was all the references to anchors and holding fast, as though there was a universal truth or some kind of titanic struggle between good and evil. She smiled to herself at the titanic reference – really not appropriate, though the chances of hitting an iceberg in the Red Sea were pretty remote.

Heather thought the nautical references were weak. Yes, anchors were there for holding fast against tide and wind –

obviously that was their purpose. But the purpose of the *Uganda* was not to hold steadfast for ever but to take people and cargoes to and from foreign lands as quickly and conveniently as possible. The ship often encountered adverse wind and tide – but only used the anchor after it had already stopped in harbour. Anyhow, who said that the flow of humanity as depicted by the metaphor of wind and tide was always wrong or always being led astray? Sometimes the best thing *was* to go with the flow – either for expediency or because it was the right thing to do.

The room was now silent and the chaplain seated; the address had evidently finished and to be fair to the Reverend Ian, he'd delivered it well. There was a tension in the atmosphere, which suggested that he'd at least been listened to and thoughts provoked, not the background of whispering and chairs scraping that suggested boredom or drifting thoughts. Now the Captain was speaking; he'd read the mood of the room and was praising the chaplain's sermon. Heather wondered whether she'd misread it, that maybe Reverend Ian was drawing upon his own experiences? Maybe it wasn't referenced to anyone else on the ship other than himself, or more generally, from what he'd seen after a few years at sea. After all, she wondered about the Indian crew – yes they mostly seemed quite happy, but then the passengers only got to see the Goanese stewards who probably had the best jobs, and just fleeting glimpses of the Lascar deckhands. Those who worked far below decks on the turbines and generators and the scores of cooks and dishwashers were never seen. What was life like for them, often thousands of miles from their homes, isolated from friends and family, working for a white officer elite who probably knew and cared little for them? The cold and wet conditions of the Atlantic would probably be quite hostile to them.

The Captain finished by referring to the sandstorm that was approaching in the afternoon, how we all had to grin and bear it, batten down the hatches, enjoy ourselves come what may, this was what we'd collectively learned during the war. It was clearly meant to be humorous, but was also an appeal to the British psyche to develop some empathy between crew and passengers. Heather watched carefully as the Captain referred to the collection for the Mission to Seafarers, left the dais, waved at a few passengers in passing, then flourished his banknote and dropped it in the second engineer's pouch. She stole a glance at Reverend Ian when he was passing their row of seats, and he responded with a slight twitch before installing himself at the doorway to the drawing room, opposite the collection pouch, to bid the congregation farewell. She thanked him when her turn came.

'Glad you came,' he replied, which Heather suspected was the same adieu he gave the previous passenger.

She arranged to meet the Carmichaels and Kirbys after the afternoon siesta then lingered in the veranda ballroom, listening to the band playing; they were very together, and technically very good but looking at them in their dinner jackets, standing upright and stoically keeping good time, Heather thought the sound too background, bright like shoe polish but lacking passion or skulduggery. The other passengers were toe tapping and nodding to the rhythm and ordering cocktails or cordials, so they were obviously popular, but it was the sort of thing that her mother would listen to on the radio or at a bandstand in Eastbourne. Heather was about to leave when a group of children arrived, being shepherded along by the same hostess she'd seen earlier that morning. Johnny ran up to his mother and grabbed her hand.

'How was the nursery?' asked Heather, stroking the hair from his hot forehead.

'They were much older than me. I've eaten 'cos you took ages.'

Some of children were lined up to make their requests to the band leader. He bent down gravely and listened to each of them in turn before writing down a list on top of a piece of sheet music and showing it to the other band members.

'Ladies and gentlemen, boys and girls, we start today with an old favourite, "Robin Hood", running through the glen with his merry men.' The band leader spoke with a strong East European accent and a slight twitch, which made it difficult for him to smile too widely. The drummer led in followed by the double bass before the shape of the song became apparent.

At this point the children started jigging around, encouraged by the hostess who held hands with a girl of about eight or nine. Some of the parents joined in as well, so the dance floor went from being empty to a mass of writhing bodies of all sizes, moving completely out of time with the music. Heather laughed at the chaos – at least there was movement and discord. She tried to drag Johnny onto the dance floor but it was only when another older boy encouraged him that he agreed. For the next song the trumpeter swapped his instrument for a violin; Johnny jumped up and down when he heard the opening notes.

'From the radio!' he shouted.

'That's right, Johnny,' Heather replied, 'from *Hello Children Everywhere*.' She couldn't remember the name of the song but as they jigged around (it wasn't really danceable) someone said 'Puffing Billy' and Heather felt annoyed not to have paid more attention to the programme at the time. After 'Davy Crockett', Heather began to feel tired and sat down at an available chair. Johnny talked a bit with the older boy, and just as Heather decided she was too hungry to stay any longer, the lunch gong sounded.

Heather had to rush her French onion soup and quiche Lorraine as Johnny was impatient and didn't have any toys with him. She was also aware that some of the passengers were staring, probably in disapproval of any child having lunch with adults in first class. The varying protocols between the two classes were becoming tiresome to Heather, and she was glad to return to the privacy of her own cabin. Johnny was too excited for a nap to start with, so Heather let him play with his soldiers whilst she took one of her anti-sickness pills and read the news-sheet for the day.

The news was as depressing as the last time she'd read the sheet: demonstrations for black rights in South Africa and America as well as daily anti-atomic bomb rallies in London, whilst at the other extreme there was the welfare of the newly born Prince Andrew and the nuptials in May of Princess Margaret and Antony Armstrong-Jones in Westminster Abbey, which would be on live television, though probably not in Kenya. Heather felt sorry for the Princess – why couldn't the Church have allowed her to marry Peter Townsend, as they'd obviously been in love? Otherwise there was discussion about the election of the democratic nomination for the US presidency between Lyndon Johnson and John Kennedy, neither of whom Heather knew much about.

She slipped into a shallow sleep and dreamed about trying to dress herself in a heavily brocaded dress with Gerald attempting to do up the zip on her back, but it got stuck so he started shaking her instead. Then Heather realised the shaking was real life calling her back and she opened her eyes to see Johnny pulling her arm.

'Wake up, Mummy! It's all dark and I'm scared!'

Johnny was right, it was *very* dark; she looked at her watch – only 3.30pm, so nowhere near nightfall. A thought about the apocalypse seeped into her brain, fizzing away along with all the gloomy news articles she'd remembered reading. Maybe one idiot had pressed the red button and then another idiot had pressed his? She walked over to the porthole and lifted up the blind; the ship was being buffeted by a strong wind from the starboard side, the side facing Africa and the Sahara, and the sun had been blocked out of the sky. Of course, she remembered with some relief, it was the sandstorm forecast for the afternoon.

'Desert sandstorm!' Heather put her hands up in exaggerated amazement. 'Nothing to worry about – shall we go and watch?'

'Cor, yeah!' he said with a big grin.

She marvelled at the speed of childrens' transition from one extreme emotion to another, from fear to joy in five seconds. They'd both fallen asleep in their day clothes, so they just brushed their teeth and combed their hair and set off, even though Johnny had a long red sleep line on one cheek, and made their way to the tourist-class lounge. Inside there was a large melee of passengers looking out of the starboard windows across the deck at the clouds of sand; their friends, the Saunders, the Carmichaels and Kirbys, were all in a cluster with the second officer in attendance.

'We're steering due east now,' said the officer, stroking his sculpted beard, 'so we can get nearer to the Arabian shore and away from the direction of the storm.'

Why doesn't he inflect his voice more? thought Heather. It would make what he had to say somehow more interesting. Outside, the sand came over from the coast in dark swirls, not unlike rain showers, with large quantities being dumped on the decks then blown across the ship in gusts. There was a continual scratching noise, especially when the sand hit glass windows, and a tinnier sound where it swirled around the masts and rigging.

'I'd like to experience it outside,' said George. 'But the wind is too strong.'

'Don't be silly, George,' said Daphne. 'We can watch perfectly well from here and have a nice drink at the same time.' A round of tea arrived, which they took whilst standing up as all the seats were taken.

The ship juddered against the wind, and was now rolling more appreciably as the horn sounded and the superstructure lighting came on. It was a surreal sight, drinking afternoon tea and peering into the darkness outside. Swirls of sand came over the railings and against the window of the drawing room, making more of a banging than scratching sound now, as the screeching noise from the squalls increased. It seemed even darker and the interior lighting came on to some 'oohs' and 'aahs'.

'Makes you realise,' Donald said to Heather, stooping over

her then taking a slurp of tea, 'that there are forces at play that are larger than us. We think we're in control of everything, but we're not really.' Heather felt his intensity squeezing out the prospects of conversation and could only meekly agree with him. 'You and Johnny have really helped with Michael,' he resumed in a rather abrupt change of mood, smiling now.

Before Heather could reply, Norman had joined them and motioned Donald over. Heather caught the last snatch of their conversation.

'How's that?' asked Norman.

'Typeface and font are synonyms you see,' replied Donald, mopping his brow with a handkerchief, thus revealing his wrists, red raw from scratching.

Norman grunted and turned to face Heather. 'Seen sandstorms in the war, the trucks weren't much shelter,' he said. 'It took an age to clean out every nook and cranny afterwards.' He winked at the rest of the group and Betty tittered.

'Sandy bottom, eh!' said a familiar voice from the other side of the lounge. It was Carruthers with a large brandy in his hand, speaking far too loudly, and making jokes with a group of men around him. His shirt had come out of his trousers and his fat hairy stomach was protruding, but he was oblivious to this as he ran his fingers around his collar, trying to loosen it.

'Don't listen to him.' Norman took Heather to one side and flexed his head over his shoulder towards Carruthers. 'He's just a big mouth. Knocks his missus about something terrible – heard them in their cabin once – especially after he's been drinking. That's what happens when you're married.'

'You should have reported him to the crew,' said Heather, staring wide-eyed at Norman.

'Well I did, actually,' he replied, 'but for something else. I heard him boasting to one of his mates last night, when he thought no one was in earshot, about setting fire to your cabin.'

Heather thought she was going to faint and gripped Norman by his forearm.

'It could have been the booze talking, but then I remembered I'd seen him hanging around the cabins at about that time. Then I wondered how he did it and went to check recent sales of lighter fuel at the shop.' Norman tapped his nose. 'Bingo! Anyhow, God knows what the Captain will do, so I thought I'd calm Carruthers down a bit by adding a little something to his drink.'

Heather placed a hand over her mouth, unable to believe what she was hearing but also horrified at Carruthers' act.

'I think he checked you were both out of the cabin first, then went in and doused the curtains, but overdid it a bit and it got out of hand. Since then it's all gone wrong for him as you got his first-class cabin and he's spent a couple of days in the can.' Norman leaned towards Heather's ear. 'Though a repeat prescription might be required by the sound of things.' There was more loud laughter and shouting behind them.

'Are you sure about all this, Norman?' Heather whispered as a gap in the darkness appeared, just a round hole in the swirls of sand; a ray of sunshine burst through making the adjacent sand particles twinkle before the gap was closed again.

'Sunshine!' shouted Johnny as another gap appeared with light beaming through.

'Don't worry, Heather,' said Norman. 'I'll make sure he keeps away from you. Not a word to anyone, mind – let's see what the Captain does.' Norman moved away to get more tea and Heather felt left in a lurch, clasping Johnny's hand tightly. She went over and rejoined her friends.

After twenty minutes, the cliffs of the African coastline were in view and blue sky and sun dominated the starboard side, though there were still the dark brown clouds on the port side. The ship assumed its southeast trajectory and rolled a lot less, and a large group of deckhands came outside and started sweeping up the sand.

They wore a mixture of turbans, neckerchiefs and straw hats with rough towels wound around their necks to keep the sand out – as a result, it was impossible to tell one from the other, though it was easy to spot the serang, who was pointing orders and opening doors with a bunch of keys. They collected up the sand in big sacks, then simply emptied them over the side. Inside, Heather could see little wisps of sand on the carpet next to the external doors where the wind must have found tiny currents of air through; she wondered about pointing these out to the crew but the deck doors still looked locked.

'We'll be late arriving in Aden then,' said George to the second officer.

Number two swayed his head from side to side, as though calculating something. 'Probably not, as we've had a following wind,' he replied eventually, motioning the wind direction with his hand. Heather noticed that Nurse Marion was also among the crowd, and she made her way through to her.

'Listen, can I come and talk to you? I'll have to bring Johnny, though.'

'Leave him in the sister's office if you like, she's only doing paperwork.'

They set off down the stairs to B deck then along the white metal alleyway to the hospital, Johnny running ahead. Heather could now differentiate areas of the ship by the smell – here it was a mixture of TCP and floor cleaner instead of the usual stale food and carpets. They went inside, Marion leading the way into one of the small consulting rooms after Johnny had been left with the sister who frowned slightly at the news. Heather felt a sense of déjà vu from her examination after the cabin fire.

Marion pointed Heather to a chair and they talked about the journey so far and whether Heather felt any ill effects from smoke inhalation. Heather then asked Marion if she was trained in gynaecology and the nurse said she'd been a midwife previously.

Marion smiled and leaned back in her chair. 'I must say, though, I did wonder.'

'This is not about me!' replied Heather, shaking her head. 'I've just had a letter from my sister and I'm a bit worried about her. She's not very good with doctors and I want to give her the right advice.'

'Go on,' said Marion, raising her eyebrows.

'She's pregnant but has light bleeding every day – is that normal?'

'Well, she really does need to see her GP and get an examination.'

Heather nodded and there was a pause whilst the two women looked at each other. Marion looked away first, swivelling sideways on her chair. 'In my experience it's not a good sign to have bleeding every day, so she should seek advice quickly.'

'Thank you.' Heather got up to go, then looked around the room. Marion smiled and stood up as well. 'Can I ask you about homosexuality?' asked Heather.

Marion laughed. 'You're not afraid of difficult issues, I'll say that for you.'

'Is there a cure I mean?'

There was another pause as Marion pursed her lips and considered her reply.

'There are medical treatments given to men, often as a trade-off to avoid prison – oestrogen injections to turn off sexual urges. The men suffer body hair loss and develop breast tissues, so it's not really a cure, more like a chemical masking tape. Why are you interested?'

'I read about the raids.'

Marion nodded slowly. 'Have you noticed, though, that all these arrests in toilets are of men?'

Heather looked up at the ceiling and pondered. 'Maybe it's not illegal for women or the police are less bothered.'

Marion hummed. 'Or, that nobody really wants to think about it too much.'

Again, the two women looked at each other, and Heather understood what was unsaid. 'Thanks, Marion. I think time's probably up with Johnny.'

Marion walked round from her desk and put her hand on the handle of the metal hospital door but didn't open it. 'It's funny, you know, this stage of the journey, it's often when the passengers open up a bit, and you get to know the real person behind each of them. I think it must be the heat or the exhaustion of having to keep up appearances for so long. The chaplain gets far more consultations when the ship's in the Red Sea and going round the Horn of Africa – he calls it a kind of flowering, when hidden colours are shown.'

Heather walked over to the door. 'Do you work quite a lot with Reverend Ian then?'

'Yes, I do the physical care, he the emotional, though, of course,' Marion replied, raising her eyebrows. 'The two are interwoven.'

They shook hands, Marion momentarily touching Heather's forearm. As she took Johnny by the hand and walked along the alleyway to their cabin, Heather wondered if Marion and Reverend Ian ever compared notes.

Chapter 21

April 1960 – Kenya

The turaco birds are starting their 'kwaw kwaw kwaw' in the trees next to the house, a kind of lament to the fading light at six in the evening. I get up from my desk and walk out to the general office to turn on the lights and notice Dorothea still sitting there, holding a sheath of papers to her face. She should get some reading glasses but won't hear of it.

Next to her, skulking low against a steel grey filing cabinet marked creditors and debtors, is a battered maroon holdall made of ancient leather with two looped handles and clothes sticking out of the top where the zip is stuck.

'Going somewhere, Dorothea?' I ask, walking over and inclining my head at the bag. I'm inquisitive as she rarely leaves the confines of the plantation and the village.

'Seeing my sister in Nairobi,' she says, sitting back and stretching her arms, her pencil and papers now on her desk.

'Do you want a lift? I thought I'd go tonight and get the early train to Mombasa.' I sit on the edge of the spare desk and eventually she looks up and smiles, showing off her gleaming teeth; she was happy when I showed her the article on teeth whitening powder from the British magazine yesterday. 'But I don't need mine to be done, surely?' she'd asked me, looking for a compliment, which I of course provided.

'No thanks,' she says, now typing something onto a label, the keys clacking. 'Jonas says he'll take me.'

'My car is much more comfortable, though.' This is another

running joke as all our cars are Land Rovers due to the state of the local roads, especially after the rains. Mine is, however, a newer model, a long wheel base with hard top, as opposed to Jonas's older, more decrepit version, which mostly runs between the plantations.

She stands up, stacks some papers and puts them into a box file, then flips the sprung clip over with a thud, the muscles standing out on her forearm. Dorothea is almost as tall as Heather but more solidly built with swinging hips; her coffee-coloured skin is much lighter than the other estate workers, and her hair less frizzy, on account of the Indian father that she never sees. 'A fine woman,' Jonas said once, watching her walking, 'but not my flavour.'

'All right then,' she says. 'I'll come with you, after I've tidied everything away.'

I arrange to pick her up later, then walk over to the bedroom in my part of the house to get my case and freshen up.

★★★

The two front seats of the Land Rover feel cramped and airless compared to the office, especially with the roads bouncing the passengers around, and reaching for the yellow knob when changing between upper and lower sets of gears invariably means banging Dorothea's knee. It doesn't seem to bother her, though; she just holds onto the side strap, and angles herself away, showing off more of her legs, and talks about her family. As we reach the flat main road in the village, she twists round to the rearview mirror and pats her newly-styled hair around the edges to make sure it's still in place; she had it cut shorter in a European style after seeing a photo in a London magazine. Then she checks her lipstick, which she presumably applied whilst waiting for me.

'Where can I drop you?' I ask as we drive through the shanties around the outskirts of the city, clouds of dust billowing behind us. The shacks are mostly of corrugated iron and rough wooden stakes and the children are squatting at the roadside, waving at any cars that pass.

'I can find my way from your hotel,' she says, smiling again.

For all the talk of her family, I don't recall a sister in Nairobi, or Dorothea ever having been to the city. As the roads become more paved I change to the upper set of gears and wind up the windows against the dust and any possible intruders. We enter the colonial part of the city with its tree-lined streets and white limestone public buildings and I park around the back of the Imperial Hotel, my usual watering hole in Nairobi.

'Fancy a drink on the veranda before you go?' I ask as we walk across the car park, hoping she will say yes. Dorothea shrugs her shoulders and we negotiate the revolving entry door together, but the space is really too small for the two of us and she pushes me in the back before sitting in a teak chair whilst I check in. Her maroon holdall is parked next to her.

We walk through the reading lounge and onto the veranda where we sit on wicker chairs overlooking the manicured lawns, the water spray clicking as the nozzle changes direction and the birds cackling with the fading light. It's hotter than up on the plantation and the streets are much noisier; beyond the iron railings of the hotel, lorries lumber by, air brakes wheezing, and two-stroke motorbikes carve their way through the traffic. A waiter comes to take our order – I have a gin sling and Dorothea frowns before ordering lemonade. She looks at the waiter who holds her gaze momentarily before he replaces his pad in a waistcoat packet and strides away, head held high.

'I often wondered what it would be like at this hotel,' she says with a wistful smile, then looks out at the traffic.

'Well, what's your verdict so far?'

She pushes her maroon holdall under the wicker table. 'I don't think I'll ever really know.'

I cannot work out exactly what this means, though I suspect

it's something to do with the way the waiter and Dorothea looked at each other. This is uncharted conversational territory for us, so I decide to ask about something else. 'What does your sister do in Nairobi?'

'She works as a housemaid for a white family,' Dorothea replies, 'but in Mombasa.'

I'm stunned by this remark and am contemplating the various permutations of meaning when Dorothea makes her breathy gentle laugh.

'Don't look so shocked, William, I can easily get Jonas to pick me up.' She turns one of her rings over, the amethyst one, then takes it off and puts it in her handbag.

I grin uncertainly, considering what to say, then Dorothea continues.

'We're not so different, William, both stuck between two cultures, both lonely.'

'What about your husband?' I ask, crossing my legs and waking up to the fact that Dorothea is making advances to me.

'He's out and my brother Winston is looking after the kids.' She leans over and places her hand on mine momentarily, then sits back again. 'Maybe I read you wrong when you asked me to book the hotel.'

I think back to that moment and remember being a bit embarrassed when she asked what kind of bed and I'd said a double. Was that a come-on? I didn't think so at the time but now I could see why she might have thought of it as a signal, and maybe underneath it all it was what I wanted anyhow. Dorothea is an attractive woman, different from the Bantu and the Maasai, quieter, more poised. She's right about the loneliness as well; I miss Heather sometimes and often feel I don't belong in either the white or black parts of the colony.

'No,' I reply, just as the drinks arrived, 'you didn't read it wrong, I just didn't realise that till now.' As the waiter leaves with a sidelong glance at Dorothea, I have an additional thought. 'We should book you a room, though.'

'For decorum,' Dorothea replies, 'and my reputation.'

We laugh, take our drinks and talk about the tea plantation, though I really want to ask about Jonas's sister but don't dare. I finish my drink first, and check with reception about an extra room, leaving Dorothea with its key before setting off for mine. It's the same room I've had before, overlooking the hills at the back of the hotel, with a balcony and a tiled floor. I hang up some clothes, place my wash bag next to the sink, and sit on the bed listening to the whirring of the ceiling fans. There's a lone gecko in one corner, in the angle between ceiling and wall, feet splayed out waiting for the evening insects; as it moves towards the nearest base of a fan there's the slightest tap on the door. Dorothea enters, swishing her hips so they glance against mine.

I offer her a drink as she drifts around the room, running her finger over the heavy wooden chest of drawers and table before stepping out onto the balcony, leaning on the wooden railing and admiring the view before returning to the room.

'Get me a whisky,' she says, running her fingers down the lapel of my dusty linen jacket, then placing one hand on my chest and looking down at my trousers. 'What is this I see?'

It's true that my erection has become rather obvious. 'I can't help it, you're a beautiful woman,' I reply, turning to retrieve two whiskies from the chilled drinks cabinet on top of a side table.

The sex isn't great at first, mostly due to my nervousness and fumbling lack of practice. But it improves considerably after another drinks' interlude when Dorothea straddles me, shuddering and moaning in Swahili as we come together. She slumps down on my front, her nipples tousling my chest hair and one arm slung carelessly around my neck. I stroke her back and she moans in appreciation before we both fall into a shallow drifting sleep.

'What will happen to you and me, William?' she asks in the hotel restaurant afterwards. We'd both chosen steaks, large flat sirloin slabs with a criss-cross grill pattern and a pat of butter on top.

'What do you mean?' I reply nervously; this kind of question always bothers me as I can never think of the right answer.

'I mean you and your job, and how it might affect me.' She cuts a slice of sirloin but leaves it poised, skewered on her fork. 'I do have a family to feed.'

We are sitting opposite each other, Dorothea reverting to her secretary pose, our hands wandering sideways to avoid each other.

I sigh. 'I want to go home but Taylor will make me stay.'

Dorothea nods. 'Jonas says he's gotten more unpleasant.'

'He's right. But then there's the big question of what will happen to a British tea plantation when Kenya becomes independent. No one talks about it.'

'I think a lot of white people will go home.' She grimaces before taking a mouthful of green beans and chewing them. 'You're a good man, William, but the world is changing fast.'

We sleep in our separate bedrooms after the meal, though Dorothea gives me a brief kiss on the lips before turning in.

Early the next morning I dream of a shipwreck on a coast in the West Cornwall of my youth; there were jagged grey granite stacks with green lichen, the angry sea draining away from high tide, the rocks angular and in vertical shards. An old freighter was in the bay, turned on its side, with men lying inert or on their knees in the foam. I was in a party which rushed out from the shore to plunder the cargo, whatever it might be; there was a woman in front of me stinking of brandy, laughing into the wind as we both ran into the water. There was a hammering in my head as she grabbed the grey hair of a man who was on all fours and thrust his head up and under her skirts.

'Get a sniff of that!' she shouted then pulled his head out again and thrust it under the sea water. 'Nothing comes free, love!' she laughed hysterically, holding him down as the waves surged over her hands.

The nightmare fades as the hammering becomes louder and I realise its coming from the door to my room. I wonder where I am for a moment then remember the Hotel Imperial, the sex and the awkwardness. As Dorothea is the only person I can think of who knows where I am, I assume it must be her in distress, so I jump out of bed and run to the door, to be faced by Jonas, his face covered in sweat.

'Jonas, what's the matter?'

'I'm so glad to have found you, boss, it's Taylor, he wants to speak to you, urgent. Luckily I managed to see where you were staying from Dorothea's diary in the office. I drove from the plantation, as I thought you might want a lift back.'

'What on earth is it?' I rub my eyes.

'He wouldn't say.'

I look at my watch and see it's 7.30am. Over Jonas's shoulder, the door to Dorothea's room opens and Dorothea looks out with a smile, then her expression freezes as she recognises Jonas.

'Is it the workers?' I ask, but too late; Jonas must have seen my eyes drifting sideways and he looks over his shoulder.

'Dorothea, what are you…' Jonas's voice trails off.

'Mr Fontwell got me a room so we could go straight to our appointments this morning.' Dorothea speaks slowly, looking straight at Jonas.

Jonas is silent and turns back to face me. Before he can speak I say, 'I should call Taylor at the office, if it's that urgent, but I need to get changed first. I'll see you at reception, Jonas,' and close the door. In my room I shut my eyes and wonder if this could get any worse, though at least Jonas didn't find us in the same room. I stare at the ceiling and listen to Jonas and Dorothea murmuring outside, without being able to make out their words over the noise of the ceiling fans. There's an additional gecko up there this morning.

I shower and put on my tropical office clothes – a beige linen suit plus blue club tie, loosely knotted – before descending to the reception. I'm shown by the receptionist to the manager's office, a cramped whitewashed room with one window overlooking reception and other the servants' corridor. At the third attempt, the operator manages to put me through to Mabroukie factory, and Taylor himself answers, managing to put more aggression and menace into the single word 'Yes' than anyone would think possible. However, after I announce myself, his manner changes completely into an unctuous church vicar tone.

'Fontwell… William, rather, had trouble tracking you down.'

'The workers?' I interject.

'Not the sodding workers.' The line crackles and I can imagine his lips curling into a sneer. 'I gather you've been sniffing around that Mombasa company we talked about.'

'Well, I went to see their port offices, all perfectly normal.'

'Don't get smart with me. Either leave it alone, or, as we discussed before, come in as an investor.'

'It's your mate Carruthers who's the fixer, isn't it?'

I can hear Taylor breathing hard before there's another line crackle.

'Look, Fontwell, this is something else you're interfering with now, which I won't tolerate, so for the last time put up or shut up or there will be consequences. Understood?'

The line noise dies away and the telephone clicks before the dialling tone returns. I wonder if someone has been listening in, then replace the receiver and emerge from the dingy office out to the reception area.

Jonas and Dorothea jump up when they see me.

'Well?' says Dorothea, staring at me.

'Just a management issue, nothing that urgent, so we can still

233

carry out our appointments. Jonas you might as well drive back to the plantation.'

Jonas nods and heads out of the hotel, trailing his knuckles across the back of some red lobby chairs. Dorothea remains, hands on hips, with her maroon holdall at her feet.

'Taylor's become very aggressive about his transport company but that's my business to sort out.'

Dorothea sucks her teeth. 'Uh huh,' is all she says.

'You could come back to Kiambethu with me later.'

'Yes, I could go and see my sister in the meantime,' says Dorothea, sucking her teeth, a smile dancing on her lips as we flop into the red chairs.

I feel that maybe my gradual drifting from religion has unrooted me somehow, adding to the loneliness. I tell Dorothea about the time I tried a Pentecostal church in Nairobi, a one-room building with a tin roof and walls and a concrete floor. There was red and ochre laundry hanging from wire lines linked to the pastor's house next door and chickens running around between the two. Inside the church, there were rows of plastic chairs with two young Africans in front leading the singing, and another accompanying them on an old sit-up piano, which sounded out of tune.

The churchgoers fidgeted in my presence and either stared at me or looked away whenever I noticed this. Although the small paperback hymnal to share was in English, most of the songs were sung in Swahili. Some of the songs were familiar and the others easy enough to follow after hearing the chorus a few times, so I'd tried to sing along where I could, but my voice was drowned out by the deep baritones of the men and the lilting sopranos of the women.

They were kind enough and kept asking me to come again, but it was so alien, with the loud singing, the people swinging and interlinking their arms, the heat and the jangling of the piano. I didn't return even after I'd grown more accustomed to working with the Africans and their ways.

My parents were Quakers and took me to the meeting house in Come-to-Good, above the Fal River, where on a still winter's day you could hear the clanking of the King Harry chain ferry. The house was small, with thick wattle and daub whitewashed walls and a thatched roof; inside I remember the coldness – even on a glorious summer there was a musty chill in the air, with the thin pages of the hymn books mottled black from the damp. Often there was silence or just one of the Friends speaking softly and my father nodding beside me, so I could lose myself in my thoughts.

'It's only religion, William,' says Dorothea, breaking the silence and placing her hand on my forearm. 'You and I know it's not that important, not like family.'

So now I tell her about the last time I saw Heather, when she waved me off from the docks in Southampton, her head above all the others as she blew me a kiss then held up Johnny so he could wave, too. But there have also been the letters since then; maybe I was a bit harsh in my last reply but Heather's letter from Malta annoyed me, on top of the fracas of her suddenly deciding to come to Kenya.

Of course, Taylor had a field day with that. 'So you threaten Doug with the shotgun and make a fuss about the girls, when they're perfectly willing,' he said. 'Well, I let that one go and decided we'd keep that side of the business away from Kiambethu. Frankly, Doug shouldn't have gone to your plantation; he got a bit carried away with that black woman, the sister of your foreman.

'But now your wife turns up out of the blue when you're due leave in August and I have to write off a load of additional expenses for no good reason. Well, you'll just have to stay on longer to pay it off.'

What on earth am I going to do now? My family are arriving soon and I'm unsure what to do with them and just at the moment when I need Taylor's help with authorising the trip, I've instead confronted him about his fraud.

'Don't feel guilty,' says Dorothea. 'It was nice in bed…' she hesitates, looking upward as though for some suitable words.

I'm expecting a 'but'. Instead she speaks slowly. 'Maybe now we can be more open, help each other.'

This seems so reasonable, so understated. Who else could help me? Heather seems so distant it's doubtful she could do much in concrete terms. We agree to meet again later in the day to drive back to the plantation, and I return to my room.

The tousled bedclothes smell of sex with Dorothea and I draw the half-open curtains to rid the room of its gloom. After months of relative inactivity at the plantation, it's as though the most recent chapter of my life has been concertinaed so hard that Dorothea's advances and Taylor's threats are all flowing into each other and nothing makes any sense.

I wash my face in the basin, dry my cheeks and forehead, then contemplate my financial and moral mess, but nothing seems resolvable with a magic wand. There might be enough time left to catch the last of breakfast, though I'm not that hungry, then check out and get a taxi to Government House. I chuck my clothes in my suitcase without caring too much if they're creased, then take a quick slug of brandy from the drinks cabinet. Poor Johnny, what will I do with him after his long and torrid journey from England?

I even pinch myself to make sure it isn't all a dream, but I sense that this might be just a mild foretaste of greater angst to come.

Chapter 22

5th April 1960 – Aden

Heather felt better without the sickness, but the bleeding was worrying her – it seemed to be getting slowly worse, so she stuffed some cotton pads in her knickers and remembered to put some in her handbag for the shore excursion that day.

They'd got up and dressed earlier this morning, in Johnny's case probably because of the excitement of going on land again, and watched as the pilot boat came alongside and the pilot stepped off and grasped the gangway. He was in a dark naval uniform, a short and stocky man who then waved confidently to his craft, which fell away from the *Uganda*. Luckily the sea was calm, and although there were clouds billowing up along the horizon of the shoreline, another hot and sticky day was forecast on the typed information sheet.

Up on the boat deck, Heather and Johnny watched the *Uganda*'s slow progress into port. Aden was not an enticing or friendly-looking place, with bare rocks rearing up behind the cranes, a prelude to the higher mountains beyond, which seemed to hold the protectorate in an unyielding cradle. There was scant sign of any vegetation or soil under such a biblical firmament.

'It looks a barren sort of place,' said Heather to the Worthingtons, who were also watching. 'Are you going ashore?'

'Oh no,' said Reg in a wheezy voice. 'I didn't feel very safe last time. The Egyptians have been stirring up the Arabs against us, and now there are all the communists to be reckoned with as well…'

'We'll do our usual bartering with the boat people,' said Honour in a more cheerful voice.

Reg chuckled. 'Only, no more wretched jellabiyas!'

They looked out over the vast oil refinery along the flat shoreline of an inner harbour; at one end there were rows of giant mushroom-like storage tanks and in the middle the grey steel towers of the main refining plant with a tangle of pipelines passing either side of it. The air had the sweet sticky stink of crude oil but also felt poisoned and heavy, with a red-brown smudge under the clouds and tall flares burning gas with orange flames and black smoke. A fat freighter aircraft painted military grey with four propeller engines passed low overhead from the sea and Heather recognised the circular RAF markings as it began a long sweeping turn and came in to land somewhere behind the port area.

Two tugs arrived either side of the ship to escort it towards the port, which consisted of a series of low-rise buildings, either modern concrete blocks or white warehouses and wooden halls built along the quayside. One of the tugs now had a line attached to the *Uganda*'s bow and the other took a position at the stern of the ship as they passed a mass of dhows all moored together, with the occasional Arab bending over fishing nets or boxes of cargo in the bilges of the dhows. The heat was already like a furnace even though it was only eight in the morning.

The ship's horn sounded to announce its arrival and as usual this made Heather and Johnny start, the boy jumping in delight. There were two oil tankers leaving the terminal behind them and heading for the open sea, both long enough to merit a tug escort; they sounded their horns in reply.

'What about you, are you going ashore?' said Reg, as they left to go down for breakfast, Honour holding onto the wide brim of her pale yellow sun hat. 'They do have cheap duty-free cameras, if you know what you're looking for.'

'I thought I'd catch our friends at breakfast, and see who's going,' said Heather, waving goodbye to them. She wondered if she should buy a camera for William as a gift, but then he'd probably complain about the money and Heather knew nothing about photography. She found Norman and Cynthia in the dining room tucking into fried eggs, bacon, sausages and tomatoes, and told them what she'd seen of their arrival.

'It seems like another war place just like Malta and Egypt,' Heather remarked. 'Isn't there an RAF base in Aden?'

'Yes,' said Norman, 'and the BP refinery, which is what Nasser wants.'

This sounded like the prelude to another one of Norman's political speeches, which Heather wasn't ready for at breakfast so she asked instead about buying cameras.

'Tell you what,' he responded, 'we can buy one and if William doesn't want it, I'll keep it. You'd better stay close to me, though; it's a bit sticky in the town, in more ways than one.'

Cynthia agreed to come as well and the three of them ordered a packed lunch; each then went to the purser's office to check what they needed to do to go ashore.

'No passports and just English money as it's a crown colony,' said Hancock from behind the glass grill of the bureau. 'Usual warnings, though,' he continued, wagging his finger. 'Don't eat or drink anything dodgy and watch out for pickpockets.'

'When does the tour leave?' asked Heather.

'No tour – you can get a taxi at the port entrance. But remember to haggle for everything.'

'God, remind me why we're doing this?' said Cynthia, shaking her head. Her face looked blotchy and she dabbed at her forehead with a handkerchief.

'Are you sure about bringing Johnny, though?' said Norman. 'White slave trade, and all that.'

'We're coming too, but without the ladies,' said George, who'd crept up unheard behind them with Bob Saunders. Johnny was offered the choice of staying on the ship with Sophie and Michael or going with his mum to Aden. As Johnny chewed his lip and

239

considered the choice, the shell door next to the bureau opened and bright sunlight burst through.

'Me stay, but don't be long,' said Johnny, frowning at the hot air coming in through the door. Heather hugged him quickly and George offered to take him back to their cabin. The shore party agreed to reconvene in fifteen minutes, giving them enough time to freshen up and change clothes for the heat.

'Nothing revealing, they're Muslims here,' said Norman, winking at Heather.

Heather rolled her eyes and returned to her cabin; she selected a knee-length pink pleated skirt and white short-sleeved top together with her sun hat, then applied a layer of sun cream to her face and arms, plus copious amounts of anti-perspirant to her underarms. She then added a small bottle of perfume to her handbag, which had a long chain she could put around her neck. That'll do, she thought, then went to the toilet, replaced her cotton pads and added some extras to her already full handbag.

They all met again at the shell door.

'Worried about losing your wallet again?' Heather asked Bob as they waited for George.

'Ha ha,' Bob replied. 'The prospect of a bargain is too good to miss, what?'

When George arrived, they went down the gangplank and the heat hit them, the dry air swirling around their legs as they descended to where Cadet Mark Edwards was waiting, clipboard in hand. Heather didn't dare touch the side of the ship for luck in case it burned her fingers. 'It's bloody hot,' she said to Mark. 'What's the temperature?'

Mark looked a bit shocked at her swearing and hesitated. 'Over a hundred forecast,' he said eventually, ticking off their names on his manifest. He pointed in the direction of the port exit and taxis.

As they started slowly walking along the quayside, trying to keep in the shade of a motionless crane, a grey Land Rover drew up.

'Want a lift to town?' said a thin man with a black pencil moustache, in the blue uniform of an RAF officer. 'Jump in then, front and back.' He motioned with his head towards the canvas cover over the rear bench seats, then smiled at their gratitude. 'Hot, eh?'

Heather got in the front next to Norman, who was in the middle seat, squashed against the long gear stick. As soon as the others had got in the back, the Land Rover jerked forward and gathered speed, a breeze coming in through the open windows.

'Like the air conditioning?' the officer shouted over the engine noise. Through the sliding plastic window they could hear Cynthia and George in the rear section sniggering at Bob who'd been flung off his seat.

'So, what's happening in Aden then?' Norman asked.

'Oh, lots of ships in port, plenty of military activity, mechanics having punch-ups, usual thing. You in the war?'

'Yes,' said Norman, 'Desert Rats and Malta.'

The officer nodded, swinging the car brusquely around a warehouse wall and stopping sharply at a red-and-white-painted exit barrier. 'Well, you'll know what it's like then,' he replied. A khaki-uniformed sentry glanced at the Land Rover, and exchanged salutes with the driver before lifting the barrier.

The officer crunched the gears and entered the town, past some older colonial-style buildings with arched windows and colonnades, then into a warren of shaded narrower streets where the buildings looked as though they'd been built up one upon the other. The Land Rover had to swerve to avoid a camel dragging a small wooden cart with fat rubber tyres, a boy standing with the reins, but then the traffic slowed in a single file between two rows of parked cars and carts. The cars were a mixture of Austin A40s, Mercedes, Morris Minors and the occasional Cadillac.

The traffic came to a complete halt and the drivers started sounding their horns. 'Best to get out here,' the officer shouted into the interconnecting window. 'Good luck,' he added to Norman and Heather.

They all tumbled out of the Land Rover, trying to avoid the women carrying carpets on their heads, old men on bicycles and younger men on motorbikes in the narrow street. There was an overpowering smell of sewage mixed with roasting meat and tobacco smoke, and the heat of the sun seemed to have been absorbed into every surface you could touch. The local Arabs were dressed very simply in a kind of tight sarong or knee-length breeches and short-sleeved shirts, with headgear either a turban wound roughly round or a white skullcap.

The five of them decided to walk around first to see what was going on before attempting any shopping. They were followed by a small group of boys, all shoeless, pleading for pennies, their hands held out with a constant incomprehensible wailing. One of them followed Heather, tugging at her dress; she stopped and looked at his dirty broken fingernails, his vest covered in dust, and shorts that were too baggy for him. She wanted to give him some money but was too frightened that a swarm of boys would follow and possibly take her purse.

Norman barked a few words in what Heather assumed was Arabic and the boys stood back, looking down at the potholed tarmac.

'That could have been Johnny,' she whispered to Cynthia, 'or Michael.'

'I know, I can't look,' she replied. They reached some shade – a tarpaulin dragged in front of what might have been a household store – whilst Norman consulted a map he'd got from the *Uganda*.

'What are you buying?' Bob asked Cynthia.

'Nothing, I just wanted to see the place – Donald's always refused to come here.'

It was difficult to walk safely; there was no pavement, just the extensions of shop fronts with the owners pestering all who passed, and the streets were full of parked cars and slow-moving traffic.

The shops were a mixture of Western goods such as soap powders and washing-up liquids, with local bottles of oils and ironmongery thrown in. The clothes on display were wrapped in loose plastic, mostly dress shirts and baggy trousers in the Arabic style.

They decided to look at an indoor food market down one side of the street; the building looked like a warehouse but opened up inside. There were heaps of vegetables – peppers of all colours and varieties, okra, chickpeas, potatoes and small onions – on mats on the floor as well as small oranges and lemons and bunches of coriander and parsley. The quality looks a lot better than at home, thought Heather, but then she smelled the meat area. She peered sideways and could see large chunks of animal parts with near naked men hacking at them with a machete; there were flies everywhere and the smell made her gag.

'Sorry, Cynth,' she muttered and rushed out of the market, pushing past people in her desperation to escape, then retching in a gutter.

Cynthia followed and found Heather on her haunches over the gutter. 'You OK?' she asked, rubbing Heather's back. In front of them was a small stray dog, a mixture of black, white and light brown. Its eyes were watery and crusty and its ribs were jutting out as it stood panting and staring at the patch of vomit in the gutter. Cynthia shooed it away and it limped off with some reluctance. At the corner of the street there was a heap of rubbish, mostly packaging and discarded food, which a young boy had set alight and was poking with a wooden stick. A thin blue line of smoke drifted over the two women. Heather stood up and wiped her mouth with one of her cotton pads. 'The meat smell just overcame me.'

The men rejoined them; Bob had his handkerchief over his mouth. A young man with a striped blue shirt hitched up to the elbows and long white trousers asked in English if he could help, then offered to act as guide. Norman spoke roughly to him in Arabic and they shook hands.

'Is there somewhere we can have a drink?' Norman asked the guide. He nodded and led them to a parallel street where there was a restaurant on the corner with a bricked-up charcoal grill in one corner, a long metal counter at the rear, and about a dozen small wooden tables. There were overhead fans swirling the air around, and the clientele was entirely men, mostly Arab but with a few Europeans and Indians. Everyone was smoking and most were talking noisily, the rest reading local or English newspapers.

A tiny woman with a headscarf pushed a couple of tables together for them, then waited for their orders; there were no menus anywhere so they just ordered a mixture of tea and lemonades. Norman muttered a few words in Arabic to the guide, who smiled.

'There's cold beer,' added Norman, 'and we can eat our packed lunch.'

Cynthia whispered to Heather, 'It's like Dante's inferno.'

Heather felt the sweat running down her spine and the dust between the toes of her sandals. 'Horrid, but amazing too, life on the edge.'

They drank their lemonades, then tackled the tea, which was extremely sweet, served in glasses from a battered metallic pot on tiny legs that was stuffed full of mint leaves. They tried not to notice that the other patrons of the restaurant were observing them not very discreetly, with the odd chuckle, especially an old man in a dirty white singlet who was permanently grinning, showing his gums and two gold teeth. Eating a packed lunch had never seemed so uncomfortable to Heather; she wanted to hide it under the table. The men drank bottles of English pale ale, though it was, of course, not as well chilled as on the *Uganda*.

When the bill came it was just a single number four written on a scrap of paper.

'Shillings,' said the guide, and they were all relieved it hadn't been pounds. Norman insisted on paying. The men decided they wanted to get the shopping over and done with and discussed what they'd like to buy. Japanese cameras were top of the list, but they had varying ideas on what models there were and how much they should pay.

'I'll take you to where the sellers are,' said the guide, and they followed him in the midday heat through the traffic and narrow streets.

Heather looked through the gaps in the shops and saw that many of the houses were of loose brick construction with rubble for a front garden. 'Do people live in there as well?' she asked Norman, pointing at some rough wooden lean-tos.

'Probably – they're packing cases from the port,' he replied, not seeming that interested. They arrived at an open warehouse area down a side street, where there were a number of men, each standing over a trailer, which contained electrical goods – radios, small television sets, cameras, record players, binoculars and telescopes. There were some other Europeans – George said they were Italians from the *Asia* that had passed the *Uganda* the day before – but the *Uganda* group was quickly surrounded by salesmen, all shouting, 'Nice goods, very cheap prices.' The Arabs wore long trousers with coloured shirts and brought samples of radios and cameras to show the group. Although out of the sun, it was very stuffy and the place stunk of engine oil and grease mixed with tobacco smoke.

Heather felt uncomfortable between her legs and hoped it was sweat rather than blood. The women were offered two small wooden chairs to sit on and they perched on the edges, as the seats looked like they would leave marks on their clothes.

The negotiations seemed to take forever and tea was handed out at one point whilst all parties calmed down a bit. George appealed to the guide for help but he just shrugged his shoulders and wandered around the other salesmen's trailers, picking up the occasional radio and examining it. Eventually, Norman agreed a

245

price for a camera, George bought a pair of binoculars and Bob settled on a telescope; packets of Craven A cigarettes, which had been agreed to make up the difference in prices, were handed out. Bob bought one six-pack of cigars and another of cigarillos and everyone seemed happy.

'I'd quite like some perfume,' said Heather, and the men all groaned and slapped their knees. 'Joke, chaps,' she added, and Bob cackled out of the side of his mouth not occupied by a cigarillo. While they were leaving, a teenager approached Heather with a bottle of Christian Dior EDT; she remembered looking at the same bottle when window shopping in Beckenham High Street after she and Johnny went to see Marjorie, and after a brief exchange gave the boy half of what he wanted, about a third of what she'd seen the price marked up at. How long ago that visit seemed now.

An afternoon offshore breeze had built up while they were bartering, bringing swirls of dust from the backstreets; Norman asked the guide to get some taxis to take them back to the port and a couple of Renault Dauphines duly arrived and deposited them at the same port security barrier they had passed earlier.

The *Uganda* was now surrounded by small open boats on one side and men with trolleys of goods on the quayside. Cadet Mark was still at the bottom of the gangway with his clipboard, accompanied by two British Military Police with red sashes around their arms. Some of the Indian deck crew were also patrolling the quayside to stop the traders causing any damage to the rope lines; as in Egypt, there were wicker baskets going up and down the ship's side with alcohol, tobacco, perfume and electrical goods, and a line of passengers either watching or taking part.

Back on board, Heather reflected that she wasn't surprised that most passengers didn't go ashore in Aden when the goods could be bought on the ship and the bargaining done at arm's length and without the heat, dust and pestering that going into town entailed. After a shower and replacing her cotton pads, she found Johnny at the nursery, then went back to their cabin where they both flopped on their beds and dozed. They were awoken by the sound of the electrical capstan winching in the mooring lines, a noise not unlike a dentist's drill, and the nudging of the ship's sides.

'Shall we go and watch the ship leaving?' Heather asked Johnny. He nodded a little grudgingly and Heather decided to go and watch from the promenade deck; by the time they'd reached this, there was already a big gap of water between ship and shore. Bob was counting a roll of notes and had a small leather suitcase with him.

'Good bit of business today,' he said. 'I'll sell it all off in Mombasa.' He showed Heather the bottles of whisky and perfume and packets of cigars he had accumulated from the bumboat men. 'Best thing is to leave the buying until just before the ship leaves, when they get desperate,' Bob added, tapping his nose, cigar ash falling in the process.

The departure was a bit of a disappointment as there was nobody cheering on the quayside as in Malta, and in the event the ship didn't really leave Aden but just moved across the harbour and tied up at a long jetty to one side of the shipping channel near the refinery; it had sheet steel sides with a covering of green slime and the odd car tyre as fender, and the concrete top was stained black around the array of hoses and pipes.

'That's why we're here – cheapest ship's fuel in the world,' said the assistant purser who had been passing up and down the deck with a bundle of mail in his hand. 'Letter for you, from the agents' offices, dropped off by the *Kenya*.'

Heather ripped open the letter and briefly scanned it; she recognised William's handwriting and it was clearly just for her rather than his usual missive for the two of them. She stuffed the letter in her handbag and asked Johnny what he wanted to do next.

'Can you read me a story?' he replied. This usually meant he was feeling tired, and was, for Heather, the right answer.

***

That evening, Heather put Johnny to bed and reflected on the day. They'd had their evening meal in first class as Heather had felt too tired to talk to anyone; in fact, the whole day had been rather an ordeal, and despite two naps in the afternoon she still felt worn out, which was unlike her. Anxiety gradually crept into her, a sense of foreboding that she couldn't put her finger on; it was surely down to her tiring day, and the unexplained continuing blood loss that was stressful in two ways: the fear that blood would start seeping down her legs and create public embarrassment, and the even greater concern that there was some underlying health problem.

And yet, as she mopped her brow and cursed not having a deluxe cabin with air conditioning, she wondered if there wasn't something else dragging her down into this slough. Heather opened her bag and retrieved the letter from William that she still hadn't read beyond the first few lines. She tapped the envelope on her bag and wondered what impact the contents would have on her mood, and whether it wouldn't be better to read it tomorrow when she might be in a more positive state of mind.

To hell with it, she thought. Why should I be frightened of a letter from my husband? It will be the same tomorrow as it is tonight. 'When things get tough, Heather,' her father had said, 'best stick out your chest and face the music.' Mother had found this vulgar but the two of them had always laughed at the phrase, whilst Marjorie had frowned and disliked being excluded from the joke.

She unfolded the letter and started to read William's small and neat handwriting, in black ink and doubtless from his favourite mottled-blue fountain pen.

Kiambethu Tea Estate
Near Limuru Town
Nairobi
Kenya

March 1960

Dear Heather,

Luckily today I'm in Mombasa to talk to the shipping agents and the Kenya is in harbour, sailing later today, so I can post this letter on the ship to catch you in Aden. Sorry not to have written earlier but leaving a letter in Malta wouldn't have worked and I wasn't sure about Suez either.

There are so many things I want to talk to you about, but as you'll be only five days from Mombasa when you read this many of them can wait! I'm really looking forward to seeing you, my love, in fact I've managed to organise a business trip to Mombasa, so will take the train down from Nairobi on 8th April and spend the next day at the agents and shippers and meet you off the Uganda *on the tenth. How romantic!*

It was lovely to get your last letter, though I was surprised to learn from your earlier telex that you'd decided to come out here with Johnny. Normally your surprises are delightful but this one was a bit of a mixed blessing. The first thing was that there was a big row with Taylor when London asked him to sanction it; then I had to ask for special family dispensation, and when it transpired you were coming anyhow it got agreed, but it means we cannot now get a paid passage home till next year. Taylor is such an awkward bastard I don't know how I'm going to work for him for another year.

There is another unpleasant issue at work; I cannot write about it easily but let's just say that it's to do with the native Kenyans and their working conditions, which are fine at Kiambethu but not so good at Mabroukie, where there are some foremen who exploit the workers and other activities involving young girls. Taylor just turns a blind eye because it suits him, but I cannot just watch this and do nothing. I know you'll say it's my Quaker background, but if you could see what I see then you'd agree with me.

I hope Johnny is enjoying the trip – are there other boys and girls for him to play with? When I last came over on the Rhodesia Castle there were quite a few children and they seemed well looked after. I'm a bit concerned, however, that his schooling is going to be interrupted; he's only just settled in the church nursery and was due to go to infants school in September. As you know, the company won't pay for boarding school in the UK, so I guess that means putting him into the British school in Nairobi for the time being, then taking him home again to another school. Have you thought about this?

I guess the main issue is that I want to return to the UK but am stuck here till some point next year – Taylor won't let me go before then and now you're coming over we're obliged to stay anyhow if we want our passage paid. Normally this wouldn't be a problem but the working conditions here are difficult – not only do I have to put up with a man I detest, but I'm powerless to do anything about his stupidities. There are also bound to be big changes when Kenya gets its independence, which will happen soon – just a case of how and on what terms; the French colonies in West Africa are already independent.

As a result, there is a lot of unrest with the local Kenyans, you can feel it in the air, especially when they already have grievances and with the history of the Mau Mau not long past. I don't mind risking my own safety, I'm used to living here, but it's different for you and Johnny.

You also talked about a sibling for Johnny. Well, this was quite a surprise for me as you've always been quite dismissive about another child. Has something happened to change your mind? I'm happy that you'd like to have another child and it certainly would

250

be good for Johnny to have a brother or sister, he's old enough now. However, having a baby then bringing up two young children here in Kiambethu would be unthinkable – healthcare is quite primitive compared to what you're used to in Kent. You'd also be stuck here all day whilst I'm away on the estate, at the factory or down in Mombasa, and there's very little to do, especially in the evening, other than staying in or visiting white neighbours. So, I'd love us to have another child, but not in Kenya; it would be much better to wait until we get home next year.

How has the journey been for you? I managed to get a look at the passenger list just now while I was in the Smith Mackenzie offices and some of them I know. George Carmichael is a bit of an old woman but quite nice and Donald is really good at his job but a bit odd I think; I've heard uncomplimentary things about Carruthers. Did you manage to get ashore at all? The food and service was brilliant the last time I was on the Uganda – it's almost like a holiday really and you do deserve a break.

Heather, I hope we can be honest with each other. I know I'm going on about this, but what has made you suddenly undertake this journey when you always said you didn't want to? Has something driven you away from the UK – a row with someone, something unpleasant? We need to talk about this – something I know I'm not good at – but for the first two weeks after your arrival I'm being sent to Nairobi by Taylor. I'm sure it will be a wild goose chase, just him wanting to get me out of the way for a while, but a bloody nuisance nevertheless, just when I wanted to show you around the estate and the local area.

Anyhow, sorry this is a bit of a ramble, done in a hurry at the agent's offices, and I'm really looking forward to seeing you again. Enjoy the rest of your trip!

Much love,
Your very own,
William

Heather felt the breath being squeezed out of her body and her heart rate increasing rapidly; she got up and started pacing around the cabin, up and down the sides of each bed, trying not to make any noise and disturb Johnny. How could she have been so stupid? She rubbed the sides of her temples and tried to stem the rising tide of panic.

There were a lot of unwelcome aspects to the letter. First, William had obviously divined that something had happened, even if he hadn't a clue about what it was; in some ways this was worse – he obviously trusted her and it hadn't occurred to him that she might be pregnant. But he would want an explanation, which would either involve further untruths or a full confession.

Second, he was pretty clear about not wanting another child – or at least, not this year and not the one Heather was carrying. Heather would have to make up the deficit in love for her unborn child herself. She wiped away a tear that had crept over her cheekbone.

And to cap it all, it sounded like sex with William over the two weeks after her arrival was going to be difficult to achieve if he was busy in Nairobi and she was stuck in the tea plantation up in the hills. So the chances of her being convincing about the baby being William's had gone from being tricky to nearly impossible.

Heather considered making a full confession to William, but even if he accepted the baby there were a lot of problems in bringing him or her up in deepest Kenya, as William had described. If she was going to confess she might as well have done it in London and brought up the baby there where at least she had her sister and the NHS to help – her trip on the *Uganda* would all have been a waste of time.

She reflected again about the one option left, which she had talked to Gerald about before they'd left; thinking his name made Heather realise how much she still loved him and how the abrupt separation, and throwing herself into the journey on the *Uganda*, had not cauterised her feelings for Gerald as she'd hoped. When she'd told him about the pregnancy test, his face had lit up as he'd talked about becoming a father. It had been a mistake by her to then talk about an illegal termination.

'Don't you still love me – and our baby?' he'd asked, waving his arms around. She'd hated upsetting him like that and tried to explain that it was *because* she loved him that she couldn't go through with it; their friendship, let alone love, would never have survived the disgrace. Really he was very naïve sometimes, which was part of his charm.

'Promise me you won't do anything rash, Heather,' he'd demanded and to which she'd acceded. And so she'd taken the only other choice available to her – the voyage to Kenya. But now things were different – what if a termination was the only way for her to survive?

Heather got up and adjusted her make-up in the mirror over the writing table. She looked pale and had a sheen from the heat that wasn't attractive, but at least her hair looked good, and she flicked away one or two errant ends and quietly left the cabin.

The ship had been back at sea a good few hours now and there was a roll in her movement that Heather found unpleasant. She thanked her lucky stars that she'd had the forethought to take so many of those pills when they were first offered and could now take them regularly to keep any sickness at bay.

The alleyways were quiet as it was after eleven at night and Heather saw no one else about before knocking on the hospital door. Marion was sitting at her desk reading a magazine, which she slipped down onto her knees when she saw Heather.

'Anyone else here?' asked Heather. The nurse shook her head. 'Well, this is an unofficial visit.'

'Now you're worrying me,' said Marion rather coolly.

Heather looked about her, just to make sure no one else was in earshot. 'Thing is, I'm pregnant, though you've probably guessed that already.' Marion just stared at Heather, so she carried on. 'I've also got this vaginal bleeding, which I'm worried about, and it seems to be getting slowly worse, and I don't want my husband to know just yet.'

'I see,' said Marion, looking sideways across her desk and chewing a corner of her lips. 'Are you on any medication?'

'Only the seasickness pills you gave me.'

'Funnily enough, they're supposed to be good for morning sickness as well, the thalidomides. Well, would you mind if I examined you, Heather?'

The nurse patted the starched white pillow on the couch and asked Heather to strip down to her underwear. There was then a long pause whilst Marion locked the door then put on some rubber gloves. She pressed all around Heather's tummy then asked her to open her legs whilst she peered with a pencil torch and took a few swabs.

'Well at this stage there's little I can see that's out of the ordinary, though you do have some bleeding. You'll just have to wait for nature to take its course and have another examination in Mombasa or Nairobi. Do you want to talk to Dr Sullivan?'

Heather shook her head and replaced her slip with the pads. 'It's difficult doing this on my own and I don't have many options, Marion.' She brushed away a tear and clenched her teeth. 'Please don't mention this to anyone.'

Marion took both her hands. 'You can always talk to me, Heather; in my experience things are never as bad as they seem.'

Heather slid off the couch and helped herself to a hospital tissue and dried her tears. 'Thank you, Marion, really.'

Marion took her arm and led her to the door before another patient arrived, then sat down again at her desk and thought about the last time she'd been in this situation, with another desperate woman, and taken the money as she'd needed it badly at the time.

On that occasion the GP had helped her surreptitiously and

things had gone well. If Heather wanted an abortion, and she seemed undecided what she wanted, then Marion would have to deal with it on her own as Sullivan was a drunken fool and she couldn't trust the other nurses. Though legally the ship was in international waters and she couldn't be prosecuted, she'd certainly lose her job if things went wrong.

Chapter 23

6th April 1960 – SS *Uganda*, Gulf of Aden

The air conditioning in the first-class dining room was a relief after the stuffiness of the cabin. Heather and Johnny had taken breakfast later than normal, rushing in just before the nine o'clock cut-off, though Heather noticed that this was not rigorously enforced. They'd managed to find a laid table next to the Worthingtons, after saying hello to Monica and Philip.

'Another hot day, but windy,' Reg said, waving a typed sheet from the purser's office. 'They reckon there'll be storms again tonight, just as bad as Biscay.'

'Any interesting activities today?' asked Heather, only half paying attention as she watched a dribble of fried egg yolk slowly descend Johnny's chin.

'Have a look,' replied Reg, getting up and handing Heather the sheet. She noticed he was short of breath and took a while to lever himself back into his chair. 'Deck games, if you like that sort of thing, music at lunchtime, then film night.'

Honour talked about them writing letters and listening to the radio, smiling before taking a sip of her coffee. Heather winced at the thought of the coffee taste and was glad she'd taken one of Marion's seasickness pills.

'Games, Mummy?' said Johnny. 'Can we?'

'Let's see how we get on,' replied Heather, finishing her omelette, and laying down her knife and fork.

'Are we nearly in Africa?' asked Johnny, glancing between Heather and Reg, his melted blue ship in one hand.

Reg laughed. 'A few days yet, young man, we're passing the Horn of Africa tonight, I think.'

'Will there be a trumpet noise?' asked Johnny. There was a pause whilst the adults reflected on the meaning of this.

Honour got it first and laughed. 'No, Johnny, it's a place, but we could ask the band leader to blow his trumpet!'

Johnny smiled and frowned at the same time then picked up a banana and looked down at his lap while he peeled it.

After breakfast, they decided to return to their cabin, get changed and go to the swimming pool to meet their friends. Heather didn't really like this plan – she wanted some time to think about William's disastrous letter and what options she had now, though this morning these seemed either very risky or flawed. If only Marjorie had been with her, she'd have known what to do. Perhaps she could talk to Reverend Ian; he did after all already know her predicament and was sworn to keep confessions to himself. But the more she thought about it the more she realised there was only one option, as there had been all along: just to carry on hiding the pregnancy and then deal with William. She'd had to confess to Marion because of her health concerns with the bleeding, but she didn't think the nurse would betray her confidence. The worst part of this plan was having to lie to William, which she'd never done before in any meaningful way, and he was always scrupulously honest with her so it seemed like a double betrayal.

'Here's your lime and soda, madam, and an orange squash for Johnny.' She looked up – it was Parminder. He was a nice-looking young man, despite his teeth, but she'd been shocked when Diaz had told her that he was already married at eighteen. His hair was slightly longer than the norm, swept back into a thick dark mass, and his skin slightly lighter than most of the Goanese and completely unblemished – indeed Heather wondered whether he even shaved yet.

They were sitting out around the first-class pool; the sea was slightly choppy with white horses topping the waves, and the odd cloud of spray coming off the bow with a clumping noise. On the starboard side there was a smudge on the horizon suggesting land, and behind the *Uganda* the stern wash had been broken up by the shifting sea. There were no other passengers about.

'Look, Mummy!' shouted Johnny, pointing out to sea as Heather was signing the chit for Parminder. 'Dolphins!'

Parminder and Heather squinted into the sun. 'Porpoises,' said Parminder. 'We see many in Goa.'

'How are they different to dolphins?' asked Heather as three of them surfaced, dark grey backs against a white flecked sea. They could just see their shapes streaking along under the water.

'No beak, a round nose instead,' said Parminder slowly, trying to think of the right words in English. 'Faster than dolphins.'

The pod overtook the *Uganda*, then veered towards the coast, quickly becoming lost to view amongst the movement of the waves.

Once they'd finished their drinks, Heather decided to go and see what their friends were doing, so they collected their bags and descended via the stairs to the tourist pool behind them, holding onto the railings as the ship pitched. Cynthia waved when she saw them and they gathered together under one of the white canvas screens that had been drawn across the pool area. George and Daphne were sharing an English newspaper George had bought in Aden, and Sophie was in a red and white polka-dot swimming costume lying face down on a lounger, scarcely moving. Cynthia was sitting on the edge of the pool supervising Michael, and Bob and Betty were dozing in their canvas chairs.

Bob woke with a snort and sat up. 'Glard yor here, Heather,' he said rubbing his eyes. 'I've pencilled you in to my team for deck games later.'

'I'm only playing if Betty does,' said Heather.

'Oh no, it's far too hot for me,' said Betty, then giggled as though she'd said something uproarious. It was true that the heat was building again, but the unpleasant humidity they'd faced in Aden was reduced by the sea breeze; it was a day for getting sunburnt without realising it, though Betty had covered virtually every part of her skin except her face and hands. She had a long skirt and a long-sleeved patterned blouse and wore a white scarf around her head and socks underneath her canvas shoes, but then she had very pale skin.

The deck door nearest to them opened and the assistant purser appeared with a clipboard in his hand and a grin on his face. 'Good morning, everyone,' he almost shouted, then asked how they all were; the replies were quite muted. 'Well, owing to the heat, the sports events scheduled for this morning are cancelled. However, the deck games set for this afternoon will take place instead in twenty minutes' time.'

'Oh, that's very disappointing,' said George in a moany voice. Heather assumed he wasn't being serious, but then he carried on. 'Why can't we just see how many people turn up? It's usually very popular.'

'Well, nobody I spoke to wanted the sports events,' said Hancock, grinning as he usually did. Heather wondered if he was making fun of George.

'Are you sure? What about in first class?'

'First-class passengers prefer their air conditioning, isn't that so, Mrs Fontwell?' said Hancock, his hands on his hips.

'Absolutely, I'm really slumming it here with this lot,' Heather replied with a wry grin. The others all groaned and Hancock then asked who'd like to do deck quoits. Bob was the only one to raise his hand.

'Well, I'll go with Johnny but only if Heather does me a favour,' said Sophie, a scowl on her face that seemed to brook further discussion.

'Yippee!' said Johnny. George slowly raised his hand.

'Excellent!' beamed the assistant purser, jotting their names down.

'Bloody cheek,' said George, after Hancock had gone.

Heather remembered what Marion had said about the passengers' real personalities coming out later in the voyage when it was hotter, and then what William had written about George being an old woman. She'd not seen that before and it was almost as if his words had presaged future events in some way. The thought of William led to her anxieties from the previous day returning; she worried about taking Johnny to the first-class nursery in case the same girl with her troll was there. None of this was helped by the ship's movements up and down beginning to make her feel queasy. She looked at Sophie who was scowling at her father and mouthing something to him. George raised his palms and sighed.

'What's the favour then, Sophie?' asked Heather, in an effort to break the tension.

Sophie smiled, and Heather was again struck by how ugly she looked when scowling and how beautiful she was when she smiled. 'I wondered if you'd take me to film night again. I'm sure Mummy can look in on Johnny.'

Daphne looked surprised by this and a bit taken aback. 'I don't think so after the last time,' she replied a little tartly.

Sophie flopped back face down on the lounger and Heather thought she could hear some stifled sobs, though George rustled the newspaper so much it was hard to tell.

The time then came for the deck games and Bob and George got up to leave, with Sophie putting on some sunglasses and reluctantly following. Johnny insisted on Michael coming with him, so the four women – Heather, Daphne, Betty and Cynthia – were left behind. Heather went back to the cabin and took more seasickness pills, adding a few extras to her handbag, and then looked in at the hospital but Marion was busy, so she left quickly after the other nurse started asking questions. Back around the swimming pool, Heather caught the end of Daphne and Betty's conversation.

'I don't know what's wrong with him the last few days,' said

Daphne. After saying hello, there was an uncomfortable silence and Heather was left with the impression they'd been referring to her in some way. She tried to relax and went over to see Cynthia who was sitting on the side of the pool again, her feet in and out of the water as it slopped back and forth with the pitching of the ship.

Cynthia told Heather about her husband seeing Dr Sullivan. 'He was quite sniffy about medication, pretty much told Donald to get his act together, which doesn't help at all. Thanks for asking, though, I can't really talk to the other two about it.' She angled her head back towards Betty and Daphne. 'They're nice enough but I can tell they disapprove.'

Heather sat down beside Cynthia and pulled her skirt up so her legs could be in the water. The cooling was very agreeable, though they were now in full sun, so Heather retrieved her sunglasses from her bag.

'How's the Graham Greene?' Heather asked after a while.

'Very good, the usual Catholic guilt trip, but I can empathise with that.' They both kicked their legs back and forth and laughed like a couple of girls.

'You don't want to swim?' asked Cynthia.

Heather shook her head and looked down at the water. Just next to her leg there was a tiny puff of red as though from a pinprick; she abruptly swivelled her legs round to take them out of the water, turning her back on Cynthia.

'Busting for the loo, sorry,' she said, walking quickly away, splashing water onto the deck and leaving messy footprints in her wake. She walked quickly past the other two women, locked herself in the cubicle, breathing heavily, then changed her cotton pads and examined her clothes for signs of any stains. Luckily there were none, so she sat on the toilet seat and practised her breathing to reduce her heartbeat. Away from the breeze on deck, the toilet felt sweaty and she mopped her brow with a handkerchief and cursed her bleeding for preventing her from swimming.

'Shall I get some more drinks?' Heather asked Daphne and Betty on her return, signalling to one of the stewards. As the drinks arrived, the others came back from the deck games and Cynthia rejoined the group, wrapping herself in a large white *Uganda* towel. Bob was smoking a cigar but was very red in the face, whilst George was holding his head up high and not saying much. Michael and Johnny were whispering to each other and giggling a lot and Sophie was shaking her hair and had one hand over her mouth, smirking.

'Everyone went a bit crazy,' she said to her mother. 'Dad was embarrassing as usual, only this time he kicked an old lady's quoit when he thought nobody was looking, so Mr Hancock disqualified him.' Sophie bent over with laughter.

'Really, George, is this true?' said Daphne, staring at her husband.

'A misunderstanding, I tripped accidentally and Hancock made a big fuss – typical of the man. I shall have to complain.'

'You'll do no such thing. It's only a game.'

'Then Dad partnered Mr Saunders in the doubles,' continued Sophie, 'and in the final round, one of their quoits disappeared when everyone was having drinks.'

'Who won the doubles then?' asked Heather.

'The old ladies,' said Johnny, grinning.

'So how did the quoit go missing?' asked Daphne, leaning forward and looking at each of them.

'Let's not go into that,' said Bob, with a final puff. 'I could do with a malt.'

'Yes, old Hancock found that very amusing,' said George, rolling his eyes, 'practically wet himself.' The two boys collapsed with laughter at this last remark whilst the rest of the group found some deckchairs to sit in, though they were all crammed together with the rising sun reducing the amount of shaded area and some other passengers coming to the pool. George went back to reading his newspaper and looked like he was sulking behind it, whilst Bob smacked his lips on his whisky. Betty patted her husband on the shoulder and he briefly smiled at her. Cynthia took the two boys to the pool, which Heather was grateful for as it looked like they needed calming down, and Daphne sighed and got out her book.

'Thanks for looking after them,' said Heather to Sophie.

'No need – they were really good fun,' she replied. There was a long period of quiet broken by the boys and Cynthia returning from the pool.

'Do you really think you're slumming it with us?' asked Daphne, peering up at Heather as she was rubbing Johnny's back dry.

'Don't be silly, it was just banter with Hancock.'

'*Carry On Nurse* is showing tonight,' said Sophie, looking at her mother.

The others all groaned or complained that they'd seen it before, as had Heather, but she thought she'd better keep quiet.

***

'Sorry I can't help you, the risks are too great,' said Marion, twisting the brown hair at the back of her bob. Heather had agreed to meet before her shift started, out on the boat deck in the lee of the lifeboats where there was no one about. Johnny was down having his early lunch. 'Now you're not going to harm yourself, are you, Heather?'

'No, I've decided to keep the baby,' said Heather as she turned her wedding ring around her finger, trying to think what else she could do. The ship lurched sideways and Heather grabbed the teak rail as a plume of spray was punched into the air. The weather was definitely worsening.

'I think you should come clean with your husband. He doesn't sound like a bad man.' Marion interlaced her arm with Heather's and they stared at the sea foaming alongside the *Uganda*. 'Promise me you won't try to treat yourself, that would just make things worse,' the nurse continued, turning close to Heather and looking right into her face. Heather could see the grey flecks in Marion's irises; she was an interesting woman.

'I promise,' said Heather, her insides churning with seasickness and the thought of such self-mutilation. 'I have to get Johnny now, but thanks anyhow.'

They both left the heat and spray of the deck and went below, Heather to the first-class veranda ballroom and Marion to the hospital. She thought about why she wasn't going to have lunch in tourist class – maybe she really was no better than those snobs in the London suburbs – then cursed herself for having such doubts; Johnny could listen to the music and she could get some time to herself. Heather felt she wasn't really much company at present with her sea-cum-morning sickness and the continual feverishness she seemed to have picked up in the last couple of days.

Johnny delighted again in the band playing for the children; as before it included 'Puffing Billy', 'Davy Crockett' and 'Robin Hood' and Heather wondered at the predictability of their routine on board. There was the same older boy with him – quite thin and stern looking – and the girl Chris, who'd had the unmentionable toy but luckily today was holding a doll with normal-looking hands. Johnny hadn't needed to be dragged to the dance floor and was disappointed when the lunch gong sounded and Heather left him to be taken by Margot to the nursery.

After a chilled gazpacho soup and half-eaten ham sandwich, Heather returned to her cabin to lie down. She couldn't remember feeling so poorly for some time; her last morning sickness hadn't been as bad as this, so it had to be the *mal de mer*, at least in part. But worse than this was the feeling of hopelessness that had descended over her relating to her pregnancy, her status as a mother, and the feeling that she was wasting her life.

Heather realised that her depression (at least she assumed that's what it was) could well be psychosomatic, particularly as she was tired much of the time and rundown by blood loss as well as the changes brought on by carrying a child. Normally, though, the blues were post-natal not antenatal, surely? Was all this because she'd been spoiled in her upbringing and didn't have the stiff upper lip attitude to get her through difficult times? This is what Marjorie had often told her, that their father had spoiled Heather by shielding her from the more pragmatic influence of their mother.

Her best memories were from holidays in Cornwall, a large Victorian hotel up on the heights overlooking Carbis Bay. They'd all eat a huge cooked breakfast every morning, then as the sun rose in a hazy sky they'd set off for the beach, taking the little steam train into St Ives. Dad would take Heather to the harbour to look at the fishermen and their wicker baskets of fish, then walk out on the grey granite breakwater to see if they could spot a seal.

'Don't you wish you had a son?' Heather had asked him once.

He laughed and tapped his pipe on the harbour wall. 'Not at all,' he'd said in that jovial way of his, and punched her on the arm. Otherwise it was the town beach where she'd happily spend hours building sandcastles or crabbing when the tide was out. Mother and Marjorie would get bored by all this and look at the work of local artists and craftsmen instead. Mother had got annoyed once on their return to the beach, as Heather and her father were playing football on the sand with a group of boys whom she'd met whilst comparing their buckets of crabs on the foreshore.

'You're too old for this now, you should be more like your sister,' Mother had said, while Dad sucked his pipe and sighed. Needless to say, things got worse as she got older.

'What do you want to do with yourself before you get married?' her mother had asked. 'Teacher, nurse or secretary?'

Heather hadn't fancied any of these. 'Can't I go to university?' she'd asked her dad later and he eventually agreed, saying she could do a degree then teach if she wanted to.

Mother had been furious. 'Why not Marj then?' she'd heard her ask her dad when they thought she wasn't listening.

'She never asked,' he'd replied. Mother had banged the dishes and slammed the door. It had been a good plan for a while as Heather studied hard at English, French and German, even through the ups and downs of her first boyfriend, whom mother had deemed unsuitable.

'Sure you wouldn't prefer secretarial college, like Susan next door?' her mother had asked on receiving her school results. 'Earn some money and treat yourself before you get married.'

Heather had compromised by going to university locally – taking the train up the branch line from their house in Exmouth to the Modern Languages faculty at Exeter. It had been wonderful, an escape, and to meet other students and find a boyfriend, before doing her PGCE. She'd met William whilst at St Luke's but it wasn't long after before she found herself pregnant.

Lying on her first-class cabin bed, Heather realised two things: first how much she still missed her father and how her mother and sister hadn't been able to help her grief. She loved Marjorie but there weren't many memories of her dad that she could share with her somehow. Mother she had to force herself to visit, down the branch line to the dead end of Exmouth, so it happened only very rarely.

She'd met William at a party on campus being held by one of his geography friends. A couple of months later he'd smuggled her into his digs on Tiverton Road but had been inept with the rubber and that was how she'd got pregnant the first time, though it wasn't till the end of the summer that she'd noticed. That was the second thing Heather realised – that her life was being defined by unplanned pregnancies. She didn't regret having Johnny, even though she'd had to give up all her teaching career plans; Dad had approved of William but Mother gave her the told-you-so life-is-pre-ordained-for-women lecture and was later sniffy about the implied sex before marriage once she'd worked it out, though of course it wasn't to be talked about more than the once.

Yet here am I again in the same situation, thought Heather; once was unlucky and forgivable, but twice, in the words of Oscar Wilde, looked like carelessness. Heather turned over and flicked through her poetry book; the verses seemed to match her mood and she started to read them more closely, starting with the Lawrence poem 'The Mystic Blue', which began:

> *Out of the darkness, fretted sometimes in its sleeping,*
> *Jets of sparks in fountains of blue come leaping*
> *To sight, revealing a secret, numberless secrets keeping.*

Heather wondered what this meant as it didn't appear very nautical – how could sparks appear in the sea? She read on and was more taken by the last verse:

> *All these pure things come foam and spray of the sea*
> *Of darkness abundant, which shaken mysteriously,*
> *Breaks into dazzle of living, as dolphins that leap from the sea*
> *Of midnight shake it to fire, so the secret of death we see.*

Well, Heather thought, I've seen the foam and spray of the sea, and the dazzle of leaping dolphins and porpoises, but there was the reference to fire again seemingly presaging death, which she didn't understand, so she wrote a few words alongside the poem and added '*Horn of Africa, 6th April*'.

She then read Robert Louis Stevenson's epitaph from his grave in Samoa, including the line '*Home is the sailor, home from sea*', but found it rather depressing and jotted a few notes to that effect next to it. 'That's enough,' she said aloud, then got up, took some sickness pills and went to fetch Johnny from the nursery for their siesta.

★★★

Johnny said he wanted to see Michael that evening, so Heather thought she ought to rejoin her friends in tourist class for dinner. She was still bothered about Daphne's question about her slumming it with them, but this was just the latest gripe in the declining relationship between her and Daphne, starting with Daphne being jealous about Norman, then annoyed about Heather undermining her relations with Sophie. This was quite unfair as nothing had happened with Norman, and Heather had been careful to support Daphne when talking to Sophie, and the Camparis she'd given the girl had always been well diluted. George had also said little to her of late and had been very peevish with Hancock, which was unlike him, and the incident with the deck games earlier that day seemed to have made him cross with Johnny.

The journey from their cabin to the dining room was punctuated with the ship juddering as large waves hit the fo'c'sle, combining with a regular rolling that made Heather feel she was inside a spin dryer, being simultaneously turned and pushed up and down. Johnny loved it and squealed with delight at each judder, and Heather struggled to hold his hand and keep her own balance by hanging onto railings and doors or whatever she could find. Inside the dining room the numbers of passengers were about a third of the norm. Of their group there was just Cynthia and Michael, Sophie and a coy-looking Norman standing by the table.

'Mind if I join you?' asked Norman. 'Most of my crowd are laying low in their cabins.'

The conversation that followed was desultory, mostly consisting of commenting on the trouble the stewards were having serving the meal. Heather was tempted to ask for crêpes suzette to see whether the tablecloth might catch fire, but as she didn't feel like eating anything, it was just a passing idle thought. In the end, the women and children went to the chilled counter and asked for a platter of sandwiches; Johnny and Michael asked for spam and tongue, which caused some mirth with the Irish chef.

'We don't have any of that,' he said, grinning at their mothers. 'Coronation chicken, egg mayonnaise with cress, or beef and horseradish, perhaps?'

Norman insisted on having boeuf bourguignon after they'd sat down again. 'Can't have sandwiches, they're for kids.'

There was a crashing noise from the galley, what sounded like a pile of plates falling over, followed by screaming from the unseen staff.

'Mum said I could go with you to *Carry on Nurse*,' said Sophie in a quiet aside to Heather at the end of the meal, 'but only after an argument.' Heather sighed and wondered if she was even more in Daphne's bad books, but didn't have the energy to decline Sophie, even though she didn't really feel like going at all.

★★★

The film was as bad as she remembered from six months previously when she and Gerald had been to see it at the Odeon in Bromley. They'd been to a Saturday matinee whilst Johnny was at a friend's birthday party. The whole event had been a nightmare; although they'd avoided Orpington where Heather had been paranoid about being recognised, she'd still kept her coat collar up and wore a scarf over her hair. Gerald had wanted to go in the evening but the childcare for that was just too awkward to arrange.

'Why all this cloak and dagger stuff?' he'd moaned. 'William wouldn't mind you going to the cinema with one of his friends.'

'But others would mind,' she'd replied, pondering how silly he was sometimes.

'And we can't even have a drink after,' he'd continued.

Heather laughed at the thought of them rolling into a pub, and Gerald joined in – he wasn't one to sulk. Once the film began,

Gerald had laughed all the way through, when they weren't stroking each other's legs and kissing. They'd parted company quickly afterwards, without any show of recognition, as Heather thought she'd spotted one of her neighbours in the foyer. That had been before the pregnancy test had changed everything.

'It's quite saucy, isn't it?' Sophie whispered to her. 'And why does that man speak in such an effeminate way?'

Heather hardly knew what to say, as she felt very queasy. The ship continued to buffet the waves in an unpleasant corkscrew motion and she wasn't paying much attention to the film anyhow, so she just dug Sophie in the ribs with her elbow and said, 'I'd take some of that laughing gas if it was on offer.'

Heather did laugh, however, when a patient's rectal thermometer was replaced by a daffodil, but this was followed by the *Uganda*'s bows rearing up then plunging down, leaving a nasty hollowed-out feeling in her stomach.

'I need to get some air,' Heather said to Sophie, bending down to avoid creating a shadow on the screen and exiting her row of chairs. She then rushed out onto deck, leaned over the teak railing and stared at the boiling sea below, the white foam visible even on a clouded wet night. The queasiness passed and Heather was breathing deep gulps of salty air when a strange light appeared in her peripheral vision.

She straightened up, turned around, and there it was, a dim blue light around the tops of all the cargo cranes and the masts around the bridge, varying in intensity as the ship rocked back and forth.

'St Elmo's fire,' said a voice beside her. It was James the engineer, wearing a bright yellow sou'wester rain jacket and squinting at her. 'Mrs Fontwell, you're getting rather wet without a coat.' He slung his jacket over her shoulders and they ran together into the shelter of the promenade deck.

'I've never seen anything like it,' said Heather, turning to look up at the glowing blue embers.

'It's quite rare, only in electrical storms,' said James leaning into her so his voice was not lost in the howling of the wind.

'So beautiful, that soft blue colour,' she replied and then remembered about the *Jets of sparks in fountains of blue* and wondered if Lawrence had seen the same phenomenon on his travels.

'Are you all right, Heather, only you look quite pale?'

'No, I'm not well.' Before he could reply she made for the deck door a few yards from them. James held the door open and as Heather handed him back his yellow sou'wester they met Sophie with Mark the cadet.

'So there you are – James has rescued you,' said Sophie, a little too coquettishly for Heather's liking. 'The film's finished – I thought we could have a drink now.'

'Sorry – I have to get Johnny, and find some dry clothes,' said Heather.

Heather and Sophie said goodbye to the two officers, Sophie waving at Mark, and together returned to the Carmichaels' cabin; the ship was still moving a lot so they had to tack across the alleyways as it rolled, grabbing onto whatever was available. Sophie screamed in delight, bumping into Heather.

When they got to the cabin, Sophie tapped on the door and went in. Heather waited outside and struggled to see into the darkness inside even though it was only about ten o'clock. Sophie leaned out of the cabin door and whispered, 'Mum says Johnny's in your cabin. I think your steward was looking in on him.' Her brown eyes were liquid in the half light, and she smelled of her mother's musty scent.

Back in Heather's first-class cabin, Johnny was fast asleep, his covers all thrown off and his legs splayed as though he were caught in the mid-action of running a race. Heather smiled and thought that there was at least one thing in her life that had gone well. She got changed, putting on a short thin nightdress, but leaving her pants and padding on, then picked up her poetry book and wondered if there were other references to St Elmo's fire that she'd missed. After a period of time flicking pages back and forth, she eventually found a line in 'The Rime of the Ancient Mariner'.

'*The death fires danced at night; the water, like a witch's oils, Burnt green and blue and white.*'

This seemed too much like a harbinger of doom to Heather, who scrawled a few words in the margin and snapped the book firmly shut. It hadn't been what she'd wanted to read before going to bed, and she sighed and went out to the toilet opposite. The bleeding seemed just as bad as before, so she replaced the pads and returned to the cabin. The alleyway seemed ghostly quiet, apart from the crashing and juddering as the ship contested the ocean, so presumably others were suffering the *mal de mer* just as much as Heather was.

As she lay on the double bed, she thought the nausea had returned as a background taste, lying in wait to be thrown up on some future occasion.

'I don't know how much more of this I can take,' she muttered to herself, as she got up, moved over to the sink, and threw back a couple of her seasickness pills with a swirl of water before one last glance at Johnny and turning off the bedside light.

Chapter 24

7th April 1960 – SS *Uganda*, Indian Ocean

Heather dreamed she was on the narrow rocky ramparts of a castle on a stormy night, dressed in a long white flowing dress with a red jacket around her shoulders. Two soldiers held out their lances over the precipice on the outer walls of the rampart.

'Take shelter, my good lady,' said one, 'for you are getting filthy wet.'

But she merely moved to the lee of one of the grey granite towers and carried on watching, drawn to the blue flames tapering up into the stormy night from the soldiers' lances. A fork of lightning appeared on the far horizon over the dark Germanic woods; the rumble of thunder came a few moments later.

The soldiers were laughing now, the blue light dancing, following the tips of their lances as they waved them. It reminded Heather of the blue part of the gas flame from her cooker at home, a million miles away.

'What means it?' said one of the soldiers to the other. They'd put down their lances and were no longer laughing.

'It bodes ill,' replied the second soldier. 'I've heard it said the stranger, yonder in white, brought it with her.'

'So she's a witch then...' His voice was drowned out in the wail of a sudden squall.

The soldiers marched over to Heather; she watched them coming and saw the intent in their bloodshot eyes but was unable to move her heavy legs. They each took her by the arm, and they were all bathed in a pool of blue miasma, shimmering in the fading afternoon light. With a collective grunt, the soldiers dragged Heather to a low ledge on the parapet, facing the rocks and stunted trees below. She could hear the roar of the river and the hissing of St Elmo as the soldiers pushed her over the edge.

Heather's stomach lurched as she somersaulted in the fall, and she woke with a strangulated cry and sat bolt upright in her bed. She recognised the cabin and tried to control her pounding heart by breathing deeply and regularly and taking account of her familiar surroundings: the same two beds, Johnny asleep in his, the porthole with the blind across showing the grey half-light of a newly dawned day, the desk and chairs, their clothes sprawled out for the morrow, and the cupboard – and yet something was wrong.

She looked down and felt the bed sheets wet around her waist and thighs and passed a finger over the stains to taste. It reminded her of wetting the bed when she was small; her mother had been furious at the extra laundry and pushed Heather's nose into the soiled sheets, but her father had hugged her and stroked her hair.

However, it was not the bitter smell of urine but the sweet metallic stickiness of blood on her tongue. Heather inhaled sharply, grabbed the edge of the top sheet and carefully peeled it across her body, looking askance in fear of what might be revealed: there was a glutinous area all over her nightdress between her legs and down over her thighs. She stifled a scream for fear of waking her son, then ripped off the top sheet and stuffed it around her waist and between her legs to try and stop the blood dripping, then set off for the toilet outside. She held onto the cabin door frame as she felt light-headed, then staggered into the toilet, which luckily was unoccupied.

The mess of paper towels from the night had to be flushed away and she did her best to wipe away the blood on her legs and around her pubic area, then wrapped up her knickers in the top sheet into a bundle, but that still left her splattered nightdress, which she couldn't take off as she had nothing to replace it with.

Heather decided to take a shower in the cubicle next to the ladies and carefully opened the door to see if anyone was about. The alleyway was empty, but just as Heather was stepping outside, a side door opened and Diaz emerged, carefully shutting the cabin door behind her. He turned and spotted Heather, his smile fading as he looked down at the blood on her nightdress.

Heather quickly stepped into the shower room and turned the latch behind her.

'What's the matter, madam?' Diaz was speaking quietly whilst tapping on the door, his ear against the wood.

'I don't know, please go to my cabin and get me a new nightdress and some towels.' Heather was crying now, a pain mounting in her lower abdomen, as she pulled her nightdress over her head and propped herself in the corner of the glass cubicle. After gathering her strength for a few moments, she turned the two taps of the shower and braced herself against the initial shock of the cold water.

The tapping stopped and Heather could hear the sound of voices in the alleyway. Diaz knocked on the open door to the Fontwell's cabin and entered; the boy was awake now, sitting on the edge of his bed and rubbing his eyes.

'Where's Mummy?' he asked.

'In shower, forgotten her clothes,' replied Diaz, in an impatient tone as he bent over and fumbled around in the chest of drawers, talking to himself in Konkani. To start with he could only find Johnny's clothes, but eventually he found what he was looking for, and pulled out the nightdress and held it up to the light to check.

'Back soon,' Diaz said. 'Please get dressed like good boy.' He shuffled down the alleyway the short distance to the linen cupboard, pulled out two large white bath towels, then returned to tapping on the shower-room door.

The shower was running freely now and steam began to mushroom around the ceiling; Heather was still propped against the glass wall, looking at the swirls of red moving around the shower tray, and the bloody streaks all down her legs. Sitting over the plughole, obstinately refusing to go down, was a small parcel of gooey tissue with stringy bits attached. It looked like the offal that her butcher gave to people to feed their dogs. Heather couldn't bear to look, so she averted her eyes and washed her abdomen and pubic area with her one free hand holding a bar of Cussons Imperial Leather. She gagged when she looked again and the sight was still over the plughole.

The tapping restarted. 'Heather, do you need help?' It was a different, woman's, voice, pleading – one that Heather didn't recognise. 'It's Monica, from the next cabin.'

Heather moved slowly to the door, the shower still running, and managed to unlock the latch before slowly sinking to her knees, one hand holding the shower door. Monica was in her long *Uganda* towelled dressing gown, her feet and lower legs bare. She drew her breath in sharply when she saw Heather and the mess in the shower but then made a little toss of her head and went to lever Heather up, holding onto the shower door, and placing her nightdress over her head and pulling it down over her body.

'Now you're decent,' Monica said.

'Thanks,' mumbled Heather, staring unfocused at the floor. Monica wrapped one towel around her waist like a sarong and dried her hair roughly with the other before draping it around her shoulders.

'Can you walk with me?' she asked, but Heather was too tall for Monica and her shoulders kept slumping to one side. As a result, Monica only managed to get Heather to sit on the toilet sideways against the cream metal wall to stop her from sliding down onto the floor.

'Wait while I get some help,' said Monica.

Heather raised one forearm in response before grasping the edge of the seat with one hand and the ivory handle on the cistern with the other. Monica left the toilet door open and spoke in Konkani to Diaz outside, who then ran down the alleyway towards the hospital whilst Monica returned to stay with Heather. Just as Diaz was leaving the first-class area he knocked into James Scott, who'd finished his breakfast in the engineers' mess room and was about to descend to the engine room to report for duty.

'What's the problem?' asked James, who'd never seen Diaz running and noticed the film of sweat around the steward's temples.

'Mrs Fontwell collapsed and I'm going hospital,' replied Diaz, breathing heavily with one hand on his knee, the other pointing down the alleyway. 'First-class ladies toilet, Mrs Doyle is with her.'

The engineer found Heather and Monica; he looked shocked at the blood on the floor of the toilet and over Heather's feet and ankles. She seemed to be only semi-conscious, responding to his touch but rolling her eyes and barely able to speak. 'Come on, let's take her to the hospital now,' said James, putting his arm across her shoulders and under her armpit, and slinging Heather's nearest arm over his shoulders. 'Heather, can you walk?' he shouted.

Heather grunted and Monica took her other arm and together they propelled her down the alleyway towards the hospital, Heather taking a few steps but her legs mostly dragging behind her. They met Marion, the sister and Diaz as they were passing the bureau; an elderly couple were scrutinising the opening times on the door and the woman's eyes widened and she put her hand over her mouth when she saw the procession pass.

After entering the hospital door sideways, they managed to lift Heather onto the bed in the consulting room and laid her down flat. The sister told Diaz to resume his normal duties.

'Where's the doctor?' James asked the sister, pointing at a side door. 'That's his room, isn't it?'

'Yes but he's on call, I'll see if I can track him down,' said the sister, leaving as she spoke. The engineer tutted and used the ship telephone on the wall to call the bridge.

'Ship's doctor to report to the hospital,' came the tannoy announcement almost immediately. James recognised the second officer's voice, calm and measured like he was announcing a train departure.

'What's wrong with her?' James asked Marion in a strained voice.

'A lot of bleeding,' replied Marion, checking Heather's breathing and heartbeat. 'It looks like a miscarriage.'

The nurse washed her hands quickly, then took the blood-pressure monitor off a shelf and bent down to talk into Heather's ear. 'Can you hear me, Heather?'

There was a grunt and fluttering of her eyes.

'Did you do anything to yourself, Heather?' she asked, placing her hand on her shoulders.

Heather's eyes focused. 'No, Marion, I promised you...' Her pupils disappeared and she sighed and turned her head.

James decided he ought to wait in the doctor's side room, but he could still hear everything that was going on.

'I'm just taking your blood pressure,' shouted Marion, putting the rubber jacket around her arm and starting to pump air into it. There was a pause as the air was gradually released and Marion took the measurements. 'That's low,' she said, then checked all around Heather's body for any other symptoms. She brought two folded blankets in from an adjoining room and put them at the end of Heather's bed, then raised her legs. Her nightdress fell back to reveal a congealed mass of pubic hair and sticky blood, which Marion started to examine. 'Just having a quick peek at you,' she said in Heather's ear.

James wondered how she could stay so detached. 'Where's the fucking doctor?' he shouted from the adjoining room.

'Indeed,' said Marion, who had now donned a pair of surgical gloves and was looking closely at the blood seeping out. 'Still in his fucking bed I should think.'

James was about to ask for an explanation for this last remark when the door opened and the tall figure of Doctor Sullivan made his entrance, followed by the sister. He was unshaven and his clothes crumpled and hair askance.

'I hope this call is really necessary...' his Scottish lilt trailed away upon seeing Heather. 'Get out of the way,' he said to Marion.

'BP is seventy over 120, pulse weak, temperature 99...' said Marion.

'Yes, yes,' interrupted the doctor who was fumbling with Heather's nightdress. 'Where's the cut?' he mumbled and James was unsure if he was talking to himself or not. 'Who found her?'

'I did,' said the engineer, stepping into the treatment room and immediately smelling the sour stale smell of whisky emanating from the doctor. James sniffed again, just to be sure.

'Stop sniffing man and tell me how you found her.'

'She was in the toilet, her steward and another passenger were helping her.' James felt hot and annoyed that he was being interrogated by a drunken doctor.

The doctor stood up and looked at Marion. 'A miscarriage I'd say, then fainted with the blood loss and the hot shower. Not much more we can do now. Did we know she was pregnant?'

'No,' said Marion, quietly.

'Her own silly fault then, eh? I'll pop by later after I've done my rounds with Sister.' The doctor opened the door, and they'd both left before Marion had the chance to say anything. His stale unwashed aroma hung in the white sanitised room like an unanswered question.

'Shit,' said James. 'What now?'

'I'll try to pack her up with surgical pads and monitor her temperature. It's already too high for my liking.' Marion set to work removing her clothes. The internal phone rang and the engineer answered.

'What's going on? Why haven't you reported for duty?' said the second officer in his flat matter-of-fact voice.

'The doctor's been and gone with the sister and I'm tidying up.'

'I see. Don't be long, the old man will be asking soon,' said the second officer and rung off.

'Dr Sullivan,' said James slowly, 'is he often like that?'

Marion turned around and shrugged her shoulders. 'War damage, I think. You'd better be going, Sister will be back soon.'

James went to put on his jacket and noticed the flecks of blood on his uniform shirt. He brushed his hair with his fingers in the mirror and turned to look at Heather again. She sighed and muttered something to herself.

'Will she be OK?' said the engineer.

'Come back later and I'll tell you,' Marion replied, touching his elbow. 'And, thanks, James.'

While he was closing the door to the hospital, the engineer reflected that she'd never called him by his Christian name before, and he made his way forward to the bridge, filled with worry and a lot of unanswered questions.

On the bridge, the second officer listened to his account of matters in the hospital whilst he checked the radar and telex traffic from Mombasa, then sent the engineer to check on the seawater pumps in the engine room then the cargo in the rear holds, which had had reports of movement in the sandstorm. It was hot work in the engine compartments and James spent most of the morning with a Lascar engine-room hand greasing some suspect valve joints and tightening them with a large wrench.

At lunchtime, James managed to get some time to return to the hospital. Heather looked much the same as before save her cheeks were a little more flushed, which at least looked better than the pale clay colour they had been before. She seemed to be sleeping, with breathing regular if a little nasal.

He could hear another nurse on duty now in the adjacent treatment room, talking to a passenger. Marion was still at her desk, looking at some patient notes.

'I think the bleeding has stopped, though I might have just covered it up. Her temperature is still too high.' Marion got up and wrote down some numbers and jottings on a clipboard, which she then attached to the frame of the bottom of the bed.

'What's happening with Johnny?'

'Her son? Oh, I think the steward and Cynthia, the lady with the son the same age, are looking after Johnny. He comes in now and again but I don't like him staying too long.'

James sat on one of the adjacent chairs and looked at Heather's chest rising up down as she breathed. Someone had brushed her hair since this morning, so she looked like she was just having a long lie-in. The floor had also been cleaned up and there was little trace of the chaos when she'd first been brought in. Maybe it would work out for her after all.

'I'll come by later then,' James said awkwardly, feeling his presence wasn't welcome somehow. Marion must have divined this and made a small twitchy smile.

'She's in good hands now you know, James.'

The engineer stood up, put his hand on Heather's arm and was surprised how hot she felt. The hairs on his arm stood up, and he moved his hand down her arm to her wrist then let go. Marion had her brow knitted as he left.

His afternoon was taken up with problems with the air-conditioning units in the first-class area where there had been a few complaints, especially from those in the deluxe cabins. James couldn't see that there was any appreciable problem in the public areas, though of course the outside temperature had risen considerably since they'd arrived in Aden.

'Just make sure it doesn't spill over into the refrigeration plant,' the chief engineer had told him in his Ulster accent. But with a few adjustments here and there, and a few small leaks stemmed, the cabin temperatures reverted to their usual 60 degrees Fahrenheit. The refrigeration plant seemed to be working normally as far as he could tell from the compression and temperature readings.

After taking butter chicken for dinner with his colleagues in the engineering officers' quarters behind the bridge, James made his way down to the hospital again. By chance he arrived at the same time as Cynthia and Michael and followed them into the treatment room. Johnny was already by his mother's bedside but there was a tension in the room that wasn't present before. Marion was looking at the patient's notes on the clipboard but kept flicking her eyes across to Heather who had propped herself up on two pillows at the head of the bed.

'Good to see you awake, Heather, how are you feeling?' said Cynthia, still holding Michael's hand, who was looking at Johnny from behind his mother's skirt.

Heather did indeed look more awake but her hairline was stuck to her forehead by a line of sweat and her cheeks were red. When Cynthia took her hand she noticed it was clammy and very warm, but she still bent down over the patient and kissed her on the brow.

'What on earth happened to you, my dear?' she whispered.

'Well, I lost my baby, the one I hardly knew I had,' she spoke softly then drew down her friend by the elbow. 'A miscarriage,' Heather whispered then collapsed back on the bed, and drew her hand across her temples; it was impossible to tell if she was wiping away sweat or tears. 'Please take Johnny away, it's not very nice for him.'

'Yes, of course. Don't upset yourself, Heather, I'm sure you just need some rest.' Cynthia turned and took Johnny by the hand. 'Do you want to play with Michael? Nursery or pool, you choose.'

Johnny nodded then rushed over to his mother's bed and buried his head on her sheets. Heather stroked his hair and kissed the top of his head. 'See you later, darling.'

Cynthia left with the two children, gently closing the white metal door behind her. The other nurse came out of her office, greeted James, then sat on the edge of Marion's desk.

'What's happening then?' asked James, looking alternately between the two nurses. Marion went over to Heather's bed and unhooked the clipboard.

'Her temperature's higher and rising and I wanted to give her antibiotics against a possible infection but Sullivan was very dismissive. Sister doesn't dare contradict him, but I'm giving her penicillin anyway, and I'd like you both to witness what I'm doing. Are you OK with that?'

The other nurse nodded in agreement.

'Yes,' said James, 'but where's the doctor now?'

'Probably having another episode,' replied Marion, shrugging her shoulders.

'Do you know what you're doing with the dosage?'

'Of course,' Marion sighed. 'I've given penicillin many times before.'

'James,' said Heather quietly from behind them. The engineer walked over to her bedside and took her hand.

'Can you get me Reverend Ian please?' Her breath was slow and stuttering. James nodded, patted her hand, then went over to the ship's telephone and called the bridge to tannoy for the chaplain.

'God, it's not that bad is it?' replied the second officer in an alarmed voice.

'No, she's just wants to talk to him.'

The call went out over the ship's PA system and James noticed that the second officer asked for Ian Tremwell, rather than the ship's chaplain, to go to the hospital. He watched Marion as she washed her hands in the sink, dried them off on a paper towel, took a vial from the fridge in the corner and a hypodermic syringe from the sterilising cabinet, then pulled the plunger to draw up the required quantity.

James thought he'd better wash his hands as well.

'Not afraid of needles?' Marion asked, with a tight grin.

Just then the door opened and Reverend Ian entered, rubbing

his hands and looking severe. 'Heather, how are you?'

Heather woke from a glazed stare and struggled to sit up. James helped her with the pillows and noticed her back was wet to touch as well. He could see red lines across her back where the edges of the surgical gown had pressed against her tanned skin, and it was all he could do to prevent himself tracing the lines with his fingers.

'Reverend Ian,' said Heather once she'd settled. 'Just to say…' she began and her eyelids began to flutter, but she took a deep breath in and continued. 'I wanted this baby but then came the bleeding and the miscarriage.' Heather sniffled and looked away.

'Yes, Heather, I understand,' replied Reverend Ian, holding her hand, staring intently at her, leaning across the bed.

'I don't know what's happened to me, but this fever…' Her eyelids closed again and she sighed. The chaplain gently shook her by the shoulders and she awoke again. 'Don't tell William, it would upset him.'

'No, of course not.'

'And please, make sure Johnny is looked after.' Heather smiled hesitantly. 'I wish… I wish… it could all have been different.' Her eyelids closed again and she eased back on her pillows and succumbed to sleep, her cheeks seeming even redder than before to James.

'I think this would be a good moment for the penicillin,' said Marion, holding the hypodermic syringe and flicking the tube with her finger to get rid of any air bubbles. The chaplain moved away from the bed.

'Just giving you some penicillin, Heather, you may notice a slight stab,' Marion almost shouted at Heather who just mumbled in reply.

Marion found a spot to inject on Heather's left upper arm, then administered the penicillin and neatly withdrew the needle, laid down the syringe, and swabbed the pinprick of blood away before applying a plaster.

James admired Marion's calmness, her methodical routine as she disposed of the swab and needle, washed the syringe and returned it to the sterilising cabinet, then washed her hands again.

James and Reverend Ian watched Heather as she breathed. Marion applied a cold compress to her forehead and wiped her face with a white flannel. 'That should do the trick,' she said, almost to herself.

'Will the fever abate?' asked the chaplain, wringing his hands.

'It should do, with the antibiotics.'

'So she lost the baby?'

'Yes,' said Marion, continuing to wipe around Heather's neck and shoulders. She seemed in a trance. 'Not much point in you both staying, if you've other things to do; she'll probably be out for a while.'

James looked down at the patient who seemed more at peace now, and admired her aquiline nose, olive skin, and even the slight cluster of freckles below her eyes. She looked poised even lying down in a hospital bed.

'James,' asked the chaplain, grasping the engineer's elbow, 'I'd just like to talk to Marion, alone.'

'Yes, of course,' he replied, looking at Heather for one last time.

Chapter 25

10th April 1960 – Mombasa, Kenya

The unbearable burden of grief hangs around me like smog, as Dorothea and I walk slowly down the quayside to berth number four where the *Uganda* is due to dock in Kilindini Harbour, both a beginning and an end for Johnny, Heather and I, compressed into the moment when the side of the ship touches the concrete wharf.

It's seven in the morning and I feel groggy with a headache coming on as I contemplate the confusion of cranes and masts and ships in front of me, the harbour water barely visible. The sky is clear out to the east but the clouds have banked up behind them, leading to a spectacular dawn with the sun's rays shining between the base of the cloud and the horizon, lighting up pencil-thin rows of orange and grey. My previous visit to Kilindini, to watch the *Kenya* leaving, seems like a memory belonging to somebody else.

Tomkinson from Smith-Max called the plantation house the day before yesterday with the news of Heather's death. He couldn't give me any details at all, other than to reassure me that Johnny was being well looked after, and this just added to the surreal atmosphere I found myself in. Dorothea burst into tears as soon as I told her and Taylor then called saying he'd had a telex and asking if there was anything he could do. I politely declined for the moment and Dorothea and I drove straight to Mombasa.

Yesterday, Dorothea helped me get the seat reservations for the three of us to travel up from the docks to Kiambethu via the midday train to Nairobi and we arranged for Jonas to bring back the Land Rover and then pick us up from the station on arrival.

I've spent two nights at the Oceanic Hotel overlooking the harbour entrance – normally one of my favourite places to stay, with the reefs and passing shipping a backdrop to the lawns and gardens sloping down to the waterside, and the comfort of a 1950s-built hotel. God knows where Dorothea stayed – I hardly dare ask her.

This time, though, I scarcely noticed anything of the Oceanic and didn't bother with evening meals; there was just the interminable hanging around between wearing trips to the ship's agents, but at least they agreed to send telexes to Heather's family and provided a warrant for the train travel. It made me impatient to return with Johnny to the plantation straight away and sort things out from there. Dorothea agreed to arrange whatever childcare was needed but she would be around the house most of the time anyhow.

Dorothea takes my arm and squeezes it. 'William,' she sighs, 'I cannot understand what has happened to your wife and why nobody wants to talk about it.'

She's right, of course, but all I can feel is the headache, a wounding of my soul and a jumble of memories. 'Indeed,' is as much as I can muster in reply. I can see quite vividly, almost too clearly, but thinking is beyond me.

Two gangways are pushed into position by the stevedores, wearing baggy half trousers, T-shirts and dirty black boots; they have red rubber gloves tucked into their belts and they move slowly in the full sunlight, mopping their glistening brows, the white of their handkerchiefs contrasting with their black skin. The transit sheds back right onto the wharves, their long low grey buildings jostling with the railway line behind. I hear the steam engine for the passenger train to Nairobi shunting backwards and forwards as it picks up coal and water, hissing and coughing up puffs of white smoke. We watch a lonely figure climbing up the access ladder on the crane nearest to us; a whine builds up as the electrical motor is started and the jib is tested with a couple of swinging movements.

287

The air smells of rotting vegetables from the loading activities in an adjacent shed.

'It's late,' says Dorothea in her matter-of-fact voice, looking back at the clock on the face of the side of the brick-built passenger terminal. Just then we hear a ship's siren and turn back to face the harbour entry, but there are so many ships docked that day – mostly in the BI colours of white with black trim and two white bands on a black funnel – that it's hard to see into the main channel with all the masts and rigging and overhanging cranes and harder still to tell which ship has just blown its whistle. There is a vessel with the distinctive white bands on the funnel just coming round the headland of Shelly Beach, entering the narrow harbour entrance towards Likoni Ferry, but this time a bigger ship with a much bigger funnel than the others. It must surely be the *Uganda* as I recognise it from the sister ship *Kenya* that I admired when it was in harbour only a few days ago, happy in my ignorance of the future.

The *Uganda* passes the row of BI vessels, its speed now very slow, with only a ripple of a bow wave and a second tug on a line to the starboard side; the first tug disappears behind the ship to push it into the narrow space left on the quayside in front of the *Karanja,* a smaller vessel with a pencil funnel. There is another blast on the ship's horn and Dorothea and I watch the bustle of deckhands around the bow and stern areas of the ship. The *Uganda*'s engines vibrate into life and there is a churning of water at the stern as it passes the *Karanja* and the ropes are thrown to the waiting linesmen.

'Not long now,' says Dorothea, watching the shell doors opening on the ship and the gangways being manoeuvred from the quayside to connect up to them. There are a few white passengers lining the promenade deck, presumably in a hurry to get off the ship and make their way through the customs shed and out into the wide open spaces of Kenya.

The gangway reaches the first shell door and is tied up by the crew as an officer jogs down to reach the quayside where he shakes hands with a tall man dressed in a cream suit and panama hat awaiting him – Tomkinson from Smith-Max.

'Let's go,' I say to Dorothea, moving forward to talk to the two men.

'Good morning, Fontwell,' says Tomkinson. 'This is the second officer. He'll look after you.' We all shake hands, with Dorothea standing apart until I introduce her as my office manager. Tomkinson and the officer just nod, with an awkward pause after.

'Please wait a moment, sir,' says the second officer, a younger man with a closely shaven black beard, 'whilst the first wave of passengers disembark.'

There is already a queue of passengers starting to make their way down, even at this early time; maybe after nineteen days you just can't wait any longer. They are struggling with suitcases and small children, with the larger luggage being carried by the stewards, all to be met by a posse of porters and carts that have suddenly appeared around the base of the gangway. The passengers then regroup around the gangway, some shaking hands and hugging each other, and others standing awkwardly apart, stretching their sea legs.

At the stern shell door, laundry baskets are manhandled off the ship followed by several large trolleys of boxes marked 'GPO mail'. The deck crew start to remove the cargo hatches and the ship's cranes twitch in anticipation.

'I'm sorry about your wife, sir,' says the second officer, turning as though he'd just remembered. 'A terrible business. Let's get on board quickly, now there's a gap,' and with this he dashes up the gangway, one arm held out with his radio in hand.

The ship seems enormous from close up as Dorothea and I follow the officer up the gangway, Dorothea slapping the cool metal side as she goes. He waits for us at the shell door, talking to one of the stewards. 'We're to go straight to the Captain's day room.'

I'm aware that the stewards are staring at me, but they avert their gaze when I look back. Is it Dorothea they're intrigued by, or just me, the newly widowed husband?

I've never been on BI before, having used the *Rhodesia Castle* and *Kenyan Castle* to come to and from London, but the smell is the same, quite unique, that mixture of cooking, laundry and beeswax, then the wafting in of brine and fuel oil from the shell door. After the plantation house, the corridors seem cramped with low ceilings and people milling about everywhere, cabin doors open with cleaning baskets outside.

We make our way forward, then climb up two decks by way of a sweeping staircase. The ship seems to have turned itself inside out, with piles of dirty laundry, trunks, cases and discarded breakfast trays lying around everywhere, passengers vacating their cabins and crew moving in to clean. Finally we get to a door marked 'Crew only'. then another short enclosed corridor with a low ceiling and another doorway leading up some steep narrow stairs. I can hear Dorothea's labouring breath behind me as we try to keep up with the second officer.

At the top, the officer knocks on the door then pushes it open, holding it with an extended arm for us to enter. 'Here we are,' he says, pointing at some armchairs, 'I'll just let him know you're here,' and he exits by another door, leaving us to survey the cabin.

Wood-panelled walls glisten with the light from the shaded windows on two sides and my attention is drawn to the writing desk in the corner where there is a photo of a woman in her forties in an evening gown next to another of the young Queen Elizabeth. There is a buff brown file marked *Heather Fontwell* in front of the chair, which I'm about to peruse when the second door opens.

The Captain enters with a scowl on his face, leading two other men behind him, one of whom I recognise but cannot remember from where. 'Ah, Mr Fontwell,' the Captain begins, extending his hand but looking behind me at the file on the desk, 'a very sad day. Please…' He gestures to the nearest armchair.

The Captain introduces the Reverend Ian Tremwell, the ship's chaplain, and Carruthers, the Mombasa harbourmaster, whom I recognised and now remember that Heather referred to in her letters. I introduce Dorothea and there are handshakes all round. I notice that the Captain does not bother to introduce himself but leans across his desk and picks up the file, then turns his writing chair around and sits down in it. The other two remain standing and lean against the long wooden side table under a glass cabinet.

'I'd just like to say, on behalf of all the crew and the British India Line, how sorry we all are about Mrs Fontwell's death,' says the Captain, opening the file. 'She was treated in our hospital where the doctor and nurses did everything they possibly could to try to save her life.' The Captain coughs then continued. 'She was admitted in a semi-conscious state after having swallowed a large number of pills and then took a fever, which we tried to combat by antibiotics but without success.' The Captain pauses for breath and glances at the other two men.

'This is not an easy message to give you, Fontwell, but we believe she took her own life by swallowing these pills. We might have saved her but for her allergic reaction to the penicillin that was administered and which she unfortunately had not warned us about in her medical statement.'

I'm shocked by this speech. Suicide? This doesn't sound like Heather at all, who told me once how she despised self-pity. I say as much but in a rather stammering and garbled voice. Dorothea puts her hand on my sleeve.

'Well, there was also the letter.' The Captain coughs again and leafs through some papers before producing what I recognised as the letter I'd written her from Mombasa. 'Look, I'm sure you didn't intend this, Fontwell, but it might have tipped her over the edge. You see, she was in a very febrile state of mind at the time, and there was an incident at the nursery as well. Mrs Fontwell appeared quite down and confessed as much to you, didn't she, Chaplain?' The

Captain swivells round in his chair to face Tremwell.

'Yes, we talked a lot over the last few days,' says the chaplain, clenching his hands in front of him and rocking them back and forth. 'She was very worried about the future, especially after the cabin fire, and was almost making herself sick. We assumed it was something domestic, though she didn't say what exactly.' The chaplain speaks with a deep and musical voice, smiling but sad at the same time.

The letter, the blasted bloody letter, which I'd dashed off in a hurry to catch the *Kenya* and which had taken on my own unhappiness and my annoyance at Heather's behaviour; could it really have poisoned Heather in this way? I was at a loss to know.

'What cabin fire?' I ask, in an effort to move on.

The Captain twitches, then leans back and closes the file. 'One of the passengers threw a lit cigarette over the side and the wind blew it into the cabin where your son was sleeping. Mrs Fontwell raised the alarm and helped put the fire out – your son had luckily been woken and got out of the cabin unharmed. She didn't have much sign of smoke inhalation but we asked her to get a check-up in Mombasa. However, it also seemed to have a psychological effect on her, and might have helped the fever progress.'

'She was very brave,' says the chaplain, 'but the incident seemed to dislocate her somehow.'

'So, we've prepared a medical report for you, as well as the certificate signed by the doctor,' says the Captain, opening the file again and handing me several sheets of paper.

I glance at them. The cause of death is marked as 'suicide' and I look away; it's all too much to take in.

'Did she leave a note?' I ask.

The three men facing me look at each other and the Captain just shakes his head. 'Not that we could find.'

'Could I speak to the doctor?' I continue.

'Well he would have liked to talk to you,' replies the Captain, one hand rubbing the back of his neck, 'but he's had to go ashore with a sick crew member.'

There is a pause whilst I consider what to do next.

'I'd like to see her now,' I say, getting up with Dorothea to leave. No one else moves and the chaplain looks at his hands.

'What do you mean?' asks the Captain softly.

What does he think I mean? It seems obvious to me. 'I want to see her remains.'

'Sorry but I thought the telex to your firm made that clear. She was buried at sea.'

'What!' I shout. 'Couldn't you wait?'

'Please don't be alarmed,' says the Captain, with a sharp intake of breath. 'It's quite normal practice, on the rare occasion that this happens, for the body to be buried at sea. We're often miles from anywhere in the tropics, without refrigeration, and the body decomposes quickly, so we have to avoid the health risk.'

'William, it was a proper Christian burial under the prescribed Church of England service for those at sea,' says the chaplain, clasping his hands together. 'The Captain officiated, and I led the service.'

'I'm sorry you didn't get the message,' says the Captain, in a slower more measured voice, 'but it is standard practice at sea.'

I wonder why neither Tomkinson nor that bastard Taylor mentioned the burial to me.

'I don't work for British India,' says Carruthers, inflating his chest, 'and just happened to be on the *Uganda* returning from leave, but I can assure you that burial at sea is normal practice. I deal with the paperwork all the time at the harbour authority.'

'Normal, even for suicides?' I ask.

'Yes,' he replies, coughing slightly.

'I understand how hard it must be,' says the chaplain, 'not being able to say goodbye to your wife. But there was a proper, well-attended service to send her away in peace.'

He seems a bit too sycophantic, this vicar, but then what do I know about such matters? The shock of not being able to see her again, no body to bury, is too much for me, and I cover my face with my hands.

'What happens next?' I hear Dorothea asking in her Swahili accent, an auditory jolt against the cut-back English vowels.

'Why don't the crew bring you Heather's personal effects,' the chaplain says to Dorothea, 'and I'll have a private chat with William?'

'Where's Johnny?' I ask, suddenly remembering the most important matter to resolve.

'He's been looked after by Mr and Mrs...' the Captain shuffles the papers in the file.

'Donald and Cynthia Kirby,' says the chaplain. 'Johnny made friends with their son, Michael. I think they're waiting for you in Heather's cabin.'

'Quite so,' says the Captain, glancing at the chaplain. 'Reverend Tremwell will take you both there.' He stands up, shifting Heather's file to one side. 'I'll say goodbye now and good luck – anything onshore can be dealt with by our agents and the chaplain will stay a little longer with you.'

'Can I see George Carmichael?' I ask. 'I know him a little from the tea factory.'

'Oh he's already gone ashore with his family,' says Carruthers. 'I saw him leaving just before coming here.'

The Captain and Carruthers shake hands with Dorothea and I, then leave to go on to the bridge. We follow the chaplain the way we came, down the narrow stairs and into the bowels of the ship, but the route is different this time and we end up in the first-class area, with the chaplain knocking on a cabin door and entering. Dorothea touches my hand with hers.

'Dadddeeeeeee,' cries Johnny, running across the cabin and hurling himself into my legs. 'Now we're in Africa!'

'Hey, Johnny, you've grown a lot, you almost knocked me over!'

I look at him; his face looks more lived-in and his hair longer. I know I cannot shed any tears in this cabin in front of everyone – it would upset my beautiful sensitive son – so I whinny like a halfwit instead and ruffle his hair.

The others laugh too but in a more restrained way, and introductions are made. Donald smiles and brings his arm across my shoulders briefly whilst his wife seems almost radiant, watching the two boys show off their toys. It could all just be a show to jolly me up, but even if it is, I appreciate their efforts.

'Thanks so much,' I say to Cynthia, 'for looking after him. Does he know…?'

'No, we thought it best to wait for you,' she whispers. 'Mummy's in the hospital.' I nod and watch as Dorothea approaches my son, her face creased into a smile.

'Hello, Johnny, I'm Dorothea, remember, from the letters?' She bends over and holds out her hand.

'You're almost black,' he replies, shaking her hand, then examining it.

'We packed up Heather and Johnny's belongings as best we could,' says Donald in a rather nervous voice, as though I was going to check.

'We'd better go then,' I say, almost like I'm thinking aloud. Events seem to be unfolding like a dream, with the bystanders acting their parts on the stage, moving towards an inevitable yet unknown conclusion.

'Are you all on the train to Nairobi?' Cynthia asks Dorothea.

'Back to the plantation house at Kiambethu,' replies Dorothea, glancing from Cynthia to Donald.

'Well, us too, so we can help you with your belongings,' Cynthia continues, beckoning to Donald who picks up one end of the box I recognise whilst I take the other.

The women and children go on ahead as we labour with the box, eventually giving up when a couple of stewards offer to help.

'What are you going to do now?' asks Donald, his question surprising me.

'No idea,' I reply after a brief pause. 'Did you go to Heather's burial?' I add, turning towards him.

'No, unfortunately,' he says and looks down at the floor and scratches his wrists, which I notice are covered in a rash. 'I was looking after Michael and Johnny.'

We make our way back to the shell door where an officer nods to me and looks away, then we descend the gangway with Johnny holding me with one hand and tapping the wooden railing with the other.

'Stinky like curry,' says Johnny, and Cynthia ahead of us laughs nervously.

On the quayside there is indeed the waft of rotting vegetables again as Donald turns against the sun and waits for us hunched under the shade of a crane. Dorothea has already commandeered two carts to take our collective luggage, which the stewards must have added to earlier. Another younger officer salutes in a rather sloppy fashion as we give our names to him.

It is much hotter now, my shirt sticking to my back and my arms clammy with sweat. I hang back from the women and children, not having the stomach to indulge in small talk, and Donald walks by my side, saying nothing as he scratches his wrists. Above the clacking and whirring of the cranes, the steam locomotive whistle blows a plaintive cry.

Johnny runs back to hold my hand, a blue plastic ship in the other. 'Africa smells,' he says, wrinkling his nose. 'When's Mummy coming out of the hospital?'

Dorothea glances back at me with a slight frown as I wonder when will be a good time to tell him, but of course there will never be such a moment. While I'm grappling with a suitable reply, Johnny adds, 'It got burnt when our cabin was fired,' his head tipped on one side.

296

I make a mental note to ask Donald more about this later, but suddenly none of these details matter any more; she's gone from me, from all of us. I look up again at the grey bulbous clouds that you only get in Africa, a bigger hotter and angrier sky, and feel my yearning for the continent, the smell of drains and decay, the acrid laterite earth tugging me away from the slopping waters of the Indian Ocean. Now I'm away from the British ship, Kenya is trying to pull me closer to its bosom as I blink away my tears but sense the dangers ahead of such an embrace, the fog of gin and the hiss of women's pity but, above all, Johnny, an innocent, his small hand slowly slipping from mine as we're sucked into the warm swaddling cradle of Africa.

'I say, Mr Fontwell!' comes a cry from behind us. I turn and am faced with a young officer with bushy sandy hair. 'Engineer Scott. I'm really sorry about your wife. This got left behind.' He hands me a large brown open envelope with a paperback book inside.

I notice the sweat on his brow and the colour in his fair-skinned cheeks. He hesitates before carrying on.

'Don't worry about the book, it's just a pretext for me to talk to you.'

He hesitates again and looks at Johnny; Donald nods, takes Johnny aside and asks the boy, 'Can I have a look at your liner?' He bends down his thin frame and grasps his knees with spread-out fingers. His voice, I notice for the first time, has a rich tone, not the loud and exaggerated falsetto many adults put on for children. Johnny squints a quick glance at Donald then thrusts forward his blue plastic model, which appears to have been bent out of shape and blackened, and gives Donald a big grin.

'I got to know your wife and son and their group of friends quite well,' Scott carries on, shaking my hand. We walk on a few steps. 'Off the record, you'll be aware that Carruthers, the Mombasa Harbourmaster, was also on the ship?'

I nod to him but with a sense of foreboding after Taylor's warning.

'Well, he had a few arguments with Heather and I think he might have set fire to her cabin.'

'So not an accident as the Captain claimed?' I reply. Scott shrugs his shoulders. 'But that didn't kill her,' I continue, my mounting anger providing me with a new focus. 'So what did?'

'Well, her suicide as the Captain said, but Carruthers didn't help.'

I remember my damned letter again and now I feel my shame mixed with the anger at Carruthers making Heather's life a misery. 'So did that bastard's behaviour push her towards suicide?'

Scott looks down at the ground and scratches the back of his shoulder. 'I don't know, she gave as good as she got.' He looks back at the ship, where the other officer at the bottom of the gangway is gesturing to him.

'Sorry, I have to go.' The engineer points at the envelope in my hands and mutters, 'There's a UK phone number on the inside cover, in case you want to talk,' then pats my shoulder before walking away quickly back to the gangway. I tip out the well-thumbed book, which is entitled *Poetry of the Sea*, and sure enough the officer's name and a phone number is pencilled on the frontispiece. The book seems to have been liberally defaced by Heather's ink handwriting, which I cannot bear to read right now, so close the book and drop the envelope onto the other rubbish strewn along the quayside.

'Did you know about Carruthers and the fire?' I ask Donald.

'Yes,' he replies, standing up from talking to Johnny.

There's another putrescence in the moist air, the sweaty stench of betrayal, the collusion of the white man – the pores on my arms and the lining of my diaphragm sense it. Donald feels it too, that's why he strokes the wrist of one hand as he hands back the bent blue boat to my son. I close my eyes and breathe in deeply to try to stem the rage, feeling a crackling in the air like dry beech burning on an autumnal bonfire. What would Heather have wanted me to do?

I open my eyes again and look down at Johnny just as he turns to me. Her clear blue eyes set in his pale unblemished face stare back at me, a shock but also a beacon, for a drifting ship at sea.

Historical Postscript

The winds of change discernible to those aboard the *Uganda* in 1960 carried on throughout the decade.

The numbers of passengers taking long sea journeys from UK ports to Africa fell from 91,300 in 1960 to 55,800 in 1970, with worldwide totals falling from 593,600 to 285,100; at the same time the number of passengers using UK airports quadrupled from 7.9 million in 1959 to 31.6 million in 1970.

The first multi-modal container ships appeared in North America in 1955–6, with ISO standards being developed over 1968–70. Over 90% of non-bulk cargo globally is now carried by these means.

The 1960s was also the period when many former British colonies gained their independence: in East Africa, Kenya became independent in 1963, Uganda in 1962 and Tanzania in 1961. Malta became independent in 1964 and followed distinctly pro-USSR policies under the premiership of Dom Mintoff, but later joined the EU in 2004.

The Aden Emergency flared up in 1963, followed by a period of instability and the withdrawal of British troops from the Protectorate in 1967, whereupon the port became part of the People's Republic of South Yemen. Aden became the location of the first Al Qaeda terrorist attack in 1992 on the Gold Mohur hotel; there then followed attacks on the US destroyer *The Sullivans* and the *USS Cole* in the year 2000. At the time of writing there is heavy fighting around Aden as part of the civil war in Yemen.

The Suez Canal was closed by an Egyptian blockade immediately following the Six-Day War in 1967 until being cleared of mines in the summer of 1975. It was then operated essentially unchanged until the opening of the New Suez Canal in August 2015, which introduced simultaneous bidirectional traffic without the Bitter Lake stopover.

The collective result of competitive air travel, the rise of container ships, the demise of the passenger/cargo ship concept, and political change led to pressure on the East African shipping line BI. When Ian Smith made his Unilateral Declaration of Independence in Rhodesia in 1965, economic sanctions were imposed by the UK that resulted in the wiping out of a major BI market. The *Uganda* was withdrawn from the East African service at the end of 1966 and Union-Castle withdrew their final two passenger-cargo liners on the UK round-Africa service a few months later. This left the *Kenya* as the sole liner on the UK East Africa service, but two years later she too was withdrawn.

There is a photo in the National Maritime Museum taken in June 1969 in Tilbury docks: the *Kenya* is disembarking her final passengers prior to being delivered to Genoa for scrap the following month. Opposite the *Kenya* and moored in Gravesend Reach is its former sister ship, the *Uganda*, now converted to a schools' cruise ship and pictured between cruises.

Educational cruising began when the UK government announced the end of troopship charters and the future use of air travel for trooping in October 1960. In the following month the last men entered National Service, with the last National Servicemen leaving the armed forces in May 1963. The transfer of one market from shipping to air ironically provided, through the availability of redundant troopships, a new market for shipping – namely educational cruising, which began in earnest in 1961 using the ex-World War Two troopships *Dunera* and *Devonia*. Another more modern troopship, the *Nevasa*, was converted and added to the BI educational cruising fleet in 1965. By 1967, the two earliest ships were due for replacement due to new marine fire regulations, and once the *Uganda*'s conversion was underway the *Dunera* and *Devonia* were sent for scrap at the end of that year.

Consequently, from early 1968 onwards, the BI educational cruising market was provided by the *Uganda* and the *Nevasa*, with a reasonable degree of financial success. However, following the fuel crisis of 1973, and the economic difficulties that followed in the UK, the *Nevasa* was withdrawn from service; despite being the larger vessel and five years newer than the *Uganda*, her fuel consumption counted against her and she was sent for scrap in April 1975. By this time, the *Uganda* was the sole surviving vessel from the once-extensive BI fleet.

***

In terms of social issues, the 1960s was also a decade of change. Although the Wolfenden Report of 1957 recommended that private homosexual acts between consenting adults away from public gaze be legalised, it was not until 1967 that private homosexual acts between consenting men, both of whom had to be over the age of twenty-one, was decriminalised in England and Wales. Scotland had to wait until 1980, and Northern Ireland 1982 for similar legislation. The age of consent was not harmonised between heterosexual and homosexual acts (i.e. sixteen years old) until the year 2000.

The Abortion Act of 1967 allowed legal abortion of foetuses under twenty-eight weeks old on a number of grounds, with free provision from the NHS. One of the main reasons for the legalisation of abortion was the thalidomide tragedy – in 1957 a German drug company launched the drug, marketing it under the trade name Contergan. It was effective against both motion sickness and morning sickness, but in early 1960 it became apparent that there might be links to defects in newly born children. This was primarily because there was only very limited testing of any new drug on unborn children and the drug had been approved for use in West Germany. Despite this, the drug enjoyed massive sales in the UK as Distaval to treat the impact of nausea and morning sickness and was also released in Australia, Canada and (for trial purposes only) the USA. Thalidomide was only withdrawn from sale in the UK in November 1961 and April 1962 in Canada. Experts estimate that 2,000 children died and another 10,000 suffered serious defects (half this number being in West Germany) due to thalidomide. The incidence of induced miscarriages is unknown.

There were 23,868 divorces in England and Wales in 1960 compared to 58,239 in 1970 and 148,301 in 1980. The Matrimonial Causes Act of 1973 significantly reformed the granting of divorce.

Britain had no legislation on racial discrimination until the Race Relations Act 1965, which was widely viewed to have been ineffective and was eventually repealed by the Race Relations Act of 1976. The first widespread public disorders with a racial motive were the Notting Hill riots of 1958, where police arrested 140 youths over disturbances lasting two weeks. The precursor to the Notting Hill Carnival was organised in 1959 as a response to the riots and the state of race relations in the UK at the time.

Note from the Author

The genesis of this book was the two months I spent on the *Uganda* in May and June 1975 between school and university, working as a School Office Assistant. This forms the background for the sequel to *The Uganda Sails Wednesday*, which is currently work in progress; some excerpts from the draft second book are included after this note.

I intend to write a third novel covering the period when the Uganda was a hospital ship in the Falklands conflict, still following the Fontwell family and other members of the crew.

I am indebted to the SS Uganda Trust who published *UGANDA The story of a very special ship* in 1998. This followed attempts by the trust to save the ship from being sold for scrap following the end of it's MOD charter in 1985 – in the event unsuccessfully. The book is some 460 pages and contains memories and technical details, which have been invaluable to me in making *The Uganda Sails Wednesday* as authentic as possible, though of course the main characters and the plot are entirely fictional. Further information about the Trust is available at www.ssuganda.co.uk.

The poems quoted or referred to in the text are as follows:

Edward Lear:	The Owl and the Pussycat
Edna St Vincent:	Millay Exiled
D.H. Lawrence:	The Sea
Henry Wadsworth Longfellow:	The Sound of the Sea
John Masefield:	Sea-Fever

Felicia Hemans: Casabianca
Lewis Carroll: The Walrus and the Carpenter
Henry Wadsworth Longfellow: Tales of a Wayside Inn
D.H. Lawrence: The Mystic Blue

They are all believed to be out of UK copyright and can be found in full on the website https://www.public-domain-poetry.com/.

I would like to thank the team at RedDoor Press including Clare Christian and Heather Boisseau for their belief, hard work and enthusiasm, and Anna Burtt for briefing and Clare Shepherd for the excellent cover design, which blew me away when I first saw it. Elisabeth Haylett Clark at The Society for Authors was also very helpful on contractual matters and Amanda Saint at Retreat West gave me hope when shortlisting a predecessor of this work for a First Novel prize.

Otherwise I should also like to acknowledge the help provided by by Andrew Hyde and Jill Thompson who read the first draft of this book and also those who have commented on draft chapters – especially those in the Chalk Circle writing group, namely Sam De Alvis, Celia Berggreen, Jayne Block, Judith Bruce, Mags Eckstein, Yvonne Hennessy and Justine Johnstone who are always very generous with their time and support. Examples of our work are available at www.chalkcircle.org.uk.

Jon Walter and Phil Harrison also helped me with earlier drafts, and I want to give special mention to my former tutors at New Writing South, Catherine Smith and Susannah Waters. I should also like to thank Lizzie Enfield for her recognition of the Uganda short story and encouragement thereafter, and Anna Hayward and her writing group. Anne-Marie Scott-Masson also assisted with nautical terminology and Dave Sims with medical credibility.

And lastly, but most of all, to my family – to Vivi, without whom none of this would be possible; to our two wonderful daughters

Emily (and husband Rob) and Olivia; to my sister Gina who has had to put up with a lot over the years, and to all my extended family in the UK and France.

Excerpt from the sequel

July 1960 Kenya

Johnny was not so keen on his new tutor to start with – I don't think he was expecting a woman, and certainly not someone as dark as Makena. In the end I could see that it meant a lot to Dorothea to have a friend at the plantation house, and she confessed that it was also a chance for her to see what a tutor did exactly. Makena, after a trial period of two weeks, now shares a bedroom with Dorothea, which isn't ideal but they both seem happy enough with this arrangement.

Johnny has, however, got used to his new tutor over the trial period; the teaching was largely based on reading, writing and arithmetic with a bit of nature thrown in. He and Makena would sometimes stay in the lounge but were more often to be seen seated at the garden table and chairs on the lawns outside in the shade of the blue flowered jacaranda tree.

Strangely enough, I've also received a letter from Gerald recently, which enclosed some cuttings for Johnny to look at. The letter itself is mostly about the usual condolences but also a lot of questions about what had happened to Heather, the fact that he didn't consider suicide at all likely and was there a note and what would be her motives? Why was the body buried at sea without any autopsy? All very good questions, which it looks increasingly likely will never get answered.

Of course, he wants to know when Johnny and I will be returning home ('surely you cannot just carry on in Kenya as though nothing has happened – and what about Johnny's education?'). Questions, nothing but questions, and all I can do is only what it's possible to do, stuck up in the hills on a tea plantation miles from anywhere or anyone other than the dreadful Taylor.

Still at least I've taken action about Carruthers; I've written a letter to Norman asking him to investigate matters and fixed a time to meet him again at the club on the day he requested. Involving Donald any further didn't seem like a good idea.

As there isn't much to do in the office and Johnny is having his lessons, I decide to go and show my face at the tea picking – the second flush of the year as the Kenyan summer is long and wet. Jonas has already driven over there with the Land Rover, so I walk over to the nearest areas of tea – with what Jonas had described as the show homes for workers. The orange laterite soils are soon sticking to my heavy work boots, which makes them heavy and tiring to walk with. I spot Jonas with my binoculars on the far side of a natural bowl of tea plants, all in neat rows following the contours and curving round in a pleasing quarter circle. He must have spotted me too and waves before getting into the Land Rover to come over; the car slithers from side to side on the rough access track and he picks me up to go over to where the workers are currently picking, baskets on their backs.

We park behind some trestle tables upon which there are industrial weighing scales with giant hooks to hold the baskets; each worker has their own pre weighed basket and the scales are checked twice a day with some solid weights.

The women seem to be concentrating on their picking and look in reasonable health, adjusting their colourful head scarves in the breeze and with the angle of the sun. Every now and again one jogs back to the scales, getting their pickings weighed and tipping the tea into a high-sided trailer. Jonas notes the results in a lined A4 notebook with the workers' names down the left-hand column.

'I keep telling them to weigh up little and often otherwise they'll get bad backs over the long run,' says Jonas, winking at the women when they come over.

'How's the harvest?'

'Not bad. See the shoots, I've measured a sample of them and they're pretty much the same as the first flush.' He holds up his wooden six-inch ruler and measures a few more.

'Is Rehema not picking today?'

Jonas sighs and puts his hands on his hips. 'She gets paid better sleeping with men, so she does that.'

'It's still going on then?'

'Uh huh. Taylor is still sending his friends.'

Another tea worker comes over and gives me a shy smile. She must be about sixteen or seventeen, slim. 'Bwana,' she says.

I smile back but hate being called this. The young woman walks quickly back onto her row with her empty sack. It's another warm day in the eighties despite our altitude of over 7000 feet, and I wonder how they can work all day in these conditions.

'Boss,' says Jonas, frowning. 'if the workers were paid a bit more and the remote houses were improved, then maybe things would be different.'

'Yes, but that means getting more money out of Taylor, when he won't even buy a new oven thermometer at Mabroukie.' As soon as I say this, an idea forms in my head.

***

I'm annoyed that Norman hasn't turned up for our lunch appointment at the same club in Nairobi. I feel foolish sitting here waiting for him and eventually give up and walk away without ordering; the waiter is suitably snooty when I give my apologies. I decide that a walk would settle me and retrace my steps to where I'm staying at the Avenue Hotel on Delamere Avenue and have lunch there instead.

In the evening, I've arranged to see Donald and Cynthia, partly to report back to Donald on my meeting with Norman and outline my plan – though how this was to be achieved in the company of Cynthia I haven't thought about much.

As I head out of the hotel to kill some time before meeting the Kirbys tonight, I reflect that luckily there is nothing to say about the meeting with Norman; I don't want to go to another club or hotel, so wander aimlessly a bit in the pleasant afternoon sunshine laced with the scent of flowers, until I see the minarets of the Khoja Mosque and remember that there is the Indian bazaar adjacent, which I'd only looked at briefly once before. I cross the road without paying much attention and fail to notice a Vauxhall Cresta hidden from view behind a double-decker London bus, which comes past trailing a dirty plume of exhaust.

The Cresta driver honks his horn and I step backwards to avoid him before he waves and shouts something at me and then pulls over. I just about recognise him and walk over to where he's parked.

'Hello, William, sorry to alarm you,' he says, leaning against the car. It's the newer Cresta PA version with red and white bodywork and whitewall tyres and US-style rear fins, not long out in Kenya. 'I just thought I'd ask if you were still pursuing that investigation of yours, you know, that one about the fake invoices?'

Of course, it's Welham the Trade Commissioner, whom I last met a few weeks past at their home, Jessop House. It seems an incredibly long time ago, and there is no point going down that road any further.

'No, I've decided to let it go.'

'Very wise,' he replies lighting up a cigarette, 'especially after recent events. Still, must get on now. You mind how you go.' With that he puts on some calf driving gloves and drives slowly away, blending into the traffic.

I've no idea what recent events he's talking about but then I don't keep up much with Nairobi club and golf club gossip, so I forget about this reference as soon as I begin looking at the Indian bazaar. It's a long street with a concrete overhang, which protects

312

the pedestrian from the sun and enables window shopping without squinting. There's a succession of units roughly the same size with their business announced on a large sign fixed to the overhang, so the shopper can see these in a line as they walk along the pavement. There are Asian people everywhere – walking on the pavement and in the various cafes, offices and shops along the street.

An Asian woman walks towards me and smiles. She's wearing an incredible outfit – a sort of trouser suit with a more traditional top over, which is cut away at the back and flows out behind her.

'Are you looking for tailoring, sir?' she asks, smiling. She's not young, but her hair is still jet black, and pulled back with an ebony comb. I realise there's a small boy following her. 'For you or your wife?' she asks, whilst I ponder what I might be looking for..

'Suits or jackets for yourself. Curtains and bedding. Nice material for the ladies,' she continues in a questioning tone with a list of shopping possibilities.

I think of giving something to Dorothea and maybe something smaller for Cynthia to thank them for helping with Johnny, though I haven't a clue what.

'I'll just have a look then.'

About the Author

Stuart Condie was a director of transport facilities but now consults part-time.

He completed the Sussex University creative writing course in 2011 and has since written some twenty-five short stories; four have been published in anthologies and another as a pamphlet. The stories have also won three different prizes and been placed twice.

The Uganda Sails Wednesday is the first of a trilogy featuring the Fontwell family and the eponymous ship. An early version was shortlisted for the Retreat West first novel prize in 2018.

Stuart is a UK French dual national and holds Master's degrees from Cambridge and City universities. He's married with two daughters and lives in Sussex.

https://www.linkedin.com/in/stuartcondie/
@StuartCondie
stuartcondie.uk

Find out more about RedDoor Press and sign up to our newsletter to hear about our **latest releases, author events,** exciting **competitions** and more at

reddoorpress.co.uk

YOU CAN ALSO FOLLOW US:

 @RedDoorBooks

 Facebook.com/RedDoorPress

 @RedDoorBooks